Also by Amelia Grey

It's All About
THE Duke

Amelia Grey

St. Martin's Paperbacks

This is a work of fiction. All of the characters, organizations, and events portrayed in this novel are either products of the author's imagination or are used fictitiously.

IT'S ALL ABOUT THE DUKE

Copyright © 2018 by Amelia Grey.

For information address St. Martin's Press, 175 Fifth Avenue, New York, NY 10010.

ISBN: 978-1-250-10253-9

Our books may be purchased in bulk for promotional, educational, or business use. Please contact your local bookseller or the Macmillan Corporate and Premium Sales Department at 1-800-221-7945, ext. 5442, or by e-mail at MacmillanSpecialMarkets@macmillan.com.

Printed in the United States of America

St. Martin's Paperbacks edition / June 2018

St. Martin's Paperbacks are published by St. Martin's Press, 175 Fifth Avenue, New York, NY 10010.

10 9 8 7 6 5 4 3 2 1

My Dear Readers,

With little more than half of the cold, damp, and snowy months of winter behind us, we must look to something that will bring us smiles and warmth. Ah, perhaps indulging in thoughts of sunshine, springtime, and invigorating gossip for the upcoming Season. Alas, the tittle-tattle won't be as embracing this year, as two of the Rakes of St. James are now married and, from what I hear, blissfully so. Be that as it may, since there is one, the Duke of Rathburne, who hasn't yet been to the altar of the happily-ever-after, hope abounds that we will be feted with much to talk about.

For all the fair young maidens who might be considering the possibility of dropping their lace-trimmed handkerchiefs at the toes of the duke's shiny knee boots, I have just published a short book that will help you decide whether you should be so daring. It is all about the duke, after all. Do try to purchase or borrow a copy of *Words Of Wisdom And Warning About Rakes, Scoundrels, Rogues, And Libertines* to read. Then choose for yourselves, dear Readers, if you want to risk your tender affections for the possibility of being smiled upon by London's most notorious rake.

MISS HONORA TRUTH'S WEEKLY SCANDAL SHEET

———◆❧❉❧◆———

Chapter 1

He could be a rake if he appears at your door
unannounced and expects you to receive him.

❧

*Miss Honora Truth's Words of Wisdom and
Warning About Rakes, Scoundrels, Rogues, and
Libertines*

Any man who boasted he had no regrets was a liar as
far as Rath was concerned. If anyone should know, it
would be him. He'd had plenty before and since he became the Duke of Rathburne more than five years ago.
Though, like most of his ilk, he'd long denied having
such a weak trait. Yet it was impossible not to when a
man had lived as recklessly as Rath had.

Coming to that confounding conclusion hadn't been
easy, but it was why he now found himself standing in
the frosty air in front of a modest house in St. James,
oddly enough, not far from his own town home, watching
a maid digging about in what was probably a recently
planted kitchen garden.

A month ago, after no short amount of drink, Rath,
who'd never sought redemption for his wicked ways, had
experienced a change of heart. Of sorts. He'd penned a

letter accepting the role of guardian for the young lady who lived beyond the door not thirty paces away. At the time of his sudden epiphany, his muddled, jug-bitten brain had thought a little penitence might be justified. After all, he'd been carrying around a fair amount of guilt for a man who hadn't yet made it to his thirtieth birthday.

It was Rath who'd suggested the unforgettable secret admirer wager that years later still haunted him and his two friends, Griffin and Hawk. At the time, he'd considered himself a lucky man not to have a sister to marry off, as was his friends' misfortune. That situation had changed overnight when his father's boyhood friend, who'd recently become extremely ill, asked Rath to take over the guardianship of his longtime ward and see her suitably wed. His first reaction had been *no.*

But then he thought maybe he owed it to his father to say yes to the old man. Rath had never done much his father approved of during his lifetime—well, except learn how to properly care for the dukedom and keep it prosperous. Perhaps doing this favor for his father's dearest friend would rectify some of Rath's misspent youth.

He remembered Miss Marlena Fast, and the memory wasn't an altogether pleasant one. The only time Rath had seen her, she'd had unruly golden-red hair and scuffed elbows as she'd glanced up at him with big green eyes, mesmerized by him—he'd thought at that moment—only to then have her thrust a frog in his face. That had been when she was twelve.

Ruffian girls rarely, if ever, became decorous young ladies. Unless Miss Fast had changed—for the better—since he'd last seen her, there was little hope any of the eligible peers would offer for her hand. Rath might have to pad her dowry quite handsomely. Which he would do.

That was preferable to remaining responsible for her welfare past the upcoming Season.

He'd had no interest in taking on the task of being her guardian and seeing to her future, until the night he'd found himself alone and blurry-minded when he came to the bottom of a brandy bottle. He'd reasoned that Griffin and Hawk had paid a price for what they'd done years ago and it could have been much higher than it was. Now it was time for Rath to do something. But there was no use going over that night again. The deed was done, and he had to carry through. While he couldn't make amends to the young ladies he'd embarrassed with the secret admirer letters that went wrong, he could help Miss Fast make a suitable marriage. And perhaps in some small way atone for them, and make up to his father for never being the proper gentleman he'd always expected his son to be.

Rath turned his attention to the front door again. He might as well get this over with. He'd always succeeded in everything he set his mind to, and he intended to triumph in this challenge as well.

After expelling an audible sigh, he strode toward the house trying to convince himself that no matter how deep in his cups he'd been at the time, he'd actually done the right thing in agreeing to this outrageous, if noble, obligation. Lifting the knocker, he rapped the door a time or two. That sound set off a yappy bark. Seconds later a small short-haired, golden-brown dog came careening around the corner acting as if he wanted to have Rath for his dinner. The dog stopped a few feet from him and took an attack stance while he continued to alternate among barks, snarls, and growls. His thin, pointy tail quivered.

"Easy there," Rath said after taking off his gloves and bending down to offer his hand for the mongrel to sniff.

But the little fellow wasn't interested in making friends just yet. He only wanted to continue his alarm and make sure everyone in the neighborhood knew someone was at his master's door.

A few moments later a stout-looking woman wearing a ruffled mobcap and clean apron opened the door, smiled generously at him, and said, "Good afternoon, sir. How may I be of service to you?"

"I'm here to see Miss Marlena Fast," he offered while removing his hat and stuffing his gloves inside before tucking it under his arm.

With the words barely out of his mouth, he heard in the distance what sounded like a young lady's voice saying, "Tut, what has you so upset?"

"Seeing her won't be a problem for you, sir," the servant said. "Sounds as if she'll be walking around that corner any second now to see what has her dog carrying on like a hound after the moon."

When Rath turned in the direction the housekeeper had nodded, he caught sight of a young lady. She was tall, of slender build, and with an easy glide to her unhurried steps. The strong afternoon breeze spread open the bottom skirt of her woolen pelisse and fluttered and flattened her aproned dress against her silhouette. He couldn't see much of her face because she was wearing a straw bonnet with a wide brim pulled low over her eyes, though there hadn't been a hint of sunshine all day.

"Quiet, Tut!" she called softly to the dog. "You're making a nuisance of yourself."

The animal looked back at her and made a quarreling sound in his throat, then barked again.

"That's quite enough," she told him with no real reprimand in her tone, while removing one of her gardening gloves. "I'm here now and can see for myself we have a guest." The dog wasn't giving up. He barked at her again. "No, I can't pick you up, my hands are full. Now quiet. You'll have this gentleman thinking you're a naughty boy and you're going to bite him if you keep that up."

Rath smiled that she might actually think he'd be intimidated by a pup who probably couldn't jump high enough to reach Rath's knees. But if it made her feel better to reassure him of Tut's temperament, Rath would stay quiet.

As she walked closer to him, she lifted her chin and he saw her face. An unexpected throb of interest simmered through him. She was downright fetching, with big, round eyes, small nose, and lips beautifully sculpted. Not even the smudge of dirt that swept across one of her delicate-looking cheeks could take away from her natural loveliness.

A narrow lavender ribbon, meant to hold on her hat, had been perfectly tied into a little bow under her chin. A small basket of trimmings from the garden dangled from one of her wrists. Unlike the housekeeper's pristine apron, hers had grass and mud stains scattered down the front of it.

It didn't surprise Rath that it was Miss Fast who had been cutting the sprigs in the garden instead of a servant or gardener. Judging from his remembrance of her, he should have known it was too much to hope that she'd gained some refinement since he'd last seen her. However, it might not be as difficult to find her a husband as he'd assumed. There was no doubt she'd grown into her beauty.

Gorgeous, green eyes filled with pleasant curiosity and the right amount of sparkle stared at him when she stopped a few feet away, smiled, and laid both her gloves into her basket. There was a wholesome, innocent flush to her cheeks that drew him immediately.

"Miss Fast," he said as Tut sniffed around the heels and soles of his recently polished boots, "I am the Duke of Rathburne."

Her slightly arched brows lifted quickly, and her beautifully shaped mouth opened slightly. She sucked in a short, startled gasp. He watched her swallow hard before making a stiff but hasty curtsy and then whispered softly, "Your Grace, what are you doing here?"

Rath took note of her intense reaction to him. With wary, searching eyes, her gaze darted from him to the front door to each side of the house as if she were looking for somewhere to hide, a way to escape, or maybe someone to come rescue her. And was she trembling, too? He was almost certain it was fear he sensed in her.

But why?

The devil take it! He hadn't meant to frighten her by his sudden and unannounced appearance.

He knew the peerage caused alarm in the hearts of some people. Many, in fact. Rath had met a few young ladies who were visibly shaken by his title, his presence, but he'd never seen one who looked as if she thought he might physically harm her. Even her rosy lips had paled.

That puzzled him. She hadn't been frightened of him until he said his name. He was sure of that. *Miss Truth's Scandal Sheet* had recently called him a notorious rake. Perhaps Miss Fast had read that.

He was so busy assessing her surprising reaction to him that he failed to respond to her, so she spoke up and asked him again, "Why are you here?" She glanced behind him to the street where his carriage was parked while moving her basket from her wrist to grasp the handle tightly with both hands in front of her. Rath had the oddest feeling that she held it as a knight would hold a shield in battle.

"Is anyone with you?" she asked anxiously.

The directness of her questions was understandable, he supposed, so the first thing he needed to do was put her at ease. Perhaps the best way to do that was to remind her that they had met so she would know he wasn't a complete stranger to her.

"I'm alone," he assured her, having no idea why it mattered. "Do you remember meeting me? Six or eight years ago?"

"Vaguely," she answered cautiously, her expression still vigilant.

From her hesitation, he had the feeling she wasn't being totally honest with him, but he decided to give her the benefit of the doubt since she looked so anguished. He certainly didn't want to add to her disconcerting attitude toward him.

Rath went on to add, "My father was good friends with your guardian, Mr. Olingworth, when they were at Eton, Oxford, and for the rest of my father's life. We were visiting Mr. Olingworth at his estate in the Cotswolds and you were there."

"Yes, but I don't remember why you were visiting."

That he could believe without doubt. "I don't, either. It could have been a business matter between them or just a visit. At the time my father was teaching me about our properties and holdings."

Her gaze restlessly searched the street behind him again. "Why are you here now?"

That same question. What was he to do? He didn't want to simply blurt out his reason while standing outside her front door or while she was still so jittery. He wasn't the most patient of men, but he wasn't an ogre, either. Though there were some who might disagree with that assertion.

As his father would have expected of him, he gave her a gentle smile, hoping to reassure her he wasn't up to mischief, and put her mind at ease about him since nothing he'd said so far had. That in itself was unusual for him. He didn't try to pacify anyone. Concerning anything. But then, he couldn't remember having ever frightened a young lady to the point of trembling before, either. Apparently he hadn't made as memorable an impact on her as she had on him that brief time when their paths crossed all those years ago.

Rath was the last person to mollycoddle anyone but, going against his nature, he said, "I'd rather not talk out here, if you don't mind. May we go inside where we'll have more privacy?"

She hesitated.

"That is," he added, "unless you are alone."

"No. My cousin is inside."

Rath had only managed to get a little information about Miss Fast from Mr. Olingworth when he visited the man last week. Thin and elderly, he'd been propped against a mountain of pillows on his bed. His voice had been raspy, feeble, and full of fondness for his longtime ward. His hands had suffered from a constant tremble as he'd fiddled with his bedcovers.

It had taken a bit of effort, but Rath had managed to learn that Olingworth had sent Miss Fast to live with her cousin in St. James almost three years ago to start preparations for her debut, which had never happened. Olingworth's declining health had kept him from joining her in London and presenting her to Society. Hence the reason Rath stood before her now.

"Then you realize you don't have to be frightened of me."

Miss Fast gave him a quizzical stare at first, and then suddenly her shoulders squared. Her chin lifted defiantly. He hadn't understood until now that she hadn't known her fear of him showed.

"Frightened?" she asked indignantly. "Me?"

"I thought it must be so," he answered honestly.

"I have no memory of the first two or three years of my life, Your Grace, but I do remember the next few quite vividly. I lived with an aunt and uncle who had five sons—all older than me. I often followed those boys' romps through muddy swamps, dark woods, and old cemeteries at night when they slipped out of the house. If losing sight of them in those places didn't frighten me, I doubt you are capable of doing so."

If that was true—and Rath had no reason to doubt her word—it was impressive for a girl so young and explained why she wasn't afraid to hold a frog when he'd first met her.

"My apologies. I didn't know you lived with a family of boys before Mr. Olingworth."

"Though I am not frightened or desperate, I think *disturbed* would be an appropriate word for how I'm feeling right now."

Maybe she was upset at first that he'd caught her in the garden? Certainly not a place a proper lady should be with a pair of clippers and cuttings in her basket. Frustrated by his failure to ease the tension between them, Rath rubbed the back of his neck once before saying, "All right. Why does my visit disturb you?"

"I've asked several times why you are here and you've ignored me each time."

"Three times I think, but wait." He paused as an idea came to him. It was completely unacceptable, not to mention risky, but he'd never let anything such as unacceptable consequences stop him. "Shh," he said softly, putting his forefinger to his lips to quiet her when she started to speak. "Be very still. You brought something from the garden with you and it's on your cheek."

Her fan-shaped brows flew up again. Uncertainty

filled her eyes before she quickly lowered her lashes and tried to look down her nose at her face.

"What is it? I don't see anything. I don't feel it crawling on me."

She took one hand off the basket and started to lift her arm, but he said, "No, don't move." He stepped closer to her.

"Is it a bee or ladybug?" she asked quietly as her hand settled near the other on the basket handle once more. "A spider then? Please tell me it's not. They are creepy and I hope it's not one. Is it still there? I don't feel it moving around."

"Shh," he said again and moved still closer.

"Or even a wasp," she continued, ignoring his soft command for her to be silent. "There are many different kinds, you know. They won't hurt you if you don't try to hurt them. Though it is much too early in the year for a bee or a wasp to be out. Not any of the insects that fly and crawl about in the garden, but I'm not afraid of them."

He believed her. A young girl who would hold a frog or follow boys into a cemetery wouldn't be worried about a bug. Though she kept talking, she remained still.

"They land on me from time to time when I'm outside. Especially on hot, dry days in midsummer. Wasps sting sometimes, but the pain doesn't last long. I've learned that a cloth dipped in vinegar helps keep down the swelling."

It usually irritated the devil out of Rath when anyone kept up a nervous chatter, but Miss Fast was entertaining him with her brave assertion that insects didn't worry her.

He pulled a neatly folded handkerchief out of his coat pocket. Without considering what the miss, or the housekeeper who stood just inside the doorway, might think, he lightly wiped across her cheek.

Her head snapped up. Her long, dark, and velvety lashes fluttered.

"There," he said in a satisfied tone.

"Is it gone?" she asked anxiously.

"Yes."

"What was it? A ladybug? Did it fly away?"

He held the bit of white cloth up and showed her the soil from her cheek.

She glanced down at the handkerchief, took it from his hand for a closer inspection, before looking up at him again. Suddenly her eyes widened with indignation. A storm of anger gathered in their depths.

"Dirt!" she huffed, squeezing the cloth into a wad in the palm of her hand. "Is that all that was on my cheek?"

He nodded.

She puffed her annoyance once more and fiddled with her gardening basket yet again. "You forced me to be still and quiet so you could—"

"Wait, wait, please," he said, holding up his hands to stop her from saying more. "You? Still? Quiet?"

"Yes," she declared, exasperation flowing from her breaths and her determined glare.

If he thought her fetching with eyes sparkling and full of curiosity when he first saw her, she was now captivating with indignant irritation swirling through her like a fierce, icy wind.

"Now, that I must take exception to, Miss Fast. You never stopped talking though I urged you to more than once."

"I'm sure I did."

She paused as if to think over what she was saying. Rath remained silent.

"Anyway," she continued. "That is neither here nor there. You are obviously guilty of everything I have heard and read about you."

"I probably am."

"No proper gentleman would ever touch a young lady without her permission."

"I do know the rules, Miss Fast, whether or not I choose to obey them."

Though truth be told, Rath wasn't a plunderer of innocents. Well, perhaps there was one—or two, maybe a few when he was a very young man—but never one that wasn't as desperately willing as he, and it was long before he realized the gravity of how little it took to break a young lady's heart. Now he had no inclination to tumble and tangle the sheets with an untouched young lady, no matter that his reputation in clubs and scandal sheets extolled otherwise.

Rath took his pleasures elsewhere. Mistresses and widows seldom put their hearts into a relationship, and certainly not out in the open for all to see as did young ladies. Experienced women were skilled, generous, accommodating, and usually eager to give and receive satisfaction without wanting much in return. For some, companionship and gratification were reward enough to keep them sated if not content. And that's the way Rath wanted it, too.

The good thing was that the fascinating Miss Fast was no longer fearful of him. Now she was incensed. That emotion was more familiar to him.

"I do have something of importance to discuss with you. We can continue to stand out here in the chill of the afternoon breeze on your front stoop, or, since your cousin is home, you can invite me inside."

"Yes, of course," she finally said, but not before giving the question more than its due consideration—again. "Please, come inside." She motioned toward the door with her free arm.

Tut barked again and rushed across the threshold as

if the invitation to enter the house had been issued directly to him. The housekeeper opened the door wider.

Rath nodded to Miss Fast and said, "After you."

She hurried past him, and Rath caught a whiff of freshly dug earth and cut herbs. There was something primal, natural about both scents that pleased him and drew him even more to the miss. He placed his hat and cloak in the housekeeper's outstretched hands and stepped inside.

"Mrs. Doddle, would you please rouse my cousin from her nap? Tell her we have a guest, ask her to join us, and then make tea."

"Right away, miss," the housekeeper responded as she laid Rath's things on the vestibule table that stood against the wall under a large, ornately framed painting of a beautiful garden whose vistas seemed to go on forever.

Once inside, Miss Fast kept her back to him and placed her basket and his soiled handkerchief on the table beside his hat. He could tell she nervously worked at the bow under her chin. He heard more than one annoyed sigh. Something told him she'd somehow managed to knot the ribbon rather than untie it when, in vexation, she pushed the hat to her back, revealing a tumble of thick, lush golden-red hair that shone as if sunlight was directly on it. Rath had a sudden urge to lift it and bury his nose in the weight of its softness.

Her hands reached around to the back of her simple sprigged-muslin day dress. He watched delicate fingers pull on the sash of the apron fitted around her slim waist. But unlike the ribbon on her hat, when she pulled the bow, the apron strings fell apart and she laid the garment on top of the basket. If she'd had problems with it, he would have risked her shock and ire again and untied it for her.

And enjoyed every second of it.

He watched her take in a deep, solid breath. Her softly

rounded shoulders lifted high and then slowly relaxed. There was a seductiveness to the nuances of watching her summon an inner strength that he'd never seen in any other lady. The lovely miss was trying to calm herself before turning to him. He admired her for that.

When she faced him her countenance was stronger, settled, and determined. That, he decided, was much better.

"My cousin will join us shortly," she said. "We'll wait for her in the drawing room."

He followed Miss Fast down the short corridor and into a small appropriately decorated room. It looked cheerful with damask-covered settees and chairs, fairly new brocade draperies, and a figurine or two on the tables beside the lamps. Her cousin didn't live in an elaborate home, but it was more than acceptable for a member of Society.

"Please, sit down." She motioned to the floral-patterned settee with its bright spring flowers. "I don't know how long my cousin will be."

"I'll stand for now," he said, noticing the knot of ribbon that rested at the hollow of her throat. It couldn't be comfortable where it lay. But what would she do if he tried to untie it for her? She was already indignant he'd touched her cheek with his handkerchief. What would she do if he reached for the ribbon?

And what would he do?

His fingertips, his knuckles, and, perhaps, even the backs of his hands would touch her delicate-looking skin. Instinctively, that thought sent a wave of tightening arousal rushing through him. Rath sucked in a hard breath. He could only attribute this awareness of her that gripped him to her being an appealing young lady and him a man. For surely he could have no designs on his ward.

"All right, Your Grace," she said, impatiently. "For the

fourth, fifth, or maybe even the sixth time, please tell me why you are here."

That was the kind of spunk he expected from a lady who liked to play outside with frogs when she was a mere girl. Though he couldn't possibly tell her the whole truth. He'd never admit that in a rare remorseful moment he'd thought about penitence for all the debauchery he'd succumbed to in his life. That for a brief time, he thought that by coming to this young lady's aid, replacing her ailing guardian, he might in some way atone for all the young ladies he'd wronged with the secret admirer letters, and for never truly appreciating his father who'd always been a gentleman, as well as keeping the dukedom prosperous.

But there were more reasons that were even harder for a man to admit. Too much brandy. The fact that his two best friends had recently married and settled into happier lives with their wives and were no longer at the clubs in the evenings or the card games that went on for days. There was no reason to tell any of that. He'd written the letter accepting Olingworth's urgent request for help and that was all that mattered.

He reached into the inside pocket of his coat, pulled out a sealed envelope, and extended it to her. "This is from Mr. Olingworth and explains why I'm here."

Taking the envelope from his grasp, she looked down at it before returning her attention to Rath. "I'm confused. How did you get a letter addressed to me from Mr. Olingworth?"

"It was included in a packet that he sent to me only yesterday."

A quiver of humor hovered at the corners of her beautiful mouth. He found himself silently asking her to go ahead and smile at him without reserve.

Instead she said, "I'm always happy to hear from him,

but why are you delivering this? I find it difficult to believe you have succumbed to becoming a common messenger."

"Well said, Miss Fast." He smiled at her. "Though I haven't read the letter, I know what it says. I thought it best that I be here when you received it in case you had questions."

"Why?"

"He's telling you that his health continues to decline and he must transfer your guardianship to another."

"Yes," she whispered while expelling a deep breath. "Well. I knew it was coming. Just not when. He's been ill for some time. I had feared he might be getting worse. His letters to me have become infrequent and almost illegible. Though I've asked several times in the past few months to be allowed to visit him, he always denies my requests."

She suddenly turned away from Rath, walked over to the window, and looked out.

Rath stayed silent, giving her time to grasp what was happening to her future in her own way. There was no rush to do what must be done. He was content to watch her standing quietly, lovely with her straw hat resting on the back of her shoulders.

Tut wandered over to him and Rath reached down. This time Tut sniffed his hand and licked his fingers. *Good boy*, he thought. Rath rewarded him with a pat on the head and a rub down his warm neck and back.

After a few moments, Miss Fast slowly turned toward Rath. Her expression was quizzical.

He gave Tut a final stroke and then straightened to face her. She met his stare a few seconds longer before looking down at the sealed envelope again and tapping it against her palm a couple of times. He watched her expression turn thoughtful, resigned, and just when he was about to believe she had reconciled the matter to her satisfaction her brows knitted closer together, her lips pursed suspiciously.

"I'm curious, Your Grace. Why are you here delivering this news rather than a solicitor or my new guardian?"

The time had come. He'd delayed it as long as possible, hoping her cousin would decide to show herself and be present before he had to give Miss Fast the news.

"I am your new guardian."

Chapter 2

He could be a rake if he looks so deeply into your
eyes you know he sees all the way to your soul.

~◦~

*Miss Honora Truth's Words of Wisdom and
Warning About Rakes, Scoundrels, Rogues, and
Libertines*

Marlena Fast stared in awe at the Duke of Rathburne. Every word she'd ever read or heard about
him was true. He was tall, broad in the shoulders, lean at the
hips, and handsome beyond belief. He wore his title, privilege, and wealth as casually as he wore his neckcloth. He
was a feast of handsome, desirous male for her eyes.

And he was to be her guardian?

Her guardian!

No, she wasn't afraid. She'd always told herself she
wasn't frightened of anything. She'd had to say it to herself many times and would probably have to tell herself
again there was no reason to be fearful. Her parents were
with her. Watching over her just as they had when she
was an infant and in danger. They had taken care of her
then and they would now that she was under yet another
guardian.

Marlena stared at the duke. No English duke should have hair that dark or eyes that penetrating. He looked more like the paintings she'd seen of dangerous pirates who captained their marauding ships on the high seas than the true highborn aristocrat she knew him to be. His waistcoat should have been made from braided wool and studded with metal buttons. Instead of fine trousers, he should be wearing trousers fashioned out of a thick, coarse burlap. A wide strip of black leather held together with a large silver buckle should have cinched his waist with the well-hammered hilt of a steel blade and a scabbard swinging by his side.

It was no wonder she'd felt light-headed, panicked even for a few moments after he'd identified himself. This man, who stood before her in all his male glory, was none other than the rake she'd written about for the past two and a half years in *Miss Honora Truth's Weekly Scandal Sheet*. She'd just published a short book filled with snippets of warning to young ladies about this man and others like him! By all the saints in heaven, and if there were any on earth, too, she should have fainted.

What was she to do?

Fate had never favored her, and now it seemed as wicked as the rake standing before her.

It was no small wonder it took her so long to regain her composure and gather her scattered wits after he announced his name. She thought he'd come to expose her as the scandal columnist Miss Honora Truth. She assumed that, after much searching, he was the Rake of St. James who had finally figured out who Miss Truth really was, and he was making it his purpose to take her straight to Newgate, the gallows, or worse—if there was worse. However, at least for now, she was convinced the duke didn't know her secret identity and he wasn't there to have her arrested.

That and thoughts of her parents watching over her had calmed her.

Somewhat.

His arrival at her front door was nothing as simple as the rake coming with a band of armed guards to shackle her hands and feet and carry her off to a faraway dungeon in the middle of a dark forest. No, he was to be her guardian!

Marlena's hands made fists. Denial rose up strong and eager inside her. She strode toward him while breathlessly whispering, "What you say can't be true."

"It is," the duke answered without any uncertainty in his tone. "Olingworth asked me, and after much deliberation—and brandy—I accepted."

Her heartbeat surged again. Rebuffing his assertion still seemed her best defense. "He wouldn't do that to me. He wouldn't put me under the care of a—"

"Rake?" the duke asked as easily as he'd told her to shush before he'd wiped her cheek. He joined her in front of the fireplace. "I know what I am, Miss Fast. I had a difficult time believing Olingworth wanted me to do it, too. And even more difficulty when, the next day, I realized I had actually consented and the letter had been posted by my butler before I could retrieve it."

"You agreed to be my guardian when you were inebriated?" she questioned in disbelief.

His ebony-dark eyes sparkled with playful mischief. "I'm afraid it's the only defense I've been able to come up with for my unusual lapse in good judgment."

"You? Good judgment?"

Marlena didn't think she could become any more offended, but she just had. Where was this man's honor? Oh, how had she forgotten, he had none. The duke was the epitome of the rogues she'd heard and read about. And had written about, too!

Now that she hadn't been carted off to a cold dungeon to await the hangman's noose, she was feeling strong and resilient.

"I can't believe you'd admit something that outrageous."

"It's true, but I feel no pleasure or guilt in telling you." He paused. "I know you're thinking I'm the last person who should be in charge of an innocent young lady's fate."

"That, as well as many other things," she answered from between tightly clinched teeth. "This is sheer madness."

"I agree."

Marlena's mind swirled with too many thoughts to properly sort them all out at the moment. She remembered how the duke had studied her intently when he first saw her. She couldn't blame him. She must have looked affright with her soiled garden apron and dirt on her cheek.

"Why would you accept this obligation for me knowing you are a scoundrel and you shouldn't even be in Society? I take it no one was holding a pistol to your head and forcing you to do this no matter the amount of swill you had ingested."

He grimaced. For a moment she thought she might have gone too far with her cutting words, but then his mouth relaxed into another smile and he chuckled softly. It was a husky, inviting, and intriguing sound that stirred her in a way she'd never felt before. He looked so natural and pleasing while finding pleasure in her discomfort that Marlena wanted to stomp her foot in frustration over the unfairness of it.

"The distiller of the brandy I drink would not take kindly to you calling his fine cognac swill, Miss Fast. But that aside, Olingworth wanted me to do this because it's what is best for you."

"Surely you jest."

"That's not in my nature."

Yes, she could see by the look in his eyes that it wasn't. She'd never know it, though, by the lack of starch in his collar and the relaxed bow in his neckcloth. Was it even a bow? She wasn't sure. It was so carelessly tied, it looked as if he hadn't even tried to manage it properly. Most noblemen wore their collar points so high and stiff they could hardly move their necks, which forced their chins into an abnormally high lift. And according to all she'd heard, titled men were usually just as rigid. The duke's chin wasn't haughty, just handsome. Maybe it was the more comfortable appearance of his clothing that added to the mesmerizing charm so many ladies in the *ton* swore he had.

"Olingworth knows my father would have done it for him if he'd still been alive. He believes because I'm my father's son and a duke I will see to it that you make a good match, and I will."

Marlena looked down at the envelope she held. Suddenly she felt as if she were choking again. She reached up and pulled on the narrow strip of satin around her neck, but knew it wasn't the weight of the straw hat on her shoulders that made it feel as if her throat were closing. It was all the raw emotions stirring inside her like an apothecary's brew in a steaming cauldron. Other than losing her parents so early in life, the Duke of Rathburne becoming her guardian was the worst thing that could have occurred.

Would she be able to continue to write about him and other rakes in her scandal sheet? Yes, she must. At least for a little longer. Until Eugenia could attend the Season and settle on a husband to take care of her so that she was no longer her sister's responsibility. Then Marlena could give it up as she'd planned after the first Season.

But what would Marlena do if the duke somehow found out *she* was Miss Truth?

No, what would *he* do?

To her?

That didn't matter right now. She couldn't stop writing the scandal sheet. There was no arguing that point with herself. It was a small amount the publisher paid Marlena, but Eugenia and her married sister, Veronica, depended on it. It helped keep the sisters in their house and living next door to Marlena. She would find a way to keep writing the scandal sheet for now.

Yet what was she to do about the duke? She had absolutely no way to fight a change in her guardianship, no way to have the freedom to control her own inheritance. She would have to concede those facts.

"Oh, I don't understand this," she whispered more to herself than the man looking at her. "Mr. Olingworth has been kind to me all these years." She placed the sealed envelope on the table beside the lamp. "He's always allowed me more freedoms than most girls and young ladies would have. Why now would he be so cruel as to put you in charge of my life?"

"If it will make you feel better, perhaps you could look at this as it was meant to punish me, not you."

"You?" Marlena exclaimed without a trace of caution in her words. His arrogance was of the highest order. But he was the typical rake, she thought. Thinking of no one but himself and his desires.

"How does this punish you? You certainly deserve to be reprimanded for all your misdeeds, but this penalizes me, not you."

His brow furrowed a little. The first sign that she was beginning to make inroads into his good nature and get under his skin. He took a step closer to her. "Surely you can't expect that it's going to be easy for me to take on the responsibility of finding a young lady a husband."

"All you had to do was say no."

"I would have if it had been as simple as stating one word," he countered. "Believe me, I have little appetite and even less desire to be in charge of anyone. Especially a lady who would rather root around in the garden and cut flowers instead of sitting in the drawing room learning how to paint them."

Marlena stood her ground. "I enjoy being in the garden, and thankfully Mr. Olingworth had no problem with me doing so whenever I stayed at his home in the Cotswolds."

"That was different," the duke insisted. "You were a young girl then. In the countryside. Now you are in fashionable London. Young ladies are supposed to let the gardener, scullery maids, or someone else cut the blossoms and herbs. You are the last person who should be doing it. You're a properly brought-up young lady with distant relatives who are nobly born and you should act accordingly."

"Which also means I am not destitute," she argued firmly, thinking he was mistaken if he thought she would so easily fall into whatever it was he wished for her. "I have an inheritance, small though it might be. I'm quite capable of finding my own husband without your help."

"And as you know," he said, his eyes narrowing in annoyance. "Someone must look after your interests until you make your debut in Society and decide on who that man will be and wed him. Olingworth chose me because he doesn't have to worry about me gambling away your dowry before you can decide on a husband. He knows, and so will all of Society, that I'll be beneficial to whomever you agree to make a match."

"All of Society you say?" she questioned slowly, thinking carefully on his words. "Is that what this is about? Is it important to *you* what the *ton* thinks about *you*?"

The duke scowled. She wondered how he could do it and still look so incredibly handsome. Almost from the moment she first looked at him she'd felt as if her legs were melting from beneath her.

"I ceased caring what Society thought of me long ago."

"It doesn't appear so to me," she maintained, giving more credence to her suggestion.

"Then you are wrong in your estimation of me."

"Somehow I don't think so. It sounded to me as if you want the *ton* to know how good you are being to the poor relation of an earl who had most of his lands confiscated by the King before I was born because he dared to criticize him for his exorbitant expenditures."

"The earl did it in public, Miss Fast. That wasn't wise."

She agreed it wasn't. She grew up hearing over and over again how dearly the earl's cutting words to the King had cost his family. But whether or not the duke cared about his standing in Society, it was a valid argument for her to explore as to why he—a known rake—had decided to be Mr. Olingworth's replacement.

"Maybe you think that by becoming my guardian you will somehow get forgiveness from Society for your secret admirer letters and regain favor in their eyes."

"Want their favor?" The duke grunted another attractive laugh and leaned in close to her. "Hell would have to freeze over before I'd welcome that sentiment."

Suddenly, with no forethought, Marlena smiled sweetly at the duke and said, "Miracles do happen, you know."

He surrendered a slight nod of admiration for her comeback, but said, "Only for the saintly, Miss Fast, and that's not a group I'm ever likely to be included in."

Unfortunately, she didn't suppose she ever would be,

either. In fact, she had some nerve taking him to task for his past misdeeds while she wrote an anonymous scandal sheet about him and others under an assumed name. Though she'd never admit it to him, some might say they were two peas in the same pod on the vine.

"I don't know your previous guardian well," the duke continued, "but my father did. He held Olingworth in high esteem."

"And what about me? Did you ask about me? Were you curious to find out more about me before or even after you accepted responsibility for me?"

"I have to admit I wasn't. I trusted Olingworth that you were highborn and in desperate need of a sponsor so that you might make your debut, enter Society, and make a match."

"Desperate?" The word came out almost as an oath. She was infuriated. If there was one thing living with her cousins had taught her, it was not to be desperate. It was to stay strong and find an answer to whatever situation you were in. "Mr. Olingworth would have never used that word concerning me. I may have lost my parents when I was a babe but I have never been desperate."

"I didn't know that you had been orphaned so long."

She could see that her words surprised him and hoped she hadn't revealed too much about herself to him.

"Though we met long ago, you and I have never really talked. Even I know that you lost your mother before you entered Oxford and your father only a few years ago."

"From the newsprint and gossip sheets no doubt. I know very well that titled gentlemen are written about more than others. However, I'll concede that perhaps it was Mr. Olingworth who was the desperate one. For you to continue your life and not be held up by his illness any longer. I am keeping my promise to him to do this for the respect I have for his and my father's years of friendship."

"You?" she asked with an exasperated breath of incredulity. "Respect? You who embarrassed twelve young ladies their first Season?"

"Yes."

"You who mortified them in front of their parents, friends, and beaus? Leaving them completely defenseless."

"Not intentionally, but yes," he admitted without complaint.

"What you did caused their loved ones to question their honesty, their virtue, and their marriage prospects."

"I can't deny any of that, and I'm sure you assume I'm guilty of much more."

"I have no doubt," Marlena said and then realized he was taking her responses to him as a challenge, not an insult.

Besting the duke would not be easy. She had no idea where she was getting the fortitude to be so bold with him. Perhaps it was because she'd written about him, taken him to task under the privacy of an assumed name in her gossip sheet for almost three years. That must be why she now felt comfortable doing it face-to-face. Or it could be as simple as knowing how Veronica had suffered because of the secret admirer letters, thereby causing Eugenia to bear the burden, too. Marlena would never forget hearing from Eugenia that neither the duke nor his two friends had ever been reprimanded by Society for those letters in any way. Because they were dukes.

"I know it doesn't help now," His Grace said. "But we never thought we'd end up proving that all the strict morals and manners that had been instilled in the young ladies from their birth would leave them at the possibility of someone being secretly in love with them. But yes, I suppose when the three of us were contemplating or even carrying out this idea one of us should have been wise enough or perhaps sober enough to say, *This isn't a good idea*. But none of us did. And it ended up every one of the ladies wanted to have a secret admirer."

"But they didn't want the whole world to know that about them."

"It was never our intent anyone but the three of us know about any of it. I admit the wager between my friends and me to see who could entice the most young ladies to meet a secret admirer should have never happened. It was wrong. But it was years ago. And quite frankly, Miss Fast, I'm tired of being haunted by it."

Marlena thought of Veronica and Eugenia again and how their lives had been affected. If it hadn't been for the letters, Veronica wouldn't have married Mr. Portington. If she hadn't married the older gentleman, she and Eugenia wouldn't be so unhappy.

But putting those thoughts aside, Marlena said, "Haunted by it? If so, that's because you never suffered any ill effects because of the letters."

The duke straightened, shrugged. "Judging the merits of my past behavior is not why I'm here. You are. As your guardian, the first thing I want to do is move you and your cousin into my Mayfair house."

"Move?" Marlena felt as if someone had punched her in the stomach, causing her to lose her breath. "To Mayfair? You can't be serious." She pulled on the ribbon around her neck. Why hadn't she been able to untie the worrisome thing?

"It's bigger than this house and completely staffed."

Marlena's heart started racing. Move from next door to Eugenia? She couldn't. Her friend was the one who saw to it *Miss Honora Truth's Scandal Sheet* made it to the publisher each week. And if Marlena moved, where would Veronica go for reassurance when a new shipment of her husband's fossils arrived and she became stricken with yet another attack of despair? If Marlena didn't write the scandal sheet, where would the sisters get the extra money needed for their household?

"I don't want to move," she told the duke hastily, refusing to give in and give up without a fight.

"I'm trying to do what's right by you, Miss Fast. Mayfair will be a better place for you to live during the Season."

No, Marlena couldn't leave St. James. Becoming friends with the sisters had been a welcomed addition to her life when she first came to London. They had needed her friendship and she needed them, too. Eugenia and Veronica were her friends. Her cousin was older and more like a governess. Justine was always telling Marlena what she must do and how she must do it. For once Marlena was taking care of someone other than herself and she wouldn't let them down. She would find a way out of moving away, as she had found her way out of the marsh, the woods, and the gravestones.

Marlena had never lacked for anything that she could remember, but she'd never wanted much. Her aunt, uncle, and cousins had never needed her when she lived with them, but she'd needed them. The boys had taught her how to be strong, resilient, and most of all to not be afraid. Having Eugenia and Veronica to help and visit with gave her things to do other than garden work, stitchery, and reading—which she enjoyed and wanted to do—while waiting around to make her debut into Society. Something that she couldn't say she was eager to do.

"You'll find you'll have no worries there. Everything will be handled for you."

Marlena put her thoughts back to the matter at hand. "I thank you for the offer, but I'd rather remain where I am. It's very generous of you to suggest a larger home. I'm quite content with my life as it is now and see no reason to change it."

The duke shifted his weight. His gaze swept up and down her face as if studying every detail of her features. She remained adamant in her stance.

"Maybe you aren't understanding me," he said softly, but without equivocating. "Olingworth only allowed you to forgo the Season the last two years because of his illness. I have no such restrictions. You're now my responsibility and I will see you suitably wed. You need to attend the Season so you can meet all the eligible gentlemen and settle on a husband. Presumably, someone you care for and someone who will adore you so you won't have to be anyone's ward but a gentleman's wife."

"But I don't want that," she insisted. "Not yet, anyway."

"That is what young ladies do, Miss Fast," he said with an edge of irritation creeping into his tone once again. "Not only is Mayfair the better place for you, you'll need someone to sponsor you and train you in all the right—"

"Train me!" Marlena had never gasped so many times in her life. "You have some nerve even for a duke, Your Grace. I am not a dog or a carnival animal to be trained."

He frowned and rubbed the back of his neck. "That was a poor choice of words."

"I'm glad you realize that."

"I'm not accustomed to arguing with young ladies about what is best for their future."

"You don't need to. Most of them already know."

"Apparently you don't. You might as well get used to the fact I may not say things the way you're used to hearing them. I'm not trying to be callous, just to get across my point that you need things I can't personally take care of for you."

"And here is my answer to you," she argued without fear of retribution. "Mr. Olingworth made sure I was well schooled in all necessary areas. I have mastered mathematics, sciences, French, the pianoforte, how to manage a household, and many other things. Everything he required of me, in fact. I don't need further *training* on any subject."

Much to her surprise, his expression softened. An attractive smile formed on the duke's lips. And much to her annoyance, it calmed her and soothed her anger.

"You were digging in the garden when I arrived, Miss Fast."

"No," she countered cautiously, and noticed that Tut wandered out of the room as if he was tired of listening to them banter. "I wasn't digging. I wasn't. Merely cutting the herbs for Mrs. Doddle. Because I enjoy it. Not because I must."

"Fine," he said, but the humor in his expression let her know he didn't believe her. "And fine, that you need no further lessons added to your accomplishments. But there are other things you do need before you curtsy before the Queen, make your debut, and enter Society. You must have connections to the proper ladies of the *ton* who can handle getting you invitations to the balls, private parties, teas, and the many other events that Society deems necessary for a young lady who is seeking a husband. You need clothing, gowns, gloves, and all that finery ladies put in their hair with feathers, beads, and ribbons to wear to balls. I don't know about these things, but I will employ someone for you who does."

Marlena had no argument for what he said. It was true. She had no connections to high Society and Justine's were limited, even though her cousin liked to think otherwise. Marlena had no proper clothing or a piece of jewelry of any kind to wear to a ball. She'd never had need of a silk gown or a velvet reticule. She didn't favor stiff, satin-covered bonnets that were worn for show. She preferred her straw hats. They were useful, malleable over time. Jewelry around her neck would probably just be a bother and become as tangled as her ribbon. She'd be pulling at it all the time. She had no use for delicate fabrics, either. They were expensive, easy to snag, and difficult to keep clean.

"I'm sure you didn't want to hear that I'm your new guardian," the duke said with a tone of finality.

"That is putting it mildly, Your Grace," she answered, her irritation at being in the unimaginable position of being the ward of the Duke of Rathburne weighing heavily on her.

"Quite frankly, I wish it wasn't so, too."

"I'm not sure that's apparent to me."

"Then let me make it clear. No matter the reason I accepted this responsibility, I am committed to taking care of you. We both must deal with this because it isn't going to change until you are wed."

"Then may I be wed quickly," she said tartly.

"The sooner the better," he quipped right back at her.

"That's the first thing you've said that I happen to agree with."

"Good," he said with fierce concentration. "Because surely even you know how damned lucky it makes you to be the ward of a duke."

They both sucked in a deep breath.

Marlena was quite simply stunned by the duke's proclamation and apparently he was, too. If he'd been looking for a way to silence their heated exchange, he'd found it. Marlena had no words to refute the duke's blunt remark. She was a practical person in all things and couldn't deny there would be many benefits to being under a duke's protection. All he said would be true—if she were anyone other than Miss Marlena Fast who wrote as Miss Honora Truth.

"And yes," he continued in a softer voice, "you might as well realize now that I sometimes swear in front of ladies. You'll have to get used to that as well."

"Contrary to what you must be thinking, it doesn't surprise me at all that you use such language in the presence of a lady."

"It looks as if we both have a lot of understanding to come to, but there's one thing that will not change. I'm in charge, Miss Fast, not you. I know you find me unsuitable to be your guardian, but I would have never thought you one to flee from a good challenge."

"Flee?" She huffed as her fighting spirit rose up within her. If she had to accept the duke as her guardian, so be it. She would, but she would do it on her terms. "I wouldn't run away from you, a wasp, or the ghost haunting the darkened hallways of a manor house. It would take a far bigger ogre than you to set me on my heels. I will agree to attend the upcoming Season to satisfy your responsibility. However, I will insist on a husband of my choice, and I want to continue to live here. I've been in this house for almost three years now and don't want to be uprooted. I know all my neighbors. They are good people. Besides, I have a special friend who lives next door. I'd be heartbroken to leave."

His eyes narrowed in displeasure. "You have a beau?"

"Of course not. Yet I'm not surprised that's where your mind immediately went. Eugenia Everard has been a good companion, and our friendship is important to me. Her mother died when she was young and her father passed on a few years ago so she lives with her sister,

Veronica, and her husband. Veronica is important to me, too. I don't want to move away from them."

"All right," he grumbled impatiently. "Since that is all you ask of me. You may continue to live here. Perhaps it will be for the best anyway, as I reside only a street away. It will be convenient for me to stop by often and check in with you."

"You live in St. James?" That wasn't what she wanted to hear. "I assumed you lived in Mayfair."

"We were called the Rakes of St. James, Miss Fast, not the Rakes of Mayfair. I prefer residing in my smaller town home closer to the clubs. Though my guests usually stay at my Mayfair house when in London."

"Oh, yes, of course," she said quietly. "I should have known a duke would have more than one home."

Without another word, the duke closed the scant distance between them. The toes of his boots brushed the hem of her dress. Heat from his powerful body reached out to her.

Before she could scream, move, or even draw a breath, she felt the duke's fingers touching her bare skin. She couldn't have been more surprised, more intrigued, more fully engaged if his lips had actually been on hers instead of his warm touch under her chin. He wasn't looking at her face but on his task at her neck.

She should have been frightened, but it wasn't fear she felt. It was something else.

Something far more worrisome.

It was attraction.

Inexplicable sensations stirred restlessly inside her. She didn't know exactly what was happening. He wasn't choking her, but she couldn't breathe. He wasn't hurting her, but she trembled. She wasn't in pain, yet she had the most intense yearning and urgency inside herself for something she couldn't describe.

"What are you doing?" she whispered, unable to look up at him.

"Kissing you deeply, madly, and thoroughly," he mumbled and continued with his undertaking.

"What?" Her gaze flew up to his face.

He smiled down so innocently at her that for a spark of a second she thought he might be serious.

"That's ridiculous," she said, reclaiming her good sense. "How can you say something like that? It's so outrageously untrue. You're doing no such thing and you know it. You aren't kissing me. You're untying the knot in my ribbon, which is highly inappropriate."

He centered his attention on his job at hand again. "If you knew what I was doing, then why did you ask?"

She didn't know. How could she think properly when the duke was this close to her? The tips of his fingers touching her. She had to say something. How could she not react to him in some way? The sensations she was having with him so near were completely new to her.

"I suppose I meant why you are doing it?" she managed to say without flinching.

He worked intensely. "So you won't strangle yourself further with all your fretting."

"Oh, you are impossible. I'm not fretting."

"You are, but perhaps you had reason to."

"I believe I did, but I refrained from doing so."

"I suppose it could have been all your talking that caused the knot to tighten."

"You make unbelievable statements, Your Grace. My talking didn't cause the knot to worsen, either. In fact, it hasn't." Her last statement was probably an exaggeration, but she'd said it and wasn't going to take it back.

"All I know, Miss Fast, is that you keep pulling on it and it's chafing a red mark on your skin."

She tried to lean away.

"Hold still," he insisted. "And quiet for now would be appreciated, too. I almost have it, and then you'll be able to breathe properly."

Marlena lowered her eyes. She didn't know if she'd ever be able to breathe properly again after his touch. She kept her eyes cast downward, onto his wide chest and the brown quilted waistcoat he wore. The buttons were covered in the same velvet fabric. Unlike the tailored garment on most gentlemen, there were no puckers or wrinkles showing around the buttons. The seams were flat and tight, proving there wasn't an ounce of extra weight around his middle.

She tried to be still, but it was impossible. She shifted her weight from one foot to the other, held her arms by her side, put them in front of her, behind her, and across her chest. The duke was just asking too much of her to be still. Didn't he know she'd never had a man stand so close to her? And certainly not for such a lengthy time. If he took much longer she'd probably find herself doing something as dreadfully inappropriate as he was doing such as trying to refashion the rumpled bow in his neckcloth.

When at last his hands stilled, Marlena lifted her lashes again. Their eyes met. An unnatural hush settled between them, but she didn't know what to say. It was as if suddenly words weren't necessary.

Her hat dropped to the floor behind her but his fingers remained still, warm, and pleasant against her skin. She didn't know why he wasn't moving away.

Why she wasn't.

As when he'd touched her cheek with his handkerchief, a now familiar prickle of awareness shuddered through her. It was intriguing, welcoming. And for reasons she didn't begin to understand she wanted to savor it. She wanted more of it. Though he was a danger to her because of her writings, something about him fascinated her. Reason and common sense were nowhere to be found. Anticipation for something she couldn't define with words ran rampant inside her. She couldn't stop whatever it was happening between them.

The duke's warm fingers slid around her neck and cupped her nape. His face moved closer to hers. His lashes lowered over his eyes. A shiver tingled over her. Instinctively, her gaze dropped to his lips, and she lifted her chin a little higher.

"Marlena, look what I just picked up for us to enjoy."

Whirling, Marlena saw Eugenia walking into the room carrying an armload of books. Her friend stumbled to a halt at the entrance when she saw the two of them standing so close together.

Tut came barking and running into the room. He stopped and jumped up on Eugenia's skirt, begging for attention.

Wide-eyed with confusion, Eugenia ignored the yelping dog and said, "Oh, I'm sorry. Am I interrupting something?"

Marlena's cheeks flamed hot as she swung back to the duke. Even though Eugenia clutched the bountiful stack of books to her chest, Marlena knew the duke could clearly read the titles of some of them if he chose to. By the saints! Why did Eugenia have to arrive at this very moment?

Was fate not through torturing her yet?

What was Marlena to do? Eugenia had their copies of *Miss Honora Truth's Words of Wisdom and Warning About Rakes, Scoundrels, Rogues, and Libertines*. The Duke of Rathburne was staring at them, and Marlena was in need of a miracle.

Chapter 3

He could be a rake if you think he only wishes
to touch your hand but tries to touch your
heart as well.

~~◆~~

*Miss Honora Truth's Words of Wisdom and
Warning About Rakes, Scoundrels, Rogues, and
Libertines*

"No, Eugenia, no," Marlena said hurriedly. "Of
course you aren't interrupting anything. Don't be
silly. The duke was helping me with, with my hat." As
soon as she spoke the words she looked around and saw,
to her horror, that the hat was on the floor quite a distance
from where she and the duke were standing.

What she told Eugenia was true but, somehow, she felt
she was guilty of much more than just allowing the duke
to help her with the ribbon. She had to thank her lucky
stars, if she had any above, it was her petite friend from
next door and not her cousin who had caught her standing
so close to the duke their noses were almost touching.

How had she let that happen anyway?

Because he's a scoundrel and knows all about seducing innocent young ladies!

She should have been outraged that he'd been so bold, so free with her. Yet despite reason and common sense, she had stood like a spineless ninny and let him help her.

Because the feelings he created inside me are so new and exciting, I want them.

"Did you say he's a duke?" Eugenia questioned softly, her anxious, light-blue gaze shifting from Marlena to the handsome man standing so quietly, watching her grip the evidence of Marlena's secret writings increasingly closer to her bosom.

As if realizing he wasn't going to get a pat on the head from Eugenia, Tut ran over to the duke and landed his front paws on the duke's shiny boots, his nails scraping the fine leather. The duke didn't seem to notice Marlena's furry friend, either.

"Yes," Marlena said, her hand going to the base of her throat and rubbing the place the duke had touched her so intimately she thought her heart might race out of her chest. "You see there was a problem with the ribbon on my hat. It became tangled, knotted really, around my neck, and I couldn't untie it. I tried countless times, pulling this way and that to no avail. You would think it would be such a simple thing, I know, but it was getting tighter and tighter. It was irritating my skin right here, and I was unable to pull it loose, and—"

"Miss Fast," the duke interjected when she paused for a quick and much-needed breath.

Marlena swung around to him, hoping he would have the prudence to help her and not make this matter worse. He bent down, picked up the straw headpiece, and laid it on the table beside the unopened envelope from Mr. Olingworth. "Why don't you save the long explanation for a later time and introduce us?"

Thankful for the respite, she gave the duke a grateful

smile and answered, "Of course, Your Grace, may I present Miss Eugenia Everard, my neighbor and close friend. Eugenia, the Duke of Rathburne."

Eugenia managed a very slight, wobbly curtsy, and took a step back before dropping all the books to the floor with a series of plops, thuds, and thumps. Her eyes rolled back in her head, and she quietly crumpled to the floor.

Tut barked and scampered toward her.

Marlena gulped.

The duke hissed an oath.

They exchanged shocked glances and then bumped elbows and shoulders in their haste to get to her stricken friend. Tut made it there before both of them and stood near Eugenia's head alternating between a bark and a whimper.

"Eugenia!" Marlena exclaimed, dropping to her knees on one side of Eugenia while the duke knelt on the other.

"Miss Everard," he said, placing a gentle hand on her shoulder and giving it a little shake. "Are you all right?"

"Quiet, Tut," Marlena scolded. "You are making matters worse. We are trying to help her. Sit."

Tut obeyed after giving another whimper.

Marlena looked down at her pale confidante. With her head moving, her lashes fluttering, Eugenia mumbled something that sounded very much like, "He finally came for us. Please don't let him take us away."

At that moment Marlena realized that, as she had first thought, Eugenia must be assuming the duke was there to confront them about the identity of Miss Honora Truth and the scandal sheet. Convinced the duke knew nothing about that part of their lives, Marlena had to do something quickly to make sure Eugenia didn't unintentionally give away their secret.

"You are fine, Eugenia," Marlena said softly. "Can you

hear me? Everything is all right. Nothing is wrong and there is no need to worry. The duke's not here to harm you."

The duke's head jerked up. He scowled in displeasure. "What did you say? Of course I won't harm her."

"I know," Marlena insisted, making it a point to meet his stare as steadily as she was capable of doing at the moment. "I'm sure of that, but it appeared to me that hearing your name frightened her and I wanted to reassure her."

"Well, it shouldn't have done anything to her," he objected. "Why would she have cause to think I'd harm her?"

"Perhaps I'm being overly cautious. I didn't want to cause her more anxiety should that be the case."

"She needs a sachet or smelling salts," he offered, looking around the room as if he expected to spot some sitting on a table. "That usually brings most ladies around to their senses after they've fainted."

"I'm afraid we don't have any. If you can help me get her to the settee, I'm sure she'll be fine."

He nodded.

Marlena thought the duke would help Eugenia to stand up and then walk her over to the settee. But no. Instead of assisting her to her feet, he gently slid one arm under Eugenia's slim shoulders and scooped the other under her knees. He then rose to his full height as if he were lifting nothing more than an empty wicker flower basket.

Eugenia's lashes fluttered again. Her eyes opened. She looked around before her muddled gaze settled on the duke's handsome face. Obviously realizing she was being carried in the man's strong arms, she promptly fainted again.

"By the devil," he rasped, gently placing her on the small settee.

Tut immediately jumped up beside her, curled near her hip, and barked once.

Marlena was worried. Eugenia was taking the duke's presence hard. Thank goodness her friend wasn't coherent enough to be asking questions about the duke or saying anything that might give away the fact that Marlena was Miss Honora Truth.

"What's wrong with her?" His Grace asked, after straightening. "Does she faint often?"

"No, of course not. I mean, I don't think so. She may not be as strong as some young ladies I'm acquainted with, but I've never known her to be this overcome by anything."

Eugenia mumbled again. Dreading what her friend might say when she came fully awake, Marlena moved to stand between the settee and the duke. Squaring her shoulders, and with as much aplomb as she could muster, she said, "Perhaps it would be best if you left me to attend to her, Your Grace."

He peered around Marlena and looked down at Eugenia with concern again. "No matter what she thinks, I'm not going to do anything that will hurt her."

"Of course not. Her fainting may not have had anything to do with you at all. I shouldn't have even suggested it."

"I don't want to leave you alone with her, Miss Fast. If she's unwell, I should stay."

"Nonsense," Marlena insisted, trying not to sound rushed but wanting to hurry him on his way. "Mrs. Doddle is here to help me should I need it, and surely my cousin will be down shortly. Really, I can handle Eugenia quite ably on my own now that she's off the floor. Thank you for that. I'm quite grateful to you."

"Then perhaps it would be best if I go so she can recover. She does seem uncommonly fragile. I've never seen a young lady faint twice in the same minute."

Marlena hadn't, either, but she understood fully why Eugenia had. Her friend had never had a strong constitution. The possibility that the duke had come for her was more than she could accept.

"I'm sure it's just that she's never met a duke before and she is still quite young. Just passed her eighteenth year. I don't fear for her well being. If I did, of course, I'd ask you to remain here with her until I could summon someone."

He seemed to study Marlena's face for a moment or two. She thought he was going to refuse her yet again, but finally he said, "In that case, please tell your cousin I'm sorry I couldn't stay any longer and meet her. I'll return another afternoon to do that."

"Yes, that would be best. I'll walk you out."

"No, Miss Fast. Don't leave your friend unattended. I'd rather you stay with her." He nodded.

Marlena watched the duke walk along the settee and turn to leave, but he stopped abruptly. She followed his gaze and saw he was staring at the pile of books scattered on the floor before him. Marlena's books. He strode over, bent down, and started picking them up.

"No, please, Your Grace." She rushed over and knelt much closer to his side than she should have, but she felt too awkward to move once she realized it. "It's not your place to do this. I can take care of them."

She reached for the books already in his hands, and her fingers covered his. A wave of something delicious washed over her. Their eyes met. Her heartbeat surged. Marlena jerked her hand away, held it to her stomach, and covered it with her other hand as if she could hide the delicious but unsettling feelings that rushed through her.

A flush of heat crept into her cheeks and slid warmly down to her neck.

"I don't mind doing it, Miss Fast. My father would say that I was seldom a gentleman, and he was right. On this occasion I will be and pick up the books."

The duke gave her the few he had in his hands and continued to gather the rest. "Did Miss Everard have to buy so many," he groused, piling more onto the stack in Marlena's hands.

"Ah—for our reading society," she said, thinking quickly. But in truth, she had no idea why Eugenia's arms had been full. She knew Mr. Trout, the owner of the publishing company, was going to give them free copies of the book but she'd thought it would be two or three at the most. Not more than half a dozen.

When the duke grabbed up the last book he held on to it and turned it over, glancing at the back cover as if expecting something to be written there before saying, "I would have thought a reading society would have chosen something a little more challenging for the mind than this kind of easy-reading fluff."

Affronted, Marlena frowned and leaned away from him. Her shoulders stiffened. She would have loved to tell him it had been quite an endeavor to write that book of quips and quotes about such men. What did she know about rakes, libertines, and all the rest of their kind who had no regard for a young lady's tender feelings? Or any kind of gentlemen, for that matter? Nothing.

She'd talked with Veronica, Justine, and most of the ladies in her sewing and reading societies to get their ideas on what constituted a rake and took their comments under advisement. Still, there were many nights she'd lain awake for hours trying to come up with things a rake shouldn't say or do concerning a young lady. And most of them had come directly from Marlena's *mind*.

She also wished she could let him know the book would have been twice as thick if she'd met him before she wrote it. There was no doubt that after a few more hours in his presence, she would have enough quotes to fill a second volume of words and wisdom! And she knew the first one she would write: *He could be a rake if every time he looks at you your heart starts fluttering.*

However, she had to put all that aside and only say, "If anyone needs to know the folly in accepting the attention of a known scoundrel or like man, it's an innocent young lady who has not yet given her hand to a gentleman. We need to be enlightened as well as educated so we don't find ourselves in ruinous circumstances."

"So I'm assuming you read penny dreadfuls, too?" he asked, with a spark of humor glinting in his eyes.

"Occasionally," she admitted awkwardly. "As well as books on poetry, history, astrology. There are simply too many other subjects to name that interest us. We have diverse tastes in our reading group."

"So it seems."

"I believe it is merely another form of entertainment for the people of London. We have plays, the opera, carnivals in the park, and gossip."

"I suppose you're right. Some people are entertained by it. They wouldn't read it if they weren't."

He kept staring at the book, so therefore she did, too. The title and her name had been beautifully scripted and stamped into the light-brown leather. It seemed to be well bound, stitched seamlessly on the edges, and not much larger than the size of his hand. A feeling of pleasure and accomplishment settled over her, and she smiled. She was quite pleased with the look of it.

And that it was hers.

Yet as the duke continued to eye it, curiosity got the

better of her and she asked, "Do you know anything about the book?"

"I can't say I do. Though someone mentioned it to me just yesterday. It's a new publication, I believe."

Marlena nodded.

"I haven't read it," he offered, thumbing through the pages with what seemed a fair amount of interest. "But I think I will."

"Why would you?" she asked cautiously. And quickly added, "Read something so unchallenging to your *mind*."

He gave her that easy smile again. The one that made her heart beat as fast as rain splattering against a windowpane during a storm.

"I wouldn't think you needed any words of wisdom or warning about such men," she advised.

The sparkle of amusement stayed in his eyes, and he shrugged. "You never can tell, Miss Fast. I might need to know how to spot a rake someday."

"Then may I suggest all you have to do is look in the mirror, Your Grace."

He laughed. "Your wit is charming, Miss Fast."

She couldn't help but return his smile, because he was genuinely pleased with her bold comment. She welcomed the humor in the duke's eyes. It softened him and made her look at him differently. Not as a commanding man but an understanding man. But she wouldn't let him know that.

"I suppose you thought you were an exception to the men in the book."

"If Society has indeed failed to make me aware of that after all these years of being the center of gossip, Miss Fast, I believe you have just set me straight on the matter. However, I'm thinking it might be helpful for me to know what a woman thinks makes a man a rake."

He thumbed through the book again, stopped on a random page, and read aloud from it: "*He could be a rake if he goes for an afternoon horseback ride with his friends instead of a carriage ride with you.*" The duke glanced over the top of the book to her and grimaced. "All young men enjoy their horses, their friends, and the young ladies. I don't see any reason why a man can't manage to do it all in the same afternoon."

"Hence the reason he is a rake, Your Grace. I'm sure the author only meant that if a gentleman is wooing a lady, his attention should be only on her and not divided with horseback riding, hunting, card playing, and those sorts of pleasures gentlemen usually enjoy. If his attention is elsewhere, he could be a rake."

The duke's expression was curious. "Hmm," he finally answered. "And he could be a gentleman who doesn't have his appointments under proper control." He held up the book. "May I?"

Marlena stayed very still but felt as if all her senses were clamoring for attention. He was asking for a copy of her book from her? The book she'd written with him and his two friends in mind. What could she say other than, "Yes. Yes, by all means, take one. As you can see, I have plenty left for my reading group."

Eugenia mumbled again. Marlena started to rise with her armload of books, and the duke reached out and took hold of her elbow to help her stand. A sensuous warmth of tingles spread throughout her body again. She felt strength in his hand and a strange sense of comfort and security in his grip. She should have recoiled or at the very least shied away from his touch, but it was simply too pleasing to withdraw from him.

"I'll return the book."

"It's not necessary to trouble yourself with doing that, Your Grace."

"It won't be any trouble. As I said earlier, I'll return

at another time to meet your cousin, and I'll be stopping by from time to time to see how you're doing. Go to your friend. I'll see myself out."

Marlena watched the duke leave the room. She had no idea why she was so affected by him unless it was because she'd written about him and the other two Rakes of St. James for so long. After hearing the front door open and close, she hurried over to a chair, dumped the load of books, and then flung herself down on the settee beside Eugenia.

"What happened?" Eugenia asked, lifting her head to look around the room.

"No, don't try to rise. You may be dizzy. You fainted." There was no need to further stress her by mentioning that she'd actually done it twice. "How are you now?"

"Fine, I think." Eugenia put her trembling hand to her forehead. "I really don't know as I'm feeling quite odd. The way I felt when Papa died and I knew I'd have to come live with Veronica. It was eight years ago but I still remember."

"Did you faint when you heard about your father's death?"

"No, but I'll never forget the feeling of thinking it can't be true. Papa can't be gone." She looked around the room. "Just as now, I could have sworn there was a gentleman here and you said he was the Duke of Rathburne, but it can't be true. No one is here."

"I wish I could tell you that he wasn't, but the duke was here."

Eugenia bolted up on her elbows. "Where is he? Has he gone for guards?"

"Lie back and stay calm, dear friend, please," Marlena urged after hearing fear in Eugenia's voice. "He left, and all is well."

"Then what was he doing here? Does he know about

us? Are we in trouble? Did he come to take us away? Is he coming back?" She plopped her head back on the settee in frustration.

"No. No. We are fine." *For today, anyway.* "Please don't worry yourself. I'm sure he doesn't know anything about what we do."

"When you said his name, I thought for sure I was about to be shackled inside a prison cart and carried away."

"I must admit that was my first thought, too, when he told me who he was. But believe me, the duke would have mentioned it if he'd known that I am Miss Honora Truth and that you conspire with me to see that the column gets to Mr. Trout to publish each week."

Eugenia placed the back of her hand onto her forehead again and expelled a loud breath of angst. "Oh, I knew I'd never be any good at this secrecy and deceit."

"Nonsense," Marlena reprimanded. "What are you talking about? We've been doing this almost three years now, and we've never had anyone come close to knowing I'm Honora Truth."

Her friend seemed to think on that for a moment and then said, "We have been lucky no one has figured it out." She paused again before saying, "The duke is more handsome than I expected him to be."

Indeed!

"But we must continue to see him as one of the men who is at the root of your sister's marriage and unhappiness, and the cause for her recurring attacks of despair."

"That's something else I'll never forget. Why was the duke here?"

"For a completely different matter, which I'll explain later. But tell me, first, why Mr. Trout sent us so many copies of my book? I almost fainted myself when I saw you walking in carrying them in your arms."

"I don't know," she said, rising on her elbows again. "It's what my maid brought in her sewing basket when she came in this morning. She had no explanation from her sister as to the amount, and there was no letter from Mr. Trout explaining."

"I suppose it could be that he wants us to give them away. Which we'll do; we can give them to our reading society. That will be good. I suppose I need to know what people think of the book."

"Do you think he gave us so many because the book's not selling very well?"

"It's only been out a little over a week, Eugenia. We must give it time. You know Mr. Trout has told us the scandal sheet is quite popular. He thought the book was a good idea and that surely everyone who reads the sheet will want a copy of the book."

Eugenia smiled, swung her feet to the floor, and sat up. "You're right. I don't know why I worry so."

"It's human nature. But let's give people time to purchase a copy of it before we get concerned."

"I promise I will. Now tell me why the Duke of Rathburne was here if not to have us arrested for writing about him." She stopped, her eyes rounded. "You don't suppose he found out about Mr. Bramwell, do you? That he and—"

"No, no, you must stop this. Do not work yourself into a faint again. The duke is not a shy man. If he knew about that he would have questioned me, and he wouldn't have left until he had the answers he wanted. Besides, he couldn't possibly have found out what Mr. Bramwell did for us. How could the duke possibly know that?"

"Perhaps someone finally recognized Mr. Bramwell as the man who started the rumor in White's."

"I don't think that's possible. Mr. Bramwell hasn't been back to White's. He'd tell us. And since your brother-in-law hasn't paid his account at White's in over two years, he'll probably never be allowed back even when he does."

"If he does," Eugenia echoed.

Marlena agreed that possibility wasn't looking good with all the money Mr. Portington was spending on his extravagances. "You don't think Mr. Bramwell would tell on himself, do you?"

A calmness seemed to settle over Eugenia. "No, of course not. He wouldn't indict himself like that."

"And he wouldn't want to see us in trouble, either."

"Never. He's a very thoughtful and intelligent man and always so kind to me." Eugenia's eyes turned dreamy, and a sad smile eased across her lips for a moment. "He would like to call on me, but Veronica would never allow it."

Eugenia had mentioned that almost every time she came over for the past couple of months. Marlena never knew what to say. Eugenia was right. Veronica would never agree. "She is only trying to take care of you the best way she knows how. She has been your mother as well as your sister for many years now."

"I wish she would just be a sister."

Marlena could have said to Eugenia that she wished she'd had a sister to care about her. Or that she wished her aunt Imogene and uncle Fergus hadn't decided to take their boys and move to America, leaving her behind with Mr. Olingworth, or when Mr. Olingworth suddenly told her she must go to London and live with a cousin she'd never met. But not wanting her friend to feel ashamed for her innocent comment, Marlena stayed silent about the feelings of abandonment that sometimes swept over her. She had managed. She'd always survived and learned how to adjust to wherever she was and accept whoever was in charge of her.

Eugenia sighed softly as if suddenly consenting to her

plight as well. "It is simply too unbelievable to comprehend that the duke was here in your house." She rose
from the sofa and looked down at Marlena. "If he doesn't
know you are Miss Honora Truth, why was he here?"

Marlena cupped her hands together in her lap. "That
is something I've yet come to terms with myself, but
know I must. He is my new guardian."

Eugenia fell back onto the settee with a plop beside
Marlena. "Guardian? How can this be? Did Mr. Olingworth—"

"No," Marlena said quickly. "He's alive, but still ill. I
assume he feels it's time to give the responsibility of seeing me enter Society to someone else. The duke's father
knew Mr. Olingworth. Apparently very well. His Grace
felt duty-bound to take over when Mr. Olingworth asked
him."

Marlena thought about the kindly old gentleman who'd
been good to her and allowed her to continue the inde-
pendent life she'd had when she lived with her aunt and
uncle and their boys. But he'd seen to it she was educated, too. He'd put few restrictions on her when she'd
arrived at his house. The few rules he'd given her were
easy to follow. She had to finish her studies, embroidery,
pianoforte practice, and any other lessons before she
could go outside. When dusk settled across the sky she
had to come in and dress properly for the evening meal.
Every night before she went up to bed, she had to play
chess with him or read for an hour. All his rules were
things she enjoyed anyway.

She swallowed a sudden lump that formed in her
throat. Shortly after she was born a fever swept through
her father's estate and almost everyone succumbed to it,
including her parents. Marlena was told she was spared
because her father had the forethought to have Marlena's
nurse take her to his brother's house, where she lived

until he wed his second wife. At that time her aunt Imogene and uncle Fergus took her to live with them and their boys. She would never forget her time with them or how following the boys around had shaped who she was today.

Much to her disappointment, when she was ten her uncle told her she must go live with Mr. Olingworth, because the family was going to America. They didn't feel it was right to take her from her homeland. She needed to be properly schooled and brought up so that when the time came for her to wed, she could make a good match with a suitable young man. Marlena hadn't understood them not wanting her to go with them, why her remaining in England was important, but after a time she'd accepted it. She'd had no choice.

When Mr. Olingworth's health started to fail, he had contacted one of Marlena's older cousins. It wasn't unusual that Marlena had never heard of Mrs. Justine Abernathy. One of her father's brothers had nine children by three different wives. Marlena had many other cousins from both sides of her family, though she knew little, if anything, about most of them. Having recently been widowed, Justine was agreeable for Marlena to move to London with her so she would be ready to prepare for her debut Season as soon as Mr. Olingworth was well enough to join her.

That hadn't happened. Mr. Olingworth's health continued to decline and Marlena's Season had been put on hold for the past two years. That was perfectly fine with Marlena. The only thing that distressed her was that Mr. Olingworth hadn't allowed her to visit him when she'd requested to do so.

"What are you going to do about the scandal sheet?" Eugenia asked softly.

Looking back at her friend, sprawled on the settee

with her head against the back cushion and her arms spread limp to each side, Marlena answered, "I don't know."

New concern clouded Eugenia's pale eyes. "You'll have to stop writing it."

"Maybe not."

"I remember you were going to discontinue it after the first Season but Mr. Trout didn't want you to and offered you more money to continue."

"It suited me to keep doing it."

"Only because you knew the money helped us. We know that, Marlena."

"That's not true it's the only reason," she defended, and then added after a prick of conscience, "Maybe at first it was. Yes, I wanted to help you. That is what friends do. Help each other. But there has always been a little of a *will-o'-the-wisp* idea that I couldn't let go."

"You're good at writing the gossip," Eugenia said with a smile of praise.

"I suppose. I do study over all the bits of gossip I hear and I'm careful with every word I write. I do feel everyone who reads the column enjoys it, and knows we really mean no lasting harm to anyone."

"Except to the three rakes," Eugenia injected with all seriousness.

Marlena pursed her lips for a moment as she remembered the handsome, forthright duke. It was really quite astounding that he admitted he hadn't been curious enough to ask Mr. Olingworth any questions about her. Maybe he'd be just as uninterested in every other aspect of her life, including Miss Truth.

"After meeting the duke this afternoon," Marlena said, "I do believe he considers the scandal sheet a bee he can't swish away."

"That is good news," Eugenia said with a satisfied huff.

"Mr. Trout says he still receives many good comments. However, you know I couldn't write it if Veronica didn't attend some of the social functions she's invited to and report back to me everything she hears. And Justine, too, of course, though she'd much rather talk about herself most of the time."

"Veronica does hear an enormous amount of gossip." Eugenia laughed softly. "I'm sure it's because she's so quiet. Most people probably don't even know she's nearby and listening to them. I only wish she were happy with Mr. Portington."

The relationship between the two of them was something neither Marlena nor Eugenia could help with. "We both thought getting a small measure of revenge on the rakes would have helped Veronica with the feelings of despondency that come over her from time to time."

Veronica had continued to attend some of the parties, refusing to give up her social life completely as her husband had after he lost his membership at White's. She hadn't found a way to remedy his obsession with his artifacts and fossils either. And she lay the blame for her hasty, unhappy marriage to the older Mr. Portington squarely at the feet of the Rakes of St. James.

Veronica had been one of the young ladies making her debut the year the rakes sent their secret admirer letters. Society went into a tailspin when they realized twelve young ladies had taken the letter seriously and had slipped away from their parents and chaperones to meet with their secret admirer. Only later to find out it was a trick created by the rakes for their personal wager and enjoyment.

There were no secret admirers for any of the ladies.

Veronica's bouts of deep melancholy were the reason Marlena had come up with the idea for *Miss Honora Truth's Scandal Sheet*. Shortly after she'd moved in next door to the two sisters, she'd become aware that Veronica was hopeless in her marriage, and blamed her situation on the rakes' letters. With a meager dowry, she'd felt as if the scandal had left her few choices when it came to marriage.

When Marlena heard that because of their titles, none of the rakes were ever held accountable, not even shunned by Society for a short time, she was upset by the unfairness of it, too. She wondered how the rakes would feel if their sisters were the marks of an ill-advised scheme their first Season?

Maybe they should find out, she'd thought. And just maybe doing so would help Veronica feel better about the decision she'd made to marry Mr. Portington.

Eager to help her new friends, Marlena had suggested they start their own scandal sheet to make sure everyone remembered what the rakes had done to the young ladies making their debuts that year. So the chickens had come home to roost for the three rakes who had so easily fooled innocent young ladies into thinking they had a secret admirer.

And thus *Miss Honora Truth's Scandal Sheet* was born.

"Surely you aren't thinking you can continue to write about the duke while he is your guardian," Eugenia said, breaking into Marlena's thoughts of the past.

"I don't know yet," Marlena answered truthfully. "That money is what helps you and your sister to continue to live in your house. You would have to move away otherwise. I must think about it."

"But what if the duke finds out?"

"And what if he doesn't," Marlena said, trying to remain optimistic. "There's no reason to assume he is even trying to find out who is writing the column or who started the rumor that the Duke of Griffin's sisters might be in danger of mischief their debut Season. Even if he did, you must not worry. I would never implicate you, Veronica, or Mr. Bramwell. I won't let anything happen to any of you."

Eugenia laid a comforting hand over Marlena's. "And we would never let you take all the blame for helping us."

"I'd want to. I would insist. Besides, what will he do to me, other than insist I marry so I'm no longer his responsibility? And he's already planning to do that."

"You marry?"

"Yes. I'll be twenty at the end of the year. Marriage is something I must start considering, as will you, as soon as the Season starts. The duke doesn't seem to be a patient man to me. I don't think he'll want the responsibility for my welfare for very long."

"And Veronica wants me to make a match this year, too. And I would if—" Eugenia stopped, sighed, and then continued. "There's one good thing about this. We'll be attending the Season together."

Marlena smiled. "Yes. We will be there for each other as we have been these past years. Now I will need you to help me keep your sister calm when I tell her who my new guardian is."

"Oh." Eugenia breathed the word out for a long time. "I guess she will have to know, too."

"Yes, but I will explain to her that she should have no worries about this and that you and I have everything under control. She will certainly understand that I have no choice in who my guardian will be. Besides, she's seen the Duke of Rathburne and the other two rakes on occasions at parties and dinners over the past years. She avoids them. That's the proper thing to do. No one in Society should ever know she harbors ill will. She would be the one punished. Not the dukes."

Eugenia nodded. "I'll reinforce to her everything you said."

"Good, because I really don't have answers to any of this, Eugenia, except I see no reason to change our routine. Veronica will continue to get the gossip from her group of friends and tell it to me. Along with the bits I pick up from Justine, I'll write the sheet and give it to you. You'll give it to your maid to hand off to her sister to leave for Mr. Trout when she cleans the publishing company in the evenings. So you see, there is no reason to worry about any of this. All will be good."

For now.

"Good afternoon, Your Grace. Terribly sorry to keep you wai—"

Marlena turned to see her widowed older cousin, Mrs. Justine Abernathy, waltz into the room with shoulders thrown back, chin arched high, and light-green skirts billowing behind her.

Chapter 4

He could be a rake if he tells you he will return
to see you rather than ask you if he may call
on you again.

—

MISS HONORA TRUTH'S WORDS OF WISDOM AND
WARNING ABOUT RAKES, SCOUNDRELS, ROGUES, AND
LIBERTINES

Both Marlena and Eugenia rose from the settee as Justine made an abrupt stop.

Marlena marveled at Justine's appearance. Surely her gown, cut low across the shoulders, was more suited for a fancy dinner party than an afternoon dress. A smoky-gold topaz dangled from a thick gold chain hung around her neck. Her ash-brown hair had been beautifully arranged on top of her head with multiple braided green ribbons gracing her crown. In one gloved hand she held a handkerchief in the perfect spot so the delicate lace trim would show.

After looking over the room carefully, Justine stared at Marlena as if she wasn't quite believing what she was seeing. "I'm sure the Duke of Rathburne was here. When Mrs. Doddle told me I didn't believe her, so I tiptoed to the top of the stairs and peeped. He was standing in the entryway talking to you. I know it was him. I've seen him many times and spoke to him at a ball just last year. He's divinely handsome."

"Yes, he was here. I'm sorry you missed him. He couldn't stay any longer and had to leave."

"Oh," Justine said, her tall, buxom figure seeming to shrink a little at the disappointing news. "I didn't think I took that long to change, but perhaps I did. I wanted to look my best. I couldn't very well come down to receive a duke dressed, dressed—like you, Marlena. My word! What were you thinking to greet a duke in such a simple day dress? You should have made yourself more presentable." She looked at Eugenia as if she started to say something about her plain gray dress but then, seeming to think better of it, gave her attention back to Marlena. "Our family may not be at the pinnacle of elite Society anymore, because of the unfortunate turn of events for our uncle, but in this house we most certainly know how to present ourselves and behave properly in front of a duke."

"Yes, of course we do," Marlena agreed, remembering how she'd taken the duke to task more than once and argued to remain in St. James. That certainly wasn't the proper way to behave. But wanting to soothe Justine's ruffled feathers with the least amount of fanfare possible, she added, "I'm afraid it was unavoidable for both of us. Eugenia had no idea the duke was here when she walked over."

"So you met him, too, did you?" Justine asked Eugenia, still sounding a little piqued she missed seeing the duke after getting dressed up to meet him and her neighbor hadn't.

"Briefly, Mrs. Abernathy," Eugenia answered timidly.

Justine harrumphed and her heavy bosom heaved.

"And I was outside and came around the corner of the

house to see him standing at our front door. It was impossible for me not to see him or he me."

"Don't tell me you were in the garden again!" Justine rolled her dark-green gaze incredulously toward the ceiling and shook her head. "Will you never learn? No, I don't want to hear it. I don't suppose I can worry about that now. It's spilled milk, as we say, and we can't put it back in the pitcher. I do hate that he couldn't wait for me after coming over to see me. I shouldn't have taken so long. We were introduced years ago and I'm quite sure I had a dance or maybe two with him before I wed Wallace. I was much younger then, you understand, and the diamond of the Season that year."

Marlena doubted the dance. There was no way she could know for sure, but she guessed the duke to be at least five years younger than Justine if not more. But according to Justine, she was the belle of every ball, the most sought-after widow at every party, and every eligible gentleman in the *ton* was just one question away from asking for her hand.

"Did the duke seem too disturbed I didn't make it down in time to greet him?"

That man? Disturbed?

He was too arrogant for such a human emotion.

"Not in the least," Marlena said honestly, and a little bit perturbed herself. "And rightly so. The duke should have made an appointment, or at least alerted us by messenger that he planned on paying us a visit. It was in poor taste that he came without making us aware of his intentions to call this afternoon."

"It doesn't matter about that, my dear," Justine stated, clearly not willing to budge an inch. "A duke can arrive at anyone's home at any time and be received. You should have immediately excused yourself to go and make yourself presentable."

She looked at Eugenia as if to add, *both of you.*

Eugenia seemed to take that as her opportunity to leave and said, "If you'll excuse me, Mrs. Abernathy, Marlena, I think I should be going back home now."

Justine nodded once.

"We'll talk later, Eugenia," Marlena whispered as her friend hurried past them with her head down, her chin almost resting on her chest. Turning back to her cousin, Marlena said, "I will take better care with my appearance in the future. I suppose both of us must, as the duke said he'd return another afternoon."

"Oh?" Justine's thick, light-brown brows lifted. She tucked her handkerchief under the sleeve of her cuff as if she were only mildly interested in what Marlena had said. "Yes, of course. I'd expect him to return. Tomorrow?"

"He didn't say when. Just that he would."

"I would assume tomorrow afternoon or the next. He didn't get to tell me what it is he wanted of me."

Marlena relaxed a little. Her cousin's softened voice was welcomed. Though Justine was only just past the half-way mark in her thirties, Marlena had never felt closeness between them. Justine wasn't unkind, her disposition not unpleasant—most of the time—but she was fastidious about routines and didn't like hers upset—unless, of course, a duke was doing it. Marlena often acquiesced to the older lady's schedule regarding when they could take a walk in the park, what time they were served dinner, or when they went out to shop for a new bonnet or pair of gloves. After all, even though they were related, she was still a guest in Justine's house. A paid guest, because Mr. Olingworth compensated Justine for taking care of Marlena.

Justine's most annoying trait was that she loved to talk about the past. It was as if she couldn't enjoy the present for always remembering the time when she was younger. She loved to talk about who had sought her hand and the many offers of marriage she declined her debut year. The list was endless. Almost any subject that came up could cause her to recall something that had happened the year she was an available miss.

"I'm pleased to hear the duke's returning," Justine continued, absently running her fingers over the large topaz. "As I told you earlier, we've met before on a number of occasions at various parties. Teas, balls, and the like. And we did have a dance. I'm sure. Though it was a few years ago." She stopped and smiled as with sweet remembrances. "I was much younger then." She repeated her earlier statement but didn't seem to notice. "He was younger, too. I was the diamond of the Season when I made my debut. Everyone said so, and I'm sure he noticed me. I had many gentlemen seeking my attention. Even Viscount Harthill. I suppose I should have married him when I had the chance. If I had I'd be living in a house in Mayfair now and not here in St. James."

Marlena knew the story well. Justine loved to tell it over and over again.

"Of course I couldn't marry the viscount. He was older than Wallace and not nearly as dashing and handsome. Every young lady wanted Wallace to offer for their hand so I had to accept when he chose me. I mean, I was the diamond of the Season. I had to marry the one gentleman every other young lady wanted." She sighed. "But I remember the viscount courting me as if it were yesterday."

"I'm sure of that, too," Marlena said, not wanting her cousin to launch into another story from the past.

Justine touched her hair and then lifted her bosom and her shoulders. "Did His Grace happen to mention why he sought me out?"

Marlena didn't know exactly how to answer that question, because Justine wanted to believe he had been there to see her. Noting the letter by the lamp, she picked it up.

"It seems the reason he came over was to bring this letter from Mr. Olingworth. After being my guardian for close to ten years, he has signed responsibility for me over to my new guardian, the Duke of Rathburne."

"What?" Justine screeched as if a rocker had just been pressed over her bare toes.

"He came to introduce himself to me." *And ended up doing so much more.*

Marlena rubbed her fingers where the duke's hand had touched hers when she'd reached for the books he was holding. As if it were happening right now, she felt his fingertips lightly caressing her skin while he untied her ribbon.

"The duke? Your guardian? He wouldn't do that. No, I can't believe it. There must be something wrong." Justine gave Marlena a skeptical glance and then eyed the letter. "Let me see that." She took the correspondence from Marlena without waiting for it to be offered. Huffing she said, "You always leave everything to me. How could you know what it says? Thunderbolts and lightning, Marlena, you haven't even opened it yet."

"His Grace told me what it said. I had no reason to doubt his word on something as important as this."

"A duke? Of course not, but I'll see for myself what this is about." She broke the wax seal and unfolded the pages. Scanning the writing, she began to mumble the words she was reading. Her eyes grew bigger, rounder. Her mumble grew louder.

Justine looked up at her and smiled. In an instant, she grabbed Marlena and smothered her up to her ample breasts, squeezing Marlena tightly. Her cousin's perfume had a heavy musky note of pine and evergreen. All the powder she'd added to her neck and shoulders wafted scents of lavender and had Marlena struggling to breathe without taking in the mixture of fragrances.

"Dear girl! Dear girl! If this is true, the saints have smiled upon us this day. This letter has changed both our lives forever. My cousin. My charge. The ward of a duke! Nothing could make me happier or more fortunate."

One moment Marlena was gasping for air in her cousin's strong grasp as she mumbled one sentence after the other and the next she'd been set free and stumbled back. Justine had never been so affectionate. Marlena was stunned.

Justine's brows lifted again. "Unless of course if I were his ward, or his . . . Never mind. Though there is the possibility of that. I do believe he's interested in me, otherwise he would have simply sent a solicitor to see us. But I must wait for that answer."

Somber once again, Justine straightened the neckline of her gown and said, "Yet I suppose we shouldn't celebrate too much until I speak to the duke myself. I mean I see it is written by Mr. Olingworth but he is ill. We don't know his state of mind. I really do need to hear from the duke that he's agreed to do this. I mean I can't be telling everyone such fortunate news only to find that it isn't true. I could never live down the embarrassment of such a mistake."

"The duke told me he had," Marlena insisted as she remembered the duke's strong words and firm expression. "He made it abundantly clear to me it was official and there would be no changing it. He even wanted us to move into his house in Mayfair."

"Oh, my, yes! I would expect he'd want us to do that. How utterly heavenly that will be." Justine clasped her hands together under her chin. "To return to Mayfair where I lived with Wallace and near my dear friend Lady Westerbrook. Yes, it is a dream come true."

Marlena knew Justine often talked about the house in Mayfair where she'd lived with her husband and the satisfying social life they'd led. After her husband had died, his uncle, who was Mr. Abernathy's benefactor, had cut Justine's allowance in half, and moved her from a larger house in Mayfair into the house in St. James. Maybe the reason Justine talked so often about the past was because she still hadn't adjusted to the change in social standing among the *ton*.

"Of course we'll move immediately. I'll have my maid start packing."

Feeling a prick of guilt to disappoint the cousin who'd been good to her, she said, "Justine, I told him no."

"No, what?" Marlena asked with a frown. "We never say no to a duke."

"I told him I won't move to Mayfair."

"Doesn't matter, dear girl," Justine said, "I want to and the duke wants us to. He offered us his home and you can't tell him no. I won't allow it."

"I'm sorry, Justine." Marlena took no pleasure in remaining firm on this, but she had to stay near Eugenia and finish the scandal sheet through this Season. "I know you would enjoy it but I wouldn't. I have declined and he's agreed. The matter is settled already. I may have to change guardians but I refuse to change houses, too."

Justine stared pensively at Marlena and looked as if she might say more on the subject but instead said, "Well, we'll leave it at that for now. As I said, we will tell no one about any of this until I speak to the duke."

"Thank you for understanding," Marlena said quietly.

"Of course," Justine said and sniffed loudly. "We'll stay here. Poor Mr. Olingworth has done right by you all these years. We shall never forget him. A sad thing for him to have passed, I know. But we won't dwell on that, will we, my dear? This news of your new guardian is too exhilarating and should be given its due significance."

"Justine, no. Mr. Olingworth hasn't passed on. He's

still with us as of now. It's just that he is making arrangements for my future while he still can."

"Oh. Well. Even better for the poor soul. How thoughtful of him to keep you out of the hands of the Chancery Court. Now, that would have been madness. Dreadful. There's no telling who they might have chosen as your guardian. You can't trust the lot of them. It's all about giving favors to their cronies and to whomever slips them the most money."

"I think I would have been better off," Marlena answered quickly. "I doubt they would have selected someone for me with the reputation of the Duke of Rathburne."

"It's true. They wouldn't have even considered asking a duke at all. The titled don't usually bother with such matters unless a very close relative is involved. That's why I must hear everything from the duke. I will speak to him about how this came about. It's probably because he remembers me from our dance and wanted to help me. I was the diamond of the Season, you know."

Marlena knew. She'd heard it several times a day since she'd come to live with Justine. At first Marlena thought she'd get used to the constant reminder. But that day hadn't come.

"I'll find out everything," Justine continued. "First, did you tell Eugenia why the duke was here?"

"Yes, of course. I tell her everything. You know that."

"I do. That is why you must head over to the Portingtons' house right now and make sure Eugenia knows she *must not* tell a soul about this. She's probably already told her sister and Mr. Portington, too, but make certain they know they must keep quiet about this."

"Justine, I don't think we need worry about that. They would never tell anything heard in this house."

Her cousin raised her eyebrows and said, "We won't take any chances. This will be my news to tell when the time is right. I'll probably tell Lady Westerbrook first. She'd like that and she can help me make a list of who to inform. Now you run along next door. I can't have them spreading this news before we are ready. We must do a little celebration tonight. Some amount is necessary, appropriate even." She stopped and shook her head as she looked at the hem of Marlena's dress. "And then up to your room and change. I see a smudge of dirt on your skirt. No doubt from the garden. I can tell by the color in your cheeks."

There hadn't been a ray of sunshine all day. It wasn't the sun that had put flush to Marlena's complexion. It was the duke.

Though Marlena knew she spent too much time outside, she tried to always wear a wide-brimmed hat even when there was no sparkling sunshine but . . . she often looked up at the sky, even if only to watch the dark gray thunder clouds to determine how long she could stay out before the raindrops started falling.

"I hope the duke didn't see the soil on the hem of your dress," Justine continued. "And I do hope that you will stay out of the garden now that it appears you have such an esteemed benefactor. I'm going to tell Mrs. Doddle we'll need a special dinner tonight. We're going to dine and celebrate as we did when I was younger." She stopped and smiled pleasantly as her bare shoulders lifted and her chest stuck proudly out once more. "You are under the protection of a duke. Which means I am, too, because I am the family member in charge of you. A duke! How good can one's life get? Tell me I am not dreaming. No, don't tell me." She turned to walk out.

"But wait," Marlena called to her. "Justine, doesn't it trouble you at all that such a man, a rake, a scoundrel, a rogue, and a libertine, will have control over my life?"

Justine blinked, clearly not expecting such a reaction

from Marlena. "Not in the least. I'm sure he's all that you say he is and more. Thunderbolts and lightning, dear girl, what's the problem? He's going to be your guardian, not your husband."

"And I thank the angels who watch over me for that," Marlena murmured under her breath.

"So what are you worried about?" Justine's brows went up again and she seemed to be studying over something while she fingered the topaz again. "Though I can't say it would be horrible if he has designs on me. And I think he might. I mean he wants to see me. And I have been married and know how to please a man."

Marlena gasped.

Justine cupped her hands under her breasts and lifted them up and then touched her hair. "Well, I won't say more on that subject. Such talk is not for your tender ears. Now please go next door before Veronica and Eugenia start gossiping and then do change into a gown. We are dining tonight as the elite of Society do. We have returned to it, my dear, and high time. We shall enjoy every moment of it while His Grace makes his intentions known to me and finds you a suitable husband. He probably already has someone in mind for you. Having the Duke of Rathburne as your guardian just made you the diamond of the Season as I was a few years ago—not too many years ago, mind you. We must rejoice!"

Justine laughed heartily as she floated out of the room. Marlena grimaced and folded her arms across her chest. The words her cousin spoke seeped into her soul.

A husband.

What would she do with a husband?

And what would she do with *Miss Honora Truth's Weekly Scandal Sheet*?

Chapter 5

He could be a rake if he goes to an inappropriate establishment and enjoys himself.

❧

Miss Honora Truth's Words of Wisdom and Warning About Rakes, Scoundrels, Rogues, and Libertines

On impulse, Rath opened the door to Miss Lola's Lacy Linens and Finer Things, surprised that with all his experiences he hadn't entered the den of frippery before. He strode inside with his usual confident step, taking off his hat as he entered. He was immediately assailed with intimate recollections from his ne'er-do-well past. The fragrances of prior conquests and mistresses assailed him at once, and momentarily he thought he'd entered into a hornet's nest of spurned lovers gathered to welcome him back into their arms.

His initial response was short-lived as he began to mentally sort the perfumes scenting the air and realized they were all illusion and not actual women.

The heady scents of warm honey, earthy minerals, summer vines, and sweet trumpet flowers seemed to explode throughout the room. There were too many different fragrances contained within these walls to distinguish them all, but he did briefly reflect on his past, with an almost visible wince of regret.

Moving forward, he didn't really know what he'd expected when he entered, but it hadn't been the explicit displays of provocative stays, silk stockings, sheer shifts, and enough lace to fill the cargo hull of a merchant's ship. Clearly everything inside was made for the precise purpose of setting a man's heart to beating faster and feeding his primal appetite for the fairer sex.

The shop, while not small, was overpowered by all the frills. Ornate handheld mirrors and silver hairbrushes, jeweled combs, and fancy gossamer gloves all graced chairs, tables, desks, and paintings that hung on the walls. Scattered among them were lace and beads woven in between the delicate items. Low-burning lamps added a soft golden glow to the room.

Obviously everything was meant to enhance and entice a lady's desire to please a man.

Rath had never seen so many feminine trappings under one roof and grew more intrigued by the second.

Thank you, Miss Fast, for the unknowing nudge.

He allowed his thoughts to stray . . . envisioning her ivory skin wrapped in nothing but a lace garland and shimmering pearls. Her glossy hair cascading across her shoulders and touching her waist where its slender nip beckoned his kiss.

"May I help you, sir?" A woman's voice stopped his fantasy cold, although the evidence of such in his breeches didn't immediately catch up.

Damnation.

He quickly shifted the hold on his hat to a more advantageous placing. Turning, he saw an older, attractive woman walking toward him. She could have been wearing her shop. Her dress was the color of lilacs and had what seemed to be mountains of lace around the neck-line and at the cuffs of her sleeves.

"Miss Lola, I presume." His greeting held warmth and regard. An enterprising woman was one he held in esteem.

"You presume correctly, sir."

"Rath. Duke of Rathburne."

"My correction, Your Grace," she said with a curtsy. Her smile was easy. Genuine. "We don't get many gentlemen in the shop. Titled or not."

He liked her instantly and gave a half snort, half laugh. Rather than prolong the moment, he questioned, "Do you carry smelling salts or must I find them in the apothecary?"

"If you'll forgive me, Your Grace, you don't look the fainthearted type. But I won't ask questions, and yes, I do indeed sell spirits to revive an attack of vapors."

Rath liked the woman's attitude, too. That she was industrious and wasn't going to let even a surprising customer walk out the door without putting in a good effort to make a sale was commendable. He didn't know much about smelling salts and sachets. Most of the women he knew weren't likely to faint at hearing his name or anything else.

He followed her to the back of the shop and caught a whiff of wildflowers as he passed an open drawer. He thought of Miss Fast again. He imagined her running through a field of tall yellow and blue blossoms, letting her fingers float along the tops of the blooms while her golden-red hair bounced on the back of her shoulders. A much more appropriate thought than his first but just as intoxicating and real.

The shopkeeper stopped in front of a long, cluttered chest where small bottles were placed among dainty satin balls, squares, and triangles all stuffed like little pillows with ribbons sewn on them so they could be hung around the wrist. That would be convenient for Miss Fast's frail friend. And no surprise to him, they were all neatly nestled among a cutting of sheer cloth, lace, and beads.

"Anything on this table would be appropriate for what you have in mind," she said, waving her hand from one end to the other. "They are guaranteed to rouse the deepest of fainters or to calm the slightest feeling of the vapors without causing a headache."

Miss Lola picked up a light-blue bottle with a fancy pewter top and opened it. She offered it for him to sniff, but Rath held up his hand and backed away. Even at a distance there was no doubt the vial had a strong scent of ammonia.

"Enough." He leaned away. "That would rouse a bear from hibernation in the middle of winter." He didn't know of a flower, fruit, or wood that could hide that scent or make it more pleasant to the nose.

"It does do what's needed in precarious situations," she assured him.

"Give me three of the bottles and three of the wrist pillows, too. I have a feeling this young lady seems to find herself in *precarious situations* more often than not."

"Very good, Your Grace. Can I tempt you to purchase one bottle of fragrance? Straight from the perfumeries in France. You know a lady can never have too much perfume."

Marlena came easily to Rath's mind yet again. He remembered her walking up to him, the wide-brimmed hat framing her lovely face, the perfectly tied bow under her chin, and the warm smile she gave him. Later, when she'd walked past him, he'd caught the scent of fresh-cut herbs, the earth, fresh air—a wholesome life. She wouldn't be one to wear perfume of any fragrance. Though for a moment, the thought of her using a liberal dose of rose water before going into the garden made him smile. There wouldn't be imaginary bees, wasps, and ladybugs dancing around her cheeks if she did that. They'd be real insects wanting to light on her.

"No perfume," he said.

"I understand. It's not for everyone. I'll take care of these for you at the counter." She picked up two of the bottles and two sachets. "I'll come back for the others."

"No need. I'll help you with them," he said and tucked his hat under his arm. He picked up the other bottle and three more of the satin pillows. If a lady couldn't have too much perfume, she couldn't have too many sachets, either.

After his purchases had been secured in a fancily trimmed package of lace and ribbons that no man would want to walk through Town carrying, he shrugged. The deed had been done. Time to make a hasty exit. But suddenly a bell chimed as the door opened and feminine chatter overtook the shop.

Familiar voices.

His stomach tightened. His steps slowed. Stopped.

The Duchess of Griffin and the Duchess of Hawksthorn walked inside, not looking in his direction at all, but immediately heading for a display of underclothing.

The wives of his two best friends and ladies he adored.

"Oh, look at these?" Loretta said. "These weren't here last time we were in." She picked up a gossamer-fine chemise, held it next to her body, and said, "What do you think of this?"

"That there's hardly anything to it," Esmeralda answered. "You can see right through it, but Hawk will love it." She then studied a very lacy corset and pondered, "I wonder if this will fit me?"

"Try it and see," Loretta suggested.

And then the ladies turned toward the counter and saw him. Loretta jerked the chemise behind her, and Esmeralda threw down the corset as if it had been a hot poker. They both stared at him in disbelief. With good reason, admittedly. He probably should have paid a little more attention to his gut instinct and kept walking when he saw the shop, but he'd let what Miss Fast needed rule his decision.

Esmeralda's golden-brown eyes widened, and Loretta's dark-blue orbs were firmly fixed on Rath's neckcloth rather than his face. Both of the ladies' delicate cheeks had turned a shade of pink. They were clearly horrified to see him, to know he'd seen and heard them. Their combined gasps had Rath wiping the corner of his mouth with his thumb in the hope of hiding his amusement. Perhaps they thought he'd never seen a pair of silk stockings, a lacy corset, or a see-through shift? By the saints, he'd probably loosened more stays and rolled down more stockings than the two of them had put together.

Be that as it may, the way Rath saw it, he had two choices. He could be himself or be as uncomfortable as the ladies were at catching him among the unmentionables and continue his hasty exit.

The choice was easy.

Rath had never been one to shy away from a situation just because it was awkward, and he'd never been one to stand on ceremony with friends. Besides, he wouldn't be the rake Society considered him to be if he let this situation pass so easily.

He didn't try to hide beneath his coat or lay aside his purchase onto the shop counter. In fact, looping a ribbon through his forefinger, he tauntingly swung the box as if it were a clock's pendulum keeping perfect time.

He smiled and said, "Esmeralda." He bowed and then

reached for her gloved hand. She slowly gave it. He kissed the back of her palm and said, "You're looking lovely this afternoon. How is Griffin?"

Without waiting for an answer, he immediately turned to Loretta and did the same thing, after she managed to wiggle the chemise enough that Esmeralda got the hint and took it from the hand she was holding behind her back, so she could extend it to Rath for his waiting kiss. "And how are you two fetching creatures today?"

Esmeralda finally took the first bite of conversation and said, "I must say it's a bit of a surprise—"

"Shock," Loretta finished.

"Indeed. To find you in here."

"Oh?" he responded, in no way deterred by the awkward shift in their stances.

He looked from one lady to the other. Their gazes kept sweeping down to stare at the purchase he'd made—both curious but neither daring to ask him what he'd bought.

Esmeralda turned to Loretta. "You know, I don't believe I see what I was looking for today. I'd like to try another shop."

"I was thinking the same thing," Loretta said just as quickly with relief washing down her lovely face. "If you'll excuse us, Rath, we'll take our leave."

He should bid them farewell without question or comment. It was the gentlemanly thing to do, but the rake inside him wouldn't acquiesce to the polite rules of Society. He'd never been any good at following them anyway, so why change now.

Even if Esmeralda and Loretta hadn't known about his reputation, his penchant for ignoring rules, before today, his presence in this shop proved his aversion to what others deemed proper. He knew letting them leave without further words or more embarrassment was the right thing to do, especially since they were the wives of his best friends and he'd dined in their homes on many occasions—but that's also what made detaining them a little longer all the merrier.

Besides, a little playful diversion might help settle their rattled nerves at seeing him in such an inappropriate place.

"What did you two come in for today?" he asked.

"Silk," Esmeralda said at the same time Loretta said, "Lace."

It took great restraint not to smile. If there was one thing this shop had plenty of, it was lace and silk. He knew they'd tell their husbands they'd seen him in here, and he'd catch hell from them for it. It wouldn't be the first time they'd peppered him with hot coals. Yet opportunities like this didn't often land in his hands.

"I came in to pick up something for my ward that *she* needed." Rath lifted the package to their eye level, innocently bobbing it for their discomfort.

"Ward?" Esmeralda exclaimed.

"Yes. A young lady."

"You?"

It appeared Esmeralda was finally regaining her composure. "What about me?" he asked inoffensively.

"Shopping for a ward in here." Loretta added, as indignant as Esmeralda had been. "You're unsuitable to be responsible for a young lady."

A feminine, "Yes, quite," from Esmeralda followed suit. "You must be teasing us."

Rath enjoyed them taking him to task. Especially now that the duchesses were getting over their astonishment at seeing him and were taking him to task. At first, he thought he'd have to bring out the smelling salts for them. Their demonstration that he lacked abilities to take proper care of Miss Fast didn't stress him nearly as much as they were anguished at the possibility of him doing it.

"I'm not trying to fool you about this, ladies, and I beg to differ with you on my qualifications to be a responsible guardian. Women like me, and I, in turn, respect and appreciate them."

"A bit too much, I'd say," Loretta's gaze remained fixed on his countenance.

Esmeralda blurted, "How did the poor unfortunate fall under your guardianship?"

"I was asked. By a family friend—who holds me in high regard." Not quite the whole truth, but close enough. "And as unthinkable as it sounds for me to be responsible for a young lady, I've embraced the idea and am ready to take it on."

"The poor lamb," Esmeralda whispered.

Loretta didn't let up, either. "What do you know about being a proper guardian to a young lady?"

"Not much," he admitted honestly. It was easy to do since he knew the ladies so well.

"Who is she?" Esmeralda asked.

"Miss Marlena Fast. She's not made her debut and I don't think you would know of her. She was the ward of my father's dearest friend. His ill health makes it impossible for him to continue."

Loretta dug her teeth in and asked, "Rath, have you told our husbands about this outrageous situation?"

"No, but I believe they will hear about this today." He feigned false encouragement. "I'll await their gallant responses and their reprimands."

Fortunately, Miss Fast was the reason he was in here, and she had given him the perfect justification to prolong this conversation a little longer and get him some much-needed help, too.

"I'm glad I ran into you today, Esmeralda."

Clearly she wasn't glad to be meeting him in Miss Lola's shop.

"I was going to stop in at Miss Mamie Fortescue's Employment Agency later today. I believe you were managing the place when you and Griffin met."

"Yes," she said warily. "That's right."

"Perhaps you could help me with something and save me the trouble of going by. If you wouldn't mind?"

"Oh, well, yes, of course, if you need me." She looked around the room quickly as if to assure herself there was no one else there to watch her continue to converse with a gentleman. "You know I'd be happy to help with anything I can—within reason. What did you have in mind?"

"I'm looking for a finishing governess for my ward." Now that he'd said the words, he wasn't sure exactly what they were called. He had little to no experience with a young lady who hadn't made her debut. The ones he knew were already properly set for Society with all they needed by the time he was introduced to them.

He really didn't know what went into getting a young lady ready for the Season other than fashions and the coveted invitations to the best parties and teas. There had to be more to it than that. Over the years he'd heard fathers talk about spending small fortunes to get their daughters ready for their debuts into Society and hopefully wedded bliss.

"I need someone who can prepare Miss Fast for the Season. Clothing, invitations to balls, Almack's. Everything. All of it. Do you know someone to suggest?"

With his sincere request for her help and genuine regard for his ward's welfare, Esmeralda's expression turned inquisitive and she asked, "How old is she?"

"Nineteen or twenty, I would say. I didn't ask. And it's for this upcoming Season."

"Oh, well that could be more difficult, Rath. I know several, of course, but whether or not they'd be available on short notice and at this late date, I'm not sure."

"I'd be most grateful if you could look into it for me. If it's not too much trouble for you."

"Not at all."

"Good, and I'd certainly make it worth the woman's time and consideration."

"I'm sure of that. It's just most of them are already prepping young ladies for this Season, but of course, yes, I'd be happy to see if anyone is available and can assist you. I'll be in touch about it when I have something to report."

"Thank you," he said with a slight bow.

"Rath," Loretta said with all seriousness, "you know we're fond of you—but perhaps you should give this duty of responsibility for a young lady over to someone with more experience."

His brow arched. "Who would you suggest has more experience with ladies and their wants?"

"Ah—with that," Esmeralda said confidently, "we must be getting on our way."

"Yes," Loretta echoed her friend's sentiments. "We've another engagement."

"Right. And we're late."

It was time to put the duchesses out of their misery and let them leave. But the devilish rake rose up inside him once more. It just wasn't in his nature to deny himself, and he had to say, "Surely you wouldn't leave without at least looking at the lace and silk?"

Rath reached over and touched a roll of lace. "The stitches are delicate. Must be Irish." His hand moved to a rack of exotic, flamboyant silks as he looked at Esmeralda. "I can tell you that your husband is quite partial to this shade of peacock blue."

"Not today," Esmeralda said, lifting her chin the way only a beautiful duchess could. "We've seen enough in here."

"But we'll be delighted to move on so you can finish your shopping," Loretta added and gave him a self-assured smile. "Should I tell Hawk you'll be over to visit him soon?"

"I'll expect him to have his best brandy open and ready."

The duo then departed without further ado, the shop bell finalizing their exit.

Rath's gaze trailed to the shop owner and he sincerely offered, "My apologies. I likely lost you a sale. Or two."

"Perhaps, but the exchange was the most interesting I've witnessed all week." Her eyes twinkled.

He laughed. "To make up for my conduct, I'll take a bottle of your best perfume."

A little while later Rath gathered his hat and packages and went out the door.

His stride, usually strong and sound, slowed. For a moment he questioned his judgment in this whole honor-bound duty of being a guardian. Being responsible for someone other than himself was a foreign affair. His carefree reputation was inarguable and he definitely wasn't the most suited to be Miss Fast's guardian.

But yes, he'd see to it Miss Fast married.

Taking up his swift pace toward his carriage once more, he tried to outrun that thought . . . because the notion of her married conjured visions of a husband he knew too well.

Himself.

Chapter 6

He could be a rake if he promises to call on you
but never does.

*Miss Honora Truth's Words of Wisdom and
Warning About Rakes, Scoundrels, Rogues, and
Libertines*

"Five days," Justine remarked in a huffing voice and
paced in front of the floral-printed settee. "Do you
know how long it's been since the duke graced us, or
rather you, with his lofty appearance?"

Oh, yes. Marlena knew exactly how many days it had
been and it wasn't because Justine had reminded her several times. For some reason she hadn't been able to get
the infuriating man out of her mind no matter what book
she read, what stitch she made on her embroidery sample, or what score she played on the pianoforte. She kept
seeing him with that hint of a smile that had made her
heart beat like the splattering of rain storming against a
window.

However, Marlena only answered her cousin with an
uninterested, "Mmm."

"It's shameful really, and I'm quite vexed about it,"

Justine continued. "He must know I need to hear from *him* that Mr. Olingworth's letter is indeed fact."

Marlena couldn't understand Justine not taking her word for it, but she'd stopped trying to convince her and had stayed quiet whenever she'd mentioned it the past several days.

"It's as if he has no manners nor respect for us, which we know can't be true. But he obviously hasn't any time for us. Most certainly because he is a duke and we are the lowly relatives of a disfavored earl. The more I ponder about this the more I'm thinking the duke has no pleasing qualities about him whatsoever." Justine stopped pacing. "Though he is quite handsome in a roguish sort of way, don't you think? He dances well, too. And if he does have designs on me, I'd have to consider him."

Marlena answered with another, "Mmm." She certainly didn't want her cousin knowing any of her own thoughts about the duke.

"But that doesn't make up for the fact I have forgone my afternoon beauty rest, dressed in my beautiful clothing, and had my maid labor over my hair almost beyond endurance every day for a week. And all for naught, mind you."

"There are seven days in a week, Justine not five," Marlena found herself saying.

Her cousin ignored her correction and walked over to the window and looked outside. "Since the duke hasn't had the civility to come by, communicate by a note, or even send a solicitor to speak to us about what his intentions are for me or his plans for you, perhaps none of this is true."

"You must give him time," Marlena answered absently while Tut lay quietly curled at her feet. He was used to Justine's rantings, too, but that didn't keep his ears from twitching every so often.

"I have."

"I'm sure he has many things to take care of throughout the day."

"Thunderbolts and lightning, Marlena. So do we. Still we take the time to dress in our finest to wait for him to call on us. And he repays us by not coming to our door."

Marlena tried to ignore her cousin's rantings and kept working on her column for next week's *Miss Truth's Scandal Sheet*. Justine never questioned Marlena about what or whom she was corresponding with when she was writing at her desk. Putting a quill in her hand and writing a letter, poetry, or even a note of thanks was the last thing Justine wanted to do. However, today had proven she was a master at the spoken word. She'd seldom stopped talking since she'd come belowstairs earlier in the afternoon.

It was difficult for Marlena to believe, but her cousin didn't even like to read. Justine had always said she was quite happy with her own thoughts and didn't need to be reading anyone else's musings. She had plenty of her own to occupy her mind. And if you thanked someone for having you to their party while you were there, she saw no reason to thank them again in a handwritten note later in the week.

Perhaps that was because Marlena had seen her script, and some of her words were truly illegible. Justine had owned up to the fact she'd never had the patience to master the art. The good thing about it was that Justine cared not a fig about how often Marlena picked up a quill to write a few words or what she wrote about. She simply had no interest in the written word, no matter who wrote it—unless, of course, someone wrote to her.

That worked out very well for Marlena not having to worry about her cousin looking over her shoulder with curiosity. Too, Marlena never added the salutation of

Dear Readers or her nom de plume at the bottom of the scandal sheet until she wrote the final draft and it was ready to be handed off to Eugenia.

Marlena picked up the wet inked sheet and silently read to herself: *The wintry season hasn't left us but the air is filled with a taste of springtime and a sunny hint of gossip.*

No, that wasn't quite salacious enough to start the column. Her readers wanted more than a hint of gossip. Marlena thought for a moment, then moved farther down the vellum and wrote again: *There may be snow clouds still gathering over London's streets and buildings but the latest rumors will be as welcomed as sunbeams streaking through an icy crusted windowpane.*

Marlena studied over that one for a few moments and decided it was better but not completely right, either. She might have to wait until Justine went abovestairs to rest before she came up with something to her liking today. The constant chattering and complaining was distracting. And for some reason it seemed to be wearing on Marlena's nerves more than usual this afternoon.

No, not *some* reason. She knew the exact reason. And that in itself was worrisome. She, too, wondered why the duke hadn't returned as he'd said he would. True, he hadn't said when he would be back to see them, but Marlena had thought it would have been within a day or two. Three or four at the most, not a day or two less than a week.

She looked up at the top shelf on the secretary. There lay the duke's handkerchief. Washed, pressed, and folded. There was no starch in it, and Marlena had told Mrs. Doddle to make sure there were no wrinkles in it, either. She wanted to return it to the duke as soft and fresh as it was when he wiped her cheek.

Glancing over at Justine, Marlena saw that her cousin

was staring out the front window as if trying to will the duke to show. Marlena picked up the handkerchief and smelled it as she had several times for the past few days. Nothing had changed. All traces of the duke's subtle, masculine scent were gone, and in its place was the arid smell a hot iron left on fine linen.

Marlena smiled and replaced the handkerchief where it would be easily seen whenever the duke decided to grace them with his present. Now that it was over, and she could think rationally about what had happened the day they met, it was humorous and made her smile. It really was quite clever of the duke to make her think she had a bee or wasp on her cheek when it was nothing more than soil from the garden. No doubt he was the kind of man who had no problem gingerly teasing a young lady.

But his tactic had also calmed her and helped her realize he wasn't there to have her arrested for writing about him. And though she was sure it wasn't his intention, he had vexed her when he untied her ribbon and his warm fingers had touched her throat. She hadn't stopped thinking about that, either. What surprised her most of all was that there was no meanness, no offensiveness or feeling of being forced to bear what he was doing. His untying the knot for her had not upset her sensibilities.

There was no impression he was being a rake, a scoundrel, or anything other than a man who wanted to help her.

"The duke said he'd get you a premier finishing governess and he hasn't bothered to do that, either," Justine complained.

"What?" Marlena asked when her cousin's words broke into her fond remembrance of the duke. "Not a premier governess, no. I never said that. I doubt there are any available at this late date. He only said that he'd hire someone who knows what to do."

"A duke can move mountains, dear girl, and we will

expect him to do exactly that for us," she said, walking back over to where Marlena sat. "There's precious little time left to get you prepared if he wants you to attend the very best parties, teas, and other events of the Season. Had we only known we could have already been working on obtaining such things, but of course Mr. Olingworth didn't keep us apprised of what he was thinking or doing so we had no idea there would be plans for you to make your debut this year. We certainly never received any money from him to get you started on your gowns. However, a duke can get whatever he wants and usually when he wants it. Best you remember that."

"I understand, Justine," Marlena answered, beginning to feel a little weary from her cousin's constant talking. "And even I know not much can be done other than clothing until everyone starts returning to London from their winter estates. Now, would you like to go to your bedchamber and rest as you usually do? There's only half an hour of proper visiting time left in the day. If you're worried the duke might come by, maybe you should keep on your dress and just be careful how you lie down. That way you'll be ready quickly should he arrive."

Justine cupped her hands under her breasts and lifted them up. "I can't lie down with these stays on. Heaven's gates, Marlena! They are pulled so tightly I'd probably stop breathing in my sleep." She touched her hair softly with her hand. "Besides, truth be told, I've hardly slept a wink since we heard the Duke of Rathburne is to be your guardian. I'm quite anxious to meet him again. Are you sure he said he'd return? Maybe you misunderstood and we were expected to seek him out for an appointment."

"I am not wrong on what he said. You are worrying too much. If you don't want to lie down, why don't you take a walk in the garden? I noticed some of the shrubs are budding."

Justine gave her a completely expressionless face. "Have you ever known me to enjoy a walk in the garden, the park, or even the street on a wintry day? Next you'll be wanting me to look through that tediously dull pamphlet you have from the Royal Horticultural Society that you are so fond of. Why you want to try to pronounce the ridiculously difficult names of what should be just a simple flower's name is beyond me."

"You are talking about *The Paradisus Londinensis* book by Richard Salisbury. And I quite enjoy reading the botanic names of flowers and plants."

"Oh, I know."

Marlena rose from her chair. "They're beautiful and lyrical."

It was Justine's time to say a very noncommittal, "Mmm."

Marlena could have added that the garden, the study of flowers helped fill the days in her life, but she wasn't sure that her cousin would understand. If Justine was thinking about Justine, she needed nothing else to occupy her time.

Being a widow with an adequate allowance, Justine had freedoms not afforded to Marlena and more things to occupy her time. She could attend parties, teas, or an afternoon of card game. Marlena must wait until she made her curtsy before the Queen and made her debut before she would be accepted at any of the social gatherings.

She and her cousin were very different in so many ways. Marlena would love to live on a sprawling estate somewhere in the countryside and have a garden so large it would take her half a day to walk through it. And she'd be happy to do it, winter or summer. She'd make sure the grounds were completely filled with shrubs, trees, plants, and flowers of every kind and color she could find. There would be arches, trellises, and waterfalls built into the landscape. Statues of the Three Graces, the four seasons, and plenty of cherubs, too. She would have a formal garden, a knot garden, and a field of wildflowers at the end.

Just thinking about it made her smile.

Perhaps a garden was something she should ask about when considering a husband. And she supposed she'd have to soon start thinking about the possibility of getting married. If the duke were to have his way. Though she truly had no interest yet in doing so. Marlena's foot started tapping at the thought of it. Surely she'd be happy living with a man and being his wife, if he had a lovely garden where she could go every day—as long as he didn't mind her helping the gardener check the soil, cut the flowers, and pull a stubborn weed or two.

"It's not wintry outside today, Justine," Marlena decided to argue politely. "It looks quite pleasant, and I'd never suggest you read any of my materials on flowers."

"Thank heavens."

"But I do think a little fresh air will do you good. You seem overwrought."

"You're right. I suppose I am. The duke knows I was the diamond of the Season, that we danced, more than once. Probably. It's simply unforgivable he's making me wait so long to see him again and renew our acquaintance and tell me his intentions for me—and you, of course. Maybe I will walk next door and say hello to Veronica and Mr. Portington and see his latest fossils, urns, tapestries, or whatever oddities have come in. I'm sure he has some since last I was there. He always does. At least the things he buys are interesting to look at and he knows how to pronounce them."

Tut's ears had perked up at the mention of Veronica and fossils. He rose and barked at Marlena, his tail quivering excitedly. If anyone was going next door, he wanted to go, too.

"That's a lovely idea. You know the sisters enjoy your visits. Perhaps Veronica has been to a party recently and has some interesting news to share with you that you can share with me."

"That would be a nice change from talking about the duke, wouldn't it? Yes. I think I will go over there."

"She does seem to know the latest on-dits. And with her husband's family being related to the Duke of Norfolk she does get invited to more dinners than most. I'm always pleased when she invites me to be her companion. Would you like to join me this afternoon?"

Marlena looked down at her writings. She didn't even have the opening sentence worked out. "No, thank you. Not this time. I'll finish what I'm working on."

"Dull as it might be," Justine said under her breath.

Marlena heard and took no offense. Her cousin's ire over her writing was to Marlena's advantage.

"No doubt you're writing about flowers again," her cousin said in a normal voice.

"I do believe Tut would like to go with you," Marlena said, putting the quill in its stand and rising from her chair. "If you don't mind. You know how he enjoys sniffing around Mr. Portington's latest crates."

"I suppose I can take him with me, but I won't be carrying him the way you do. He'll have to walk."

Did Justine really think that after almost three years of living with her Marlena didn't know that Justine had never once picked up Tut, rubbed his back, patted his head, or even offered to let him out in the back garden for a scratch, sniff, and search around the grounds? But it was best not to say anything and ignore Justine's comment. Now that she'd decided to go next door for a little while, Marlena didn't want to hinder her with more chatter and delay her.

"He really prefers to walk anyway so he can do a little exploring along the way."

"You will send for me immediately if the duke arrives."

"I promise to send Mrs. Doddle for you."

Chapter 7

He could be a rake if he brings a young lady a gift
she can't show to her mother.

~~~

*MISS HONORA TRUTH'S WORDS OF WISDOM AND
WARNING ABOUT RAKES, SCOUNDRELS, ROGUES, AND
LIBERTINES*

A few minutes after Justine and Tut left, Marlena had
finally settled on the first few lines of her article. It
was so much easier to concentrate when she had silence.
But after a few more sentences, she decided Justine had
disturbed her thoughts so much she needed to take a
walk in the back garden herself. Sometimes during the
winter months it was difficult to come up with new gossip because most of Society wintered at their country
estates. The parties in London were few. At those times
she'd rely on a new twist to an old story to get her past
the weeks neither Veronica nor Justine had anything new
to tell her.

She supposed that is what she'd have to do today.

Usually she'd have the sheet finished and given to Eugenia before dark but she wasn't sure that would happen. Not that it mattered much either way. Marlena could

always use what they called their *night plan*. There was a side gate in the fence between their two houses. They often stopped there to chat, or to exchange books or other things during the day. It was also where, when necessary, their clandestine meetings took place.

When the scandal sheet was finished, Marlena would light a lamp in her bedchamber before taking Tut out for the last time in the evening. That was Eugenia's sign that Marlena would be waiting at the gate for her with article in hand. Since it was a weekly sheet and not a daily one, as Mr. Trout had wanted her to do, their timing always seemed to work out. On the rare occasions they needed to have a nighttime exchange, it hadn't been a problem.

Marlena opened the desk drawer, slipped her sheet of musings inside, and closed it. After capping the ink jar, she headed toward the back door to don her cape and gloves. Just after entering the corridor she heard a knock at the front door.

She stopped and listened. Her heart pounding in her ears was the only thing she heard.

Could it be the duke? Justine's friend Lady Westerbrook? It could even be Mr. Bramwell since he lived next door.

Mrs. Doddle came out of the kitchen with flour on her hands, her apron, and her face.

"I'll get that for you," she told the housekeeper.

"Are you sure?" Mrs. Doddle asked. "It won't take me long to clean my hands."

"I'm sure," she answered, realizing there was a knot of anticipation in her stomach. "You continue making the bread."

After several deep breaths and much more expectancy than she should be feeling Marlena walked to the front door and opened it. She caught the duke with his hand midair, obviously ready to hit the door knocker again. He smiled at her and she would have sworn to anyone in the world that her heart flipped over in her chest.

There couldn't be a man alive who was more handsome than the one standing before her in a three-tiered black cloak, his white neckcloth showing above it, looking as dashing, dangerous, and devilish as the rogues she wrote about. Feminine desires Marlena hadn't known existed until she'd met the duke made themselves known again. Her pulse increased rapidly, her breaths grew short, and her lower abdomen clinched reflexively.

He removed his hat and said, "Miss Fast."

She curtsied. "Your Grace."

"May I come in?" he asked with a hint of humor in his tone. "Or should we stand on the steps for a few minutes and converse as we did the last time I was here?"

So as she remembered, he was a man who liked to tease and obviously not one to hold a grudge, either. She could accept that quite nicely. What she didn't know was if she could handle the fast beating of her heart and the womanly desires curling inside her every time she saw him.

"Well, it is an unusually sunny afternoon," she answered in the same light tone and easy smile he used. She deliberately looked past him to see a light-blue sky above the rooftops. "And it's so near springtime there are probably a few bees buzzing about in the garden. I know of no reason for us to hurry inside, except I believe my cousin would be quite perturbed with me if I didn't insist you join me in the drawing room without delay."

"Then I shall."

Marlena opened the door wider, stepped aside, and allowed him to enter. That's when she noticed he was holding an unusual package. Something about the size of a loaf of bread, wrapped in white lace and tied with a fancy blue ribbon.

She shut the door behind him and said, "Allow me to take your hat and cloak."

"I'll handle it."

He put his hat and the package on the side table and swung his expensive-looking woolen cloak off his wide shoulders, laying it beside the hat. He wore a dark-brown wool coat and a lighter-brown waistcoat. His neckcloth didn't seem to be tied any better than it had been the last time she saw him, but there was something about the careless bow that added to his charm. Most gentlemen were very precise in how their neckcloths were secured, but obviously that wasn't a concern for this duke. That more relaxed appearance appealed to her.

"I expected Tut to meet me at the door," he said, looking down the corridor past her. "He must be in the back garden."

"No," she said, pleased that he'd missed her beloved pet and expected to see him. "He's with my cousin visiting a neighbor."

The duke then picked up the package and said, "This is for you, Miss Fast."

Marlena looked at it. Flowers, confections, and books were about the only gifts appropriate to give a young lady, and this didn't appear to be any of those things. But no matter that, she was fairly certain that nothing should be wrapped in such a fine stitching of lace. She reluctantly took it from his hands.

It wasn't heavy, so it couldn't be books. In fact, it was very light. Confections, she would have thought, but still asked, "What is it?"

"Why don't we go into the drawing room and you can open it and see for yourself?"

"All right."

The corridor wasn't long but it was wide and the duke walked right beside her. Though their shoulders never brushed, she felt his warmth, sensed his strength, and matched the determination with which he took every step.

At the entrance to the drawing room she stopped, looked up at him, and said, "If you'll excuse me for a moment, Your Grace, I need to ask Mrs. Doddle to go next door and let my cousin know you're here. She's been most anxious to talk to you again."

"Again?" he questioned. "I don't believe I met her the last time I was here."

"No, you didn't. Not then. She says the two of you met some time ago. A few years, I think. And danced. She's recently seen you at some parties as well."

He seemed to study on that. "I'm not sure I remember her. Mr. Olingworth only said that your widowed cousin was your companion. What's her name?"

"Mrs. Justine Abernathy."

He gave her another slight smile. "If she says we've met, I'm sure I'll remember her when I see her."

"Make yourself comfortable inside. I'll return shortly."

Marlena stared down at the package as she walked into the kitchen. She decided it had to be fruit tarts. As for the lace covering, perhaps that's how dukes chose to wrap their gifts. Though it was still extravagant.

"Mrs. Doddle?"

The woman looked up from the kitchen table where she was thoroughly working a mound of dough. "Yes, miss. Do you need me?"

"I'd like for you to go over to Mrs. Portington's house and tell Mrs. Abernathy the duke is here." And then, having no idea as to why, her hands tightened on the lace box and she added, "Please feel free to finish what you're doing first."

"Thank you, miss. I'd like to get this in the bowl to rise. And then I'll go as soon as I can wash."

Marlena nodded and headed back to the drawing room feeling as if she'd done something decidedly wicked and yet feeling quite giddy about it at the same time. She'd deliberately given herself more time alone with the duke before Justine returned. Which, of course, was an utterly ridiculous thing to do!

It was impulsive, too, but she couldn't bring herself to be upset that she'd done it.

In truth, the less time she spent with the duke, the better for her. She must remember he was the main gentleman she wrote about in her scandal sheet. She must be careful around him at all times, and manipulating a reason to be alone with him, no matter the length of time, was the last thing she should be doing.

Reprimanding herself about it didn't help, either. She still wasn't sorry she'd done it.

The duke stood in front of the fireplace when she walked inside the drawing room and heaven help her, she swore her heart flipped again at the sight of him. He stood tall, comfortable, and so divinely inviting. She didn't want to take her eyes off him.

She would have to do something drastic to change her unexpected feelings and desires. So she walked straight over to him, extended the package, and said, "I thank you, Your Grace, but I really don't think it's appropriate for me to receive a gift from you."

A wrinkle formed along the top of his brows. "I am your guardian."

"Still, I don't think I should accept."

He relaxed his stance and continued to gaze into her eyes, clearly not wanting to give up without a fight. "It's not a personal item, Miss Fast. It's a necessity."

That sounded rather odd to her. "A necessity?" she questioned. "What does that mean?"

He folded his arms across his chest and gave the kind

of roguish grin she'd seen on the faces of the pirates she'd seen in paintings. And it was tantalizing.

"I guess you're going to have to open it and find out."

Marlena sighed. "You aren't making this easy for me, but all right." She pulled on the ribbon and the lace fell away from a plain tin box. After dropping the ribbon and lace onto a nearby chair she took the lid off and was immediately struck by such strong scents they almost took her breath away. There were several little satin pillows and three beautiful, colorful bottles of perfume.

Stunned, she looked up at him. "Contrary to what *you* think, perfume is not a necessity for a lady. Nor is it appropriate. I can't accept this from you and you should realize that."

The wrinkle suddenly extended to between his eyebrows and deepened. His bit of smile faded. "The only thing not appropriate about the package was me walking down the street to my carriage carrying it, but I did for you. Besides, it's not perfume, Miss Fast. It's smelling salts. I thought you might benefit from having some on hand in case Miss Everard faints again."

"Smelling salts come in a small clear or brown vial with a plain cork stopper, not in a beautifully shaped crystal bottle with a silver closure!"

The duke shrugged in a noncommittal way. "I suppose that depends on whether you go to an apothecary's shop for it or a la—" The duke stopped abruptly for a second or two and then continued. "Or a different kind of shop. It doesn't matter where they came from. I assure you they are smelling salts."

In what appeared to be one seamless motion he reached down, picked up one of the bottles, pulled out the stopper, and waved it swiftly under Marlena's nose.

A strong, offensive whiff assailed her. "Heavens!" She

quickly turned her head away but not before her eyes watered and she coughed. "What is that?"

"Mostly ammonia, I would assume. Now do you believe me when I say it's not perfume?" he asked, replacing the top and settling the bottle back between the sachet pillows again.

Marlena coughed again. "You—you have vividly made your point, Your Grace, but there are three bottles and at least four or five sachets in here. How many did you think I needed?"

"I don't know," he said innocently.

He was impossible. "Well, let me enlighten you. This is enough for almost every house on this street to have one."

Seeming to remain quite comfortable with the conversation as it was going, he said, "Miss Everard faints a lot."

"No," Marlena said, wanting to stomp her foot in frustration at the imposing man. She managed to resist the urge. "I told you she really doesn't. Except that one time."

"Twice," he reminded her as one side of his mouth lifted with an attractive grin again. "She fainted twice."

"All right," Marlena agreed, reluctantly, and found herself giving in to a smile as well. "But the second time she woke with a strange man carrying her in his arms. I'm sure that would unsettle anyone."

"She seemed terrified."

He was right, but that was one admission Marlena would take to her grave. "She was dazed." Which was also true.

"Then perhaps she simply needs to eat more, Miss Fast. She's slight and fragile-looking. She hardly weighs more than a few feathers. It might do her good to go into the garden with you once in a while and get some natural color to her cheeks as you have. Whether or not it's fashionable to do so."

Marlena lifted a hand to her face, and her fingers caressed her cheeks.

"Yes," he said softly, his dark-brown gaze sweeping slowly up and down her face. He stepped closer to her. "You look as if someone dipped a paintbrush in gold dust and skimmed it across your cheeks."

A strange and wonderful feeling washed over Marlena. Her breasts tingled, her abdomen tightened, and her stomach did a slow enticing roll. Something was blooming inside her. She could feel it. His expression, the way his gaze combed her face, made her feel as if the duke was staring at her and thinking to himself that she was the most beautiful lady he'd ever seen.

Why was she so attracted to him?

It seemed unfair she even wanted him in the same room with her, much less enjoyed their banter. He shouldn't be making her feel these wonderful sensations. He was a known rake. He'd ruined Veronica's life with his selfish prank years ago and thereby Eugenia's, too, for she had to live with Veronica and see how unhappy she was every day. Knowing that, Marlena should be appalled at the very sight of the duke. She'd always thought she would be should she ever meet him.

But she wasn't. She found it difficult to be upset that he'd teased her about an insect on her cheek, and even now his charm was soothing and enjoyable.

To cover the intense, pleasurable sensations budding inside her, she coughed again and cleared her throat. "None of that is here nor there at the moment, Your Grace. What is—" She looked down at the tin of beautiful bottles and satin pouches in her hands and extended it toward him for the second time. "—is this. As thoughtful and considerate as it was of you to think of my dear friend and her needs, I can't accept anything this personal from you. No matter what is in the bottles, they are beautiful and have expensive silver stoppers."

He didn't make a move to take back the package; instead, he clasped his hands together behind his back. "They are pewter, Miss Fast. You're mixing your metals."

Determined he take the box, she stepped closer to him, extending the box so close it almost touched the velvet-covered buttons on his waistcoat. "And you are mincing your words."

"I'm forced to when I'm with you," he answered.

"Because you seem to ignore the accepted rules of propriety and I have to remind you."

He moved so that the tin pressed against his middle and he leaned into it. Marlena hadn't expected him to do that and for a moment her throat seemed to close on her. Should she accept his challenge and hold the tin firm against him or pull away?

No, she wasn't going to surrender. She held her ground.

Keeping his hands behind his back, he pressed harder against the box between them. "You know, you're still as precocious as you were when we met long ago," he said.

"You're still as overly confident," she countered.

"You've been given too much freedom to speak your mind."

"Yet it impresses you that I do."

"It does," he admitted, his gaze remaining on her face as he leaned even more into her. "Your eyes are still as big and bright as they were when you were twelve."

Oh, he wasn't making it easy for her senses or her strength. She tightened the muscles in her hands and arms and held steady against his pressing weight. "I was ten."

"Your hair was unruly."

"It was uncombed."

"You held a frog."

Marlena didn't know how much longer she could defend herself. He was strong and he kept leaning harder and harder against the package. "It was a toad," she assured him.

The duke's brows squeezed closer together and the corners of his eyes narrowed. He straightened but didn't step away. "Good Lord, can you really tell the difference in the two?"

Marlena laughed a little. Her arms relaxed as his weight left her. She realized they were trembly from trying to hold her own with the duke—with dialogue and somewhat with strength, too.

"Actually, I can. Toads' legs are shorter and their skin is thicker and tougher than a frog's."

"I know the difference, Miss Fast. I'm just surprised you do, but I don't suppose I should be."

She relaxed. "I've always liked to read. I especially enjoy reading about gardens and all the things that grow and live in them." Fond memories washed over her and she smiled. "It was my cousins who helped me develop a joy for being outside. They insisted that before I could play with them I must catch a toad. Several frogs later, my aunt had mercy on me and told me the difference between the two."

"It sounds as if they little imps, but you didn't mind."

She nodded. "They were and no I didn't mind."

"And apparently you like reading about rakes, scoundrels, rogues, and—" He hesitated.

The duke seemed to be searching for the other word in the title of her book so, she said, "Libertines."

"Yes, that's it."

A fluttering started in her chest and moved up into her throat. Marlena didn't want to question him, shouldn't question him, but her natural curiosity wouldn't allow her to stay silent.

She had to ask, "Did you read the book?"

"Not yet."

That admission piqued her tremendously.

Not yet?

"You asked for a copy to read," she said hesitantly, trying not to sound petulant or even inquisitive.

She considered it downright shameful that he hadn't bothered to open the book after he'd asked her for a copy. He'd had it a week—almost. She had no doubt he could breeze through the pages in less than an hour if he'd simply take the time to sit down and do it. Even if he were a slow reader, which she was sure he wasn't, because he was so fast with his wit.

So why hadn't he? Other than to irritate her.

"I'll read it one day," he offered casually.

One day!

She was miffed again. Affronted even. If he were holding the book right now she'd rip it from his grasp. How dare he ask for a copy of *her* book and then not have the *manners* to read it.

He was truly devilish.

And she couldn't let it go, saying, "It's quite informative," sounding a little more peeved than she should have, but who wouldn't be a little upset at his lack of respect for the effort she put into every word.

"I'm sure most ladies will find it so." He moved closer to her again.

"I expect they will."

"But you know if I read it, I won't have any excuses for not changing my wicked ways. Miss Truth will have told me everything about the proper way to behave toward a lady."

"Then you'd best get to reading, Your Grace, because you have a lot to learn."

He slowly shook his head as his gaze held on hers once again. "Would you like to hear what I'm thinking right now?"

"That there are some things I know more about than you do."

"No, that I want to kiss you."

Chapter 8

Marlena suddenly felt so light she didn't know if she was still standing on the floor or floating just above it.

The duke wanted to kiss her? What did she think about that?

Yes!

He pulled his hands from around his back and caressed her cheek with the tips of his fingers.

That startled Marlena but she didn't back away. She couldn't have moved if she'd wanted to. His touch was warm, tender. Neither Mr. Olingworth nor any other man had ever touched her in such a sensual way. Not her hand, not her cheek, and certainly not her heart, but . . .

No. She would not allow her thoughts to go there.

The duke wanted to kiss her!

And someone help her, instead of being affronted, she wanted him to.

This was wrong. Madness even. She was drawn to one of the Rakes of St. James in a wanton way. And worst of all, she was having difficulty controlling her desire for him.

It was her common sense that finally rallied to save her. She stepped back and her legs and buttocks hit the edge of her secretary. She could go no farther.

The duke smiled mischievously. He was enjoying this battle with her and it looked as if he was set to win. That roguish, victorious expression he gave her boosted her courage.

One of the many things her cousins had taught her was to never cower and she wouldn't. She lifted her chin. Her breaths were shallow and fast. Her chest heaved as her gaze locked onto his. Yes, she had courage, but it was weak.

"That would be highly inappropriate, Your Grace," she managed to say past her raging thoughts and her breathless feelings.

"I know."

"Then why would you want to do it?"

He lowered his head, bringing his face very close to hers. "Human nature, Miss Fast. You are a young lady and I'm a man. But you are also beautiful, bold, and your wit is commendable and pleasing. I find all those traits desirable."

"Mr. Olingworth was my guardian and he never said he found me desirable or that he wanted to kiss me." Though there were times a hug or a pat on the top of her head would have been nice when she'd picked flowers and given them to him. "In fact, in all the years I was with him, he never touched me at all. And you touched me twice the first day we met."

The duke lowered his head toward her upturned face. "I'm pleased to know Mr. Olingworth is a true gentleman, as was my father. I am not. I want to kiss you. I don't mind telling you, and I think you want me to kiss you."

Oh, yes, she did.

But she couldn't. He couldn't.

"You can't kiss me," she managed to whisper.

"I know," he said, though his face kept coming closer to hers. "I'm not going to, but you can kiss me."

"Me kiss you?"

He nodded and the scent of windswept shores and rugged cliffs suddenly filled the air around her, making her feel languid and dreamy. Her breaths became deep and heavy with wanting what he was suggesting. She wasn't afraid to kiss him. It was just the thought that she shouldn't want to that held her back.

Yet her desire to feel his lips on hers was great, and he was so close.

So maybe she could kiss him. Not a long kiss of course. Just a brief touch of her lips upon his. Just once.

Only to solve the mystery of what a kiss would be like. As when the boys had encouraged her to touch her first snake, climb her first tree, and wade in her first icy pond without her shoes and stockings. She could consider the kiss a learning experience that she very much wanted to accomplish. When she went to Mr. Olingworth's house she'd been taught to dance, ride a horse, and manage a household. Shouldn't she be familiar with a kiss as well?

Marlena's lashes lowered over her eyes. She felt herself rising up on her toes to meet him. His breath lightly caressed her lips. She was only a second or two away from receiving her first kiss and it was a heady feeling.

Holding the tin tightly to her midriff with one hand, she splayed the other on the desk behind her to steady herself. Her palm landed on a piece of linen. She caught it up in her grasp and quickly shoved it between her face and the duke's.

"I have your handkerchief," she said breathlessly.

The duke slowly straightened again. He blew out a soft laugh and nodded. "So you do."

Marlena didn't know if she was relieved or if she would be forever regretful that she'd spoiled her chance for a kiss.

He took the handkerchief from her and slipped it into his coat pocket. "That was very clever."

It was her escape but she still wasn't sure she'd wanted to be set free.

"I know we shouldn't kiss," he said.

"That's good to hear," she agreed.

"It doesn't keep me from wanting to."

She wanted it, too, though she wasn't as courageous as he. She would keep silent with her answer.

He took a step away from her. "I know well my responsibility to you. I will abide by it with all the honor it requires of me. I'm your guardian, your provider, and your protector as surely as Mr. Olingworth and your other guardians before him have been."

"Thank you."

He glanced at the box in her hands. "Tell me, Miss Fast, would you have accepted that if Mr. Olingworth had given it to you?"

She looked down at the strong-smelling items in her hands. She wouldn't have blinked an eye if Mr. Olingworth had brought her the smelling salts in such beautiful packaging. But somehow with them coming from this man who from the moment she first saw him made her feel so feminine and desirable, she thought it must be inappropriate.

Being truthful, she answered, "I would have."

"Then I don't know what more I can say about what I brought today," he said calmly.

After taking in a long deep breath and then expelling it slowly, Marlena said, "I'll accept them as you intended them. A household necessity."

Since her secretary was right behind her she turned and opened the top drawer, wanting to hide the tin from Justine for, at least, the time being. There in plain sight for the duke to see as clearly as she could was her writing draft of *Miss Honora Truth's Scandal Sheet*. Marlena thought she might stop breathing, and for a moment she couldn't seem to move. Seconds ticked by before she slammed the drawer shut. She turned and leaned against the desk again, praying the duke hadn't had time to read many of the words on the page.

"Is something wrong?" he asked.

"No, I realized that the drawer is full and the tin won't fit," she fibbed, but with no small amount of guilt.

That was too close.

How could it have not dawned on her that her scandal sheet was in there? Because the duke had somehow bewitched her. He had her feeling strange sensations, wanting even stranger things like kisses and being held against that wide, strong chest. She'd have to be more careful. Justine might not care what she wrote, but the man she wrote about certainly would.

"I can help you rearrange the things in there so it will fit, if you like." He put his hand on the drawer to open it again.

"No, thank you, no." Without thinking, Marlena laid her hand on top of his to stop him. A shudder of awareness shivered through her. His skin was warm and she had the urge to give his fingers a gentle squeeze but instead she lifted her hand and said, "I believe it will work nicely in the second drawer." Nervously, she opened the next one down and tried to place the tin inside but the depth was too shallow.

Marlena couldn't believe the bad luck she was suddenly having.

Trying to stay calm, she softly closed it and opened the bottom one. Thankfully the tin settled in perfectly. She closed the drawer. Facing the duke again, she realized he was still scandalously near her. She backed up against the desk again.

"You're flushed," he said.

"Yes, I am," she answered, thinking quickly. "I'm not used to a gentleman telling me he wants to kiss me." *Or me wanting him to do it.*

"I agree, most of them wouldn't tell you, but believe me when I say they'd all be thinking it."

Marlena heard the back door open and she jumped. Tut barked. She heard his nails clicking on the wood floor as he ran down the corridor. Marlena silently sighed, knowing Justine was right behind him. Tut came running into the room and straight over to the duke to bark up at him. Marlena grabbed up the lace wrapping and ribbon from the tin box. She shoved them on top of the scandal sheet while the duke bent down to greet Tut with a pat on the head and a few rubs down his back.

Justine swept into the drawing room with her feathered headpiece all askew and completely out of breath. She must have run the entire way from the Portingtons' house.

She curtsied as if she were bowing before a king instead of a duke. When she rose there was a smile like none Marlena had ever seen on her face. She held her hand out as she walked toward him.

Yet by the duke's reaction and expression, Marlena believed he had no recollection of ever having met Justine.

Showing he was a gentleman, though, he took her proffered hand and lightly kissed the back of it.

"Mrs. Abernathy," he said as politely as the finest of gentlemen. "It's good to see you—again."

"Your Grace, I'm so glad you remembered me and our dance." Justine splayed her other hand across her bosom. "It wasn't that long ago, was it? Seems like just yesterday. I must say, I'm quite flattered and more than pleased. Honored, too, that you sought me out in order to help my dear cousin during her time of need. Thank you. Please, please sit down. Marlena, dear, did you order tea for us? Or would you prefer something stronger?"

There was no doubt, Justine was smitten by the duke.

And Marlena understood why. Heaven help her, she'd wanted the rake to kiss her.

"Nothing, thank you. I can't stay. I only came by to drop off a—a message that I have a friend looking into finding someone who can help Miss Fast through the intricacies of the Season. I hope to return with a name soon."

"So it is true," she said clasping her hands together in front of her. "You are Marlena's new guardian. Splendid!"

The duke gave Marlena a questioning glance so she said, "I was unable to convince Justine. She wanted to hear it from you."

"Naturally I didn't want to tell anyone until you confirmed Mr. Olingworth's letter," Justine defended. "I mean, the man's been quite ill and I have no way of knowing if he is of sound mind or delusional. I had to make sure he knew what he was writing and not just assuming." Justine stopped and smiled sweetly. "I mean one must not be too careful where an innocent young lady and a duke is concerned."

"No explanation necessary, Mrs. Abernathy. I understand."

"Well, then! This is superb, Your Grace. Of course I've taught Marlena everything I can, but entrance into Almack's and invitations to the most important and sought-after parties of the Season can be very difficult to obtain." She cleared her throat. "Even though I was the diamond of the Season my debut year, some in Society choose to ignore that honor." She smiled and lifted her chin. "I'm sure you remember. Still, you know that the dear ladies who control tickets and invitations for those events protect them as if they were made from pure gold."

"You need have no worry on that account. I'll see Miss Fast is invited to whatever is most advantageous for her."

"Excellent! And I assume you will still want me to be her companion and chaperone?" she asked in a softer voice.

"As long as you and Miss Fast are happy with the arrangement."

"Oh, we are, we are. We get along quite well. And while you're here, if I may make you aware that we really could do with a coach-and-four to be at our disposal as well as another servant or two."

"Justine," Marlena said. "We are perfectly fine without either."

Her cousin ignored Marlena and continued. "Mrs. Doddle has been with me for years, and my lady's maid, too. We have managed with just the two and no conveyance of our own, but now that Marlena will be entering Society, she will need more." Justine fluttered her lashes.

Marlena wanted to say, *What more?* but, deciding not to embarrass her cousin further in front of the duke, she remained silent and steamed that Justine would say something that was so obviously untrue. They had no need of more servants. They had managed quite well for almost three years. And why have a coach when all the shopping one could do was an easy walk if Justine would just do it.

"I understand, Mrs. Abernathy. I'll see that's done, too."

"Wonderful." She smiled broadly and rolled her shoulders in a flirtatious way. "Mr. Olingworth has been kind but he had limitations as to what he could provide for us. I assume we'll have no such limitations where you're concerned, Your Grace."

The duke glanced at Marlena but said nothing before turning his attention to Justine again and saying, "Well, if there's nothing else, I'll take my leave." He turned to walk away.

"Ah, Your Grace, yes, there is one more thing I would like to mention before you go, if you don't mind?"

He stopped and looked at her but remained quiet.

"Marlena said you had offered us the opportunity to live in your larger home in Mayfair, but she declined."

"Justine." Marlena spoke up without hesitation this time, knowing where her cousin was going with the comment. Rude or not, embarrassing to Justine or not, she would not let her control this. "You know I declined and I still do. It was kind of His Grace to offer but we will not accept. I like living near Eugenia. I made it clear to both of you I will acquiesce to a lot of things in order to attend the Season, however unwillingly, and become some man's wife so the duke will not have to care for me indefinitely, but on this issue I will remain adamant."

"Yes, yes, of course, dear girl. I know how close you and Eugenia are, and I do enjoy a visit with her and her sister from time to time myself. I only wanted to make sure you didn't have second thoughts about the idea and apparently you haven't so I'll just thank the duke for his generous offer to allow us to live in his much larger home." Justine smiled sweetly at the duke again. "Thank you, Your Grace. Now I'll walk you to the door."

Justine fluttered by Marlena.

The duke gave Marlena a touch of a grin and a nod before he followed her cousin out of the room.

All Marlena could think was that he had almost kissed her.

He could have read the start of her scandal sheet, but if he knew what he was reading he gave no indication.

Marlena suddenly felt as if she'd somehow just dodged the balls of two pistols that were fired at her chest.

Chapter 9

He could be a rake if he tells his friends about a
conversation he had with a young lady.

❧

*MISS HONORA TRUTH'S WORDS OF WISDOM AND
WARNING ABOUT RAKES, SCOUNDRELS, ROGUES, AND
LIBERTINES*

Hell's teeth, Rath thought as he opened the front door
of his town house. Miss Fast would be the death of
his sanity. He had wanted to kiss her. She had wanted to
kiss him. And would have if not for her good sense to
stick the handkerchief between them just before their
lips touched. He knew it was wrong to allow a kiss but
he would have.

A smile twitched the corner of his mouth. Thankfully
she'd found a rather sobering and amusing way to say no.
He could say that had never happened to him before.

She was his ward. A very appealing ward. He'd meant
those things he'd told her about providing for and pro-
tecting her. Even against himself. He'd thought on it all the
way home—which admittedly was a very short carriage
ride—why, when he could probably kiss any available mistress, lady, or widow in London, had he felt so desperate

to taste the lips of the one female who was completely off limits to him?

"Ah, that's the problem," he muttered to himself, plopping his hat down on the entryway table.

Forbidden fruit.

It had always been the most desirable, the tastiest, and the hardest to deny oneself. What he needed was a glass of port and a few minutes to relax quietly in front of the fire with his feet propped up so he could get his primal urges under control.

Too, it was best if from now on he spent as little time as possible at Miss Fast's house. He didn't need to be filled with the desire to ravish her. Not only was she his ward, but long ago he had taken an oath not to dally with innocent young ladies. And so far, he'd managed to keep that oath. He had no plans to break it now that he was nearing thirty and trying to make amends for proposing to Hawk and Griffin they send those damned secret admirer letters.

He couldn't think about his ward as anything but a responsibility and an obligation that he must fulfill. And the hell of it was that it would be a whole lot easier if she still looked like the gangly youth holding a frog—*toad*—he'd first met.

Rath started taking off his leather gloves. Another irritation crossed his mind. Who the devil would have ever thought smelling salts were an objectionable item? They were a common product that should be in every household. And what did it matter what kind of bottle they were put in? He thought all women liked pretty things sitting around their houses.

"Hell's teeth," he murmured again under his breath. Rath was beginning to see why Mr. Olingworth allowed Miss Fast to have her way in so many things. Her previous guardian was a smart man. It probably didn't take him long to figure out how much easier it would be to agree with her and let her have her way than debate her.

It was no wonder she had the mettle to speak with such confidence. Following five boys around a country estate for a few years would bolster anyone's courage. Not that he minded her pert answers during their conversations. He actually enjoyed them, which in itself was unusual for him. The only ladies who'd spoken their minds to him so freely were his best friends' sisters, Lady Vera, Lady Sara, and Lady Adele. And that was because he'd always thought of them and treated them as if they were his sisters, too.

Though his mother had died when he was way too young to remember her, Rath had still been around women all his life. He enjoyed them. They enjoyed him. He was good to them and in turn, they were good to him. From his nurse, to his governesses, to servants, and in later years mistresses, widows, and young ladies. But not even his friends' sisters Lady Vera, Lady Sara, and Lady Adele had questioned him or challenged to the extent Miss Fast had. And she did so without contemplation, fear, or regret.

"Your Grace, let me help you with that," Sneeds said, rushing into the vestibule as fast as his short, sturdy legs would carry his rotund body. "I didn't hear your carriage drive up or I would have been at the door waiting for you."

His new butler was another person who didn't seem to listen to him, Rath thought, throwing his gloves onto the top of his hat. But after his verbal boxing rounds with Miss Fast, he was in no mood to tell the eager-to-please Sneeds one more time that he needed no help removing his cloak, hat, or gloves. There were just some things a man wanted to do for himself.

"Your colleagues the Duke of Griffin and the Duke of Hawksthorn are here to see you."

Rath inhaled a deep silent breath. He expected them. Just not this soon. So much for his hope of a few minutes of leisurely time alone in front of a warm fire with a strong drink to think about the feelings Miss Fast had stirred inside him. It certainly hadn't taken Esmeralda and Loretta long to inform their husbands about his venture into the unknown lion's den earlier in the day.

"I did as you instructed me last time they were here and settled them in your book room with a bottle of your best brandy," he said, helping to pull the cloak from Rath's shoulders. "Would you like for me to pour a glass for you or would you prefer to be alone with them as before?"

"Alone, Sneeds. I'll let you know if I need anything."

"Of course, Your Grace."

Rath walked down the corridor, taking off his coat and then rolling his shoulders a few times. If there was one thing he could be in his own home, in front of his boyhood friends, it was comfortable. Though this day he didn't know how comfortable their conversation would be.

But he'd handle it. He always had.

The three dukes had been friends since Rath's first year at Oxford. He was a year younger than Griffin and Hawk, but it hadn't taken him long to discover those were the two he wanted as his friends. They were the smartest in the class, courageous, and fair. They loved a good escapade, and a little bit of trouble, as much as he did.

Though a strong friendship had already been established between Griffin and Hawk, Rath knew how to get their attention. He'd hidden a bottle of port in the fake bottom of his satchel. They were more than happy to help him drink it then—and all the other times he'd managed to slip a flask or two into the school without any of the headmasters knowing.

Their friendships hadn't ended but their long nights

of drinking, gaming, and voraciously indulging in extravagant behavior of the previous ten years had. The other two rakes had married. In all their experiences together over the years there had been many times one had tried to beat the other two, whether it be a wager about gaming, shooting, racing their horses, or the favor of a woman, but they'd never had a lasting quarrel.

He hoped tonight wouldn't be the first.

Rath strode into his book room seeing a familiar sight. Hawk and Griffin sat on opposite sides of the dark-blue velvet-covered settee. Both were tall, well-built, and handsome men, some would say. Unlike most dukes and other peers, they weren't stiff or haughty in their appearance or ways. They wore their privilege as easily as most gentlemen wore their neckcloths. There really wasn't much difference in the two, save for the fact that Griffin had dark-brown hair and blue eyes while Hawk's hair was a lighter shade and his eyes decidedly green.

Both held a glass of brandy. Griffin had one booted foot resting on the opposite knee, while Hawk's legs stretched out before him with his feet crossed at the ankles. There was no doubt his friends felt at ease in his house. They always had, and he in theirs. What surprised Rath was that they didn't look as if they wanted to rain hellfire down on his head for being caught by their wives in a ladies' unmentionables shop.

"Do either of you need a refill?" he asked, throwing his coat on his desk and making his way over to the opposite side, where the brandy was sitting on a tray.

"Not me," Griffin said.

"I'm good," Hawk added.

Rath poured a generous splash of the amber liquid into a glass and took a sizable swallow before turning around. He swung one of the upholstered wingback chairs away from the low-burning fire to face his friends. After settling himself onto the cushion, he took another drink from his glass and waited. He wasn't going to bring up the subject that was most assuredly on everyone's minds.

Finally, Griffin said, "So you have a ward?"

A ward?

Why yes. He did have one, but that's not the first question he expected to hear from either of the other two rakes. He supposed he should just be grateful he wasn't being cursed, so he simply nodded.

"A young lady," Hawk added.

Griffin's brows knitted a little between his eyes. "Who is set to make her debut this Season?"

Rath nodded again. He saw no reason to answer anything they weren't asking.

"Then why the hell didn't you tell us?" Griffin asked, leaning forward in his seat.

Rath shrugged. "It was only settled a few days ago. I kept thinking I'd see one of you this week at White's."

"We don't go out to the clubs as often as we used to," Griffin admitted.

Rath knew and understood why. But he was still a bachelor and had different pursuits from the two husbands. They now had other duties to attend in the evenings, and they seemed more contented men for it. He was happy for them. At times he'd wondered what it would be like to go home to a wife and children running up to grab him around the legs. But usually when those thoughts came to his mind, he dismissed them quickly.

"We should have been the first to know," Hawk added in a perturbed tone. "Not the last."

"Surely long before our wives," Griffin finished on an aggravated note before settling back against the settee again. "It shouldn't have happened they knew before us."

Other than Esmeralda and Loretta, Rath had told no one but Miss Fast and her cousin. He had no idea how many people they might have told. It couldn't have been many. There had been no mention of it that he'd heard at White's or any of the other clubs where he'd spent time the past few days.

"It wasn't my intention, it's just the way it happened. I had good reason for mentioning my ward to Esmeralda today."

"So she told me," Griffin said and then cleared his throat.

Hawk took a drink from his glass but never took his gaze off Rath and asked, "Who is she?"

Griffin leaned forward again. "What I want to know is how did you become her guardian?"

"You didn't do anything that caused you to be tricked into doing this for someone, did you?"

"Did this come about because you lost a wager?"

"Or won one?" Hawk questioned.

Rath held up his hand to stop the barrage of questions and huffed a tired laugh. Not that he hadn't been capable of being in that position in the past—he had and more than once—but like the other two rakes sitting in front of him, he'd mended his ways. Somewhat, anyway. Surely not to the extent they had. He might not have a mistress, but he did fill his nights at the gaming tables with a stout drink by his side.

"Nothing of the kind. You both know I might have been guilty of such behavior in my younger days, but now I'm more sensible. I don't wager horses, houses, businesses, or women."

"Then what?" Griffin asked.

"It's a long story."

Griffin made himself comfortable again while he and Hawk looked at each other and then at Rath. He knew exactly what that meant. They weren't going anywhere until they heard everything they wanted. Now he was wishing they were talking to him about their wives finding him at Miss Lola's rather than his blunder of accepting responsibility of the alluring and intriguing Miss Fast.

"The truth of it is there are many reasons I became her guardian." He shifted in the chair. It was never easy to explain oneself even to the people who knew you best.

"We've time to hear them all."

Rath untied the bow in his neckcloth and loosened the fabric at his throat, something his father would have strongly objected to. A gentleman stayed completely dressed until he was ready to change or retire for the evening. But Rath had never tried to be the gentleman his father had been or commanded Rath to be. Much to his father's disappointment. It simply wasn't in Rath's nature to always be properly dressed, to always say the polite thing whether or not it was true. Perhaps if his mother had lived past his sixth birthday, he would have been a better gentleman. She was a soft-spoken, gentle lady. A bright spot in his life that dimmed too quickly and went out. If she had been there to soothingly encourage him to do the right thing, instead of his father's demanding ways, maybe Rath would have been a different man.

After another sip of his drink, Rath considered being completely truthful, but did he really want to rattle off all the possible reasons he'd written that letter to Mr. Olingworth that night? *Because my father would have expected me to finally step up, be a gentleman, and do it for the old man. Guilt because the secret admirer letters were my idea. Guilt because after the wager went awry the two of you had the obligations of your sisters to marry off and I didn't. Feeling that in some way if I could help one young lady I might atone for the ones we embarrassed because of those letters.*

And endless more.

No. Whether it was one reason or a host of reasons

didn't matter. He would keep them all to himself. There were some things that didn't need to be shared even with men he'd known for what seemed like most of his life.

"Late one night, after having a few glasses of this"—he held up his brandy—"here in this room, I opened a letter from a man my father admired very much. Mr. Harold Olingworth. He'd written asking me to do it because his illness was progressing to the point he could no longer do so himself. By the time the bottle was empty, I'd picked up a quill and agreed to accept responsibility for her. The next day I had a clearer head and had come to my senses. I came in here to destroy the letter only to find that my new, eager-to-please butler had already posted it and was delighted to tell me it was on the early-morning mail coach already heading on its way out of town."

Griffin smiled. "When you were a younger man you wouldn't have made a mistake like that."

Hawk chuckled low in his throat. "So after all these years, fate finally decided to stop smiling on you at every turn and there was something you botched."

Rath took a drink. Fate wasn't something he thought a lot about. And he was no longer sure he'd *botched* this. Miss Fast was a challenge, and that suited him right now.

"You could have gone to see the old man and explained that you'd made a rash decision and couldn't possibly be trustworthy for an innocent young lady's welfare."

Always the levelheaded one of the three rakes, Rath expected a comment like that from Griffin. None of them were saints when they entered Oxford or Society. Instead of appreciating and revering their titles, the three had chased only what they desired, and that was drinking, wagering, gambling, and ladies of the evening.

"I did go to see the man right away." Rath leaned forward and put his elbows on his knees. "I had all intentions of forsaking my honor and going back on my word to take responsibility for her no matter how much the man might plead for me not to. Surely he would understand what a mistake he'd made in asking and me in accepting. I was not suitable to take care of a young lady and I was determined not to be swayed."

"I hear a silent *but* at the end of that sentence."

"With good reason," Rath admitted. "Olingworth was so ill it was impossible for me to disavow the commitment I'd accepted. He could hardly draw a breath but kept trying to—thanking me for accepting her guardianship, telling me how strong-minded yet sweet she was, and all I wanted him to do was stop trying to talk and breathe at the same time. I had to leave things as they were."

"So it was that bad?"

Worse.

Rath settled back in the chair and sipped his brandy again. It wasn't a scene he wanted to repeat. Ever. Miss Fast had told him she wanted to go see Mr. Olingworth but he wouldn't allow it. Rath could understand the man not wanting her to see him in that condition. Not wanting anyone to see him.

"What's her name?" Griffin asked, swirling the small amount of drink in the bottom of his glass.

"Marlena Fast. She's from a respectable family. Her dowry is small, but I'll enhance it."

"Is she pleasant to look at?" Hawk asked.

Very, and spirited, and wholesome, and quite bold.

"Yes," Rath answered.

"So you have no reason to think you'll have a problem helping her make a match?"

Rath swallowed hard. Miss Fast getting married wasn't something he wanted to think about, either. It didn't matter that doing exactly that was his primary duty for her welfare—finding a husband to take care of her the rest of her life. He turned his head and gazed at the fire through the brandy in his glass. It reminded him of the colors that heightened her cheeks. When he'd touched them, they were as soft as he'd imagined they'd be. None of the scents in Miss Lola's shop could compare to the natural, womanly scent of Miss Fast.

He probably shouldn't have told her he wanted to kiss her, but he was glad he had. She needed to know he was attracted to her. It was best she be wary of him. A nudge of admiration flared through him and along with it a hint of a smile. She was clearly up to the task of keeping him away—with a handkerchief!

"There should be no reason she can't make a good match," Rath said with no enthusiasm for the task. "She does have a determined streak. If she decides no man will suit, I have no doubt she won't accept any offers no matter how good they might be. But I gave up long ago trying to figure out a lady's mind."

"Yet you went into a ladies' shop today," Griffin said casually. "Did you hope to find some answers in there?"

At last his friends had gotten around to the real reason they were in his home.

"You do know what you did was tantamount to a lady entering a gentleman's club and walking around looking at all the men assembled there, don't you?" Hawk added.

"If I didn't, I certainly do now," Rath quipped, making light of his venture into the private world of ladies' underclothing.

"You do also know there are just some places a man and a woman shouldn't be seen together?"

Rath had no idea how much Esmeralda and Loretta had told their husbands, but he was fairly sure Griffin and Hawk hadn't wanted him watching their wives looking at unmentionables. He had to admit that part of their meeting was a little disconcerting to him, too. He thought of the duchesses as he did Hawk and Griffin's sisters. Having no siblings of his own, they were his family. Otherwise, he would have never annoyed them, but done the proper gentlemanly thing and walked past them without showing a smidgen of recognition.

In truth, he didn't think they would have liked that any more than he would have.

"My father tried hard to make a gentleman out of me, but as no one knows better than you two, he didn't succeed." Rath shrugged. "Besides, if they only wanted certain people to enter the shop, they should put a lock on the door or station an attendant at the front to keep out interlopers and lurkers as the clubs do."

Griffin snorted. "They probably thought there'd never be a chance in hell a gentleman would ever be brave enough to walk through the door of such an establishment."

Hawk smiled. "Why the devil did you?"

His best friends were having a good time at his expense. He'd done the same to their wives so he really couldn't say anything. Rath would let it pass and take his due. Besides, it was better than them being fighting mad at him.

"Smelling salts are for ladies," he defended. "I needed some and it seemed the perfect place to get them."

"Did you think about stopping by the apothecary?" Hawk asked. "Or asking your housekeeper to take care of getting them for you?"

No, to both questions.

"It was an impulsive decision," Rath admitted with no shame. "I was walking by, saw the sign, and entered. Damnation, do you think I'd have gone inside if I'd had any idea that your wives would be entering later? Or that the shop had such, such—"

"What?" his friends said in unison.

Thinking quickly, he said, "—an array of smelling

salts and sachets, which is exactly what I went in for."
He would not mention the sheer fabrics and mountains
of lace fashioned to titillate a man's natural desires.
"However, I'm sorry if I embarrassed and upset either of
Esmeralda or Loretta by being in there and talking to
them rather than passing by as if they were not right in
front of my eyes."

"Upset?" Hawk questioned.

Griffin huffed a laugh. "They weren't upset."

"Loretta was laughing when she told me about the expression on your face when you saw her holding an un-
dergarment, and she tried to hide it from you."

My face? What about hers?

"Esmeralda said you were so surprised your package
was shaking in your hands."

What little mischiefs their wives were to get back at
him in such a fashion.

The ladies had turned the tables on him and told the
story so that he was the one uncomfortable and awkward.
How clever. He should have known, or at least suspected,
they would. Neither Griffin nor Hawk would have married
a lady who wasn't up to the challenge of taking on a man
no matter the situation or where they were. Still, he was
quite impressed they had thought to make him the one
unnerved by the chance meeting.

Rath eyed both men carefully. They were telling the
truth as they knew it. So be it. He was all right with however the ladies explained the encounter to their husbands. He would never contradict the two duchesses.

"Esmeralda was amused about the incident," Griffin
said, "though she admitted to being a bit astonished to
see you in there at first."

Horrified at first is more like it.

"She said that after a moment or two you collected
yourself and the three of you had a nice conversation."

I had to collect myself?

"Loretta admitted she didn't know if she'd ever go into that shop again," Hawk said. "She had no idea you frequented the place."

He was pretty sure he'd learned his lesson about entering a lady's domain, too.

"That would be a shame for Miss Lola. There are some very desirable things in there."

"Yes, but apparently they both said they didn't want to be looking at ladies' undergarments at the same time you or any other man was looking at them."

Rath held up his drink to his friends and gave them a toast. "On that we all agree."

"Why were you needing smelling salts?" Griffin asked. "Is your new mistress prone to the vapors?"

"I have no mistresses at the moment and am quite content on my own for now." Rath had grown tired of their constant desire to please him and the fact there was no challenge in his relationships with them. "The smelling salts are another long story."

They both gave him the same expression as when he'd said becoming Miss Fast's guardian was a long story, and Hawk quipped, "Those are the kind that are always best told over a glass of brandy and in front of a warm fire among friends."

"And maybe it is long but I have a feeling it won't be boring," Griffin reminded him.

"Your exploits never are," Hawk added. He rose from the settee and walked over to Rath's decanter without seeking permission. He brought it back and poured a splash into each of the three glasses before replacing it and then returning to his seat. "We have nowhere to go, so take all the time you need to tell us about it."

"But before we get to that story," Griffin said with all

seriousness as he once again leaned forward in his seat, "I have one burning question that I must ask."

Ah, as Rath suspected. They were interested in knowing what kind of things were in Miss Lola's shop after all. He'd be very careful what he said, given that Esmeralda and Loretta had already reshaped what had happened to suit their desires. And it wasn't as if there was anything in the shop that Hawk and Griffin hadn't ever seen before, if maybe not in such an abundance of embellishments, scents, and styles. But he'd be willing to tell them a few details.

"Ask away," Rath said and took another sip of his drink. "After all these years with you two, I have nothing to hide."

Griffin's eyes narrowed and his brow wrinkled with determination as if he had to get to the bottom of something pressing. "Do you really think Esmeralda should buy a silk chemise in peacock blue?"

Rath sprayed brandy all over the toes of their boots and the floor, too.

All three of the rakes burst into laughter.

My Dear Readers,

Though the wintry days of Christmastide are long past, it's with good tidings of great joy I bring you the latest scandalbroth scattering throughout the clubs, homes, streets, and parks around London like flakes of falling snow. It's time to stir your imaginations and make you pant for springtime and the approaching Season. I have it on the most authoritative source available that the Duke of Rathburne, the only bachelor left of the Rakes of St. James, is now guardian to a young lady set to make her debut this spring. Perhaps he thought he didn't have to worry about revenge against him because he had no sister. Now he has a ward. I am fortunate enough to know her name and will share it: Miss Marlena Fast. So not only will we have the Duke of Griffin's unmarried sister, Lady Vera, attending her third Season, we now have the ward of the Duke of Rathburne. We will be watching and listening to be the first to know if either young lady settles on a husband this year. We will also be keeping our concentration steady on the rumor that was first repeated here two years ago to see if there will be revenge against the rakes heaped upon Lady Vera or Miss Fast—innocent though they are—for the dukes' past deeds.

MISS HONORA TRUTH'S WEEKLY SCANDAL SHEET

Chapter 10

He could be a rake if he doesn't understand that it
doesn't take much to make a lady cry.

~ひゃ~

MISS HONORA TRUTH'S WORDS OF WISDOM AND
WARNING ABOUT RAKES, SCOUNDRELS, ROGUES, AND
LIBERTINES

Though it was unnatural for her, Marlena was nervous.

For more than one reason. First, there was the duke.
He'd consumed her thoughts. Marlena hadn't been able
to get him off her mind since, in a moment of disquiet
at the prospect of such a forbidden act as a kiss, she'd
thrust his handkerchief between the two of them to
avoid it when she'd very much wanted the kiss.

She kept asking herself why she hadn't let their lips
touch when she had been so eager to do exactly that.
She'd thought about kisses before. With gentlemen who
had no defined features. Now she had a face in her thoughts
and fanciful notions. It was the duke's roguishly handsome features that confronted her, and they wouldn't leave
her alone and give her peace.

Surely it wouldn't have been so horrible to have allowed one little buss. If she had, the mystery of it would be solved. End of the story the way it was when she'd been in the woods with her cousins and they looked under a dead tree branch to see what insects were crawling around beneath it or when she's explored the attic of Mr. Olingworth's house. Surely there was nothing wrong in simply satisfying one's curiosity about something that was unknown. She'd know how it felt to have a man's lips pressed against hers. She kept asking herself why she hadn't let the kiss happen. Why had she placed the handkerchief between them?

And then there was the *other* reason Marlena was nervous today. Miss Honora Truth. Her latest scandal sheet had come out earlier today. The first since the duke became her guardian. Eugenia was on her way to buy one at the bookshop she and Marlena frequented, and to casually ask how *Words of Wisdom and Warning* was selling.

Or if it is selling.

Marlena was waiting for Eugenia to return by using one of Justine's annoying habits. Pacing in front of the fireplace and occasionally mumbling to herself.

When Marlena, Eugenia, and Veronica had first started this venture into the gossip writing world, they'd decided that Marlena must never be seen buying a copy of the scandal sheet, in the hope she could never be connected to it. And Eugenia seldom purchased one, but Marlena wanted to see this one in print.

She hadn't been this worried since the third or fourth one hit the streets. The one where she'd mentioned the rumor Mr. Bramwell had started at White's. That's when the sales of the sheet seemed to take off.

After the duke had left her house a couple of days ago, she knew exactly what she had to write. Once that decision was made it wasn't difficult to finish. The strange thing was that she'd never written about herself. She would be seeing her name in print and not someone else's. She'd never suspected she'd have a reason to write about herself.

In fact, she'd never written about anyone she'd ever met or had even seen until she'd met the duke. Now that she could put a face and a personality to the Duke of Rathburne's name, everything about the short weekly column seemed different. What had seemed more like a made-up story about people she didn't know was suddenly very real.

She'd quickly finished the piece and handed it over to Eugenia to give to her maid, but Marlena had worried about it ever since. She'd had to mention herself and the duke. She couldn't let a whole week pass without doing it. By then it would already be all over town that she was the Duke of Rathburne's ward. Justine was seeing to that. If she didn't get it to print, the gossip would be considered interesting but old news. Sales would go down and the monthly payment for Eugenia and Veronica would be less. She couldn't let that happen.

There had been no other options to consider. Once Justine had heard from the duke himself that Mr. Olingworth's letter was indeed true, she couldn't contain her excitement any longer. The very next day she was out all afternoon visiting with Lady Westerbrook and Mrs. Barnes; she had even called on the Duke of Griffin's unmarried sister, Lady Vera. The two had met at parties, but Justine admitted she didn't know Lady Vera well. Yet Justine wanted the duke's sister to know Marlena would be entering Society and they would look forward to having her over for tea at an appropriate time during the Season.

Marlena was already dreading the prospects of that meeting and many others when she started attending the afternoon card parties, balls in the Great Hall, at Almack's, and too many other social occasions to think about. She'd written about Lady Vera, and her twin sister, Lady Sara, before she married. Marlena didn't write about anyone once nuptials were said. And it wasn't that she'd ever written anything truly bad about the twins. She hadn't.

Though Marlena wasn't guiltless by any means. She'd been behind the rumor that had Society thinking there might be retaliation against the twins because of their brother's past misdeeds. That gossip had probably disturbed Lady Sara and Lady Vera's Season. Thankfully, nothing had ever happened to the twins. She hadn't expected it to. They were sisters of a duke. Who would be foolish enough to try and harm them or even ruin their Season?

Marlena had never been happy with herself for asking Mr. Bramwell to start that rumor. And she had expected to stop writing the column after the first Season, but Eugenia and Veronica's plight continued to get worse not better as she'd hoped. She couldn't bring herself to stop helping them.

Now that the time was drawing near, Marlena wasn't looking forward to meeting anyone she'd written about. When she started the scandal sheet it hadn't dawned on her that one day she'd enter Society and be meeting the very people she was gossiping about. Realizing that put an entirely different burden on her—and another measure of guilt, too. Just as she had after the first Season came to a close, Marlena was feeling the need to shut down the column once the upcoming Season was over, and hopefully Eugenia would be betrothed.

The back door opened and slammed shut immediately. Who would do something like that? Certainly not Eugenia or Justine. Tut went running from the room barking like a fiend. Before she could take the first step to see what was going on, Marlena heard footsteps bounding down the corridor. Veronica came charging around the entryway and into the drawing room. She flung herself face down on the settee and started weeping uncontrollably.

Tut came back in with her and continued to bark.

"Veronica, what's wrong?" Marlena asked, dropping to her knees beside the settee. "What's happened?"

There was only more weeping from her friend. Tut put his paws on the settee beside Veronica's head and barked again. This wasn't the first time either of them had seen Veronica storm over crying but it always upset Tut when it happened.

"Shush," she told her pet. "I'm trying to calm her." He whimpered at her and then barked again.

Mrs. Doddle rushed into the room, drying her hands on an apron that had goose feathers and dumpling flour all over it. "What's wrong with Mrs. Portington this time?"

Marlena looked up at her housekeeper. "I don't know yet. She doesn't look injured so I'm sure she's just upset about something again." Marlena grabbed hold of Tut and reached to hand him up to Mrs. Doddle. "Would you please take him out to the back garden for me and I'll find out?"

"Of course." She bent down and took Tut in her arms. He scrambled to get down, knowing he was about to be put outside and miss the drama. Mrs. Doddle held firm. "Let me know if I can help the poor lady. She seems to have more than her share of distresses in her life, doesn't she?"

Marlena smiled at her tenderhearted housekeeper and nodded. "I'll let you know if there's anything you can do. Thank you."

Marlena laid a comforting hand on Veronica's shoul-

der but she made no move to stop crying or look up so
Marlena gave her a slight shake. "Veronica, you must tell
me what's wrong."

With her face hidden in the cushion, she mumbled a
few words. The only word Marlena could make out was
Eugenia.

A slight chill raced over Marlena and she shuddered.
"Has something happened to your sister?"

Veronica nodded.

Marlena felt her whole body shake. "What?" Had she
and Eugenia been found out? Had someone finally figured out they were responsible for *Miss Truth's Scandal
Sheet*?

There was no answer forthcoming so Marlena tried
again. "Was she arrested? Was she struck by a carriage?
Did she get hit on the head with something? Veronica, you
must stop crying, sit up, and tell me. Where is Eugenia?"

Slowly, Veronica quieted and rose to a sitting position,
shaking her head, sniffing, and wiping her big, pale-blue
eyes. "No, she's fine I'm sure. It's Mr. Portington who's
not."

Confused, Marlena shook her head. "But I don't understand. When I asked you if something had happened
to Eugenia you nodded. So what is this about? Is Mr. Portington hurt? I can't help you if you don't give me details
about what is wrong."

She sniffed again. "Mr. Portington bought some eggs."

Heaven give me patience!

Marlena struggled to hold her tongue. She'd long
known that Veronica was emotionally delicate, predis-
posed to spells of crying, to having days when she wouldn't
eat or get out of bed, but it was ridiculous to be this
upset over something as simple and everyday as buying
eggs.

And Marlena wanted to tell her that.

But she couldn't. Certainly not in Veronica's current state anyway.

Giving herself a few seconds to change her frame of mind from wanting to tell Veronica how silly she was being to cry over this and throw herself into a fit of despair, Marlena rose from her knees. Spouting unkind things wouldn't help her friend feel better and could very well make her state of mind worse.

With a silent sigh, Marlena seated herself on the settee beside her distraught neighbor, and asked, "Why would his buying food of any kind disturb you so badly?"

"Because they're Megalosaurus eggs!" she exclaimed, and then covered her face with her hands and started wailing again.

Marlena wasn't familiar with that word but undoubtedly it was some new type of rooster, chicken, or perhaps a bird that Mr. Portington had heard about. Threatening her friend was the last thing she wanted to do, but at this point, she had to be firm.

"Stop crying please, Veronica, or I'll have to leave the room until you get control of yourself."

At that, Veronica dried her eyes, dropped her hands into her lap, and quieted to sniffles again.

"Now, I don't know what you mean by these Megalo—"

"Megalosaurus eggs," she responded softly, sniffing into a handkerchief she pulled from beneath her long sleeve.

"Yes. Why is that so bad?"

Veronica kept her gaze down on her hands resting in her lap. "Mr. Portington took the money I was to pay the modiste for Eugenia's gowns, gloves, capes." She twisted her fingers together. "All the clothing she needed for the Season. And he bought the eggs with them."

Marlena still didn't see why this was so disconcerting

to her friend. There was quite a bit of difference in the price of a few eggs and a few gowns. He couldn't have possibly used all the money Eugenia's father had set aside for her Season.

"What exactly is a Megalosaurus?" Marlena asked.

"A giant reptile that lived millions of years ago. Bigger than an elephant and taller than a giraffe."

Speechless for a few seconds, Marlena could do nothing but blink. Rapidly. "I've read about large bones and fossils of these bones being discovered in quarries and other places around England and throughout the world, but not the creature's eggs. I haven't ever heard of the word *Megalosaurus* before."

"One of Mr. Portington's friends, Mr. William Buckland, said the reptile hasn't been officially named by the scientific community yet, but it means 'great lizard.' He came up with it and hopes they'll approve the name he's chosen before the end of the year. Soon anyway. He found the bones but not the eggs. It was a different friend who found those and talked Mr. Portington into buying them, assuring him they are indeed fossilized Megalosaurus eggs from one of these giant creatures. He said that once it has been named and cataloged as such by the Royal Society of Paleontology, the value of the eggs will increase tenfold or more."

Marlena didn't know enough about this subject to even talk about it. She did know Mr. Portington had purchased some strange things and all of them were sitting around his house. There was the purported fossil of the extinct and legendary dodo bird, which had cost him a large sum a year or two ago. One of his prized possessions was a burial cloth he claimed came from the tomb of an Egyptian soldier that dated from the times of Ramses II, and there was a tusk from a long-extinct animal that looked very much like an elephant tusk to Marlena.

"What do the eggs look like?" she asked Veronica.

"Dark-gray lumps of coal. They're about the size of my hands cupped together. They are packed tightly in what looks like a fossilized breadbasket."

"Oh," Marlena said, not knowing what else to say about that for now.

She would have to do some reading about this subject before she could really understand what Veronica was talking about. However, that wouldn't help with the fact that Mr. Portington had used the money Eugenia's father set aside long ago for her debut.

Marlena knew Mr. Portington had managed to spend all the money left to Veronica by her parents and now he'd obviously started on Eugenia's. Veronica had lamented to him about his gross expenditures on fossils and artifacts hunts for years to no avail. It was as if he were deaf. Either his eyes and nose were in an article or book about fossils, he was looking at one through a magnifying glass, or he was corresponding by letter with someone about them.

"Are you sure he used all of Eugenia's inheritance?"

She nodded. "I asked him for money to pay the modiste and he told me he'd spent the rest of it on the eggs. I don't know what I'm going to do," Veronica said. "Eugenia can't attend the Season this year if she's not properly gowned."

"We won't worry about the possibility of losing all the gowns and other things she needs just yet. The Season is still weeks away and there may be something we can do to purchase some of them. At least a couple. Maybe not all the capes, gloves, and headpieces but enough to keep her properly dressed. We won't know what we can do until we have time to think about this."

"I don't know of anything we can do that will give us that much money."

Marlena didn't, either. Not right now, anyway, but

knew she would try to come up with something. Despondency seeped into Veronica's demeanor. Whenever her shoulders hunched and her chin sank toward her chest, she usually spent a day or two in bed. The last time she was in such a state was when Eugenia had told her the Duke of Rathburne was Marlena's new guardian. Marlena had finally convinced Veronica that his guardianship of her would in no way affect the scandal sheet or what Marlena was doing to help the sisters stay in their house and keep up appearances in Society. Veronica was desperate for Eugenia to attend the Season, make a match, and have happiness and her own home.

"Veronica, look at me and smile," Marlena said lightheartedly. "Come on, look at me. Smile. This is not a situation we can't handle. We took on three rakes with the scandal sheet and we'll come up with a plan to take care of this, too. We always do, don't we?"

She faced Marlena but didn't smile. Her eyes were red and puffy. Dull and distant.

"Let me have some time to work on this," Marlena said earnestly. "I don't know whether we'll make much or any money from the book I wrote. I'll write Mr. Trout a note and put it in with the next scandal sheet and ask. Listen to me," she said, taking hold of Veronica's shoulders. "You cannot take to your bed over this. Do you understand? Eugenia needs you to help her. So you'll stay strong, right?"

She nodded again.

"Good. I'll also ask Mr. Trout if he can pay us an advance for the scandal sheets. That's a possibility. I've not missed a week writing them so I do believe he'll do that for us. And perhaps if the book has sold a few copies, he'll give us some payment on that as well. So we have hope and prospects to getting enough money to pay for some of the clothing."

"I know the book is selling well," Veronica said, seeming to perk up a little.

"Really?" Marlena asked curiously. "How?"

"I hear ladies talking about it," she answered, brushing her dark-blond hair away from the side of her face. "They are enjoying it and recommending it to other friends, mothers, and aunts. Grandmothers and cousins."

"Oh." This information lifted Marlena's spirits immensely. Didn't Veronica think this was something that Marlena would have wanted to know? But rather than scold her friend for not sharing the news, she simply said, "Thank you for telling me. Now, it's important we don't mention to Eugenia that Mr. Portington spent money that was intended for her. We don't want her worrying unnecessarily that she may not get the new gowns and other things she needs."

"Yes. All right. I don't want her to know what he did."

"Good," Marlena said, and then repeated, "Do not take to your bed over this and don't say a word to Eugenia. Somehow I will see that all is well."

"She must attend the Season, Marlena, and find a man who is not like Mr. Portington. I will not have her as miserable as I have been for all these years. I'd rather she spend her life unwed."

"There's no reason she should have to do either. You know, she's quite fond of Mr. Bramwell. He's young, handsome, and prosperous now that he's inherited his father's tailoring business. I'm told that his easy charm and intelligence have made the company even more successful."

Veronica looked at her aghast. "He is a tradesman. Eugenia couldn't possibly consider marrying him. I've seen her watching him in the mornings. He walks past our house every day on his way to work. And they talk over the hedge when they think I'm not watching, but I am. I believe he's quite fond of her, too."

"He is," Marlena agreed.

"I appreciate his help, and we don't mind if they visit over the hedge, but she can't marry him. You know she'd never be accepted back in Society if she doesn't marry a gentleman."

Marlena wanted to say, *Would you rather she marry a gentleman like Mr. Portington who has no mind for business, no heart for home or family, or would you rather she marry a man like Mr. Bramwell who works a successful business, doesn't buy odd things, and is good to his mother?* But she held her tongue. She couldn't step into the sisters' affairs any further than she already had. Writing the column and the book, giving them the money she made from them, was all she could do.

"You're right, of course," Marlena said. "I wasn't thinking."

And what was she thinking when she started writing about three gentlemen and other people she'd never met? The same thing she was thinking now: Veronica and Eugenia needed her. They had from the moment she'd met them. And though it was trying at times, she wanted to be needed by someone.

She'd thought Veronica would feel better, do better if she knew they were not letting Society forget what the Rakes of St. James had done to young ladies with their secret admirer letters. But Veronica hadn't changed. She still had periods of hysterics and the depression that followed. The constant reminder to Society of what the rakes had done hadn't helped her despair.

When Marlena wrote the first four columns and took them to Mr. Trout as a sample of what she could do, she'd never dreamed she'd still be writing them almost three years later. But what else could she do when her friends needed the money because Mr. Portington was so reckless with his allowance that the family was at times in dire financial straits? She was forced to keep doing it for their benefit.

It wasn't fair Veronica's husband had become so reclusive and didn't take better care of his family. What was wrong with him? He was supposed to put his wife and her welfare first. Not take from his sister-in-law's inheritance and send them all to the poorhouse because he bought *giant lizard eggs*!

With that thought, an idea came to Marlena. She didn't know if she could actually do anything, but she would try. Turning to Veronica, she squared her shoulders and asked, "What is the name of the friend who sold Mr. Portington the eggs?"

Chapter 11

He could be a rake if he hesitates when a young
lady makes a simple request.

~◆~

MISS HONORA TRUTH'S WORDS OF WISDOM AND
WARNING ABOUT RAKES, SCOUNDRELS, ROGUES, AND
LIBERTINES

It seemed as if every carriage in London was on the
same street as Rath's. His driver was inching the
horses and landau along with the usual occasional
jolts, bumps, and sudden stops. The many shouts from
frustrated people up and down the long stream of con-
veyances did little to speed up the process.

Rath had forgotten there would be an end of winter
carnival in Hyde Park later in the day. Everyone must
have left their houses at the same time in the hope of
getting to the park early enough to stake out a prime
place to enjoy the afternoon and evening with family and
friends. Not that Rath was minding the slower pace today.
The longer-than-normal ride from his solicitor's office to
St. James gave him more time to study the papers in his
hand before arriving at Miss Fast's house.

Shuffling through the loose pages, Rath's eyes kept

capturing the same information time and time again. Mr. William Buckland was a highly intelligent and well-learned man. Noted for being a clergyman, a fossil hunter, and a geologist. He'd recently been elected a fellow into the Royal Society. That was no small accomplishment. Rath was sure it had been a boost to his reputation and his rapid rise to prominence in his chosen fields of study, because he had the Prince's ear. Thereby, the Regent's monetary support as well. But the main thing that caught Rath's attention—the man was also a bachelor.

The probe into Mr. Herbert Wentfield's life had been an entirely different story. And that was odd.

It was perplexing to Rath why Miss Fast wanted to know so much about the two men. Why did Mr. Buckland's obsession with diggings in the earth for scientific purposes in order to prove historical facts, or to look for animal bones and fossils interest her? Not to mention all the explorations he'd conducted and the honors he'd been given because of them.

Rath hit his knee with the stack of papers. Was she interested in making a match with either of the men? That thought didn't sit well with him.

And if she had such notions, what was she thinking to send Rath a note asking that he obtain *any and all* information possible for her on Mr. Buckland and Mr. Wentfield? Did she consider Rath her personal secretary to do her bidding on gentlemen she might be interested in for marriage just because he was her guardian?

He blew out a grunted laugh. That was precisely what he was supposed to do. And he had. If making a match with either of these men was her consideration, didn't she know Buckland was too old for her? He was probably closer to four score than three. He did wonder how she knew about the unknown Wentfield when Rath's solicitor couldn't find out anything about him.

Rath started out not even responding to her unusual and cheeky request of him. Nevertheless, in the end, his responsibility to her and no small amount of curiosity had gotten the best of him. After a couple of days stewing about her note and rereading it numerous times, he'd had his solicitor find all the articles available that had been written about Buckland and the ones the man himself had written. And then Rath had to read the damned stuff to make sure it was appropriate for her to see. He couldn't allow her to be inquiring about someone who might have led a life completely unsuitable for her to read about. Rath certainly wouldn't want an innocent young lady reading about his own life.

Though it wasn't a natural inclination for young ladies, Miss Fast had admitted she liked to till the ground around the flowers and cut the blooms rather than just walk in the garden and enjoy the beauty. Maybe it wasn't unusual she'd be interested in someone who liked to dig deep below the earth's surface for ancient carcasses. After all, she'd lived in a house with boys and followed them around until the day she moved to Mr. Olingworth's. He could see her cousins had great influence in her life. And not in a bad way.

Once Rath had gotten over his reluctance to do so, he'd done what she asked, and now she was going to do the same. And tell him why she'd wanted the details on these men's lives and work.

There was another reason he'd wanted to get the facts on Buckland and Westfield, though it took a while for him to admit it to himself. Being Marlena's guardian had given him a challenge unlike any he'd ever accepted before. Over the years of his youth and beyond there had been many dares and gambles from friends and foes alike. Every one he'd met, and most of them he'd won.

The most stimulating had come from his father. For as long as Rath could remember, he knew he'd be a duke one day and in charge of lands, companies, people, and wealth. But it wasn't until his father had challenged him to be proficient in all the inner workings of the entailed property's businesses after he left Oxford that he'd set his mind to learning about them all.

And he had.

Rath caught on quickly as he and his father traveled the estates, met the tenants, and surveyed the lands. Often his father had praised him for his intuition, cleverness, and financial skills in all the ventures that kept the estates prosperous. Learning the holdings of the farmlands and the mining companies had pleased his father. The knowledge of all that was easy for Rath to absorb but managing his neckcloth, his time, and his social pursuits was not.

That was where he and his father had parted ways and no amount of challenge could change Rath's mind. He cared little for high fashion and it showed. No amount of pleading from his father had convinced him to keep his neckcloth properly tied or his coat and waistcoat matching. As soon as Rath was old enough to do so, he'd refused to have a valet dress him or have starch in his collar. Rath wanted to be comfortable, not trussed up like a dandy attending his first ball. His father had never forgiven him for that lax attitude in his clothing, or for the fact that he'd chosen the life of a rake over a gentleman.

At the time, Rath was too eager to taste what was afforded to him. He was only interested in what gave him pleasure and not what his father demanded. Rath felt a sense of peace that his father knew, even though he lingered for months with a broken body after being thrown from a horse, before he died that Rath could manage the dukedom well whether or not his neckcloth was properly tied.

Looking out the carriage window, he tapped the papers against his leg for the second time. Right now, his challenge was the responsibility of taking care of Marlena. It wasn't coming as easy to him as learning about his estates. Women were capricious. Estates were not. But looking after Miss Fast was giving him an unexpected and immense sense of pleasure.

When the carriage finally stopped at Marlena's house, Rath stepped out into the bright sunlight of a cool afternoon with the ends of the sheets of vellum and newsprint fluttering in his hand. He started up the stone path but his steps slowed as he noticed the patches of blue sky. Without really thinking about it, he changed direction from the front door and headed around the corner to the back of the house.

Tut heard his approach and raced to the fence barking. The little dog made it to the wooden gate before Rath. Just as he'd suspected, Marlena was in the garden wearing her straw hat. A wine-colored shawl was spread over her slender shoulders and knotted perfectly between her breasts. Tut continued to jump on the fence and bark until Miss Fast made it over to unlock the gate.

Stepping inside, Rath swiped off his hat and shoved it under his arm as he reached down to pet the excited dog. He looked up at Marlena and said, "Good afternoon, Miss Fast."

"Your Grace," she answered with a curtsy.

Oh, yes. She was as lovely as the first day he saw her. Maybe even more so. Usually he'd rather a young lady not wear a hat or bonnet to cover her hair, but with Marlena, the hat seemed to flaunt how stunning she was.

"I thought I'd find you out here on this sunny afternoon," he said while Tut danced on his hind legs, begging for more attention.

"Much preferable to being inside. And it is the warmest day we've had in quite a few months."

Her gaze strayed to the papers he held in his hand. He sensed by the gleam in her eyes she was anxious to know what he had. That left him even more intrigued than he was before. If they were so important to her, they were important to him, too.

"Actually," she continued, "I should have said it's wonderful for me to be outside. I know you prefer to be indoors so we can go into the drawing room. I'll have Mrs. Doddle make some tea. We'll leave Tut outside so he'll stop jumping on you."

"I'm good out here, Miss Fast," he said, giving the head of the small dog another friendly pat. "And Tut isn't bothering me."

"Tut, behave," she admonished. The dog looked at her and gave her a quarreling bark. "Go," she said and pointed toward the back of the garden. Tut wagged his tail and looked at her but didn't move.

Marlena turned her attention back to Rath. "He's not well trained. My fault, I have to admit. If you'll stop showing him attention, I'm sure he'll leave you alone and go find a grasshopper to chase or something to sniff in the grass."

"I don't mind a welcoming dog or a watchdog."

"He's certainly both," she answered, always willing to talk about Tut. "I'm indebted to Justine for allowing me to accept him from a child on the street who was trying to give him away. He's brought me immense pleasure since I've been in London."

"That was kind of her."

"Tell me," Marlena said, "were you able to find some information for me?"

Nothing like getting right to the point of the matter. Rath couldn't help himself. He had to grin. She was polite enough to ask and not assume what he held was for her.

"You were very specific in your note to me, Miss Fast. *Any and all information*, you directed."

She moistened her lips nervously. "Yes, I believe I said that, but I hope it didn't sound like a demand."

It was on the tip of his tongue to deny it, but then he knew she'd want the truth, so he said, "It did."

"I didn't mean my words how you read them. It was a request."

Her eyes were caressing his face, and Rath was taking in the way she was appealing to him. He didn't mind her fighting spirit. It was fascinating and he even encouraged it, but he wanted her to look at him with her softer side, too.

He held up the papers. "And it was accomplished."

"Thank you. That's wonderful. I'm most grateful to you."

Marlena held out her hand to him. Her eagerness to get the material intrigued him more than it should. He'd had no plans of getting wrapped up in his ward's life until he met her. Now she was all he could think about. He had to know what her interest was in the famed Buckland and the unknown Wentfield.

Rath's grip tightened on the pages he held by his side and his arm didn't move. "I'm afraid I need more information from you before I can give you these, Miss Fast."

It was slight but she lifted her chin and stiffened. "What do you mean?"

He rolled the sheets, pushed aside his cloak, and then

stuffed them into the side pocket of his coat. "To begin with," he said without any hint of annoyance, "I'd like to know why you thought to use me as your researcher, and ask me to gather this information for you."

"You're my guardian," she answered without equivocation.

He couldn't argue with that. "But not your personal secretary."

"No, of course not. I never thought—I mean it would be very difficult for me to do it myself. I needed your help."

His stomach tightened. She needed him. That washed over him as soothing as watching the sun melt into the water in the late afternoon. But he couldn't let those feelings disturb his inquiry.

"Why is that? All of this is available to anyone willing to look through old issues of newsprint, journals, and pamphlets."

"Yes, that's true, I'm sure. But rarely am I allowed to go anywhere without Justine."

"So you wouldn't want her to see this?" He touched his side where the papers were.

"I wouldn't. Not because it's something inappropriate. If I made her privy to the fact I wanted the articles on the men, she would want to know why."

He could only assume that if she didn't want Justine to know why she wanted the information, she probably wouldn't want him to know, either. So why ask him to do it? That only made him more determined not to leave until he found out.

"It might not be a bad idea if she knows," Rath added.

"I'm not sure she would have allowed me to go about getting the information even if I had told her why I needed it. She doesn't always place value on the same things I do. I thought to avoid any confrontation with her about this. Since you are my guardian, I decided to ask you to do it for me."

She was unbelievable. "And you didn't think I'd want to know why you required this?"

She pulled on the edges of her shawl and tightened it around her. "Not really. It was, as you said, a simple thing to get and maybe not even interesting to most."

Rath felt a twitch between his shoulder blades. He wondered again if she might have designs on the men. That irritated him, and made him ask, "Did it dawn on you that I might have more important things to do with my time than chase down gentlemen for you? Such as taking care of problems and issues that arise with my lands, tenants, and businesses. Meetings with members of Parliament who are forever seeking my favor as well as my advice and a host of other things."

"Including a card game or two, several rounds of billiards I'm sure, and a few tankards of ale at White's or some other club that is happy to have your membership no doubt," she said tartly.

Oh, she was quick and tempting beyond what he thought possible. Rath folded his arms across his chest and smiled. He liked that she refused to be intimidated by him.

"That, too," he agreed.

"And truth be told," she added, obviously not enjoying the conversation as much as he was, "I never expected you would go searching for the particulars yourself but have someone do it for you."

Which is exactly what he did. "What is your reason for wanting this information?"

She remained silent. The breeze blew through his hair and fluttered the ribbons under her chin. She pushed her hat farther up her forehead, and a golden-red strand of hair fell from underneath it. The sun made it shimmer as if it were winking at him, enticing him to touch it.

Without thinking, he asked, "Are you interested in making a match between yourself and Buckland or Wentfield?"

"What?" she gasped. "That's absurd. Of course not. I've never met either man. They could both be married for all I know about them."

The passion in her voice and expression of denial on her face told him she was being truthful. Her answer pleased him and he asked, "Then why?"

Rath received only silence from her again, but he could tell she was thinking seriously. But what about? Was she thinking to continue eluding his questions or saying less than the truth?

"If you don't tell me, Miss Fast, I can refuse to give you the information. I saw the gleam in your eyes. You're most eager to get your hands on these articles."

"I am. Why would I ask for it otherwise, Your Grace?" She inhaled a long deep breath and then folded her arms across her chest. "I suppose there's no reason I can't tell you, except for the fact it's not my story to divulge. But if I make you aware of this problem, you must promise to stay quiet about it."

That surprised him. "I *must* stay quiet about it?" That word, *must*, didn't sit well with Rath. "You certainly demand a lot for someone who is at my mercy."

"Perhaps that's because you are a troublesome guardian and I must strive to continually be a step ahead of you."

She had more pluck than the King's army, but he supposed she'd have to have been strong to have followed five boys around a country estate before the age of ten. "I do appreciate the fact you don't mind your words when you are talking to me. Apparently, Mr. Olingworth never asked you any questions about the things you wanted him to obtain for you."

"He trusted me."

Rath nodded. "So do I, but I'm also curious. Perhaps we would work well together on this if you were only trying to stay equal with me rather than ahead of me."

She tapped her foot, Tut wandered away, and Rath waited. He didn't mind that she was taking her time to think it over. It not only showed courage, but showed strength and intelligence, too. And it showed him she was a lady to be regarded for her abilities.

"All right," she finally said, her eyebrows furrowing. "I want to know what Mr. Buckland and Mr. Wentfield have to say about Megalosaurus eggs."

"What in the hell —" *fire*, he finished silently, as Marlena's brows shot up in surprise.

Chapter 12

He could be a rake if all he has to do to seduce you
is look into your eyes.

~∽⊙∾~

*MISS HONORA TRUTH'S WORDS OF WISDOM AND
WARNING ABOUT RAKES, SCOUNDRELS, ROGUES, AND
LIBERTINES*

Rath truly had to watch his language more closely around her and try to be more gentlemanly as his father would have expected him to do. Most of the women he had extended conversations with didn't mind if a *hell* or *damnation* or two slipped past his lips—or any other disrespectful words for that matter.

"What kind of eggs are they?"

"Fossilized eggs from a gigantic reptile that once roamed the earth—thousands of years ago."

Rath eyed her carefully. She seemed to be serious about what she was saying. "I've not seen or heard of this reptile, and there's no mention of it in the papers I have."

"I would hope you haven't seen one." A smile twitched her lips. "I'd hate to think we had a creature that large walking the earth today but are you sure there's no mention of it?"

"I've read every word."

"I suppose that's because Megalosaurus isn't the official or scientific name for the ancient reptiles. They don't have one. Not yet anyway, but Mr. Buckland hopes they will soon. He recently found the giant bones and is still doing his examination of them. It was Mr. Herbert Wentfield who discovered the creature's eggs and the dragon bones."

"Dragon bones?" Rath asked in disbelief as he stepped a little closer to her.

"Yes," she answered truthfully

"Miss Fast, I've read that big bones were unearthed a few years ago up north, and some believed them to be from dragons. Scientists determined those bones were actually from ancient Roman military elephants that were brought over here long ago. There never was such a thing as a dragon."

"I'm not saying I believe there are such bones in existence from legendary beasts such as dragons, Megalosauruses, or unicorns that might have lived long ago," she argued. "Only that some people do. Mr. Portington and Mr. Wentfield do."

Another man?

Rath was doing his best to follow this conversation. "And who is Mr. Portington?"

She moved her hat even farther up her forehead. Rath knew such action was why she usually had a golden glow to her cheeks.

"He's my neighbor and Eugenia's brother-in-law. She lives with him and her sister, Veronica. All three men are collectors of fossils, bones, and various other artifacts from all over the world. As for the bones of a dragon, all I can say to that is what Mr. Portington told me when I questioned him about them. He said there was a time when some people thought the world was flat and that a balloon filled with hot air couldn't possibly take people into the air, fly them around as if they were birds, and bring them safely back to the ground again."

The more she told him, the more interested he became in this outrageous story. "You seem to know many things about these men already, so I'm wondering why you wanted to know more." He looked around the garden and saw a small bench under a barren tree. "Why don't we sit down over there and you can explain what all this is about?"

"I'm not sure Justine would approve of me sitting alone in the garden with a gentleman."

"I am your guardian. I can be alone with you, and call you Marlena by the way. I see your eyebrows go up sometimes when I do."

"It feels inappropriate."

"What did Mr. Olingworth call you?"

She studied on that for a few seconds before saying, "Marlena, but I was a still a girl with braids in my hair and freckles across my nose when I went to live with him."

Rath gave her an expression that would surely let her know he'd gotten the best of that conversation, and said, "I'm willing for Mrs. Abernathy to be out here while we talk. Where is she?"

Marlena smiled at him and shook her head. "She is riding around town in the extravagant carriage *you* had delivered yesterday. She's quite pleased to have it and wants everyone she knows to see her in it. I don't think she'll ever walk anywhere again."

"Now she doesn't have to. You didn't want to go with her?"

Marlena's softened gaze stared into his eyes, and that warm feeling washed over him again. "I've told you before that I like being outside. I've missed living in the

countryside, first with my cousins and then Mr. Olingworth. I also prefer walking to riding in a stuffy coach."

He didn't know why but it pleased him that fancy trappings didn't interest her. "And do you believe me when I
say Mrs. Abernathy will not mind us being out here together because I am your guardian?"

"I suppose that does make it acceptable. I was often
alone with Mr. Olingworth. Except, of course, for the servants. But he wasn't—" She hesitated and her gaze fell
softly on his again.

He was fairly certain he knew what she started to say,
and he should be a gentleman and let it pass. The rake
inside him wouldn't allow that. "What? You are not shy,
Marlena, finish your sentence."

She gazed into his eyes without wavering. "Not as
young and handsome as you are. Not as . . ."

"Desirable?"

Marlena inhaled deeply. He'd told her what she was
thinking. What she was too embarrassed by her womanly
emotions to say out loud?

"Mr. Olingworth was a gentleman at all times."

"Ah, a gentleman. Which was a good thing. I'm glad."

Rath extended his hand toward the bench and they
walked over to it. He took off his cloak and spread it on
the seat before they made themselves comfortable. It
wasn't a long bench so there wasn't much distance between them. Rath took the papers out of his pocket and
laid them beside him with his hat on top so the breeze
wouldn't blow them across the garden.

He listened to Marlena's tale about Miss Everard's
brother-in-law and his penchant for collecting fossils and
unusual specimens and artifacts. And how he'd gotten so
carried away that he'd spent what was left of Miss Everard's inheritance—the money intended for her upcoming Season—on the Megalosaurus eggs.

"So you see, Mr. Wentfield is the one I'm most interested in as he was paid a large sum for the eggs. I was hoping to find him, write to him about what Mr. Portington had done, and ask him to buy back the eggs so Eugenia can have her Season. I know Justine would have insisted I stay out of their affairs so I didn't want to ask her for help."

"I agree she would have and rightly so. I should do the same thing."

"But I won't stay out of it. I've told you before that Eugenia is dear to me. I must help her and Veronica if I can."

"That's what I thought." He leaned against the seat back and watched Marlena. Determination was written all over her face. "It's kind of you to want to help Miss Everard, but I'm afraid my solicitor reached an empty bottom concerning Mr. Wentfield. He couldn't find any reference to the man."

She blinked slowly, letting his words sink in. "Not anywhere? Not even an article written by him? What school he attended? An address?" She looked down at the thick stack sitting under Rath's hat. "All of that and none of it about Mr. Wentfield?"

Rath wasn't getting a good feeling about Wentfield. "Not a word." Tut had wandered over, and he reached down and gave him pat on his shoulder. The dog then settled down by Rath's boots and curled into a ball to nap.

"I find that hard to believe." Marlena huffed. "Mr. Portington has purchased things from him before—there were the dragon bones just a few months ago. I—I just assumed he was as well known in the field as Mr. Buckland."

Rath didn't want to tell Marlena he was beginning to believe that Mr. Portington had been tricked. Using a made-up name was essential if a person wanted to lure an unsuspecting chap into a scheme and abscond with his money—especially if the person was as gullible as Mr. Portington seemed to be. The only thing Rath knew to do was hire a thief taker from Bow Street to see if he could find out enough about Wentfield to locate the man.

Marlena's fan-shaped brows furrowed again and she bit down on her bottom lip before saying, "I wonder how it can be that nothing was found about him. Perhaps the—"

"No," he said. "My solicitor was quite thorough, but I'll have the matter looked into again."

"I would be most grateful for any assistance you can give me—I mean give Eugenia—on this. I really don't know how to help her. She needs to have a Season."

"Are you sure Mr. Portington used all of her inheritance?"

"Veronica says it's so. She's very disturbed about what her husband has done. She's not a strong person, and sometimes I fear for her well-being."

He could tell by Marlena's expression that she wasn't exaggerating her concern for her neighbor and friend. "That sounds serious."

"I do believe it is for her. The past few years Mr. Portington has become increasingly more reckless with spending his allowance, and obviously he's spent Eugenia's, too. He purchases so many unusual things, and there's really not room in the house for more, yet he keeps buying. He doesn't seem to notice how it disturbs Veronica and Eugenia."

"So Mr. Portington isn't concerned about their distress?"

Her eyes widened and she quickly said, "I don't think I should have disclosed that much to you. I really hate that I have to be talking about their private life at all."

Rath put her at ease by saying, "I am not one to spread

gossip about people, Miss Fast. So anything you say will go no further than my hearing."

Seeming bothered by his words, she quickly looked away from him and said, "Yes, gossip can spread quickly." She turned back to him and added, "That is an admirable way to be, Your Grace. In any case, I must help the sisters if possible. Mr. Portington seems unwilling to do anything to change his destructive ways."

Rath had listened carefully to all her story. Her eyes, her expression told him she believed every word she was saying. He knew many men with gambling and drinking habits they couldn't control even though it appeared some tried hard to do so. It was a damnable thing he was sure. Some were not able or perhaps just not willing to give up their mistresses or tavern wenches when they married and no longer had need for such services. But he'd never heard of one that had a penchant for collecting oddities. A man should never let anything take control of him.

But all he said to Marlena was, "Or perhaps it's that he's incapable of changing his ways."

"Can't or won't. Either way it is a sad situation for the sisters."

She clasped her hands in her lap and looked down at them.

"I can see this bothers you greatly."

"More than I can say. I've helped them in little ways since I moved next door, but the task gets harder."

She didn't lift her lashes and look into his eyes. She wasn't telling him everything. There was still something she didn't want him to know. He sensed it but he wouldn't press her at this time. He could be patient—the mark of a gentleman, his father always said.

"It's kind of you to want to help, but I agree you are limited in what you can do."

"Yes. That's a good way to say it. I need to find Mr. Wentfield and ask him to buy back the eggs."

Portington was obviously an odd boot. No wonder Miss Everard was so fainthearted. And the man's wife, too. Looking at Marlena, with the breeze stirring her hair, making her nose a little red and her cheeks pink, Rath knew he would never let her marry such a man as Portington.

That thought caused Rath's gut to twist. He didn't want to think about her marrying at all right now. He only wanted to consider what he could do for her. It was noble to help her friends. She was kind and loyal to them, and he wanted to be that way for her.

"It's not wise for you to approach either man. I don't know Wentfield, but I'd bet a gold coin he's not going to buy back the eggs. Perhaps I can speak to Mr. Portington if you would like?"

Her attention returned to Rath. "Oh, I don't think that would be wise, either. He probably wouldn't like it if he knew Veronica had told me or I'd told you he had spent his sister-in-law's inheritance on questionable reptile eggs."

Rath loved the way her eyes sparkled when she perceived something was wrong. "Nothing as confrontational as that, I assure you. No, I was thinking along the lines of asking him if I could examine his fossil collection."

"Are you interested in such things?"

"I can't say that I am, but I don't have to tell Mr. Portington that. I can suggest to him that I want to buy some of his collection? Enough to see to it your friend can have a proper Season."

Marlena's face filled with hope. "Would you do that?"

He chuckled. "I don't think you're happy unless you

are taking issue with me about something. Everything. I just offered to do it, but it would be up to Miss Everard's sister to see to it Portington used it for its intended purpose."

"I'm sure she would. I don't know what to say. I never expected to hear you suggest helping someone you don't know. I mean, you're a duke."

"I admit it's a rarity, but I have been known to be kind once or twice in my life and do something for someone without having been asked."

Her face lit with happiness. "That would be too wonderful for words," she exclaimed, and then she reached over and hugged him with the softest feminine strength he'd ever felt.

Rath didn't know if he had ever been so surprised to have slender, womanly arms stretched around his neck. Marlena clutched at his shoulders with gentle hands. Her cheek grazed his and her hat fell to the back of her shoulders as she buried her cold nose against the warmth of his neck. A throb of sensual hunger flowed through him when he felt her breath on his skin.

She leaned into his chest for a few seconds and his heart pounded. Through his velvet waistcoat and linen shirt, he felt her soft breasts pressing against him. His body responded quickly again. Though she held him tightly for only a few seconds, it was long enough for him to know he wanted more of her arms around him.

And her in his arms.

Just as he moved to catch her up to his chest and kiss her soundly on the lips, she slowly pushed away from him. Her arms slid from around his neck, the tips of her fingers tickling his skin. Her hands then skimmed over his shoulders, down his upper arms, and across his forearms before her touch left him. It took all the will and strength he could muster to let her draw away and not pull her back into his embrace and demand the kiss he was longing for.

"I probably shouldn't have done that," she said, clasping her hands together in her lap again as if to keep herself from touching him. "It was very forward of me. My only excuse is that I'm used to hugging Eugenia when she does things for me and makes me happy."

He could tell she'd shocked herself as much as she had him by her unexpected affectionate display. "No need to explain. It's a nice way to say thank you."

"I—I, all right," she answered a little shyly. "What would you do with the fossils if Mr. Portington allowed you to purchase any of them?"

Rath didn't know. He hadn't thought that far ahead about what he'd offered to do. Right now he was more interested in feeling Marlena's arms around him again than pondering what he'd do with ancient reptile bones and fossilized eggs.

"I'm not certain," he answered, and as soon as he said that, an idea came to him. "One possibility is that I could probably donate them to the Ashmolean Museum at Oxford. If they could authenticate them and wanted them. That might be a commendable way to make amends to the institution for all the trouble I caused when I was there."

She smiled and a small, soft burst of laughter passed her lips. She looked enchanting.

"You were a troublemaker?"

He nodded guiltily. "Of the worst kind, I'm afraid. I encouraged others to join my pursuits. The headmaster told my father more than once they should throw me out for leading other young men to stray from the strict rules they demanded we follow."

"Then it sounds as if a gift from you might be appreciated by them."

Rath stared at Marlena and wondered how long it had

been since he'd seduced a woman. Not for many years anyway. He never had to. They always seduced him. From the moment he'd walk through the doorway of a mistress' house or a widow's drawing room, they were set to seducing him. He let them, of course. It didn't mean he wasn't willing or that he had no care for the woman's pleasure. He just never had to pursue a lady anymore.

But now he wanted to pursue his ward.

He shouldn't.

He couldn't.

Rath reached into his coat pocket and extended his folded handkerchief to Marlena.

She looked at it curiously and said, "I'm not going to cry over this, Your Grace. Though I'm distressed for Eugenia's and Veronica's plight, I think I can manage not to get teary-eyed about their situation."

"I didn't think you were. That's not why I'm trying to give you my handkerchief."

She laughed softly and relaxed against the back of the bench, seeming more at ease than she'd been since his arrival. Rath was certain he'd never seen anyone as lovely as Marlena on a sunny day wearing a straw hat on her shoulders and smiling at him, not because she wanted something—his attention, his power, his favor—but because she was simply enjoying time with him.

He never expected it of his ward, but he was enamored by her. He wanted to hold her supple body next to his, feel her in his arms, and kiss her beautifully shaped lips, no matter of the wrongness of it.

"I can tell you right now, Your Grace, you will never fool me again as you did the first day you came to my house. Even though we are in the garden, I know I don't have a bee, a ladybug, or anything else on my cheek. So if there is dirt, a grass stain, or even a piece of dried leaf or twig on my face, it can stay there."

"That is a clever assessment, Marlena, but I'm not trying to fool you this time. I am being truthful."

Rath leaned toward her and lowered his head closer to hers. Despite knowing it was not the right thing to do, he wanted to kiss her. He simply didn't want to stop himself.

And he wouldn't.

She would have to do it, and she'd proved herself capable before.

Rath laid the handkerchief on top of her hands, which were still resting in her lap. "This was a very effective tool to remind me we shouldn't kiss. I'm giving it back to you so you can use it now to keep yourself from kissing me."

"Me kiss you?"

He nodded.

She looked down at the handkerchief resting on the top of her fingers and then back to his eyes. There wasn't an immediate answer from her. He took that as a good sign. She was contemplating. He had no doubt she wanted to kiss him, but he didn't know if she would give in to the desire that was so very strong between them and do it.

"That is," Rath added, "if you want to kiss me."

Chapter 13

He could be a rake if he offers a lady his
handkerchief.

❧

*MISS HONORA TRUTH'S WORDS OF WISDOM AND
WARNING ABOUT RAKES, SCOUNDRELS, ROGUES, AND
LIBERTINES*

Oh, he was a rake of the highest order.

Of course, she wanted to kiss him.

But shouldn't he just catch her up against his chest and
kiss her madly, force a kiss on her whether or not she
wanted him to? He was a rake. Shouldn't he act like one?

Apparently not.

He knew she wanted him to kiss her. Was dying for
him to kiss her. Why couldn't he just do it? Without her
making the first move. Wasn't that what rakes were supposed to do?

Marlena sat silent.

And so did the duke.

It wasn't fair. He had been the one promising her a kiss
almost from the first day he arrived at her door with his
short, captivating glances, long compelling gazes, and
provocative words that kept her wanting more and more

attention from him. Why did he want it to be her decision whether or not they kissed? And how could she once again be contemplating it at all? She should be feeling nothing but shame over her desire for him.

He was a rake, a rascal, and a scoundrel! But more than that, he was indirectly responsibility for Veronica marrying Mr. Portington. And Marlena had no idea how many of the other young ladies' lives the Rakes of St. James had upended by their secret admirer letters.

And why, after all his years of being a scoundrel of the highest order, would he decide at this very moment to be a gentleman and not kiss her?

Maybe this was his plan all along, because he was a master of seduction? For surely he knew that denying her his kiss made her want it all the more. Her outrage over his past couldn't extinguish the continuing attraction she had for him. He stirred emotions inside her that were too complicated for her to understand right now.

Marlena kept her hands still, the handkerchief resting on top of them. "Why are you making this my decision?"

"You are an innocent."

"Why does that matter to you? You have kissed innocent young ladies before, haven't you?"

His gaze searched hers. "Not for a long time."

"Because?"

"You don't mind asking personal questions, do you, Marlena?"

"It's the usual way one gets answers."

A grin broke across his masculine features and she realized she liked it when he looked at her like that. He quirked his head a little as a breeze scattered his dark locks across his forehead, reminding her of a brazen pirate yet again.

"All right," he said. "I'll tell you. Long ago I made a vow not to pursue innocent young ladies."

She turned her head back to him. "After the secret admirer letters?"

"No, before then. When I realized young ladies' hearts are too easily given and too easily broken. When I found out they believed a few kisses was a promise of marriage."

"Did that happen to you? A young lady thought you intended marriage because you kissed her."

"Twice, much to my father's dismay, before I understood that it was best to seek comfort in the arms of a mistress or widow who had no illusions of marriage between us."

Marlena cleared her throat. "Perhaps that was more than I wanted to know. I'm surprised you admitted it to me."

"I think you understand men more than you realize, Marlena."

"What makes you say that?"

"You would have never followed your cousins into a swamp or a cemetery unless you were quite sure they were looking out for you and would see to it you returned home safely. Since there were five of them, no doubt two of them stayed behind watching over you while the other three ran ahead of you."

"Perhaps they did." She smiled, remembering that her parents were watching over her, too. "It's true the boys taught me more than just the difference between a frog and a toad and how to get down from a tree once I had climbed up it. I've missed them."

"Where are they now? Are you still in touch with them?"

"No, I haven't heard from my aunt in several years now. My uncle had a restless spirit, I think. He wanted to take his family to America and seek their fortunes there." She sighed softly. "My aunt wasn't happy but wouldn't defy her husband. She didn't think it fair to take me from my homeland and the life my parents expected me to have. That's when my uncle arranged for me to live with Mr. Olingworth."

"You've missed being part of a big family?"

Oh, yes, she had. She'd cried quietly in her room for weeks.

"Terribly at first. But Mr. Olingworth was kind and allowed me to play outside and roam about his spacious gardens. It made me feel closer to them, helped me remember them. And then it wasn't long before Mr. Olingworth had me busy most days learning my lessons, reading, and sewing. All the things a proper young lady needs to know, but I never forgot chasing after the boys. Yelling for them to wait for me. Proving to them I wasn't afraid of a worm, the dark, or tomorrow." She stopped and smiled with sweet remembrance of those wonderful carefree days that helped make her strong. Strong enough to take on three dukes—even if it was anonymously.

"But all in your uncle's family were safe in America last you heard?"

"Yes. A place called Boston at first. But the last I heard from them, which was years ago now, they were planning to move west and would be in touch."

"But you didn't hear from them again."

A sadness gripped Marlena. "No, I didn't." She'd never forget the boys or the lessons they taught her.

Marlena looked over at the gate that stood in the middle of the side fence. The one that she, Eugenia, and Veronica had used many times to go back and forth between their houses. How could she be telling and revealing so much about herself to this man? It was his actions that had ruined Veronica and Eugenia's lives and prompted her to start *Miss Truth's Scandal Sheet*. Why was it that when she was with him like this, he seemed nothing like the rake, the rogue she always thought him to be? Expected him to be.

She faced him. "If you knew young ladies' hearts became involved so easily, why did you send letters asking them to meet a secret admirer?"

Her sudden accusation didn't cause him to blink. "I can't explain the foolish actions of a young man who was so full of drink and arrogance he cared for nothing other than his own pleasures."

"I find that hard to believe," she said softly. "You have offered to help Eugenia."

"I have no reason to lie to you about it. About anything. I was that young man." His shoulders relaxed, and he placed his elbow on the top of the bench. "You know that what happened years ago was never about the letters. It was about a wager among three friends. We truly thought most of the young ladies would throw our notes into the fire and never think of them again. We couldn't believe that every one of them went to meet their secret admirer."

"And then you bragged about it."

"No," he said quietly, earnestly. "I want you to know the truth. We were not bragging when our conversation was overheard."

"Yet you offered the man money not to tell."

The duke slowly shook his head. "That may well be what you heard, but Mr. Howard Drayton wanted us to pay him money not to tell. A handsome sum from each of us every month. He saw it as a good way to sustain his mounting gambling debts. In hindsight, we should have given in to his demands, but it went against our nature to be intimidated by the man or any man. We knew it would do no good to threaten him because he had the Prince's ear. Now it seems we were foolish not to pay. But we had no glimpse of the future. If we'd had any idea how long this scandal would follow us, and that it would actually outlive Mr. Drayton, we would have paid him. It would have been better if we had."

"I suppose we all have regrets," she commented, knowing she had a few of her own.

"Some of us more than others."

"You say you haven't pursued an innocent young lady for a long time, but you have been pursuing me every time you look at me, Your Grace, and with almost every word you say to me."

She saw in his expression that her comment surprised him. "Is that truly how you feel?"

"I have no reason to lie to you about it," she answered.

His expression turned to something between a grimace and a smile. "I've not deliberately done that—well, perhaps on an occasion or two. When I touched your cheek at your front door and when I had your back against the secretary in the drawing room."

"More times than that and you know it," she insisted, not taking her gaze from his. "I know all the reasons I shouldn't but I want you to give me my first kiss. I believe you want that, too."

"No doubt. I do. But I also know that I am the last person who should do it, because I am your guardian. I'm supposed to keep you safe from men just like me."

"I trust you not to take advantage of me."

A husky, intimate chuckle passed his lips. "I'm not sure you should."

He reached up and placed one hand to the side of her neck. Its warmth soothed her instantly. She turned her head to more fully settle into his palm. His thumb caressed the skin under her chin before moving down the column of her throat to the top of her dress and back up again. The feather-light tenderness of his touch sizzled through her.

His penetrating gaze never left her face. "That's asking a lot from me. From someone who's never had to restrain himself when it came to anything he wanted."

His touch, his expression, the way he looked at her made her breathless. Slow waves of pleasure expanded and grew inside. The heat of his touch seeped deeply into her soul.

"I don't believe you've ever forced your attentions on a lady or anyone else."

"I've never had to," he answered without a hint of arrogance in his low tone.

The woodsy scent of his shaving soap stirred her senses. Marlena moistened her lips in anticipation. "I assume you've been kissed many times before, Your Grace, but I have not. So, of course, I'm curious about what makes kisses so stirring that poets write endlessly about them, people have clandestine meetings to kiss, and others have endangered their reputations for a stolen few."

"Some have even risked scandal and death in order to have a few kisses from their lover, Marlena."

"Yes, I believe that's true," she agreed.

"I am not stopping you from having your first kiss."

No, he was encouraging her. His hand continued to cup her neck, and his fingers moved to caress the sensitive area behind her ear while his thumb moved up and over her jawline until it stilled at the corner of her lips. He lightly let the weight of his forearm rest between her breasts. Every soft, slow movement he made had her breathing deeper, her chest growing tighter, and the stirring between her legs feeling more wanton.

She gazed into his eyes. He wasn't denying her, yet he wasn't kissing her, either. She looked down. The handkerchief was there. Between them. A shield of sorts, but not one she wanted to use. The wind blew the corners of the linen but it wasn't going anywhere unless she took hold of it. It had saved her from her great desire to kiss him once before. All she had to do was close her fingers around it and lift it between them. She had all faith he'd back away from her.

Marlena looked up into the duke's dark eyes again. He stared at her with such rapt attention it made her feel as if she meant the world to him, and he would do every-thing within his power to give her her heart's desire.

Yet he made no move toward her to do so.

Suddenly she understood. Because of his vow or honor or whatever it was that held him back, she had to make the first move. They both wanted the kiss, but she had to be the aggressor.

So be it.

Doing her best to settle her jittery stomach, to slow her racing heartbeat, Marlena lifted her hands. The handker-chief fell away. Kissing couldn't be all that hard to do, she told herself. People did it all the time.

Reaching up, she slipped her arms around the duke's neck and clasped her fingers together at his nape. She lifted her face to his and placed her closed lips against his. They were warm. Soft. They didn't move and neither did hers. Just two sets of lips pressed together.

However, she was very much aware she was kissing a man for the first time so she let her lips stay against his for several seconds to prolong the momentous occasion. Her heart was pounding to the same beat that had her stomach jumping, but she wasn't feeling the eager, spi-raling sensations of desire she thought would be a part of the mating of their lips.

When she lifted her lashes, their eyes met and held. Marlena slowly broke the kiss, let her arms slowly drop to her sides and leaned away. She looked deeply into his eyes.

"Are you disappointed in your first kiss?" he asked.

Was she?

Perhaps a little she thought, but said, "I don't think so. I wanted you to kiss me."

"My beautiful, innocent Marlena, I didn't kiss you. You kissed me."

She frowned. She did, but—A tremor raced through her. "Were you disappointed with the kiss?" she asked, suddenly fearful she hadn't done something right.

A hint of a smile lifted one corner of his mouth. "Not at all. It was refreshing. It's been a long time since I've been kissed by someone who doesn't know how to do it."

She thought on what he said for a few seconds. "I suppose that's true. It's not something I've been taught the way I learned dancing, manners, reading, or even how to catch a fish."

"Fishing? Did your cousins teach you how to do that, too?"

"They tried. I wanted to be with them and do whatever they did. I wasn't any good at it." She smiled. "I've had no tutors for kissing."

The duke chuckled softly. "It's best there are none for that. It comes naturally with practice."

"I would assume you know how to kiss very well. That you've had a lot of practice."

One corner of his mouth lifted in a grin. "You aren't going to fool me into telling you anything about that, Marlena."

"I'm not trying to. I was going to ask if you would kiss me this time and show me how it's done properly."

With his mouth hovering above hers, his gaze locked on hers, and his warm hand still resting ever so lightly against her neck, he asked, "Do you want a kiss from me because you are curious about how it's usually done or because you have a burning desire to feel my lips on yours once again?"

"Both."

A sparkle of surprise seemed to light in his dark-brown eyes. "Your answer will do—for now."

The duke circled her waist and placed his hands in the center of her back, bringing her up close to his hard chest. Marlena felt strength in his arms as they surrounded her and warmth from his body as she settled into his embrace.

He lowered his head, closed his eyes, and softly placed his slightly parted mouth on hers. Just as before, his lips were pliant and moist, but this time her stomach quivered deliciously. Tingles of sensation shivered across her breasts and tightened her nipples. The duke didn't just press his lips to hers and leave them there. No, he slanted them over hers and moved them back and forth, over and across hers. Slowly, generously, and softly, as if he were caressing the most prized bolt of velvet with his lips. She felt as if she could kiss him all day and not grow tired of doing it.

"Move your lips with mine," he whispered without breaking contact with her.

Marlena did so as her arms once again circled his neck.

She felt him smile in answer, and then he kissed her again and again, moving his lips seductively, smoothly, confidently, and effortlessly over hers. It was stimulating and she felt every fiber of her being participating. She savored the experience of being held in the arms of a man for the first time. Her body seemed to melt closer and closer to his. She allowed her hands to explore his wide shoulders and broad back beneath the fine wool of his coat.

Marlena was swept away by new sensations twirling, curling, and tumbling inside her. He created such thrilling and intense feelings rippling inside her she was almost afraid to draw breath for fear they would disappear and never return.

How could it be that she'd spent almost three years of her life trying to make his life miserable? And now with his touch on her lips, on her skin, he was giving her pleasure she hadn't known existed until she'd met him.

The duke raised his head and looked down into her eyes. Her heart fluttered. Her lashes blinked against his beckoning stare.

"Now do you see how much different a kiss can be?"

Almost dizzily, she answered, "Yes. Much better than mine to you. I'm wondering what comes next."

"If only I could show you, but alas, I can't. We'll have to settle for another kiss and that will have to do."

His lips came down to hers and lightly brushed across them. The contact was alluring, brief, and inviting. With a trembling sigh Marlena surrendered into his embrace again. Kissing was really very easy now that she knew what to do and much more pleasurable than her effort. Her fingers played in the thick, soft hair at the back of his head. She breathed in deeply, trying to take in every second of being in his arms and memorizing them all.

"You smell like sunshine," he whispered against her lips.

Marlena laughed softly between short eager kisses and though she loved the smell of him, the taste of him, and the feel of him holding her so close to his strong, warm chest, she answered, "Sunshine has no scent."

"Oh, but it does. It smells just like you—a warm breeze on a cool, sunny day. The fragrance is warmth, beauty, and goodness."

"You are making that up. And I am not good, Your Grace," she admitted honestly, knowing he didn't know who she was, what she had done, and what she continued to do as Miss Honora Truth—and at the moment praying he never would.

"You feel good in my arms."

He kissed her cheeks, her eyes, over her jawline and down her neck. Passion burst quickly between them. Gone were the sweet soft kisses and in their place were eager, desperate, and hungry kisses. His arms held her tighter. And as if it was the most natural thing to do, Marlena opened her mouth and the duke's tongue entered to tease, to play, and to seek hers.

Marlena's stomach, her abdomen, and between her legs tightened at the thrilling spirals of need cascading through her.

Sensations that she had never experienced shot to the core of her being as a tingling warmth settled over her, filling her with an eagerness to know more, to feel more, and to give more in return. She had no idea how or why she had such wanton, wonderful feelings.

Feelings aroused from the touch of a rake. A man who knew just how to kiss her, hold her, and tempt her beyond her control to stop him.

He wasn't forcing her to do anything. He hadn't even reached for her. She had initiated their kisses.

She wanted this.

Something she could have never expected, never have dreamed had happened with the Duke of Rathburne. The man in whom she'd done her best to inspire shame, guilt, and penance with her writings.

The duke's hand slid up her waist to cup and caress her breast beneath the sprigged muslin of her dress. Marlena gasped at the desire that flooded her entire body. She moaned faintly at the exploding pleasure overcoming her. Now she finally knew what the poets meant when they wrote about ravishing their lovers.

Marlena wanted the rake to ravish her.

Their kisses became more passionate with each breath. His tongue lightly probed and stroked in and out of her mouth, teasing her. His kisses filled her with a hunger she didn't understand but somehow knew only the duke could satisfy. All she was aware of was how the duke was making her feel and hoping it would go on forever.

Suddenly the side gate burst open wih a bang.

"Marlena! I have our article and its wonder—"

Marlena and the duke sprang apart as if a shot had been fired between them. She felt as if her heart had entered her throat. Had Eugenia said *our* article in front of the duke? Had she seen them kissing? Of course, she had!

"Oh, I didn't know you were here," Eugenia squeaked, clutching at her skirt with one hand and tightly holding a sheet of newsprint in the other. Her gaze solidly on the duke.

"He's not," Marlena said without thinking. "I mean. Yes, yes, he's here. We're here. We were just sitting in the garden."

Eugenia seemed frozen when she said, "You were wrapped in each other's arms."

"Yes, I suppose we were," Marlena said guiltily and jumped up off the bench while the duke slowly rose and remained quiet. "But I can explain that." She looked over at the duke, hoping he would step in and help her. Surely he was more used to a situation like this than she was, but he was watching Eugenia.

"You were kissing him," her friend said.

"Yes," Marlena answered and feeling quite incapable of doing so, added, "And I can explain that, too."

Eugenia's surprised expression suddenly turned to one of fear. "How? Was he attacking you?"

Marlena gasped. "No, no! Of course not. I mean I know he's a rake, but he's not a brute."

The duke held out his hand toward Eugenia, and calmly said, "Nothing is wrong, Miss Everard. There is no cause for alarm."

"You were kissing her," she said again but not nearly as loud as before. "With such passion that I—I . . ." Her words seemed to trail off into the air and disappear.

"I have not hurt Miss Fast and I won't harm you. Miss Fast wanted to know what it would— No, don't faint, Miss Everard, listen to me, do not faint."

"Eugenia, no!" Marlena called to her friend.

But it was too late for either of them to say or do anything to help. Eugenia's eyes rolled into the back of her head, and she crumpled to the ground before they could reach her. The scandal sheet she'd been holding floated down into the dead grass beside her.

Marlena and the duke rushed to her side and knelt down.

"Eugenia, are you all right?" Marlena looked over at him and asked, "Is she all right?"

Instead of answering, he said, "Do you still want to tell me she doesn't faint often?"

"I swear she doesn't," Marlena insisted. "I mean, of course, she would faint this time. Heavens to mercy! She saw us kissing."

"I'm well aware of that, Marlena."

"That would put anyone over the brink."

"Maybe." He looked down at Eugenia and then over to the scandal sheet. "What did she mean by *our* article?"

Marlena's throat constricted again. Suddenly she felt as cautious as she had the first afternoon the duke arrived at her house. As if he knew she was Miss Truth.

"It means that we share the price and buy just one," Marlena said, thinking quickly. "We bought it together so it's ours."

"Oh."

"Is she hurt?" Marlena asked, wanting to steer the conversation away from the scandal sheet as quickly as possible.

"She shouldn't be. The ground is soft here and she didn't appear to hit her head on anything as she went down." Rath added, "Will she tell your cousin we were kissing?"

That thought hadn't crossed Marlena's mind. "Eugenia tell Justine? No. No, she wouldn't tell Justine anything. She wouldn't even tell her sister. Unlike me, Eugenia is quite timid about most things and wouldn't want to create any trouble for me or anyone. I have no fear of her tattling."

"I'll take your word for it," the duke said. "She does seem quite timorous."

He reached over and picked up the article that had tumbled to the earth with Eugenia.

The duke turned to Marlena. "Apparently the two of you enjoy Miss Truth's books and her scandal sheets."

"Yes," she answered after swallowing a lot more guilt.

"Do you read it every week?"

She nodded.

"I haven't read this one," he said and his eyes drifted back to the paper.

Merciful heavens! Was he going to read it right in front of her?

It was horrifying to have the duke holding the scandal sheet in his hand. Knowing as he did that both their names were written in it. And that she had been the one who'd written them.

Would he remember any of the words from the writings he'd seen that day in the drawer of her secretary? Was she about to be found out and have to admit she was the writer of the scandal sheet that had haunted him for almost three years?

Seconds passed and he didn't accuse her so she asked, "Do you really read them?"

He looked over at her and said, "Most of the time. They're never longer than a paragraph or two. It's not like reading a book. I suppose you have read her book by now, too."

Guiltily, she nodded again.

"I haven't read it yet," he offered.

How long could it take to read such a simple book, she groused silently to herself!

"I heard it's selling rather briskly, which surprised me," he said.

That surprised Marlena, too, when Veronica had told her.

"There's really no reason you should bother yourself with such trivial entertainment," she answered honestly. "You probably wouldn't enjoy it anyway."

"But you did," he said. "Your reading group as well?"

Marlena was forced to nod for the third time, certain her throat was too dry to speak again.

Looking at him, with the breeze stirring his dark hair, Marlena remembered the passion she'd felt in his arms and she wanted the ground to open and swallow her. Her double life was catching up with her, but she couldn't let it scare her. What she'd done, what she was doing might be wrong but she had to remember it was for a worthy cause.

"Apparently, Miss Truth has heard that I am now your guardian. Does that bother you? To have your name printed in here."

Yes, it bothered her. Just as it now bothered her to write about him. It was much easier before she could put a face to the name of the Duke of Rathburne.

"I suppose it had to be done. Justine has been telling

everyone," Marlena said, more breathlessly than she would have liked to sound.

The duke glanced back to her. "Does she know who Miss Truth is?"

"I hope not."

He gave her a puzzled glance. "Why is that?"

"She would probably tell everyone about that, too."

He smiled. "And you wouldn't like that. You'd then have one less scandal sheet to read."

Eugenia rolled her head back and forth and started mumbling words that thankfully Marlena couldn't understand. How was she ever going to explain what happened between her and the duke to her friend?

The duke held the sheet toward Marlena. "Here, you take this. Since your name is printed in it along with mine, I'm sure you don't want to lose it." He extended the scandal sheet to her. "You carry it and I'll carry Miss Everard into the house. It's time to try your smelling salts."

Chapter 14

He could be a rake if he fails to detect a young
lady's distress.

❧❧

*MISS HONORA TRUTH'S WORDS OF WISDOM AND
WARNING ABOUT RAKES, SCOUNDRELS, ROGUES, AND
LIBERTINES*

Now again," Justine said. "Step forward, left, left,
back on the right, forward on the right, twirl, clap,
and curtsy. That's good. Keep going. Now again, step
forward—"

"No, no, Justine," Marlena said, walking over to the
pianoforte, wiping her forehead, though it was chilly in
the music room. "Please, I need to rest. You've had me
dancing for over an hour now."

Justine kept playing. "Only an hour? And you complain? You'll be dancing all night, every night during the
Season, dear girl, so I don't want to hear your protest
until you can dance for that long. Now back to the center
of the room with you and let's continue."

"At a ball I won't be dancing by myself to the same
tune over and over again and it won't be one dance right
after the other without a break in between sets. I'll have

time to rest, have a cup of punch, and hopefully a conversation or two."

Justine took her hands off the keys and leaned an arm on top of the pianoforte as she stared at Marlena with no softening in her determined features. "I would hope not."

"Really?" Marlena asked, confused by her cousin's remark.

"If you're going to be the diamond of the Season, *as I was*, you must be on the floor for every dance. All the acceptable and eligible bachelors should be lining up to dance with you and trying to gain your favor. Besides, I've been sitting here playing the pianoforte for you for over an hour. You don't hear me complaining that my fingers are tired and need a rest, do you?" She started the melody again. "See. They are still moving, but you are not still dancing."

"There's quite a bit of difference between what you are doing and what I'm doing," Marlena argued, though it wasn't so much that she minded the dancing. She wasn't actually tired, either, but she was nervous—again. She'd turned in another scandal sheet that morning, and hoped she'd made it outrageous enough everyone in London would want their own copy. If Mr. Trout saw the sales going up maybe he'd be more inclined to advance the money she'd written to him and asked about. Veronica was talking about *Words of Wisdom* to her ladies' groups, but Justine had refused, saying she delighted in telling everyone she hadn't read it and didn't intend to. Even the duke had said he'd heard it was selling well.

Marlena didn't know anything else to do to get enough money to help Eugenia purchase two or three gowns for the Season. Since the duke admitted to carrying the package of smelling salts down the street, it wasn't a far stretch to assume someone had seen him doing it. Though she didn't expect he'd be happy Miss Truth had written about it. There was no way Marlena would have if it weren't necessary for her to help the sisters.

Since she couldn't stop thinking about the duke, his kisses, or the very revealing scandal sheet she'd turned in yesterday, she'd decided to work on a complicated stitchery that happened to remind her even more of the duke. With a sharpened lead pencil, she'd painstakingly sketched a garden scene on a fine linen fabric suitable for framing.

First, she'd drawn the grass. Tall swaying blades tightly nestled by shorter straight ones and a few wide sprigs, too. Next, she'd added flowers springing up from the grass. Big ones with wide-open petals, tiny ones with little closed blooms, and even a blossom or two that was falling away from the stem. When she had the garden lightly sketched the way she wanted it, she'd added a bee, a wasp, a ladybug, and two butterflies. One in flight over the top of what would be colorful flowers and the other sitting on a petal.

It had taken her almost as long to pick out all the colors of embroidery thread she wanted to use as it had to sketch the entire scene. She was threading her first needle, eager to get started with her stitches and thinking about the duke, when Justine burst into the room and announced Marlena must practice her dancing. There had been no persuading her differently.

Marlena had also wanted to think on her conversation with Eugenia about why she was kissing the duke. To Marlena's surprise, Eugenia had understood Marlena's desire to be kissed. It was good to know other young ladies had great curiosity about it. Her friend admitted she'd often wanted Mr. Bramwell to forget propriety and kiss her, too, but it hadn't happened yet. What Eugenia hadn't understood was why it was the duke giving Marlena her first kiss. That had been harder to explain. She wasn't sure Eugenia believed her when she'd told her the truth: Marlena was the one who'd kissed the duke first.

"Did you hear me?" Justine asked.

"No, I'm sorry," Marlena said, honestly. "I was thinking about the embroidery sample I was working on when you interrupted me for a dance. What did you say?"

Justine continued playing the practice tune. "If you'd had the good sense to agree to move into the duke's home in Mayfair we both would have—"

"Thank you, Justine," Marlena said, interrupting her. She would rather dance than hear her cousin complain once again about not getting to move to Mayfair. Marlena turned and walked back over to the center of the room to wait for her cousin to give her the prompt to start.

"I'm ready whenever you are."

"Perhaps you will marry well. A man who has a home there and he'll allow me to move in with you."

"Would you really want to do that? Give up your home here?"

"That, or if it were possible, to continue to have a coach like the duke has provided for us so I could visit with my friends there anytime I wanted."

"You could walk. It's really not that far."

Justine sighed heavily. "Still so much to teach you. I can't be seen walking around Mayfair with all my friends now that I have the duke's coach. Appearances are so important to Society. I've received so many invitations since the duke has become your guardian, I feel as if I'm the diamond of the Season again."

That Marlena did know.

After playing a few more moments Justine said, "One. Two. Three. Begin. Step forward, left, left, back on the right, forward on the left, twirl, clap, and curtsy. That's right. And again. Step—"

"Excuse me, Mrs. Abernathy."

"What is it, Mrs. Doddle?" Justine asked, but she didn't stop playing or turn to face the housekeeper.

"Begging your pardon, but the Duke of Rathburne is here to see you and Miss Fast."

All ten of Justine's fingers landed on the keys at the same time, making a dreadful sound.

Eager anticipation gripped Marlena. She rose very slowly from her curtsy, suddenly more out of breath than she should be. The duke was here. Every sensation she'd felt when he held and kissed her came rushing back to excite her.

"Oh, how absolutely wonderful!" Justine jumped up from the stool and walked away from the pianoforte. "I must have been playing so loud I didn't hear the door. He was just here a few days ago. I thought for certain it'd be weeks before we'd see him again. He's such a rogue." She lifted her breasts to make sure an ample amount of flesh showed from beneath the neckline of her silk dress, and then pressed her hands down the front of her skirt. She looked over at Marlena and said, "How does my hair look? Is any of it out of place?" She touched the sides, top, and the back of it. "Are there any wrinkles in my clothing?"

"You are very presentable," Marlena said, having no doubt how she must look after an hour of skipping, twirling, and bowing from one end of the room to the other.

"Good. You may show him in, Mrs. Doddle, and then please make tea for us."

Justine turned to Marlena. "Some of your hair has fallen out of your chignon but I suppose there's nothing for us to do about that now. You've not time to completely redo it. Quickly brush it behind your ears and we'll hope it will stay."

Marlena was far more worried about how her insides were jumping than about her unruly locks. It wasn't the first time the duke had seen her with tangles in her hair, as he'd reminded her. She doubted it had been combed at all the morning she'd first seen him all those years ago. Now she was older and should be able to keep her hair under control, but some days it was as if it had a mind of its own. She tucked the loose strands behind her ears and moistened her lips.

Seeing the duke again shouldn't make her feel this happy. Thrilled even. But it did.

The Duke of Rathburne strode into the drawing room as if with a purpose in mind. His gaze settled immediately on Marlena and she felt as if her heart melted in her chest and slowly flowed all the way down to her toes. The way looking at him made her feel couldn't be explained by words. It was more comforting than a blazing-hot fire on the coldest of nights. There was a rich and lush appeal to him. He was devilishly handsome dressed in his coat of deep-ocean blue, boots that covered his knees, and an expression that told her he was pleased to see her, too.

After greetings were appropriately taken care of, the duke said, "I heard a melody when I came into the house. I hope I'm not interrupting anything."

"No, not at all," Justine said, walking closer to him. "I was playing for Marlena so she could work on her dance steps. The Season isn't far away now and she still has much to learn."

Marlena had known the steps to every dance since she was sixteen. She opened her mouth to contradict her cousin but the duke spoke first.

"The Season is why I'm here. But first"—he extended a box to Justine—"I brought you some sweets."

Justine's face lit up as if a thousand candles were shining on it. Marlena couldn't help but think her cousin's heart was melting, too.

"For me?" Justine took the box with one hand while the other flattened on her ample bosom. Her lashes fluttered. "How lovely. Thank you, Your Grace. Look, Marlena. Something sweet for us to enjoy."

Marlena watched Justine tear into the package and murmured, "Lovely indeed," though his gift to her cousin irritated Marlena beyond sensible reason.

How dare he. She had received very inappropriate, expensively bottled smelling salts from the duke and Justine was given confections. Confections that were properly wrapped in brown paper and tied with a common string. Not expensive lace and pretty blue ribbons. And to bring Justine sweets after he'd kissed Marlena. Kissed her so thoroughly she would never forget his touch.

What nerve he had! Not that Marlena cared, of course. He could bring Justine all the sweets he wanted to.

The more the better.

What he did or didn't give Justine, or how he chose to present it to her, meant nothing to Marlena. She'd told him she wanted him to give her her first kiss and he had. The mystery of what a kiss would be like was solved. That was the end of it, and that was the way she wanted it.

But her mind reminded her she hadn't expected the kiss to be so powerful, so delicious that she couldn't stop thinking about it. Couldn't stop thinking about the possibility of the duke kissing her again.

"Oh, my, so tempting," Justine said as she looked at the bounty nestled in the box. "Small apricot tarts glazed with sugar. You must have remembered they're my favorite from my first Season. They'll be divine."

The duke acknowledged her gratitude and then gave his attention to Marlena. "Back to the reason I'm here,

Miss Fast," he said. "I told you a friend was helping me find someone to guide and provide you with the things I couldn't do for you during the Season."

"Of course we remember," Justine answered for Marlena with another generous smile to the duke. "We've been patiently waiting to hear from you about this."

He nodded to Justine and then gave his attention back to Marlena. "I had a note from her this morning telling me she'd found someone and asked that I meet her here at your house this afternoon. She's bringing the person to meet you."

"Splendid." Justine beamed. "We are most appreciative, Your Grace. Perhaps it's Mrs. Seagrove. She's the best, I'm told. Or Miss Provost. Though she never married, I've heard outstanding things about her as well. Either would be perfect."

"Who is she?" Marlena asked him, suddenly feeling wary.

"I don't know who the Duchess of Griffin has found. She didn't say, but I trust Esmeralda. You'd have no reason to know this, but Her Grace once worked with an employment agency. She's very familiar with most of the women who know what to do."

The Duchess of Griffin was coming to her house? Marlena knew very well about the duchess. She had written about her in *Miss Honora Truth's Scandal Sheet* for a Season. And now Her Grace was on her way to meet Marlena. Face-to-face. Marlena's stomach quaked at the thought, but she managed to mumble, "It was kind of the duchess to take the time to find someone."

When Marlena continued the scandal sheet after the first Season she should have known it would come back to haunt her in some way, but at the time she was only thinking she had to continue to help Eugenia and Veronica.

At the back of her mind, Marlena was furiously trying to remember exactly what she'd written about the duchess when she was the chaperone for the Duke of Griffin's twin sisters. It was impossible to recall it all. It was more than two years ago and she'd written many columns since then.

Yet, some of the sentences she'd written came back to her. *Perhaps the most scintillating gossip from the first ball of the Season wasn't about the Duke of Griffin or his sisters. It centered on their intriguing young chaperone, Miss Esmeralda Swift.*

That wasn't a bad thing to say. It was actually nice. Marlena remembered she'd commented on the announcement of the duchess' engagement, too:

The Duke of Griffin has made his intentions known, and the maiden who made the prized catch of the Season is none other than the chaperone for his twin sisters, Miss Esmeralda Swift.

Marlena couldn't remember saying anything unkind about the duchess. Thankfully, her rebukes were usually reserved for the Rakes of St. James and not others she mentioned in her scandal sheet.

The front door knocker sounded. Justine's eyes lit up again. "That must be the duchess. I do hate to bring it to your attention again, Your Grace, but this is a perfect example why we need more servants in the house. Mrs. Doddle is making tea but will have to stop and go answer the door because we don't have enough servants to fulfill all the duties around here."

"I'll help her with the tea," Marlena said, wanting to prolong meeting the duchess and quite happy to leave the duke's presence for a few minutes to collect her thoughts.

"Thunderbolts and lightning, Marlena." Justine placed the box of tarts on a nearby table. "That will never do. Neither of us should have to do it, but it will be better if

I take care of this until other arrangements can be made for us. It's my house. Imagine one of us having to answer the door for a duchess!" She turned to the duke and smiled. "If you'll excuse me, Your Grace."

He nodded.

"I'll take care of the door, Mrs. Doddle," Justine called as she swept out the room with her tiered skirts billowing behind her. "You continue in the kitchen and add two more cups to the tray."

The duke walked closer to Marlena. "You are looking quite fetching today, Miss Fast."

"Am I?" she asked, tilting her chin up and realizing she still felt a little miffed at him about the sweets even though she didn't want to care enough about him to feel that way.

"I should have said you are fetching every time I see you, but your cheeks are a little more flushed today and your hair is curling beautifully about your face."

She made a move to swipe her hair behind her ear again.

He softly grabbed her wrist to stop her. "No, don't change it. There's something enchanting about it."

Marlena looked down at his hand on her. It was warm. There was strength in his fingers even though he wasn't holding her tight. Little pricks of delight were dancing inside her.

When she met his gaze, he said, "I like it the way it is now."

"And how is that, Your Grace? Untidy? No," she answered herself. "I believe your word was *unruly*."

The duke chuckled huskily, and all the pleasurable feelings swirling inside her multiplied.

"Yes. It reminds me you are innocent, wholesome. Desirable."

"I suppose Justine is quite desirable, too," she responded, unable to stop herself from saying it, though she knew she shouldn't. Why did it bother her so and why was she letting him know?

His eyes narrowed. "Most ladies are, Marlena."

"So after you kissed me quite thoroughly you bring Justine confections and me smelling salts."

The amusement he was so obviously experiencing didn't leave his features. And she was too wrought to do anything about it other than continue her annoyance at him.

"Is that a jealous remark, Marlena?"

"What? Jealous of you favoring Justine? Of course not. I was simply stating a fact."

"You are piqued at me for bringing her sweets and not you." His thumb gently rubbed the underside of her wrist.

Marlena was. It was ridiculous. It was horrifying that he knew it. And the duke was enjoying her distress about it. What was wrong with her? Why should it bother her a fig if he brought Justine confections, flowers, or sachets?

It should mean nothing to her.

Yet it did.

He was her guardian, not a beau. Yes, they had kissed. And kissed. Touched, too, but there was a certain amount of curiosity in it. A small amount perhaps but it was there.

"I'm still upset that you brought so many smelling salts," she said, giving him half of the truth. "Wrapped so lovely. In such beautiful bottles. I will never have to buy more during my lifetime."

His attractive grin was letting her know she wasn't fooling him for a moment.

"And I thought a box of confections was the least I could do for Mrs. Abernathy because I didn't remember our first meeting or the dance she and I had."

Marlena wanted to tell him that was probably because

neither of them had ever happened. Justine not only lived to remember the year of her first Season, but embellished it to suit herself.

He let go of her wrist. "I should have brought some for your young friend Miss Everard, too, for always making her faint. How is she? Did she recover with no aftereffects from the strong smell of the salts or witnessing our kiss?"

"She's perfectly fine," she answered truthfully. "We didn't go into any details about that. It was easier for us to just avoid an in-depth reflection about what she saw."

"I find that unusual, Marlena, considering the effect it had on her. How was that accomplished? I would think our kiss would be the first thing she wanted you to explain when she was feeling better."

"She's very shy. I know she didn't want to pry too much. I, in turn, didn't want to have to confess anything other than the truth, which was that I had first kissed you. Never having had a kiss herself, she understood my inquisitiveness."

"Your capability of amazing me amazes me. Inquisitiveness, was it?"

"Yes. I'm sure there'll come a time when she and I will talk about it in more depth. When she's a little older. Maybe after she's had her first kiss. My answer for what she'd seen between us seemed to satisfy her for the time being. Now I hope it satisfies you and we don't have to mention it again, either."

"No, Marlena. We will talk about kissing again."

She was afraid of that.

No, she couldn't fool herself. She wasn't afraid they'd talk about it again. She was hoping they would.

Feminine voices drifted in from the corridor.

"But not today," he added. "However, there is something you can do for me."

"If I can," she said, feeling a little wary at having no idea what he might ask of her.

"Could you arrange it so I can visit Mr. Portington and inquire about his collection at a time Miss Everard isn't home? I would hate to arrive at her door and distress her in her own home."

"Yes, of course," Marlena said, thinking Eugenia and Veronica needed to be away from the house and not see the duke. "That's very thoughtful of you."

"I'm only keeping my promise to see if I can persuade him to relinquish some of his fossils and artifacts so that money might be returned and Miss Everard can have her Season as planned."

"I'm grateful—as you know." She cleared her throat and clasped her hands together before she did something foolish like hug him as she had in the garden a few days ago. Though this time she wasn't fearful the hug would end in a kiss. But she could very well be caught in his arms. "Let's plan it for tomorrow afternoon. I'll prepare a picnic and take Veronica and Eugenia to the park at half past two. Would that work for you?"

He nodded. "And then, since you are right next door, I'll come to your house and wait for your return so I can fill you in on what I find out."

"Yes, yes, thank you." Excitement that she might be able to help Eugenia make the Season bubbled inside Marlena. "I'd like that very much if we can find a way to get Justine to give us a few minutes alone."

He smiled. "I'll think of something."

"I have no doubt you will," Marlena said, and looked up to see two beautiful ladies walk into the drawing room. What startled her for a moment was that both were so young. She expected one of them, the one who would be assisting her with the Season, to be much older than the duchess and even older than Justine. Both these ladies were younger than her cousin.

The duke greeted them: the Duchess of Griffin and *Lady Vera*. After she heard that name the rest of the introductions were like a reverberating echo in her ears. Lady Vera was one of the Duke of Griffin's twin sisters. She was another young lady Marlena had written about.

Heaven help her! What was Lady Vera doing here? Maybe the duke knew she was Miss Honora Truth after all, and he was proving it by bringing these two ladies to taunt her. Marlena went through the motions of following the introductions even though she was once again swamped with guilt.

Coming face-to-face with the duchess and her sister-in-law was even worse than meeting the duke for the first time. He deserved being written about in the scandal sheets after the secret admirer letters. The two ladies standing in front of her were completely innocent of any wrongdoing, yet she'd splashed their names all across London and beyond with her quill.

Marlena's thoughts scrambled again as she tried to remember what she'd written about Lady Vera. She couldn't remember it word for word but something about: *It was Lady Vera and Lady Sara's misfortune that it was up to their brother, the Duke of Griffin, to see they married. And it may be his twin sisters who pay the price of his misdeeds.*

Oh, my. Marlena wanted to sink through the floor. The fear the sisters must have felt, thinking someone might want to do them harm or ruin their Season. There was no doubt that the worst thing she and Eugenia had done was to talk Mr. Bramwell into going to White's with Mr. Portington to start that rumor.

She remembered clearly what she'd told Mr. Bramwell to say because she'd taken such pains with the wording:

The Rakes of St. James never had to pay a price for their scandalous behavior of sending the secret admirer letters. Maybe it is time they did. Would it be fitting if something happened to ruin the Duke of Griffin's sisters' first Season?

Why had Marlena ever thought that was a good idea? Was it because she was a young, rash seventeen-year-old who thought to do something good and punish someone who'd done something bad? Was it because she was in London with nothing to do but wait for her debut into Society? Was it because at heart she was a horrible person?

No. She didn't want to believe she was a horrible person. Maybe it was only that she'd been too zealous in her approach to help her neighbors. She really didn't know, but she had to remain calm. And remembering that her parents were watching over her was always a good way to settle conflicting emotions.

"Miss Fast," the duchess said.

"Yes, Your Grace." Marlena answered the duchess with what she hoped wasn't a hint of the turmoil leaping in her thoughts.

"I was telling Lady Vera about you. How the Duke of Rathburne was now your guardian and I mentioned you needed someone who could help you with your Season. Lady Vera offered to do that for you."

Marlena looked at the lovely young lady with light-brown hair and eyes as blue as the sky. "You're to be my finishing governess?"

"Heaven's gates, Marlena," Justine exclaimed. "Lady Vera is not a governess of any kind for anyone."

"Indeed I am not," Lady Vera answered pertly. "I can understand why you thought I might be since I offered to help you with the particulars."

"I meant no disrespect, my lady," Marlena said.

"None taken. I am not shocked, offended, or embarrassed easily, Miss Fast." And as if to prove it, she walked over and slid her arm around the duke's elbow, and looked into his eyes. "I am doing this for Rath. He knows I adore him and I've wanted him to marry me for years. He won't give me the pleasure of offering for my hand. Perhaps my helping him with you will entice him to favor me."

"You have and always will have my favor," the duke said to her.

Marlena watched Rath smile down at Lady Vera and felt her whole body stiffen. It was quite clear the duke and Lady Vera knew each other very well. The way she smiled at him, spoke so brazenly to him, and had touched him. Marlena was astounded by how forward Lady Vera was being, and that the duke had responded so honestly. That was when Marlena realized she *was* jealous!

Jealous of Justine.

Jealous of Lady Vera.

Jealous of any other lady who tried to lay claim to the duke.

That was maddening.

It was time for Marlena to get her feelings under control, and fast. The duke would have many ladies seeking his attention and favor and she shouldn't be one of them.

Justine cleared her throat rather loudly. Obviously she'd hadn't approved of Lady Vera's open display of affection either.

The duke took hold of Lady Vera's wrist and slid her arm from around his, placing it down by her side. "You know I can't marry you because I think of you as my sister."

"That has never bothered me," she added with a smile most men would be more than happy to receive from a duke's sister.

"But it would me," he said affectionately.

"Well, I always like to try in case there is any chance you've changed your mind about me." Lady Vera turned to Marlena. "I will be attending my third Season, Miss Fast, and if anyone knows gowns, parties, and *gentlemen*, and their way around them all, it's me. I'll be glad to guide you through and tell you all the gossip I know about everyone."

Marlena was certain she must have gulped before she repeated the word, "Gossip?"

Good heavens! Did the duke, Lady Vera, and the duchess know she was Miss Truth or was she just feeling so guilty that everything they said made her feel that way?

She sought out the duke's face. His gaze was on her, too. She took in a long, deep breath and felt better for it. The duke wasn't one to hold his tongue. Of that she was sure. If he suspected her dual life, he wouldn't be playing this game with her. He would just ask her about it. She was being overly suspicious for no reason. If they knew she was Miss Truth they wouldn't be so polite to her. And right now she wished she wasn't. It simply hadn't been clear in her mind that she might one day meet the people she was writing about in her scandal sheet. And regret it.

"Why don't I try explaining it a little better, Miss Fast," the duchess said, glancing at her sister-in-law with an indulgent expression. "First, I'll do my best to see Lady Vera doesn't teach you anything you shouldn't know. Since you really don't need any lessons, nor do you have need of a chaperone because of Mrs. Abernathy, I thought having someone near your age would be best for you when deciding fabrics, patterns, and all the latest fashion of clothing. And Lady Vera will certainly know which parties you need to attend and how to get the invitations for you."

"And I also know which gentlemen are really looking

for a bride and which ones are merely looking," Lady Vera then glanced at the duchess and added, "And there will be a few other things I will tell you along the way."

"You'll be just perfect for her," Justine said, clasping her hands together at her waist. "We can't thank you enough for offering to do this for her, Lady Vera."

"Yes, Your Grace, Lady Vera, I'm delighted that both of you are so willing to help me."

"Good," Lady Vera answered. "We'll start tomorrow. I'll arrive for you and Mrs. Abernathy at half past twelve."

"Could we please make that the day after, my lady? I've already made plans for tomorrow."

"What?" Justine asked.

"I'm taking Eugenia and Veronica for a picnic in the park. I failed to mention that to you today." Marlena turned to Lady Vera again. "Will the day after work for you?"

She smiled. "Of course. We will go to my modiste first so she can get started making your gowns. I have some wonderful colors in mind already that will go beautifully with your hair."

Marlena reached deep and pulled up her courage. It appeared she and Lady Vera were going to be spending quite a bit of time together. She might as well get used to it. She'd brought this burden on herself by trying to help Veronica and now she'd have to find a way to accept the consequences.

Lady Vera turned her attention back to the duke, put her arm through his again, smiled, and said, "I take it we have no limits concerning your plump pockets, Your Grace."

"I would never put those kinds of limitations on you, Lady Vera. It would do me no good anyway."

"That's what I wanted to hear."

"That's what I wanted to hear, too," Justine added with

a broad smile. "Ah, the tea has arrived. Let's all sit down and have some."

Marlena looked over at the duke and saw that he was watching her. His brows drew together. Maybe he sensed her misgivings about Lady Vera. Maybe he sensed her jealousy. Maybe he felt she hadn't been gracious enough for the help Lady Vera was going to give her.

And then for a moment or two as their gazes were locked together across the room, Marlena wondered what it would be like if he wasn't her guardian and she wasn't Miss Truth. Would they then be able to look at each other as they had when she'd rounded the corner of her house and looked up to see him standing on her front steps? The way they had looked at each other before she knew he was the Duke of Rathburne.

My Dear Readers,

My latest wisp of scandal will come as no surprise to any of you, unless perhaps if you have been on the Grand Tour. And then, even so, I'm assured this weekly column makes its way to France, Portugal, and many countries beyond. Though I'm told, some devoted fans refuse to read anything about their homeland while traveling so as not to disturb their entertainment and pleasure.

Today it is with abundant fanfare and much ado that I tell you the latest I've gleaned about the notorious rake, the Duke of Rathburne. I have it on the most privy authority that the duke was seen coming out of a ladies' shop carrying a ribbon-and-lace-covered package! That he entered a ladies' shop is scandalous enough, but that he walked down the street to his carriage carrying his purchase goes beyond the pale. My source tried to follow him to see where he was going with an item from an unacceptable place for a gentleman to enter, but the duke's landau was much too fast. If anyone hears who received a gift from the duke, let me know. I'll tell it right here next week.

MISS HONORA TRUTH'S WEEKLY SCANDAL SHEET

Chapter 15

He could be a rake if he fails to take a lady at her
word that a situation is serious.

No rain fell and the gray skies didn't appear threatening as Rath stepped down from his carriage. He was proceeding with his plan to pay a call on Mr. Portington as arranged with Marlena. If something had happened and Marlena hadn't been able to leave with Miss Everard, maybe she wouldn't faint if she knew her brother-in-law was there to protect her. And if she fainted again, maybe Portington could shed some light on why.

Not much puzzled Rath. Miss Everard did. She was an odd young lady. He wanted to know if she was truly frightened of him. If her fainting had only happened once, maybe he could rationalize it with the knowledge that she'd never met a duke before. But not three times now. He could just ask her, but she would probably faint before she got her answer out.

Rath thought back over the two times he'd seen her as

he entered Portington's gate and headed up the stone steps to the man's front door. She had carried something written by Miss Honora Truth both times. Was that the problem? Obviously Miss Everard knew Miss Truth constantly wrote about Rath and had written about his friends before they married. Had she been so embarrassed she was carrying such rubbish authored by the gossipmonger that the thought of him knowing made her faint? That seemed plausible to him.

Rath had glanced at the scandal sheet when he'd picked it up off the ground where it had fallen beside Miss Everard the last time she'd curled her toes and collapsed. The words seemed familiar when he'd read them. Probably because the woman wrote that Marlena was now his ward. And he was most definitely kissing Marlena. Maybe she was right and that was enough to make Miss Everard faint again.

He didn't know why people kept reading the gossip sheet. Why he did. The Rakes of St. James were never punished according to Miss Truth. Fine. He could live with her, and the rest of London, thinking that guilt wasn't a fitting punishment. He was also fairly certain Miss Truth wouldn't have started her war on the rakes if it hadn't been for the man who suggested the chickens should come home to roost for the rakes and perhaps someone should make mischief for Griffin's twin sisters during their debut Season.

Rath would love to get his hands on that man or all the men who'd been in on that, he thought as he lifted the door knocker and rapped the iron a couple of times. There had been many times, more than he could count, when Rath hadn't been a gentleman where a lady was concerned, especially not up to his father's standards, but he'd never threaten to harm a lady's reputation, or willingly do so.

Thankfully, nothing of serious consequence had happened to either of Griffin's sisters, and Lady Vera had more than proven she could hold her own against someone out to ruin her reputation. And now Miss Truth had suggested in her last column that Lady Vera and Marlena might be at risk during the upcoming Season.

The thought that some man might want to put his hands on either lady or in some way ruin their reputation for the Season gnawed at him. He didn't even want to imagine Marlena dancing and twirling about the dance floor with other men, their arms gliding down hers, squeezing her fingertips and caressing her back as they moved through the steps. He had accused her of being jealous, but maybe he was the one whose heart was stricken.

The door opened and Rath looked upon a reasonably tall, solidly built gentleman who in no way looked as if he could be the neighbor Marlena had described. Rath was expecting a much older looking man. His light-brown hair showed no signs of gray and his face was clean-shaven. Both were unusual for a man past forty. In fact, the man appeared to be in excellent shape. He wasn't balding or stooped in the shoulders, and there were no spectacles sitting across the bridge of his nose. There weren't even any stains on his neckcloth or waistcoat.

"Mr. Portington?" Rath asked.

"Yes," he answered, staring at Rath in a quizzical manner.

"I am the Duke of Rathburne. May I come inside?"

"Your Grace." He bowed. "If you're sure it's my door you're looking for." He patted his pockets and looked around as if he'd lost something.

"I am certain," Rath assured him.

"You are?" he said, clearly flustered. "Then please come in. It's my pleasure."

"Thank you."

Portington stepped back and Rath walked into what he thought would be the vestibule of the house. All he could see was a dimly lit, narrow path. The walls of the walkway were lined with crates that had been stacked floor-to-ceiling. Rath moved aside and allowed Portington to lead the way through the tunnel until they came to a small room where a settee and two chairs were placed in front of a fireplace.

Behind the living space were more crates stacked high and an abundance of urns, statuary, armor with and without pikes, shields, bones, tusks, and carpets. Littered among all the things shoved against one another on the floor and shelving was a varying mishmash of stuffed birds and animals. There were several statues of cherubs, busts, and figurines that had been carved and fashioned out of marble, agate, bronze, and more stones than he could identify.

Marlena wasn't kidding when she said the man had fossils and relics in his house of everything anyone could imagine—and then more. Rath had never seen anything like it. Where could the man have purchased such a large assortment?

"I apologize there's so little room for entertaining, Your Grace," the man said without any embarrassment. "But my work takes up a great deal of space."

To say the least.

"May I—may I take your cloak and hat and offer you a seat? I have port. It's been open awhile, a month or two. Maybe longer. I don't drink it often, but it should still have a bit of taste to it."

Rath couldn't remember a time he'd drunk stale port, but he'd promised Marlena he'd handle this and so he would. Even if it meant downing every drop of the fortified wine whether or not it tasted like vinegar.

"Yes. I'd like to have a drink with you."

Portington smiled, lifted his shoulders, and started looking around the room. He touched the pockets of his coat as if he thought the port might be in them. "It must be in another room. The kitchen probably. Would you give me a minute?"

"No hurry," Rath said, as he removed his cloak and laid it across the back of his chair. "Is it all right if I look around?"

"Please do," he answered. "Most of the fossils are crated, you understand. They can be fragile, and I have to keep them safe. I'll be right back."

Scanning the area around him, Rath realized he was looking at an unorganized warehouse, filled with priceless rare antiquities as well as possibly fake items from all over the world. There were shelves of china, figurines, clocks, and books stacked to the heavens. Rocks—large and small. He saw piles of white, dried-out bones. Some large enough to have come from an elephant or maybe a giraffe. In some of the open crates he saw insects and small animals forever cast in stone and now nestled in beds of straw. One of the fossils etched in a gray slab was hauntingly intriguing. A lizard had caught the head of a butterfly in its mouth. Both of them had become the prey of time.

Rath couldn't say he knew much about the authenticity of the man's collection, but Portington had so many items, some of them had to be valuable. He could now comprehend what Marlena was talking about when she said the man had an obsession. That was an understatement. And he could also empathize with Portington's wife—to have to live with the man who had such a penchant.

The problem was going to be getting Portington to part with some of his possessions.

"Here we go, Your Grace." He handed the small glass to Rath and pointed to the crowded seating area.

Rath took the glass and the chair. He held up the drink to his host and said, "Cheers, Portington. You have many fascinating artifacts in your possession."

"Quite proud of it all." His host smiled and then sipped his drink. "Mrs. Portington frequently complains about it, but I don't know why. I do my best to keep her comfortable. Everything I purchase is of great value. Sometimes not so much as what I pay for it, but it's value to our culture and the history of mankind."

"That's understandable. It's why I'm here."

Portington made himself comfortable in a chair. "You're a collector, too, I gather."

"Not yet. Right now, I'm only looking into the possibility of becoming one. I was hoping you could help me get started."

"Ah, now I understand the reason for your visit." He smiled at Rath. "There are several gentlemen I work with to procure the things that interest me. I'd be happy to put you in touch with any of them. For instance Mr. Layton trades in potteries and Mr. Hillsburg trades only in statuary."

"Good. I believe Mr. Herbert Wentfield is one."

"Oh, you know him?"

"No." He took a sip of the port and almost winced as he swallowed. He'd have to remember to send the man over a new bottle. "I've heard his name and about some of the fossils he has."

"Yes." Portington nodded. "I've sent him two letters in the past few days with no response. Usually he's quick with an answer. I took myself over to his house yesterday and it was empty—everything cleaned out as if he'd never been there. I don't know where the man's gone. None of the neighbors seemed to know, either. There must have been an emergency. Perhaps with a family member. I feel sure he'll write and let me know where he is."

The information about Wentfield, if that was indeed the man's name, didn't surprise Rath.

"Do you happen to know where he is?" Portington asked.

"No. I was hoping you could tell me. Do let me know if you hear from him, and I'll do the same."

He nodded. "Now that I know of your interest in starting a collection, I will."

"I've seen many artifacts here in your house that could help me start accumulating some treasure of my own. If you'd be interested in selling any of them."

Portington chuckled. "That's kind of you to offer, and I'm honored you think so highly of my collection, but I really couldn't part with any of it. You see, I only purchase things that speak to me. And I must have them when they do. I have cataloged everything as to what it is, its value to history, where it came from, how much I paid for it, and the date I bought it. And I couldn't willingly sell or give up any of it."

That was not the answer Rath wanted to hear. "So you have all of this listed in a ledger?"

"My notes fill several ledgers. It's quite extensive, and takes time to keep up with. I can show you one of them if you'd like. And I'd happily show you the rest of the things I have."

"You have more than what is in the front of the house and in this room?"

"My, yes. I've been collecting since I was a young boy, but only on rare occasions back then, of course. My father sealed my interest when he obtained one of the first marbles from the Parthenon. Of course, that was long before Lord Elgin raided the stones in Athens and caused such a stir that no one can get near them now. And rightfully so."

Rath took another sip of the port and looked at the man so innocently admitting he had something of such a great value and rarity in a private home—and yet he'd also bought things that Rath considered as worthless as Megalosaurus eggs.

"Where is the marble?" Rath asked.

"Not in this room, and not where I could easily get to it, or I'd show you. It has to be kept crated and wrapped so it won't get broken, you understand. I keep most of my fossils crated, too."

"Yes, you're wise to do so."

"Would you like to see what I have in the other rooms of the house?"

"Yes," Rath said honestly. "I find all these possessions fascinating. I'd like to see more."

Half an hour later, Portington walked Rath back to the sitting room.

"Your knowledge about all you have is astounding, Mr. Portington."

The man bowed. "I thank you for being so kind with your words, Your Grace. It humbles me."

"Are you sure I can't tempt you to help me get my collection started? I'd be most generous."

Portington patted his pockets again. "Not with anything I have, but I'll be happy to guide you on whatever you decide to purchase. It's as much the seeking out the rare items as it is obtaining them."

"Yes, I can see that it is for you."

"I'll send you a list of the traders, if you'd like?"

"I would." Rath swung his cloak over his shoulders and picked up his hat and gloves. He reached for Mr. Portington's hand when he heard the front door open and ladies' voices.

Hellfire! Had he been at the man's house that long? He'd been trying to hurry but the man had so many relics to look at it was impossible to rush through them.

Mr. Portington shook his hand as Marlena, Miss Everard, and another lady, whom he assumed was Mrs. Portington, walked into the small space. He was fairly sure he'd seen her at a party or ball before, but certain he'd never had a reason to be introduced to her. She looked almost as pale-faced and frightened to see him as her sister.

Without thinking, Rath said, "Don't faint, Miss Everard."

"Faint?" Portington laughed and let go of Rath's hand. "Eugenia's never fainted in her life. Strong as they come, that one. It's her sister who's delicate. If you don't mind, Your Grace, may I present my wife, Mrs. Veronica Portington."

The ladies quietly acknowledged him with a curtsy and he nodded to them. Rath didn't know how Portington could say Miss Everard had never fainted. She looked very much on the verge of it again, and so did her sister. They huddled close to each other. Rath assumed the man was as oblivious to his wife's and sister-in-law's dismay as he was to the massive collection of artifacts surrounding him like an ancient tomb.

But what caused Miss Everard—and now her sister— to be so disturbed by him was a mystery Rath had yet to solve. Was he such an ogre? Had Miss Truth's weekly writings made him such a villain in London that young ladies were now becoming fearful of him?

"Fog came in and we had to cut our picnic short," Marlena offered on a rushed breath of air. "We'll have to go back another day."

"That's disappointing," Mr. Portington said. "Days in

the park are good for Veronica. She always enjoys the outings."

The ladies remained silent, watching him. Rath thought it best for him to excuse himself and make a hasty exit. "I was just leaving." He nodded to them again. "Mr. Portington, thank you for your help." He turned to Marlena and reached for the basket she held. "Miss Fast, I'm on my way out. I'll walk you home."

"All right. Yes, thank you, but I'll leave the refreshments. Mrs. Doddle made the sweet cakes and cinnamon butter especially for them. I can get the basket later."

After Marlena said her good-byes, they stepped out of the house and into fog so dense, Rath could barely see the rooftops of the neighboring houses. It was best the ladies had come home while they could still see to cross the streets. The blinding fog was moving in fast.

Marlena started down the stone pathway that led to the front gate, but Rath touched her arm. She stopped and looked up at him. Though the vapor enclosed them, he had no problem seeing her. She wore a black bonnet with a short brim that allowed him to see all her face. Her cheeks were damp from the heavy mist. Her beautiful eyes were sparkling like emeralds though there wasn't a spot of light anywhere around them. Even surrounded by a gray, thick haze, she was beautiful.

"Are you cold?" he asked.

"Not so much. We had a brisk walk from the park."

"Just in case," he said. Reaching over, he lifted the small collar of her wool cape and tucked it securely around her throat. His hand skimmed across the top of her shoulders and drifted down her arms. Emotions he didn't want to think about were stirring inside him. "I don't want you getting moisture down your neck. You might get chilled."

"Thank you."

"Let's take the side entrance," he said, moving his head to the left. "The one you and Miss Everard use."

"How did you—never mind. I remember." She turned away and started walking again.

Rath fell in step beside her. "Did you hear Portington say Miss Everard never fainted in her life? That she was strong."

"Yes, I've said as much," she answered, glancing over at him. "What did Mr. Portington have to say about his collection and the possibility of parting with some of it?"

It was bothersome how easily Marlena could dismiss Miss Everard's reaction to Rath, but he decided to let it go for the time being and discuss what was on Marlena's mind.

"First, everything you said about Portington is true. He doesn't have the look of someone extremely eccentric, but he is. I'm not an expert but I believe many of the artifacts he has are valuable, though some aren't."

"That's my thought as well."

Rath opened the gate for her and she walked through, stopping while he secured the latch behind them.

"Second, I don't believe there is a Mr. Wentfield."

"What? There has to be. I don't think Mr. Portington would make up a story about those eggs."

"I believe there is a real man, but he's not using his real name. When I asked about Mr. Wentfield, Portington told me the man has moved and no one knows where he is. It's not unusual for such men to prey on people like Portington who are devoted to their passion, taking them for a large sum of money and then skipping to another town with another name and another worthless artifact to sell."

"So you don't believe the eggs are real?"

"I am not an expert in such things."

Marlena stopped near the steps of the back door. "It's disturbing to hear you believe he was taken advantage of in that way. And with Eugenia's money. I just find it hard to believe he'd be so foolish with what was left to her. It wasn't his money to lose."

"I know," he said softly and lifted her chin with the tips of his fingers. Moisture was forming on her black bonnet and her face. "Why don't we move under the eave of the house? It will shield us a little from the fog, and I'll tell you more of what he said."

"All right," she agreed and, as soon as she'd stepped under the protection of the extended roof, said, "Will he allow you to purchase anything from him so you can help Eugenia?"

"No." It wasn't the answer he'd wanted to give her. She was trying so hard to help her friend. He wanted to help her do it. "I tried. He won't consider selling one piece."

"Then try harder," she insisted irritably. "You're a duke. You are supposed to be able to make people do things they don't want to do."

He understood her sharpness and let it pass. "In business, Marlena. In Parliament maybe, but it's usually because there is a reason for someone to compromise with me. I offer something in exchange for what I want them to give me. Even if I had something Portington wanted, I don't think he'd do an exchange. He'd just want to buy what I had."

"No," she said, refusing to accept defeat so easily.

"Yes." He gently took hold of her shoulders. "Marlena, I don't know if I can explain it adequately. It's as if he considers each piece he has as a part of himself, and his work as saving what's left of the past for mankind's future. Valuable or rubbish, I'm certain he'll never sell any of what he has. The man has cataloged and written about every damned piece of it."

She remained quiet, clearly upset, so he added, "I can give Eugenia the money to have her—"

"No," Marlena interrupted. "Don't say that. You can't. They'd never accept your help and I wouldn't want you offer." Marlena's lashes lowered and a sigh passed her lips. "Eugenia doesn't even know about this yet, and I'm certain Veronica would rather her sister not have a Season than to consider your charity."

He looked at her curiously. "Most people would be happy for a duke to sponsor them."

"Some. Justine is certainly happy to accept all the gifts you want to bestow on her."

He rubbed his hands up and down her arms. "So you are still unhappy about the sweets I brought her."

"Actually, I'd forgotten about that. I was thinking of the carriage that is at her disposal. She thinks it's divine. Her station in Society has risen considerably and she's quite pleased to pick up Lady Westerbrook and others and take them for rides in the park." Marlena paused and shook her head. "I don't mean to sound ungrateful. I know you will do well by me, but the thought of Eugenia not attending the Season is troubling. She needs to have the opportunity to dance and talk with all the gentlemen, too."

"I understand your compassion for your friend. It's admirable. Don't give up hope yet. I had an idea when I was talking to Portington, but nothing I want to discuss until I check into a couple of things."

Her gaze lifted back to his and she inhaled deeply. "If there's one thing living with my cousins taught me it was not to give up without a fight. We—that is, Veronica and I—have some ideas, too."

"What?" he asked, knowing there wasn't anything a lady could do to earn money.

"Nothing I want to talk about right now, either."

"I suggest you not do anything rash, Marlena."

She shook her head slowly and looked down at the ground. "I should have been told that long ago." She lifted her face and met his gaze. "I shouldn't have been ill tempered with you, but I'm—"

"Shh," he whispered. "No need to explain."

Marlena smiled at him and his heart started pumping as hard as a steam engine he'd recently seen. He'd never tried to hide or deny his attraction to her and he certainly didn't want to now. There were times a man had to go with his instincts. This was one of them.

"You know what I'm thinking?"

"How could I possibly know," she said in a light-hearted tone. "I can't see inside your head."

It was his turn to smile at her. "I know because we are thinking the same thing."

"We couldn't be."

"I have the kisses we shared the other day on my mind."

Her gaze swept his face. "I told you I wanted to forget that happened and not talk about kissing anymore."

Rath stepped in closer to her. A tremor of arousal threaded through him. He wanted to kiss her until she surrendered everything to his will. "But can you forget?"

She flattened her back against the side of the house. "I had until you mentioned it just now."

"I believe that is what some would call fibbing, Marlena."

"No, I—No. Maybe I thought about the kisses a time or two, and that's all I'm going to say about them." She wiggled her shoulders just a little as if to shake off what she'd just said. "Besides, you should have never let the kisses and touches happen between us."

"Me?" He blew out a soft, brief chuckle. "So it was my fault? Even though I gave you my handkerchief to stop me."

"Entirely your lapse in judgment, yes," she insisted with a smile. "You knew I wanted the kiss, that I had never been kissed, that I was eager and curious to have my first one. You should have remained strong and denied me for my own good."

"Your own good? You are so unbelievable at times, my lovely Marlena, that I find myself wondering how you will astound me next," he said, hoping she could see the respect and the desire he had for her in his expression. "How could I have done that when I wanted the kiss as much as you, if not more?" He moved a little closer to her, keeping his gaze steadily, firmly on hers. "I want to have more kisses with you. Right now."

She moistened her lips and swallowed. "If that is the case, Your Grace, you will have to do it."

With pleasure.

"I'll consider that permission, but from here on, you will call me Rath. Not Your Grace."

Her eyes widened. "I shouldn't."

"All you need is permission to do so and I just gave it. We have become too close for you to continue being so formal."

He could no longer bear not touching her. He caressed her damp cheek with the backs of his fingers, letting them slowly trace down to her jawline and then over to her lips. Just touching her face caused his lower stomach to tighten and a surge of longing to catch impatiently between his legs.

Rath's hands parted her cape and his arms slid beneath it to circle her waist and pull her close. He immediately felt her soothing warmth and leaned into her, enjoying the feel of her in his arms. He stroked her back and shoulders while reaching down to kiss her forehead and then both cheeks before letting his lips trail first to one side of her mouth and then the other.

He lifted his head and smiled at her. "Your face is wet from the mist."

"Does that bother you?" she questioned.

It arouses me.

"No," he answered with a smile. "I'm sure mine is the same."

Keeping her gaze steadfast on his, Marlena reached up and touched his cheek with her gloved hand.

That was all the invitation he needed. Rath bent his head and brushed his lips tenderly across hers. They were soft and enticing. But that one sweet pleasurable kiss was not nearly enough to satisfy the hunger he had for her, and he sensed she had an equal appetite for him. He kissed her again, lingeringly at first, taking his time to fully taste her lips before easing his tongue into her mouth.

The streets and houses around them were silent, the deep fog having sent everyone inside. All he heard was the strong, increasingly erratic beat of his heart and their mingled moans of pleasure. A burning heat surged through him and a longing to make her his filled him with an overwhelming eagerness. He didn't want to tamp down his growing desire for her.

He sought her sweet, yielding mouth again and again. Their tongues met. Their breaths mingled. Each kiss dissolved into the next. With her clothing between them, he continued to rub his hands along the contour of her back, around to her hidden breasts, and then down her waist to the lean lines of her hips and thighs. She was beautifully shaped, womanly soft, and heavenly to taste. It was as if time weren't moving. All he could think, all that mattered was how good she felt in his arms and beneath his hands.

A tremor shook her body. That sent a slow spread of delicious warmth sizzling through him. It pleased him that his hands exploring her body thrilled her as much as it pleasured him. He continued to caress her, loving the feel of her against his hands. Touching her helped ease the intense hunger he had for her and gave him such pleasure that he wanted more and more from her.

She stretched her arms up and around his neck and leaned into his chest. In place of the mist on the back of his neck, Rath felt her velvety-cotton-gloved hands. Her warm, eager acceptance of his touch pleased him. He held her tighter, urging her to fit her softness more fully against the strength of his body. He lifted his hips toward her.

Their kisses deepened even more. Rath loved the way she responded to him, and in turn he was consumed with hot, throbbing desire for her. It scorched through him fast, making him want to give her more and demand more in turn. Without letting his lips leave her skin, he kissed her cheek, behind her ear, and then back to her lips to tempt her with short, sweet kisses that moved agonizingly slowly over her mouth.

"Rath," she whispered against his lips. "You are making me feel things I never knew existed."

At the sound of her whispering his name, a shiver stole over him. He had visions of her waking in the bed beside him in the morning, leaning over his bare chest and softly calling his name. Rushing down the stairs in the afternoon when he returned home from his duties at Parliament, calling his name. Lying beneath him during the culmination of their passion and tenderly whispering his name.

Those thoughts jolted Rath. He wasn't ready to think

that way about Marlena or any lady. And yet he wanted Marlena more than he'd ever wanted any other woman. He didn't know why but he felt differently about her than all the others.

He didn't know what he was going to do. The problem was that he didn't know who was risking more if they continued on the course they were on.

Marlena or him.

Chapter 16

He could be a rake if he kisses you and makes you swoon, and then never calls on you again.

~∽᙭∾~

MISS HONORA TRUTH'S WORDS OF WISDOM AND WARNING ABOUT RAKES, SCOUNDRELS, ROGUES, AND LIBERTINES

Marlena stood on a box and looked at herself in the tall wall mirror of Mrs. Musgrove's Dressmaking Shop. The famous modiste was, indeed, a French woman who had married a Londoner a year ago. At his insistence, she'd changed the name of her shop to suit her new husband. Lady Vera claimed she was still the person to use in Town, because she could work miracles with fabrics, colors, and trims.

After little more than a whirlwind of a week of choosing fabrics, ribbon, lace, and a host of other things, Marlena was trying on her fifth gown of the day. The one she had on was exquisite. Her underdress was a simple dark-pink satin shift. The fine silk overskirt was a gossamer layer of the palest pink froth Marlena had ever seen. The high waist, short capped sleeves, and hem were banded with dark-pink velvet ribbon. Tiny little sweetheart bows had been sewn all over the skirt. Marlena looked at the overly adorned dress and wondered if there was any way she could get out of ever having to wear it. She wasn't adverse to bows, but there must have been fifty on the gown.

And she'd certainly never had a dress cut so low. Lady Vera and Mrs. Musgrove insisted she not be shy about showing off to all the gentlemen, those available and those not, what nature had beautifully given her. Marlena would have to get used to that, along with the abundance of bows.

Still staring into the mirror, her gaze strayed to what was behind her. More gowns. More ruffles, flounces, ribbons, and delicate, handmade silk roses sewn onto skirts that were sprigged, tufted, gathered, or scalloped at the hem. And all of them had been made for her in a short span of time.

It was almost too much for her to take in.

Her dresses had always been good fabrics, well stitched but simple, void of what she considered unnecessary frippery. Marlena's clothing was always very wearable. In the house, in the garden, or in the park. The gown she had on and the ones hanging on the wall behind her looked as if they were far too fragile to touch, let alone wear anywhere outside her bedchamber.

One thing Marlena had learned during the past week was that when Lady Vera spoke, people listened and acted. Mrs. Musgrove had more than a dozen women working for her, too. As soon as a pattern and fabric had been chosen, the dress was assigned to a seamstress and it was started immediately.

Marlena looked at herself in the gown again. It did make her look pretty. Made her feel pretty. She turned her body and watched the skirt float and swish delicately from side to side. Maybe there weren't too many pink bows on it after all.

She'd never worn a ball gown. She'd never been to a ball. And why-oh-why, now that she was going to be attending them, did she want to be on the arm of the Duke of Rathburne. Why did she want to be in his arms again? Held tight. Feeling his lips on hers, his warm breath on her neck. If she was going to fall in love, why did it have to be with this man?

Fall in love? Heaven have mercy on her. Had she fallen in love with the duke?

Fate must be punishing her for writing the scandal sheet. Writing about innocent people like the lovely Lady Vera and causing them worry about what might be said about them next.

Marlena closed her eyes, as she had so many times in the past few days, and remembered the duke's passionate kisses in the cover of the fog. His body had been so warm. His mouth and lips had tasted so good. She'd felt as if her body were melting into his as they kissed and kissed, and then kissed again. But then her eyes opened. The duke's sudden, whispered words that he must go had left her feeling shocked, empty, and bereft as he'd quickly disappeared into the gray mist.

And he hadn't been back to her house.

She'd done something wrong. But what? Had she allowed him too much liberty? Did he think her a loose woman because they'd kissed so deeply and touched so freely? She shouldn't have allowed it but she wasn't sorry she had. The memories were too important to her. She wouldn't want to give them up.

What upset her most of all was that she must continue to write about him for now even though he was trying to help Veronica and Eugenia. If Eugenia made a good match during the Season perhaps her husband could then help her take care of Veronica.

Marlena swallowed past a tight throat. She didn't know what she was going to do about herself. The duke was going to expect her to choose a husband as well. That chilling thought was too disturbing to dwell on.

"You look quite stunning in that gown, Miss Fast, but you are also looking pensive," Lady Vera said, walking into the fitting room with all the elegance one would expect from the sister of a handsome duke.

"Thank you for the compliment," she answered softly. "And I suppose I am pensive. I'm not sure I'm ready to look for a husband, and I can't figure out where I would ever go that I'd need so many gowns, carriage and day dresses, and traveling outfits. Not to mention all the gloves, capes, headpieces, and underthings to go with each one. I know the Season is several weeks, but surely I can wear a gown more than once."

"Indeed, you can. Are there pins in the one you are wearing now?" Lady Vera asked.

"No. Mrs. Musgrove said it was perfect."

"I think so, too." She reached her hand out for Marlena. "Let me help you step down. Come sit on the settee with me while we wait for Justine to finish looking at the fabrics and lace."

Marlena took her hand and stepped down from the box.

After they made themselves comfortable on the settee, Lady Vera said, "You will have many places to wear your gowns, Miss Fast. We are fitting you for clothing not only for the Season but for your marriage as well."

"Oh, my." Marlena eased onto the settee beside Lady Vera.

"You know that is what the Season is for. The marriage mart, remember? But only if you should find the right match." She smiled. "Should you accept an offer early, which is quite possible given how lovely you are, your intended may want to marry quickly, and if so, you will already have all your clothing prepared."

Marry quickly?

That sent another chill racing over Marlena.

"It is Rath's duty to see you wed."

"Yes, of course. I know I must marry. Sometime. It's just that I don't think about it often."

"I find that interesting, Miss Fast."

"Why? I've not had many opportunities to be around gentlemen. I have other things to occupy my time and my thoughts."

"Marriage is something *most* young ladies think about all the time. Getting an offer from the right man, leaving their parents' home, making a life of their own with their husband, and having his children. But there is no reason you have to dwell on such. It's just that most young ladies do because they want to marry their first Season. My sister Sara did. She is very happy and expecting her first child."

"That is lovely for her. I'm glad her life is settled and that she's happy."

"She is," Lady Vera said with a clear carefree attitude. "I, on the other hand, am still waiting for the man I want to spend the rest of my life attached to. The longer I wait the harder it gets to choose."

Marlena's chest tightened as that horrifying feeling of jealousy gripped her again. "Is that because the Duke of Rathburne hasn't offered for your hand yet?"

Lady Vera laughed softly. "So that is the reason you don't like me, Miss Fast. Because of my relationship with Rath?"

"What?" Marlena exclaimed. Was Lady Vera serious? "No, it's not true. I like you very much. I don't know how you can say that. And with a smile on your face."

"It is true, but I don't mind now that I know why."

"You are being unkind," Marlena insisted. "I have the utmost respect for you. For how bold and honest you are about your feelings. I wish we all could be so engaging. I don't dislike you. I—I." She stopped, not wanting to lay open her feelings.

"What?"

"If you must know I am jealous, but I don't dislike you at all. It's surprising to me as well, but I enjoy being with you."

"That's nice to hear." Lady Vera's smile remained in place. "A little jealousy is good. Not too much, mind you, but a small amount. Are you envious because I am so carefree with Rath, or is it because I am the sister of the Duke of Griffin and feel I don't have to marry just because it's expected of me or that my brother wants me to?"

"Rath, of course," Marlena answered, knowing Lady Vera already knew but was giving her a way to deny it if she wanted to. Why should she? After writing about Lady Vera in the scandal sheet two years ago the least Marlena could do was be honest with her now.

"I should have guessed earlier. I noticed the way the two of you kept looking at each other the afternoon you and I met. I thought it was because it shocked you that I wanted to assist with your Season. Unlike you, I don't have a lot of things to occupy me. I've quite enjoyed the challenge of helping you."

"I will understand if you want to stop assisting me now that you know I have developed feelings for the duke, too."

Lady Vera laughed. "I can see you don't know me at all, Miss Fast. If I saw you as competition for anyone I was interested in, I would still help you but make sure you wore the most hideous gowns Mrs. Musgrove could make."

Marlena chuckled. Lady Vera was right. She could not compete with her. "You are beautiful and intelligent. You're the sister of a duke with a dowry I'm sure no other young lady could match. You have no competition, Lady Vera."

"Rath doesn't need nor does he desire any lady's dowry, so you can put that thought out of your mind. Tell me, why don't you seek Rath's affection? You have the perfect opportunity."

"How?"

"He is already dedicated to taking care of you."

Marlena looked over at the mirror and saw all the gowns she would be wearing to attract gentlemen—but there was only one she wanted to notice her. The one who wasn't a rake after all. He was a gentleman. He was good to Justine. He was trying to help Eugenia—a young lady he didn't even know. He had kissed her, yes. Not something a gentleman should do, but she had invited his kisses and touches. He hadn't forced them on her. It had been her decision to make whether they kissed from the first day when she was backed against her secretary.

It was useless to think about trying to win affection from Rath. Though she hadn't known it at the time, she had sealed her fate about that possibility when she became Miss Truth.

"I would never try."

"What's this?" Lady Vera exclaimed. "Are you telling me you want the attentions of a gentleman you aren't willing to fight for? Because if you are, I'd tell you that you don't deserve a man you aren't willing to fight for."

"If it were only a lady I had to fight, I'd be willing. That's not the reason. There are other things. Things in my past that I don't want to discuss."

"You are being honest about that. I can see something troubles you."

"Yes, and it's not something I can change."

"Sometimes it is easier to embrace things than change them, Miss Fast."

"That's not possible either. Other people are involved, but I thank you for being kind about it. Tell me, have you known the duke long?"

"Since I was a little girl. Hawk and Rath would come home from Oxford with Griffin. And sometimes he'd go home with one of them. Sara and I would miss their visits. Once we even wrote them very childish letters."

"So that is why you are so free with him. Touching him."

Lady Vera relaxed against the back in the settee, crossed one leg over the other, and started swinging her foot. Marlena was amazed to see a lady be so casual.

"Rath used to give me rides on his back. Sara would get on Hawk's back and they would race to a certain spot to see who would win. Hawk and Rath were so handsome, tall, and strong. Sara and I gave them no peace while they were with Griffin but still they would come for a visit. I know they enjoyed our attention—for a little while anyway."

"That sounds wonderful," Marlena said wistfully. "I lived with my cousins for a few years and I can remember taking turns riding on their backs, too. They were so good about me pestering them. But they moved away and I went to live with Mr. Olingworth. There were no children to play with at his house so I spent my time in the garden talking to flowers and sometimes the insects that crawl on them."

"Flowers are beautiful friends," Lady Vera said.

"Yes," Marlena admitted. "I never felt lonely when I was in the garden. Flowers don't last, though they do come back the next year, and that's always a comfort. Tell me, Lady Vera, do you really want to marry Rath?"

"Of course I do. What lady wouldn't? But I never will. Not because I don't love him dearly. I do. But as a brother, and he loves me as a sister as he's said. We will never marry, but we will always be close. Rath would come to my aid if I ever needed him. Hawk, too."

"Three brothers then. You are blessed."

Lady Vera let out a satisfied smile. "I am. You may not remember or may not have even known that a couple of years ago, when Sara and I made our debuts, there was a revival of Griffin's, Hawk's, and Rath's secret admirer letters in a scandal sheet."

Marlena went still. That old fear of being caught assailed her.

"It said something along the lines that Sara and I might bear the brunt of revenge for Griffin's and the other rakes' misdeeds," Lady Vera continued. "And someone might want to disrupt our Season to get back at them. Do you remember anything about that?"

Very guiltily Marlena swallowed hard and answered, "Yes, I do. I'm sure it must have made you and Lady Sara suspicious of every gentleman you met, but I hope nothing tarnished you or your sister because of that rumor."

"Oh, we weren't suspicious of anyone," she insisted.

Marlena gasped. "How can that be true?"

"We were cautious as all ladies should be about how a gentleman is treating her. Being twins we were always the center of attention. And if we weren't, we'd do something to make sure we were. We thrived on it. The more the better."

"I'm pleased that you weren't upset about the rumor and its possible consequences."

Lady Vera waved her hand dismissively. "Both twins living to our age are a rarity as I'm sure you know. Sara and I had been the topic of discussion as long as we could remember. We wouldn't have wanted our first Season be any different. Far from the scandal sheet ruining our lives, it enhanced them. We enjoyed every moment of the Season."

That surprised Marlena. "And you never felt you were in danger of anyone trying to ruin your Season or your reputation?"

"Not in the least. From the first, we never believed anyone wanted to harm us and no one did. Oh, no, wait. That's not exactly true. There was one. Lord Henry, a young bachelor who was so handsome he could make birds sing just by looking at them. He still can. But he is an ogre in gentleman's clothing. One afternoon he thought to make good on that rumor and was trying to force me to kiss him, but I took care of him with a few whacks on his head with my parasol."

Marlena was astonished. "Did you really?"

"I did and was quite proud of myself. I taught him that when a lady says no, she means no. The poor man was bleeding all over his white shirt and neckcloth. Every time I think about it now, I smile. He had to stay in hiding for over a week to let the bruising heal."

"I think that's wonderful," Marlena said, and then suddenly realized how that must have sounded and added, "I mean that he learned a valuable lesson about how to treat a lady. I hope the experience wasn't too frightening."

"Only for Lord Henry. You'll probably meet him at the first ball. I hear he's now a perfect gentleman when he takes a young lady for a ride in the park. And neither of us make mention of the incident when we meet. He bows, kisses my hand, and says hello every time he sees me."

"And Lady Sara? Did she have any ill effects from the rumor?"

"None at all. From the first mention of the rumor she and I thought the intent of it was to worry poor Griffin. And it did concern him tremendously. Hawk and Rath, too. In fact, Hawk was so concerned he helped his sister make a match before her debut started so she wouldn't be set upon by mischief-makers wanting to ruin her Season."

So the rakes had been worried but the twin sisters had not. Marlena couldn't help but feel a little prick of triumph for Veronica and the other ladies who'd been embarrassed by the secret admirer letters. She was also impressed by Lady Vera and glad she had enough wits about herself to take care of the misbehaving Lord Henry. However, Marlena only said, "I'm glad to hear the rumors didn't disturb you greatly."

"If what I believe is true, whoever started the rumor should be quite satisfied with himself because the trio of rakes have been worried and probably will remain so until I marry. They would all love to know who was behind it."

"Why?" Marlena asked cautiously, thinking of the kind and gentle Mr. Bramwell. "It was so long ago."

"Well, you know it's said there are two things a man will wait forever for."

"No," Marlena said even though she was fearful of the answer.

"Love and revenge."

Marlena moistened her lips. Even if she was found out, she'd have to be very careful that Mr. Bramwell was never implicated.

"You look disturbed, Miss Fast. Are you thinking there may be retribution against you this Season because you are now Rath's ward?"

"Me?" Marlena smiled and tried to relax. "No. That never entered my mind."

"Good, because I would hate for your Season to be troubled."

Guilt flooded Marlena. Lady Vera was truly concerned about her. And yes, the rumor would indeed hurt Marlena's Season—not for the reasons Lady Vera was thinking, but because of Marlena herself. She could never admit her role as Miss Truth, and because of that, she couldn't let Rath know how she felt about him.

"It won't be," Marlena fibbed.

"I don't know if you are aware," Lady Vera continued, "but Miss Honora Truth has a book out. Have you read it?"

Welcoming the chance to change the subject even if it was about her book, Marlena said, "Yes, I have."

"Quite entertaining, don't you think?"

Marlena nodded honestly as another wave of guilt washed over her. Lady Vera letting her know the rakes had worried about their sisters welfare had helped Marlena know that Veronica had received a measure of revenge for the secret admirer letter but Marlena wasn't sure the price she'd paid was worth it.

"I only wish I knew the woman. Or man."

Marlena blinked rapidly. "A man?"

"Yes, some believe the scandal sheet and the book are actually written by one of the men who works at the publishing house. Whoever she or he or they are, I wish I knew them. With two Seasons behind me, I could certainly add a lot to the writings in the book."

That caught Marlena's interest, and she asked. "Such as?"

"He could be a rake if he looks at you from across the room and smiles at you, but never approaches you."

"Oh, my. Yes, that is a very good one."

Lady Vera leaned closer to Marlena. *"He could be a rake if he pursues you even when your father has told him to stay away."*

"I like that one, too, and I'm sure that's true," Marlena said, wishing she'd had Lady Vera's help to write the book.

"How about this one," Lady Vera said excitedly. "*He could be a rake if he smiles when you slap him for kissing you.*"

"That one is wonderful!"

"Now you tell me one."

Marlena thought for a moment. "How about, *He could be a rake if he ignores your tender affections for him and pursues another lady.*"

"Oh, that one is perfect," Lady Vera said with a laugh. "I know that some people are disturbed by scandal sheets but others see value in them. They are entertained by the gossip whether or not any of it is true. Many are, I believe. Some, like me relish it and love seeing our names in the columns."

Lady Vera's perspective didn't exonerate Marlena but it certainly made her feel a little better. Marlena then leaned back in the settee, crossed one leg over the other as casually as Lady Vera had, and started swinging her foot, too.

It was so pleasing to have a lighthearted conversation with a young lady who had no fears to haunt her. No dark lonely nights disturbing her peace. A lady who was happy and settled where she was in life. Marlena had Veronica and Eugenia. She was devoted to them but their lives were not happy or easy. There was seldom peace, humor, or laughter between them. Their lives were in a constant upheaval.

Eugenia was too timid to say much about Mr. Bramwell, even though Marlena knew she pined for him and he longed for her. Veronica was never happy with anything Mr. Portington did. They were her friends but they weren't happy.

Lady Vera could have been a true friend for Marlena if not for Miss Truth. There was no use in wondering if Lady Vera would ever forgive Marlena should she find out that Marlena was Miss Truth. It didn't matter. Marlena was beginning to wonder if she could ever forgive herself for writing about such a lovely person—or for being obligated to keep writing about the duke.

Chapter 17

He could be a rake if he feels he is wasting his time
in the presence of any lady.

❦

*Miss Honora Truth's Words of Wisdom and
Warning About Rakes, Scoundrels, Rogues, and
Libertines*

"I know it's heavy, Mrs. Doddle." Marlena rested her
hands on her hips and huffed. "But if you managed
to help me get the trunk belowstairs you can certainly
help me now drag it to the bottom of the steps."

"It wore me out just to do that much and I've yet to
get your dinner cooking. I'm not used to lifting anything
so heavy."

"It's not heavy and you know it. Merely cumbersome
and too much to handle on my own. Besides, we didn't
carry it. We dragged it most of the way. It's only a little
farther. Now let's do it."

"Why is it you won't tell me what you have in the
trunk?" the housekeeper asked.

"Because you really don't want to know and I don't
want you to know."

"It's heavy enough you could have Mrs. Abernathy

stuffed in there and that's why you don't want to tell me. And you're trying to get rid of it before anyone finds out."

Marlena burst into laughter. It felt so good to be amused. "Thank you for that, Mrs. Doddle. I haven't laughed that hard in a long time. But I must say again, I don't want you to tell my cousin anything about this trunk no matter what you think might be inside. Now let's get it down the steps before she returns from her ride in the park."

They each took hold of a handle on the ends of the trunk and with a heave and a step started down the five steps to the garden. Mrs. Doddle grunted all the way but they managed to get it to the bottom. Tut wandered over to sniff around it.

Marlena breathed in deeply and Mrs. Doddle said, "I think I'm going to have myself a cup of tea and put my feet up for a spell after doing all that lifting."

"I want you to, but after you go next door and ask Eugenia and Veronica to come over while I get the rest of the things from inside."

Mrs. Doddle looked from the trunk to Marlena. "What things?"

"You never mind about that. Go now. Tell them I want them to come right away."

The housekeeper walked away mumbling to herself, and Marlena turned and went back into the house. She raced up the stairs to her room and gathered the things she hadn't been able to fit into the trunk. She wrapped them in her black cape and then hurried back out to the garden to wait for Eugenia and Veronica.

A few moments later, Mrs. Doddle came walking through the side gate that she'd left open. "They're on their way. They asked if it was urgent and I told them it was."

"Thank you, Mrs. Doddle."

The housekeeper stopped and deliberately eyed Marlena's cape. "I suppose you aren't going to tell me what's in there, either, are you?"

Marlena smiled and shook her head. "Now make yourself a cup of tea. You deserve a rest."

"Marlena!" Eugenia called as she ran through the gate with Veronica on her heels. "What's wrong?" She threw her arms around Marlena and hugged her.

"I'm fine," she said and returned the hug. "I didn't mean for Mrs. Doddle to frighten you."

"She said it was urgent," Veronica said, rushing up to stand beside her sister.

"Yes, but only because I wanted to do this before Justine returns." Marlena extended the folded cape to Eugenia. "These are for you. And what's in the trunk, too."

"What is it?" she said taking the garment.

"Don't open it here," Marlena told Eugenia as she glanced at Veronica. "It's clothing. I wanted to give you these things. There are gowns in the trunk and I want you to have them. It's something I want to do."

Eugenia's pale blue eyes searched Marlena's. "Why are you giving me your old clothing?"

"No, no, they aren't old. I mean the cape they're wrapped in is. But you can return that. I couldn't fit everything in the trunk. Everything I'm giving you is new."

"I still don't understand."

How could she tell her she felt sorry for her because her brother-in-law had spent the money that was intended for her? It was up to Veronica to do that. All Marlena knew to do was help her friend look as prosperous as most of the young ladies who would be attending the Season.

"You know I've been going to dressmakers and fittings with Lady Vera and Justine every day recently. They are constantly saying I must have this and this. I keep saying I don't need any more, but they are quite deaf to my pleadings. I—Eugenia, I have so much clothing for the Season. I wanted to share some of the things with you for your Season."

"Oh," Eugenia said softly. "I suppose my gowns aren't as stunning as yours, and I certainly don't have many. Three I think."

Marlena felt as if a lump had swelled in her chest. She glanced at Veronica. Marlena really needed her sister to help right now. "I'm not doing this because I don't think what you have is as good or beautiful as mine. It's because you are my friend, my partner. No, more than that." She hoped Eugenia could see the sincerity in her expression. "I think of you as the sister I never had and always wanted. Even when I lived with my aunt and uncle you know I only had boys to play with. I loved them, but now I have you and Veronica. I want to share with you as I would with a sister."

"Thank you, Marlena," Veronica said. Tears clouded her eyes. "We are grateful and it will help Eugenia. I had wondered how we could make her the diamond of the Season and you've just settled that for me. We are happy to take these things and alter them to fit her."

"And you can change the colors of the bows, move the lace, and shorten the sleeves. There are many things you can do to make the gowns look different and no one will ever know."

Veronica nodded. "I understand, and I'll make sure we rework them."

"So you think it's all right for me to accept them?" Eugenia asked her sister.

"I certainly do," Veronica said joyfully. She sniffed and wiped the corners of her eyes. "We'll consider Marlena your sister and benefactor, too. Most young ladies entering the Season have one, don't they?"

"Yes, Veronica, they do," Marlena said, grateful that she had finally caught on to what Marlena was trying to do. But Eugenia looked no happier. In fact, she looked sad.

Marlena touched Eugenia's shoulder affectionately. "But you don't have to accept them."

"No, no, I will," Eugenia said wistfully, "I want to. It's just I find it difficult to get excited about the Season. I had hoped to avoid it for a couple of years, as you did. Until I'm older."

"Oh, but you must start looking for a husband," Veronica said earnestly. "So you can have a house and family of your own."

"I know," Eugenia said even softer.

Marlena then realized Eugenia was thinking about Mr. Bramwell from across the street. She had already found the man she wanted to marry and have a home and family with, but Veronica would never accept Mr. Bramwell for her sister.

Marlena looked over at the bench where she had her first kiss with Rath. She remembered the touch of his lips on hers. His fingers caressing her cheeks, his strong arms and warm embrace making her feel cared for, desired.

Suddenly she knew she was feeling the same way Eugenia did.

Chapter 18

He could be a rake if he sees an opportunity to
have some time alone with a lady and takes it.

Spring was inching closer. Temperatures were getting warmer. Today a heavy mist had settled over London. It was early afternoon but the skies were so gray the lamps had just been lit in the card room at White's when Rath sat down at a table with Hawk and Griffin. He was looking forward to a long afternoon of laughing, winning, drinking, and companionship. He hadn't seen both his friends together since he'd walked into his house and found them enjoying his brandy—and a fair amount of gossip about him—in front of the fire in his book room.

He knew this afternoon wouldn't end the way they used to when the three got together. In the past they'd stayed up all night drinking, playing cards, throwing dice, shooting billiards, and reliving stories from their misspent youth. Stories that he was sure had been told so many times they no longer resembled the truth. Their days of debauchery had ended once Griffin and then Hawk had married.

And that was probably for the best.

The crowd at White's was thin, which was to Rath's liking. It was that time when most gentlemen were paying calls at the homes of friends or still trying to recover from their overindulgence into a bottle of brandy, port, or wine from the night before. Tankards of ale were placed before Rath, Hawk, and Griffin while they exchanged the usual pleasantries about Esmeralda and Loretta, members of Parliament, and the Lord Mayor's latest scandal before Griffin asked Rath, "How long has it been since you've seen Miss Fast?"

Thirteen days and twenty-three hours, give or take a few minutes either way.

It was madness that he actually knew how long it had been. He knew because he'd had to force himself not to go see her. Every time he looked at her, he wanted her, and she'd left him with no doubt that she wanted him, too. He didn't pursue innocents. That was one of the few rules he didn't break.

With her being his ward, under his protection, it wasn't just the trouble it would cause him, it was a matter of his honor. His father had never really believed he was a gentleman. And in most instances he wasn't. On this one, he'd always wanted to remain true. So far he had. Though in truth no other young lady had tempted him to the point Marlena had to break that oath. Every time he saw her.

It was best he stay away from her for her own good. His, too. He didn't want to have to be explaining to anyone why he'd taken advantage of his ward.

Rath shrugged off Griffin's question, dug into his pocket, pulled out a gold coin, and tossed it on the center of the table. "I'll go first," he said. Picking up the deck of cards, he started shuffling them.

"Has it been recently?" Hawk asked.

A sly smile lifted one corner of Rath's mouth. "Remind me what you consider recent. Two hours ago? Two days? Two weeks? A month?"

Griffin grinned, too. "That means he saw her last night."

Rath wished that were true. "No. So you'll leave me alone about her, it's been a while. Well over a week."

"All right," Hawk said, "But why would you think we are going to leave you alone about her?"

"Don't you think Miss Truth's damned scandal sheet is enough? Must you two pester me, too?"

"I do believe the gentleman protests too much, Griffin."

Griffin nodded, "You must have known someone would see you coming out of the shop."

"And then the owner was likely paid a tidy sum to give up the information on you," Hawk offered.

If Miss Lola had been given money, Rath was all right with that. Because of him, the woman had most likely lost whatever business Loretta and Esmeralda would have given her over the years. But why did Miss Truth have to write about it two weeks in a row? If he knew who she was he'd tell her it was smelling salts in the package!

"I would have sworn the last time we talked that you had more than a passing interest in Miss Fast," Griffin said, changing the subject back to Marlena.

I do.

But Rath wasn't going to tell them that. He cut the deck and fanned the ends together once again.

"So why has it been so long since you've seen her? She lives almost a stone's throw from you."

"I've had many things to attend to," he said.

Griffin and Hawk laughed and Rath nodded his agreement. It was a cheap answer and not worth the breath he expended to say it. For a moment he thought about telling them about Portington and how the man lived and what Rath was planning to do for the man, his wife, and his sister-in-law to make their lives a little better. But Hawk and Griffin would know in an instant that he was doing it for Marlena more than for her neighbors. Best he get more of the matter settled first. There were things that still needed to be done before Rath told anyone, including Portington and Marlena, about his idea.

"I believe I told you both that Marlena has a friend who faints every time she sees me," Rath said, changing the direction of the conversation to suit what was on his mind.

"I believe you told us she fainted twice the first time she saw you," Griffin said with a bit of a grin. "Really, Rath. Has your reputation become so debauched you now make ladies faint at the sight of you?"

"Yes," Hawk agreed. "That was the reason for the smelling salts, which led to Miss Lacy's Lace and Fine Fancy Lace or whatever the name is. It didn't help you in any way for the *ton* to read about your escapade into that ladies' shop."

"Her name is Miss Lola," Rath corrected.

"And to carry your package down the street to your carriage. Couldn't you have at least had it delivered? You must have known someone would see you and it would end up in *Miss Truth's Scandal Sheet*," Griffin added with a little censure in his voice.

"Thank you for not leaving anything out, my friends," Rath grumbled and started dealing the cards. "I'm still perplexed as to why Marlena's neighbor fainted the second time she saw me with Marlena."

"Does that make three times?" Hawk asked.

Rath nodded.

"Do you think she has a condition?" Griffin asked, scooping up all his cards in one swoop. "Maybe a weak constitution? Maybe her stays are too tight?"

"Or," Hawk said, casually picking up his cards one at a time, "Perhaps she saw you kissing *Marlena* and that made her faint."

"I didn't catch that, Hawk," Griffin said. "I didn't notice he was calling her by her given name."

"A man doesn't usually do that unless he's shared a few kisses with a young lady," Hawk said and then took a drink from his ale.

It was so damned hard to hide anything from these two. Rath didn't even know why he tried.

"She's your ward. Is that wise?" Griffin asked, spreading his cards between both hands.

No. Which was why Rath hadn't seen her in almost two weeks.

He ignored their comments about kissing and said, "There has to be a reason Miss Everard faints every time she sees me. It's not natural. Even her brother-in-law, Mr. Portington, said she never faints. So what is it about me that makes her collapse?"

"Everything," Hawk quipped with a grin.

"Everard, you say?" Griffin asked, his eyes narrowing as a grimace formed on his lips. "And Portington?"

"Yes," Rath answered, trying to make a connection before Griffin explained. "They are Marlena's neighbors Miss Everard lives with her sister Mrs. Portington and her husband. Why? Do you know them?"

"I can't say I know them. I know *of* them. If her sister is Veronica Portington, she is one of the young ladies who received one of our secret admirer letters."

Rath slid his fanned cards together and cupped them in his hand. "Are you sure? I don't remember the name."

"We each sent letters to four ladies, remember? Veronica Everard was one of my four."

Rath's hands stilled on his cards as he took in the impact of Griffin's words.

Hawk added, "Yes, it was two years ago when we were trying to find out who'd started the rumor that someone might want to ruin Griffin's sisters' Season, so we checked on the twelve ladies to see how they were doing—if they seemed happy, settled. We did all we could do to make sure we hadn't caused any one of them lasting harm by what we'd done."

Rath would never forget that rumor. He still longed to get his hands around the necks of the men who started it and scare the devil out of them.

"Mrs. Portington was one of the ladies on my list and from what I could find out she seemed happily married. Her husband appeared to be in somewhat of a financial bind at the time, but she still attended social functions."

"Every lady who received a letter from us was checked on and they all seemed to be carrying on with their lives," Hawk added.

Rath tamped the ends of his cards on the table. Griffin took another drink from his ale, and Hawk leaned his chair back on two legs.

According to Marlena, Mrs. Portington wasn't happy. It might appear she was to an outsider, but all one had to do was step inside her house to know that neither Mrs. Portington, Miss Everard, nor any lady Rath knew, would be happy living there. What lady wanted to reside where the rooms were filled to the rafters with stuffed birds, elephant tusks, dried bones, and fossils?

Rath could understand—maybe—Miss Everard fainting the first time she heard his name. Especially if she felt he'd wronged her sister. Mrs. Portington had definitely been distressed to see him in her home, yet she hadn't fainted. Suddenly, what Rath was trying to do for Portington seemed even more important now and it would no longer be just for Marlena.

A few things were beginning to make sense, but not

enough, Rath thought, as he fanned his cards again so he could look at them. Griffin and Hawk did likewise and their table quieted as they each decided which card to lay down.

An attendant stopped at their table and said, "Excuse me, Your Graces, I don't like interrupting your game but I have a message for the Duke of Rathburne."

"What is it?" Rath asked.

"There's a young man outside. He says a Mrs. Justine Abernathy asked that you come to her house right away."

Rath's hands tightened on his cards. Was something wrong with Marlena?

"Isn't that Miss Fast's companion?"

Rath nodded to Griffin. Surely, if anything was wrong, Mrs. Abernathy would have said more. Still, a spiral of concern started in Rath's chest. He looked up at the attendant. "Did the man make it sound urgent?"

"I can't say, Your Grace. Only that he said right away."

"We'll come with you," Hawk said, and pushed his chair back from the table.

"No." Rath rose. "Mrs. Abernathy can make a small matter seem large. I'm thinking this isn't pressing, but I'll go and make sure."

"You'll send for us if you need our help?" Griffin asked.

"That you can be sure of." Rath turned away but turned back when Griffin called his name.

Hawk tossed the coin to Rath and he caught it in one hand.

At the front door, the attendant was holding Rath's hat, cloak, and gloves. "Where is the young man?"

"I don't know, Your Grace. I don't see him now. He must have left when I went to tell you about his message. I took the liberty of calling your coach, but perhaps I shouldn't have."

"No, thank you. I'm glad you did. I want to go and see what this is about."

Though it seemed to take longer, less than ten minutes later Rath strode into Marlena's drawing room. His gaze found her first, standing in front of the fireplace. Relief washed down him at the sight of her. She didn't seem to be harmed or frightened. He would have sworn to anyone that Marlena was tapping her foot in frustration, though he couldn't see the toes of her shoes because her skirt swept the floor. Her arms lay folded across her chest and she appeared annoyed, though the corners of her mouth lifted slightly at the sight of him.

Mrs. Abernathy was seated on the settee with her feet up and a blanket covering her legs. His first thought was that she must have fallen and injured herself, but Marlena didn't seem upset so whatever was wrong with her cousin wasn't a problem for Marlena.

A young man Rath didn't recognize, as well as Mr. and Mrs. Portington and Miss Everard were all in the room. He tried not to even look at Miss Everard for fear she'd faint. The gentlemen bowed and the ladies curtsied, but no one smiled. They all looked nervous. Something was going on.

"Please forgive me for not standing, Your Grace," Mrs. Abernathy said and touched her forehead with a lace-trimmed handkerchief. "I simply can't put one foot on the floor."

"And I apologize for Justine sending Mr. Bramwell to look for you," Marlena said, walking closer to him. "It wasn't necessary. I tried to keep her from it."

Keeping his gaze on Marlena's, he asked, "What's wrong?"

"It appears we have a rodent problem," she answered and then sighed.

Rodents?

He didn't know what he expected to hear, but it wasn't that.

"Oh, I do hate that she even has to say such a word," Mrs. Abernathy complained. "Thank you for coming so quickly, Your Grace. I've had to take a tonic to settle my anxieties. You make the introductions and tell him what happened, Marlena, I can't bear to even say it."

Marlena hesitated only a moment before presenting Mr. Stephen Bramwell to him and adding that he was her neighbor in the house opposite to the Portingtons'.

"Are you the one who came to the club to get me?"

"Yes, Your Grace," he said stiffly, holding his head high and his hands behind his back. "I gave the message Mrs. Abernathy asked me to deliver and then came straight back here in case I could be of further assistance."

Rath turned back to Marlena. He wanted to smile at her, let her know it made him feel good to see her, that he'd wanted to spend time with her. Instead he said, "Perhaps you should tell me more about this."

"Justine saw a mouse."

"Mice," Mrs. Abernathy said from her perch on the settee. "Mice. Please tell it right, Marlena. About half a dozen of them scampering across the floor as if they owned the place."

"I saw no more than two," Marlena argued. "Justine was screaming and screeching so loudly."

"Screeching!" Mrs. Abernathy interjected. "I'll have you know I don't screech."

Marlena cleared her throat and said, "Perhaps I heard wrong. Tut was barking so fiercely, trying to get at the mouse that everyone came rushing over to see what was going on and to offer help. I had to put Tut in the garden and when I came back Justine had already sent Mr. Bramwell to find you. I told her it was completely unnecessary. All her scre—noise had already scared all the mice away and half the neighbors, too. But she's been on the settee with her feet up ever since, refusing to move."

Rath frowned. Mrs. Abernathy had taken him away from a card game with friends he seldom spent time with anymore because of a mouse. He'd bet the gold piece that Griffin tossed back to him that every house in London had mice in it. There was only one reason he'd forgive Mrs. Abernathy for disturbing his well-planned afternoon, and it was because it gave him an opportunity to see and talk with Marlena.

Looking at her perturbed expression made him smile. It didn't surprise him a mouse scampering past her toes wouldn't scare her.

"You didn't see all the mice because most of them had scurried away by the time you looked around," Mrs. Abernathy grumbled.

"No matter the number, I am not afraid of a mouse, Justine. The way you are acting, anyone would have thought the mice had danced up your skirts."

Mrs. Abernathy harrumphed. Rath and Mr. Portington chuckled. Mr. Bramwell, he noticed, gave no sign of seeing the humor in Marlena's remark and remained as stiff as a wooden soldier.

"You can come stay with us, Mrs. Abernathy," Mrs. Portington offered softly.

There wasn't room for the three of them in that house, let alone two more, Rath thought as he looked at her pale face. Yet Rath was touched by how kind it was of her to offer shelter from what little space she had. He was more determined than ever to make sure that his plan for Portington worked out.

"Thank you, Veronica," Mrs. Abernathy said. "It's so dear of you, but we really couldn't impose on your hospitality. The duke will take care of us."

"The offer stands," Mr. Portington said confidently.

"We'll do what we can to help. Now, Your Grace, if you think we can be of further assistance to you, we'll be happy to stay. If not, we'll take our leave and allow you to handle this for Mrs. Abernathy and Miss Fast."

"There's nothing more you can do. Thank you for coming to her aid, Mr. Portington. And you, Mr. Bramwell."

"Yes, thank you, gentlemen, Veronica, and Eugenia," Marlena agreed. "I'll see you out."

"What dear neighbors you all are," Mrs. Abernathy called as they filed out of the room. She then turned to Rath. "I'm so glad you came so quickly, too. I simply didn't know what to do."

"Miss Fast is right. A mouse cannot hurt you. They are way too small and are much more frightened of you than you are of them."

"No. No, that is not true. I cannot possibly get off the settee and put my feet on the floor. We have an infestation here, and I simply can't abide it. We can't stay here. I don't want to live with mice. And worse, what would we do if Marlena had a gentleman caller over? Perhaps a viscount wooing her. What would we do if a mouse ran across his boots? What horror that would be!"

"No man would be horrified over a mouse. They are seen in the finest homes and on every street all over London."

"He's right, Justine," Marlena said, walking back into the room. "It's not likely anyone will have a mouse near their feet in this house. Give the tonic you drank time to settle you and you'll be fine."

"Not in this house, I won't. I can't allow Marlena to live here, Your Grace. Whether or not she's afraid of the little creatures, I am. We will have to move into your Mayfair home after all. Marlena will simply have to adjust and manage without seeing Eugenia every day."

"Justine, how many times do I have to say no to that?" Marlena exclaimed. "We are not moving."

"I'm afraid that's not possible anyway, Mrs. Abernathy. My house in Mayfair is no longer available."

Mrs. Abernathy rose up straighter. "What do you mean? Why not? You offered. Are you rescinding your invitation?"

"When it became clear Miss Fast didn't want to move there, I allowed the family of one of my cousins to move in for the Season as I usually do."

"Why didn't you tell us?" Justine sounded peeved.

"I don't feel it necessary to tell you about decisions I make concerning my family or my properties, Mrs. Abernathy."

"But you'd offered it to us," Justine argued.

"And the offer was declined," the duke reminded her firmly. "I doubt I could even find a place to lease for you this late. Everyone has their plans for the Season set."

"Well, no matter," she said, lifting her chin. "You can ask your cousin's family to leave now that you know your ward and I have need of it. It will be perfectly understandable to them."

"Justine!" Marlena exclaimed. "How can you be so cruel to suggest such a thing? Throw someone out?"

"It's not cruel. The duke had no way of knowing you'd have need of the place. You are his ward. You should come first."

"Mrs. Abernathy," Rath said, moving closer to Marlena. "I won't ask them to leave. They're all settled in and that is the end of it."

Mrs. Abernathy swung her feet off the settee and stood up, lifting her chest high as she did so. "Don't you have another home in Mayfair we can go to?"

"I'm afraid not," he said.

"We can't go to an inn," Mrs. Abernathy declared.

"Heaven only knows what kind of people we'd have living there with us. I don't want to even think about that. And we simply can't stay in this house until we're sure the mice have been dealt with. If you have no other home we can go to, we shall move into your house in St. James with you."

Marlena glared at her cousin in disbelief. "Justine, you are being impossible. We can't do such a thing, and you know it. It's absurd for you to even suggest such madness. An unmarried lady under the same roof as a—a." She looked at Rath. "A rake."

Rath smiled at her. He saw her frustration at her cousin's antics melt away after he did. He liked the fact that he could settle her with a smile. Mrs. Abernathy had no idea what she'd just done, but Rath knew and so did Marlena. Her cousin had given him the perfect gift for a rake. The opportunity for Marlena to live in his home.

With him.

The thought was heady. His breathing kicked up.

"Thunderbolts and lighting, Marlena. He is your guardian. It is his responsibility to see to it that you live in a safe and suitable home, and right now, this one isn't. It will be quite all right for a few days until this rodent infestation has been dealt with."

Listening to them, watching Marlena, Rath breathed in deeply and relaxed. The rake inside him wanted to accept Mrs. Abernathy's plan no matter his honor, no matter the consequences. No matter that his father would have disapproved and challenged him to do what was right and be a gentleman.

But how often had he listened to his father unless it was concerning the dukedom? Mastering the business of their estates, companies, and lands had been easy. Accomplished with his father's approval before he died. Mastering being a gentlemen had never been easy for

Rath, and his father took the failure of trying to teach him to his grave. Being circumspect in all things wasn't easy for a man who enjoyed indulging in the guilty pleasures life offered, such as spending a week at someone's house doing nothing other than drinking, playing cards, and making himself available to willing women.

But now his thoughts were only on Marlena.

"Mrs. Abernathy is right. I, more so than others, know the definition of scandal, Miss Fast. I assure you, I'll make your stay at my house as short-lived as possible."

Marlena's surprised gasp pleased him.

"Thank you, Your Grace," Mrs. Abernathy said with a smile. "I knew you would see reason and be kind and hospitable to us during our hour of need. How can Society balk when we have been overrun by mice? Everyone will understand the peril we're in."

"I'm sure they would, Mrs. Abernathy, if that were to be the case. I'll make arrangements for you and Miss Fast to be moved into my home this afternoon. However, as a gentleman and her guardian, I won't do anything to tarnish Miss Fast's reputation. Mice or no mice. I'll stay at one of my clubs until you and Miss Fast are back here in your own home."

"Oh, the perfect gentleman indeed," she exclaimed. "I knew you would be. Yes, yes. That would be much more appropriate but, of course, I'd never ask you to leave your own home."

"And neither would I," Marlena argued. "Your Grace, this is madness. There is no reason for us to leave *our* home and certainly no reason for you to leave yours for us. It was a mouse. They are everywhere, including in the walls of your home."

He smiled. "I know, but I think you need to do this for Mrs. Abernathy's well-being."

"Her well-being would be best served by staying here.

The first ball of the Season is only a few days away! You can't imagine what we'd have to pack. I don't even want to think about it!"

"A minor inconvenience, Marlena. We now have more staff because of the duke and it will take them no time. All will be well." Justine smiled at the duke. "I'm grateful you, at least, understand my delicate nerves, Your Grace. And as for you," Mrs. Abernathy said, turning back to Marlena, "don't look at the duke as if you want to snap him in two for being so kind and humoring me by letting us have *his* house. He remembers I was the diamond of the Season and appreciates my delicate sensibilities." Justine lifted her chest even higher. "Besides, I'm sure the duke has a garden that has started to bud. No doubt you will find it fascinating to walk around in and look at all his gardener has planted. Soon you will forget all about your dear friends next door."

Rath stared at Marlena for a moment or two. She didn't give in easily to Justine or anything. An admirable trait that pleased him. Suddenly a hunger for her engulfed him. Though at first it had bothered him, he really didn't mind her being in the garden if it gave her pleasure. He liked gardens, too. He enjoyed the scent of fragrant herbs, rich, freshly plowed soil, and he loved the smell of sunshine on Marlena. Gardens were beautiful places for walks, talks, and most of all, for forbidden kisses and caresses.

Being a gentleman was damned hard.

Chapter 19

He could be a rake if he tries to gain your
attention by doing something unexpectedly nice
for someone you care for.

~∘∘∘~

*MISS HONORA TRUTH'S WORDS OF WISDOM AND
WARNING ABOUT RAKES, SCOUNDRELS, ROGUES, AND
LIBERTINES*

Do tell him to be careful with my trunks, Sneeds,"
Justine said as she and Marlena stood in the entryway of the duke's St. James home. "I would be devastated
to hear any of my perfume bottles breaking."

"Really, Justine," Marlena whispered, holding Tut's
warm body in her arms. "The duke's staff knows how to
handle your baggage. I'm sure everything will be fine."

"We can hope," Justine answered and turned back to
the butler. "I should like to know what the duke's favorite scent is."

The short man looked aghast and snapped his hands
behind his back. "I don't discuss anything about the duke,
madam."

"Hmm. Very well. I'll find out for myself." Justine
looked toward the two men carrying her trunk up the

stairs. "You did tell them that I should be settled in the duke's chambers, didn't you?"

Sneeds pulled up his thin shoulders, lifted his square chin, and rose up on his toes. He was still no match for Justine's superior height and breadth. "Certainly not."

"Then you should. The duke would want me to occupy his suite of rooms. Wait," she called to the men who were about to reach the landing at the top of the stairs. "You there, with my trunk, wait, please."

The men stopped and turned their heads toward her. "That will go in the duke's rooms."

"No, it will not," Sneeds said, also looking up at the men. "Put it in the room where you were told it would go."

"Now, see here," Justine said to Sneeds. "The duke would want me to have the bigger rooms."

Holding himself stiffly, the butler insisted, "I can't allow that, madam."

"Thunderbolts and lightning! Why not? The duke won't be using the rooms while we are here." She paused and then added under her breath, "Not unless he wants to, of course."

Marlena's grip tightened around Tut in frustration. "Justine, please be careful what you say."

"I said nothing wrong, my dear girl. Merely the truth."

"The duke would have to give permission, Mrs. Abernathy. He hasn't done so. I'm afraid it's not possible for you to be allowed to use his private chambers."

"Sneeds is right, Justine," Marlena added, hoping to put this unpleasant conversation to an end. "You have no right to invade the duke's private chambers. We will only be in the house a few days. It doesn't matter the room you're given."

"I have no idea how long we will be staying. However, I intend to enjoy my time here, and I intend to do it from the duke's chambers. He has given us the freedom of his house and I intend to use it."

Marlena shook her head. Sometimes there was just no way to make her cousin see reason.

Sneeds looked back up to the men who still stood on the stairs close to the landing and said, "Be off with you to the guest room as you were told and stop tarrying."

"Now, see here, Sneeds," Justine said, sternly. "While I am here I will be mistress of this house and you will do well to remember that."

"I've not been informed of that information, either, madam," he answered quickly. "And until I am, those men are under my command, not yours."

"We'll see about that. Furthermore—"

The front door opened. Tut barked and squirmed. Justine stopped mid-sentence as Rath stepped inside, removing his hat as he entered. Marlena knew she'd never tire of seeing him. It was as if something bright shone inside her at the sight of him. She breathed a sigh of relief. He could now handle this situation between Justine and his butler.

"Good afternoon, Mrs. Abernathy, Miss Fast, Sneeds." He nodded to them all as he spoke their names. "I wanted to check in and make sure you'd arrived."

"And just in time, Your Grace," Justine said with a satisfied smile.

"Your Grace, let me help you with that," Sneeds said, reaching for the duke's cloak.

Rath's gaze swept back to Marlena and lingered on her face. Tut barked again. "It seems I failed to speak to Tut." He took the dog from her arms. "And how are you today?" Rath asked. "Are you enjoying sniffing around my house?"

Marlena watched Rath rub Tut's head and pat his

shoulders and back with firm caring strokes. It pleased her that Rath took the time to give Tut attention.

"I haven't put him down," she answered. "We just arrived and we're not settled yet."

"And I was just saying to Sneeds," Justine said, moving to stand between Marlena and the duke, "that I believed you would expect me to make myself comfortable in your chambers while I'm here. Since, of course, you won't be."

That wasn't exactly the way Justine had said it to the butler but Marlena thought it best to stay quiet. Still, she wouldn't let her cousin obstruct her view of the duke. She moved to the side so she could see him. Rath looked down at Tut again and lightly scratched the dog behind his ears. Tut yawned his pleasure.

"I think perhaps you should inspect all the rooms before you make that decision, Mrs. Abernathy."

Justine smiled at the duke, and then at Marlena, and lastly at Sneeds before saying, "That's not necessary, Your Grace. I'm sure yours will be perfect. I should be quite content residing in your chambers."

"Still, I insist." Rath nodded to Sneeds. "Show Mrs. Abernathy all the rooms and allow her to choose the one she wants."

"*All* the rooms?" the butler questioned.

Rath nodded.

"Yes, Your Grace." The butler stiffly turned to Justine and waved his arm toward the staircase. "After you, Mrs. Abernathy."

Marlena watched her cousin walk away the victor. "Justine seemed be floating," Marlena said. "It was very kind of you to give in to her wishes, yet again."

He shrugged. "It's a small thing."

"Maybe for you but not for her. I don't think she's

forgiven me for not agreeing for us to move into your Mayfair home when we had the chance."

"Then maybe this will encourage her to look kindly on you once more. Besides, having her look at *all* the rooms gives me the opportunity to spend some time alone with you."

Marlena's heart started beating a little faster. She gave him a teasing smile. "For Justine, I think it feeds the designs she has for you. I think she intends to catch you in a snare."

The duke's brow wrinkled. "I think Mrs. Abernathy has sights set on no one but herself." His frown turned to a pleasant grin. "And a rake can't be caught unless he wants to."

"Oh, you must have read my—" Marlena almost choked on the word *my.* She cleared her throat. "That is, *my* copy that I gave you of Miss Truth's book that day you were at my house."

"No, I haven't read it yet."

Marlena's spirits fell. Why did she keep expecting he would read it? Why did she want him to read the book? She shouldn't. She should hope he'd never read it.

"I thought perhaps since you mentioned a rake that you might have more insight about them now. But as I said before, there is no reason for you to read it. If anyone knows rakes, it's you."

He laughed softly and patted Tut's head again. "Since you still have your coat and bonnet on, let's take Tut out to explore the garden. There's something I want to tell you."

A feeling of anticipation washed over her. "What?" she asked as they started down the corridor. "Or maybe I don't want to know. Is it good news or bad?"

"It's not about rakes or Mrs. Abernathy for sure."

"Then it can't be too bad, can it?" Marlena smiled at

him, and a shiver of awareness shook her when he returned the smile.

As soon as Rath opened the door, Tut was squirming to be put down. He scampered down the steps and into the garden barking, letting the neighbors know there was a new dog on the street.

Marlena walked down the steps beside Rath looking at the grounds spread before her. Late-afternoon clouds had darkened, and daylight was waning. The chilling breeze she'd felt when she'd entered the house earlier had calmed. But then she remembered she always felt warmer when she was with Rath.

It surprised her that the garden wasn't much larger than Justine's. Definitely wider, but not any longer. There were shrubs, plants, and small trees showing their new growth, and the tops of many flowers were peeking from below the ground. In the center of the garden stood a fountain with three cherubs in the middle. Tut sniffed around the bottom of it.

She and Rath started leisurely walking down the stone path that led directly to the back gate. "What is it you want to tell me?" she asked.

"So you are eager to know?"

"Of course I am. I'm hoping you've found Mr. Wentfield so we can get Mr. Portington's money back for the giant reptile eggs."

"I don't believe we will ever find that man—not under that name anyway."

"Well, I must say I don't believe I'd ever show my face in public again, either, if I'd had the gall to sell someone the supposed remains of a reptile that probably never existed."

Rath chuckled low under his breath. "The man was shrewd about it. I found out from the Royal Society that

Mr. Portington wasn't the only one tricked by Mr. Went-field in the last year. There were others."

"That's disheartening news."

"For the few men who were taken in by him. But that's not what I wanted to tell you."

They had made it to the back of the garden. Marlena stopped and stared up into his eyes. "So it is something serious then?"

"You might think it is, but I'm hoping not."

A lump formed in her throat. "What is it?"

"After I left you and Mrs. Abernathy today I went to talk to Mr. Portington."

Marlena's breathing became deep and heavy. "Why?"

"A couple of reasons." He paused. "I hadn't planned to talk to him so soon. I'd wanted to wait until I had more plans in place, but this afternoon I decided to go ahead and tell Mr. Portington I wanted to finance a museum for him to put his collection in so it could be open for all to see. What he has, most of it, shouldn't be kept in his home and hidden in crates. I suggested The Portington Museum of History."

A museum?

Marlena understood what Rath was saying but not why. She searched his face. His dark eyes were looking straight into hers. "That seems as if it would be a tremendous investment."

"It will, but I have a couple of friends who are dukes that I think might be willing to help me with this project."

"The other rakes," she said with no fondness in her voice.

"Yes."

"Why would you want to do this?"

He smiled softly. "Several reasons. Portington didn't want to sell anything," Rath said. "This way he doesn't have to. Everything will continue to be his and he will be the owner and curator of it. I had the idea after I visited his house but didn't mention it because I didn't know what such a creation would entail. I still don't know all I need to. I asked him if someone from The Royal Society could visit him and he agreed. They assured me, from what I told them, that the man indeed has many items museum-worthy. Meticulously documented. And they agreed that some things would probably need to be kept in storage until they can be researched more."

"The Megalosaurus eggs?"

"Among other things."

"I don't know what to say except thank you. I'm grateful you're being so kind and generous to him, but—"

"But you're wondering how this helps Mr. Portington get the money back from the eggs so that Miss Everard can have her Season in the most fashionable way?"

"Yes."

"It doesn't. That is what I needed to tell you and once again offer to take care of her Season myself. Her benefactor can remain anonymous."

Marlena stared into his eyes and wanted desperately to touch his cheek and kiss his lips. Instead she said, "I don't think you are the rake you want everyone to believe you are."

"Do not doubt that, Marlena. I am."

"Well, then, I must ask you not to offer your help. Eugenia will be properly gowned for the balls and any of the teas or card parties she wants to attend."

His gaze searched her face. "What did you—You gave her clothing, didn't you?"

"It was much easier when I stopped arguing with Lady Vera and Justine about what I needed and let them purchase whatever they wanted for me. I had more than enough to share. Veronica and her maid will make alterations so that Lady Vera and Justine won't recognize the gowns."

"That was very clever of you. So you didn't need my help after all."

Marlena appreciated the admiration that shone in his eyes. "It helps knowing how to be resourceful and to have a generous sponsor myself."

Rath bent his head and placed a short, sweet kiss on Marlena's lips.

"What if Justine had seen you do that?"

"She would have been upset. I would have had a lot of explaining to do, but I couldn't let you come to my house without giving you at least one kiss. A rake likes to take chances, after all. What good is it being one if I can't steal a kiss or two in my own garden?"

Suddenly he caught her up to his chest, held her tightly, and kissed her long and hard and deeply. Marlena melted against him and sighed as he slowly let her go and stepped away.

My Dear Readers,

The days are warming up nicely and much to my delight so is the gossip. Some in Society are calling the latest news about the Duke of Rathburne a scandal while others are saying it is perfectly innocent and the gentlemanly thing for him to do. I will leave it up to you, dear Readers, to decide for yourselves which you choose because it's fact not rumor. The duke has moved out of his home in St. James for a few days in order to accommodate his ward, Miss Fast, and her companion while their house undergoes an inspection. I'm not usually one to give credence to anyone who misquotes Shakespeare even by a word or two, but I do think I agree with the person who said he thought he smelled a rat.

MISS HONORA TRUTH'S WEEKLY SCANDAL SHEET

Chapter 20

He could be a rake if he steals a kiss from you in
the garden and doesn't ask you for a dance at the
ball.

~∞~

*MISS HONORA TRUTH'S WORDS OF WISDOM AND
WARNING ABOUT RAKES, SCOUNDRELS, ROGUES, AND
LIBERTINES*

Marlena stepped down from the carriage Justine was
so fond of, and a feeling of awe almost took her
breath. The Great Hall was glimmering from the win-
dows and open doors. It was teeming with beautifully
gowned ladies and splendidly dressed gentlemen walking up the wide steps to the entranceway. She heard chatter and music coming from inside, and the clip-clop of
horses' hooves and carriage wheels grinding on the road
behind her.

The air was crisp but she wasn't cold wrapped in her
black velvet cape. Her underdress had been made of a
warm soft velvet and overlaid with the most beautiful
alabaster-covered silk she'd ever seen. The trim on her
capped sleeves and the band of her high-waisted gown
was a gold-threaded brocade that also banded the hem
of the three flounces of her dress and her headpiece.

"When I come here I always feel as if I'm eighteen and starting my first Season all over again," Justine said as she walked up beside Marlena. Her black cape opened to reveal a puce-colored gown that had small silk roses trimming the neckline, and the crown in her hair.

Marlena turned to her cousin and smiled. She definitely seemed to have the same look of awe about the Great Hall that Marlena was feeling. Still, she laughed softly and said, "Justine, you always feel eighteen. I've never known you to act, talk, or look as if you were a widow ready to take your place sitting around the dance floor watching all the other beautiful ladies dance and enjoy themselves."

"Thunderbolts and lightning. I hope I never shall, but tell me, since you have never been to a ball, how do you know about the wall of widows?"

"The tutor who Mr. Olingworth employed for me told me everything about balls. She was quite thorough, I believe. She was very good at teaching me to dance, which is why I really needed no further lessons though you insisted. She explained what I should expect, whom I should speak to first, how to sip my first glass of champagne, and that I should never have more than two glasses. I should never have two dances with the same gentleman in one evening and no more than two rides in the park with the same gentleman until I was sure I wanted to marry him."

Justine harrumphed. "Only two glasses of champagne? That wouldn't do for me. But I suppose she's right since you aren't used to it yet and have no idea how it will affect you."

"A headache," she said.

"For some," Justine added. "Thankfully not me. Now my toes are beginning to feel the cold. Let's go inside."

If Marlena thought the outside of the Great Hall was

a masterpiece of inviting warmth, the ballroom far exceeded her expectations. Light from what seemed to be hundreds of chandeliers and thousands of candles lit the room with a bright golden glow. It took her a few moments to realize it was tall mirrors that made the room seem as if it had so many crystals hanging from the ceiling and so many tulle-and-flower-draped Corinthian columns outlining the dance floor. She had never seen so many statues of Greek gods and goddesses in one place. There were more urns of beautiful fragrant flowers than she could count.

Already many people filled the dance floor enjoying the melodious tune. The swirl of ladies dressed in jewel-colored gowns mingled with gentlemen clothed in black and white made for a scene no tutor could have prepared her for. The precision with which they all took each step made her wonder if she was indeed as ready for the dancing as she'd always thought.

The duke came easily to her mind. She let her eyesight land on each gentleman on the dance floor and then to those she could see standing around the room. There were a few she couldn't see but Rath wasn't among those she could. A sudden streak of disappointment struck her. She'd never asked Rath if planned to attend the first ball of the Season. It had always been her assumption he would.

"Tell me, dear girl. Do you feel like a princess? As you look out over the gentlemen, do see any you think might be your prince?"

"I really can't say, Justine. I have no idea which of them might already be spoken for or even married."

"Let's remedy that right now, shall we? I see Lord Henry walking this way." Justine breathed in deeply.

"Lord Henry?" Marlena said and let her gaze follow Justine's.

"Yes. He's the most handsome of all the eligible bachelors. He's one gentleman you can depend on to treat you properly and not step on your toes or your sensibilities. He would be a match made in heaven for any young lady. Lord Henry," Justine called to him as he passed.

Justine was right. The man had the fine-looking classical features of the paintings she'd seen of Michelangelo's *David* in one of Mr. Olingworth's books of art. Lord Henry's hair was cut in the same style, complete with the same thick waves. But Lord Henry was also the man Lady Vera had to pound with her parasol. Obviously Justine didn't know about that and Marlena wasn't going to be the one to tell her.

"Lord Henry, do you mind if I stop you or are you in a terrible hurry?"

"Not at all, Mrs. Abernathy." He reached to kiss her hand as his eyes shifted to Marlena.

"So kind of you. I'd like to present my cousin, Miss Marlena Fast."

They greeted each other and Marlena had to admit the man was filled with charm and perfect manners, commenting on her beauty as well as asking how she was enjoying her first ball. When he heard she'd just arrived he said he'd be honored to guide her through her first dance. Marlena hesitated. She'd hoped, wanted to have her first dance with Rath, but she hadn't seen him and wasn't sure he was attending the ball.

"She'd love to," Justine said after Marlena failed to answer promptly. "Come for her when the next set starts."

"Yes," Marlena added. "Thank you, Lord Henry."

He excused himself and Marlena turned to Justine. "I'm perfectly capable of accepting or declining my own dances."

"Then you should have spoken up quicker. Thunderbolts and lightning, Marlena, what young lady wouldn't want her first dance to be with Lord Henry. Ah, there's

Lady Bellehaven coming inside. Let's go talk to her. Her nephew will be here tonight. She says he's a handsome fellow and he's looking to make a match. I'll ask her if he's here yet."

Marlena looked around the room again. She didn't see Rath or Eugenia and Veronica, but she saw someone else she wanted to speak to. "Do you mind if I join you in a few minutes, Justine? I see Lady Vera and would like to say hello to her first."

"Yes, do. I'll go with you."

Marlena hoped Justine didn't plan to hover over her the entire evening and make all her decisions for her. "No, best you find out about Lady Bellehaven's handsome nephew for me, don't you think?"

"Oh, yes. Let me do that and then I'll join you and Lady Vera."

Justine walked away and Marlena scanned the ballroom again as she walked over to Lady Vera, who seemed to be searching for something in her beaded reticule.

"Lady Vera, I hope I'm not interrupting."

The lady glanced up at her and Marlena knew immediately it wasn't Lady Vera. Her eyes were different. Softer. Her features a little more pleasant than Lady Vera's when she smiled.

"I'm not Lady Vera. I'm Lady Sara, her twin sister, and who might you be?"

"I'm sorry, Lady Sara." Marlena curtsied. "I'm Miss Marlena Fast. Lady Vera—"

"Yes, I know who you are. Vera told me all about you. She's had such a grand time helping you prepare for the Season." She looked Marlena over from head to toe. "It looks as if she took excellent care of you. Your gown not only fits you perfectly, it complements your hair and your countenance as well."

"Thank you. She was very kind. I've been told you

two look very much alike, but even more so than I'd expected."

"Well, we won't for long." She took her hand and pressed her high-waisted dress against her stomach.

Marlena saw the small swell of her babe and realized she didn't know what to say except, "How wonderful. You must be very happy."

"Extremely so. And how is your first ball?"

"I haven't been here long but I don't think I was prepared for the opulence of the hall, the gowns, and the people."

"Believe it or not, I felt that way my first ball, too."

"You? The daughter and sister of a duke?"

"We are all human, Miss Fast."

Marlena watched a tall, broad-shouldered, and quite handsome man approach Lady Sara and lovingly kiss her hand. Marlena assumed it was her husband until she heard him say, "How is my dear sister tonight? I didn't expect you'd come."

A shiver stole over Marlena. She was looking at Lady Sara and Lady Vera's brother, the Duke of Griffin. The first rake she'd written about. Like Rath, he didn't look like the ogre she'd always imagined him to be. He didn't sound harsh. There were no piercing gleams of folly or meanness in his eyes. He looked quite normally, quite lovingly at his sister, and he was almost as handsome as Rath.

"I was just showing Miss Fast how my dress conceals my condition. Have you met her?"

The duke's gaze landed on Marlena's and she was sure he noticed she swallowed with difficulty. What had she written about him? A quote flashed through her mind. *It is my hearty belief that most everyone in Society agrees that it is Lady Sara and Lady Vera's misfortune that it's up to their brother, the Duke of Griffin, to see them suitably wed. That the duke is now the protector of innocent young ladies is dismaying but may prove to be the punishment that long escaped him and perhaps force a measure of penitence upon him.*

Marlena could weaken as she had the first time she found herself lost in the woods chasing after her cousins, or she could be as she had the second time it happened and not wait to be rescued. She reached deep inside herself and remembered her parents were watching over her. The boys had taught her to be strong and stand up for herself. Mr. Olingworth had seen she was taught the proper manners. Her shoulders lifted a little higher. She knew what to do and she would do it.

"I haven't had the pleasure," the duke said.

"Then may I present Miss Marlena Fast," Lady Sara said. "Miss Fast, my brother, the Duke of Griffin."

Marlena smiled, curtsied, and responded, "Your Grace."

"I've heard much about you, Miss Fast."

"As I have you."

"Ah yes," he said. "I fear I have a reputation I'll never live down."

"Lady Vera speaks highly of you," Marlena said. "I'm sure Lady Sara does as well."

The duke chuckled. "A clever answer, Miss Fast. I know you met Esmeralda, my wife, when you met Lady Vera, too."

"Yes. It was an honor. She's beautiful and was very kind to me."

He nodded. "And how about the Duke of Rathburne? Is he treating you well?"

"I have no complaints, Your Grace," she answered.

"That's good to hear. I would be happy to speak to him on your behalf should that ever change."

Marlena kept her gaze steady on the duke's, feeling amazed. He wasn't just making conversation with her. He wasn't just telling her what he thought she wanted to hear. She could see he was sincere in his offer. That shocked her. Why should he care how she was treated by anyone? She always believed him to have no care for a young lady's feelings—other than his own sisters, of course. But as Rath was not as she expected him to be, neither was the Duke of Griffin.

"There you are, Griffin, and Lady Sara." He kissed her hand. "I'm surprised to see you tonight. Are you sure it's wise for you to be out?"

Marlena found herself staring at yet another magnificent-looking man. She had looked around the room, more than once, searching for Rath, and most of the gentlemen she'd seen were not as tall and handsome as Rath, Lord Henry, or the Duke of Griffin, but here was another man who stood as tall, handsome, and powerful-looking.

"Wise and helpful," Lady Sara said, "I haven't received this much attention since my debut Season."

"You know we only want to take care of you," the new gentleman said, before looking Marlena's way.

As soon as she looked into his eyes she knew he was the third Rake of St. James. Instinct told her no man could wear his title, privilege, self-confidence as strikingly as the rakes.

Another quote that Marlena had written as Miss Truth suddenly flashed through her mind. *Rumors still abound that mischief is in the air. And said mischief could be directed against Lady Adele and Lady Vera because of their brothers' past misdeeds as the Rakes of St. James.*

"Lady Sara, may I do the honors?" the Duke of Griffin asked.

"Please do," she answered.

The introduction to the Duke of Hawksthorn went as smoothly as the one to the Duke of Griffin. Marlena stood with them, trembling inside because they didn't know who she was and what she had done. She didn't want them to know.

"I remember your cousin Mrs. Abernathy. We had a dance a few years ago."

"Really?" she asked.

"You seem surprised."

"No. Not at all. I mean most ladies remember their dances with a duke. I'm thinking she may have confused you with the Duke of Rathburne and thought she'd danced with him."

Hawk quirked his head and smiled. "He probably told her it was him."

She smiled, too. "Perhaps he did."

Their conversation continued and Marlena answered their questions but at the back of her mind was the fact she'd written gossip about them before they married. Still wrote gossip about Rath. She'd always considered these men to be scoundrels of the highest order, having no care or even respect for a young lady. Yet here they were being considerate, asking about her well-being, the issue she had at her house with the rodents, though neither of them ever said *that* word aloud.

"Yes," she answered quietly. "I feel certain we'll be back in our home within the next couple of days. Justine is now feeling more comfortable the problem has been eradicated."

"Lady Sara."

Marlena turned to see Lord Henry bow to Lady Sara. He then turned, bowed, and spoke to the two dukes, and lastly he turned to her. "Miss Fast, they've called for the dance and I believe you promised it to me."

Grateful for anything to get her away from the dukes and her turbulent feelings, she smiled and said, "Yes, of course."

"Lord Henry," the Duke of Griffin said. "I wonder if you might relinquish your dance with Miss Fast to me. You don't mind, do you, Miss Fast?"

Yes! She did. She wanted to get away from him, Lady Sara, and the Duke of Hawksthorn, too. In truth, she wanted to get away from *Miss Truth's Scandal Sheet.*

"No, let me have the honor, Griffin," the Duke of Hawksthorn said. "You stay here and visit with your sister. You don't mind, do you, Miss Fast?"

Feeling her insides turning over and over, the only thing she knew to say was, "I don't, no, of course, but I, but Lord Henry asked."

Lord Henry took a step back, gave a humorless smile, and bowed first to the Duke of Griffin and then the Duke of Hawksthorn. "Another time, Miss Fast."

That's when Marlena understood. The dukes knew how he'd treated Lady Vera and they were showing him that Marlena was under their protection and Lord Henry wasn't to pursue her. If she hadn't been so stunned, tears would have filled her eyes.

"This way, Miss Fast," the duke said.

Marlena didn't know how her legs were moving as she walked beside the duke. Her feet, her whole body felt numb. How was she ever going to manage a dance? A waltz?

As they took their place on the dance floor and waited for the music to begin, Rath came up beside the Duke of Hawksthorn. "I'll take over from here."

"I was beginning to wonder if you were going to show up in time."

"I had to make sure you were going to do your duty first," Rath replied with a hint of a grin.

"It was my pleasure," the duke said to him, and smiled at Marlena before walking away.

It always calmed her to look at Rath. Her jittering

stomach settled down. She felt her legs strong beneath her once more as he took hold of her hand and they took the waltz stance just as the music began.

Suddenly they were gliding across the floor in perfect time to the music. The duke's frame was strong and she felt light, protected; even though many couples swept, twirled, and passed by them, for a moment she imagined she and Rath were the only ones on the dance floor.

A couple bumped into Rath's shoulder. He paid them no mind but Marlena noticed the lady staring at her. Marlena smiled and the lady's eyebrows rose. Did she think it wrong for Marlena to dance with her guardian?

Marlena kept her gaze on the people surrounding the dance floor as they moved in a circular motion. Everyone was looking at them. Some were talking behind their hands, some their fans, and others were openly staring—but she felt sure they were all talking about Marlena and the duke's dance.

"I believe everyone is staring at us, Your Grace."

"They probably are. I'm sure they are thinking it's scandalous of me to be dancing with my ward."

"Is it?"

He smiled and led her into a twirl under his arm. "Not to me. You were looking tense before I arrived, Miss Fast. Almost the way you appeared the first day we met at your door. *Disturbed* I think is the word you wanted to use."

The humor in his eyes and twitch at the corner of his mouth told her he was teasing her. "Not only did I find myself in the presence of Lady Sara and two dukes I had never met, this is my first ball, my first dance, *and*," she emphasized, "I was looking for Eugenia. I haven't seen her and I want to make sure she is here and enjoying herself, too."

"Ah, yes. Miss Everard. I should have known she was your priority."

"You know she's delicate and—" Marlena hesitated. "And may not easily meet strange gentlemen."

"Yes, but I saw her on my way inside the ballroom. She's lovely in a dress with yellow bows on the skirt and four or five in her hair. She's quite fetching."

Marlena's heart lifted. "Yellow? Good. You didn't speak to her, did you?"

His eyes sparkled with mischief. "I admit I thought about it but didn't know whether or not the Great Hall had smelling salts so I decided against approaching her for a dance."

Marlena laughed. "You are teasing me."

"About the dance, yes. That I saw her, no. If you are concerned I can discreetly see to it that she is asked for a dance or two."

"Would you do that for her? Discreetly?"

"Consider it done."

"I—don't know what to say other than thank you. I'm grateful once again that you have come to her aid."

"It is difficult for some gentlemen to approach a timid-looking lady. They don't want to be turned down. All it will take is a dance or two and other gentlemen will start asking her to dance."

"I'm thrilled. Thank you. I want her to feel beautiful. Tell me, does the gown fit her well?"

Rath laughed and led Marlena into a twirl under his arm. "Yes. As I said, she is lovely but not as lovely as you, Marlena." His gaze stayed tightly on hers as they danced. "No one here is as beautiful as you. There is no one, *no one* I'd rather dance with than you."

Her heart fluttered, her abdomen tightened, and his expression told her he meant what he'd said. She wanted to echo his words, started to, but then she remembered she was Miss Truth. She had to keep silent about that and about her feelings for him.

Chapter 21

He could be a rake if he plans a rendezvous
with a young lady.

~◦~

*Miss Honora Truth's Words of Wisdom and
Warning About Rakes, Scoundrels, Rogues, and
Libertines*

Marlena opened the front door to her house and Tut ran inside barking as if he'd seen another mouse. She hoped not. That would give Justine reason to stay longer in Rath's house, and though he hadn't mentioned it at the ball or any other time, she was sure he was ready to return to his own home.

Tut scuttled down the corridor and out of sight. No use in calling out to Mrs. Doddle, she thought. Tut had announced their arrival in grand style. Stopping in the vestibule to remove her cape, bonnet, and gloves, she wondered how her little dog could have missed home so much when he had such a large patch of ground to scratch, sniff, and explore at the duke's house.

Unfastening the hook of her new, dark-blue cape, she smiled to herself, thinking how easily she'd adjusted to living at Rath's home. Justine had also settled into the duke's house, after an unpleasant start of acting as if she were the duchess moving in. She'd had Sneeds, the duke's butler, in a huff ever since, making demand after demand. It was time she and Justine moved back to her home.

Marlena laid her wrap on the table and removed her matching gloves, loving the feel of the fine fabric Lady Vera had helped her select. Though Marlena had never thought they needed to move out of their house just because a mouse or two had decided to make it their residence, too, it had been good to be at the duke's home. She'd seen him almost every day since. There were always reasons for him to stop by early in the afternoon, before she left with Lady Vera for her daily fittings and shopping.

There were the account books he needed one day, documents for his solicitor the next, and a certain greatcoat he wanted for a special event another day. Rath always took the time to smile at her, chat with her, and gaze so intently into her eyes she thought she might jump into his arms and kiss him right in front of Justine.

Thankfully, she'd managed to control herself.

It was as if her cousin knew something was developing between the two of them. Justine never left them alone for a moment. The duke had tried more than once to get Marlena alone for a few minutes of private talk. He'd suggested they take a walk in the garden but Justine, who never went outside, said she'd love to go, too. He'd had Sneeds come in and say that he needed her attention on a matter but she'd told him it would have to wait. There had been no getting out from under her nose except the first day they'd arrived. Marlena feared the tension that had been building between her and the duke had not been lost on Justine.

Marlena laid her bonnet on top of her gloves and cape and, from the corner of her eyes, saw movement. She turned to see Rath walking down the corridor carrying Tut.

Her breath quickened in her lungs. "Your Grace, you startled me."

"I didn't mean to."

"No, of course you didn't. I was expecting Mrs. Doddle or her new kitchen helper. Not you."

"I wondered if you'd be surprised I'm here."

She gave him a quizzical look as he stopped in front of her and bent down to place Tut on the floor, giving him a rub on the head as he did so.

That's when she noticed he didn't have on a coat or neckcloth. She hadn't known how fully his strong arms and wide chest filled out his white shirt. Or just how slim his hips were. Rath looked magnificent. He was looking her over, too. She was glad she was wearing one of her new dresses: a pale-green, long-sleeved, lightweight wool with a scooped neckline.

"You don't have a coat on," she said. "Is something wrong?"

Tut barked and jumped from Marlena's skirts to the duke's legs, trying to get one of them to show him attention. Both ignored him.

"No. Most gentlemen put their coats on in the mornings and don't remove them until they are in their bedchambers in the evening, thinking it ungentlemanly to remove them for any reason. Certainly not in the presence of a lady. I have no such fears. There are times I prefer to be more comfortable and remove my coat and neckcloth. I hope it doesn't offend you overly much that I'm not properly attired."

To the contrary. She felt as if she were devouring every inch of him with her eyes.

"Not at all. But I am wondering what you're doing here?"

"I was told the men who were taking care of the rodent problem had declared the house empty of the mice and ready for your return. Mrs. Abernathy has refused to take their word for it. Apparently she is enjoying the attention she is receiving from the *ton* by living in my home and is in no hurry to leave."

"I can attest to that fact."

"Which is why I decided I must come over and check it out for myself. Make sure none of the harassing little devils were left and impress upon her that it is safe to return."

Marlena laughed softly. "You nor anyone else has discovered a way of looking within walls to make sure there are no mice or anything else lurking around inside."

"You're right. But Mrs. Abernathy doesn't seem to know that. I'm hoping it will make her feel more satisfied and ready to vacate my home if I tell her I've checked all the rooms myself."

"I'm sorry she's been such a bother. I know you must feel as if you have two wards instead of one."

Rath walked closer to her. His eyes skimmed down her face, and her whole body tingled invitingly. "That's never crossed my mind."

Tut continued to jump from her skirt to Rath's legs.

"Tut, stop," she said, glancing down at him. "Sit. You're making a nuisance of yourself. Sit, I say." He barked at her and wagged his tail but didn't follow her order.

"Do you want to know the true reason I'm here, Marlena?"

"Yes, of course."

"I heard you tell Mrs. Abernathy yesterday that you would be coming over today to see Miss Everard and to check on Mrs. Doddle and see how she is getting along with the new members of your staff."

"I did." She looked down the corridor. "I haven't seen anyone since I arrived. Do you know where they are?"

"I don't know," he answered. "I told them I had to inspect every room in the house and I'd prefer to be alone while doing it. I added that I didn't know how long it would take, so I gave them the day and evening off, with enough money to buy their supper, and told them not to return before midnight."

Marlena smiled. "What a nice thing to do, but why would you do that when—" She stopped.

"When I can't see inside the walls anyway?"

She loved it when his gaze feathered down her face and sent chills of desire soaring through her. "That's why you thought I might not be surprised to see you."

He nodded. "I did it so I could wait for you to come here. I wanted to see you. Alone."

Marlena's breaths became more labored. The rhythm of her heartbeat changed to a slow hard thump. Yes, she wanted that, too.

Rath reached down and picked up her dog. "Come on, Tut. It's time for you to leave, too." He looked at Marlena with a determination in his features. "I'll be right back."

From the vestibule in front of the stairs she watched Rath walk down the corridor, open the back door, and shoo Tut outside. She then watched him turn toward her. He was tall, lean, and never more handsome than when he was looking at her with desperate desire for her in his expression. It stirred her longing to be in his strong embrace again, and in that moment she knew why she couldn't get him off her mind, out of her thoughts or dreams. She loved him with all her heart. He was the man she wanted. She knew all the reasons why she shouldn't love him. Most notably that she was Miss Truth and didn't want him to ever know that.

Rath strode back down the corridor with long purposeful steps, straight toward her, and didn't stop until he caught her up in his arms.

His lips came down on hers in a long hard, ravishing kiss that stunned her with the intensity of his passion. Her lips parted and his tongue swept inside her mouth, plundering its depth over and over again. With warm lips he kissed both corners of her mouth and then glided his lips across her cheek, over her chin, down to the neckline of her dress to kiss the swell of her breasts, and back up again. It was glorious to know he wanted her kisses as madly as she wanted his.

"I thought you'd never get here so I could take you in my arms," he whispered between kisses.

"Why didn't you tell me you'd be waiting?"

"I wanted to surprise you."

Their ragged breaths flowed together easily, deeply, as they kissed. Rath's tongue slipped back inside her mouth and she moaned her approval as his hands explored her back, and then fondled her breasts with soothing, titillating strokes. He cupped her buttocks, lifting her to his lower body. She welcomed the hard feel of him and eagerly pressed against him, too.

Rath kissed his way down to the neckline of her dress again. Gently pulling on it, he slid the sleeve of the bodice off one shoulder and kissed her chest, the crest of her breast. Marlena softly whispered, "Yes," and tilted her head up and arched her back, giving him all the access he wanted. He ran the palm of his hand and tips of his fingers over her naked shoulder, around her neck, down her breast, and back up again as he kissed her, heating their passions even more until ever so slowly the depth of his kisses eased. His kisses softened, his caresses were so tender, all she wanted to do was lie with him and let him continue to touch her so gently.

Without letting his lips leave her skin, Rath found his way up to her forehead, kissed it, and then laid his own forehead against it. He held her tightly for a moment, calming his breathing before lifting his head.

He kissed her softly and whispered, "I must stop, Marlena. I can't go with you where we are headed."

She moistened her lips. "Why?"

One hand moved soothingly up and down her back. "Don't pretend you don't know the answer to that."

Dipping his head, he covered her mouth with his in a long, sweet kiss as he covered her dress over her shoulder once again. He then stared down into her eyes while rubbing his hands up and down her arms. "I've told you, I don't take innocents to my bed. And as much, as desperately, as I want to make you mine right now, I can't."

Marlena turned her head and looked at the staircase right behind them. It suddenly looked wide, beautiful, and glorious. Her bedchamber was only a few steps past the top of it.

Turning back to Rath, she said, "I agree. You can't."

He nodded. She lowered her lashes over her eyes, but he immediately lifted her chin with his fingers, bent his head, and slanted his lips over hers in a slow tender kiss. The longing and the passion inside her was intense and she felt it just as vibrant inside him. She leaned into him, wanting him to know the depth of her feelings for him. He deepened the kiss again for only a few seconds before backing away again.

"You know that I want to," he insisted when his lips left hers.

"I do," she answered. "And you won't be taking me to your bed." Her breath trembled in her throat, and anticipation filled her.

Did she had the nerve to finish what she really wanted to say?

If she was ever going to, this was the time. She smiled. "I'm going to take you to mine."

"Ah, Marlena." He shook his head and cupped each cheek with his hands and kissed her softly, sweetly several times. "You are mixing your words. No matter if it is said my way or yours, it means the same thing. I am trying to be a gentleman. You aren't making it easy on me."

"I don't intend to."

"I need your help. You are my ward, an innocent. I can't do this to you."

She rose on her toes and clasped her hands together at the back of his neck. He remained still and let her kiss his lips, his cheeks, and the warmth of his neck before dropping her arms to her side and resting on her feet again.

Marlena had no doubts, no misgivings. He wanted to be with her as much as she wanted to be with him. She wasn't asking for forever. She knew because of their pasts that was impossible. But they could have this afternoon. That's all she was asking for.

"I can do it," she said. "You're not taking anything. I am giving."

Marlena reached out her hand to him. "Third door on the right."

Time ticked by. He didn't reach for her though she saw in the dark depths of his eyes he wanted to. More seconds passed. She feared he was going to walk out the door and deny her. Should she chase him as she had her cousins so many years ago and demand he not run away from her? Should she back away and honor his request?

Just as her spirits dropped Rath swooped down and covered her mouth with his in a ravishing kiss that stole her breath. Then, as if she weighed no more than a stone, he bent down, scooped her up in his arms, and headed up the stairs with her.

Within seconds they were in her room with the door closed. He laid her on the bed and covered her body with his. Their desire for each other was too frantic to be slow. With impatient hands and fierce kisses, they quickly stripped off her clothing and then disposed of his as eagerly. Rath stretched his lean, nude body next to hers, and she turned to face him.

"No, wait," he said huskily. "I want to look at you first."

Slowly, she rolled to her back. He rose up over her. Rath stared into her eyes for a long moment before touching her face with his fingertips. He gave her a pleasing smile, and then his gaze and his hand drifted down her face to her breasts, her stomach, between her legs before sweeping back up to her face again.

"You're beautiful," he said and pulled the two combs out of her hair and settled its length around her shoulders.

"I'm glad you think so."

She ran her palms over his wide, smooth chest, his broad shoulders, and then moved her hands up and down his muscular back. It was exciting to feel his bare, warm skin. She stared at his rippled midriff, and slim hips, and touched him again.

"You're strong," Marlena whispered.

"And you are not an easy lady to say no to, Marlena."

"I want to keep it that way, Rath," she said as he captured her lips beneath his.

Rath's hand traced the line of her shoulder, down her arm to the plane of her hip, and back up again and again. He continued to kiss her, caress her. Marlena relaxed, surrendering her body totally to him so he could show her all he knew about loving a woman. He kissed her tenderly, slowly, while caressing her breasts, her waist, and down her legs. A tremor of expectancy shivered through her. Delightful shivers of pleasure tingled along her spine, down her abdomen to settle and gather in her most womanly part.

"Your touch is always so light and gentle with me. I thought when we were alone like this . . . you might be rough."

He looked at her curiously. "Why would you think that?"

"You are a rake. I thought you might be rough or harsh and not gentle."

"You amaze me, Marlena. You thought I might be rough with you and yet you still wanted me in your bed?"

"I admit I really didn't know what to expect, but I am very happy with the way you touch me and how you make me feel."

He kissed her lips softly and whispered, "Rakes might be heartless, but they are not harsh."

"I'm glad I know the difference now."

"So am I."

At his touch, ripples of desire flooded her once more. Pleasure swept over her. He placed one hand on her waist, and with the other, he supported his weight as he fitted himself against her. A soft tremor shook her and she gasped softly when the weight of his body settled on hers.

Rath made love to her with tenderness that overwhelmed her. His movements were slow, sensual, and worshipful. He kissed her, stroked her body, and moved gently on top of her. An inexpressible, eager wanting kept increasing between her legs and caused her to join the rhythm of his hips meeting hers.

Rath continued his tender assault on her senses, gently moving until she whispered his name in unexpected wonder at what she was experiencing. As the extraordinary feelings ebbed, she murmured a blissfully contented sigh and watched Rath release his own passion. Marlena closed her eyes and hugged him to her as she buried her face in his neck, celebrating the feeling of strength and joy in his body.

They lay there side by side in the afternoon light, not moving. She was too filled with the wonder of everything she'd felt to think about the future. What would she do now that she was no longer innocent? She slowly shook her head. *Innocent?* Was she trying to fool herself? She hadn't been innocent for a long time. Not since she became Miss Truth.

Rath raised up on his elbow and looked down at her. "Did I just hear you laugh?"

He was so handsome with his dark hair rumpled and his dark eyes staring into hers. "Probably. I was just telling myself that I would think about tomorrow—tomorrow."

"No," he said, and with the tips of his fingers under her chin he kissed her sweetly on the lips. "Let's talk about it today. Right now. I'll start by telling you I don't want to be your guardian anymore."

She swallowed hard. Though his words came as a shock to her, she understood why he'd said them. It wouldn't be proper for him to continue. "I don't think you ever wanted to be, did you?"

Rath brushed a strand of tangled hair away from her face. "No." He smiled softly at her. "I've decided I do want to be your husband."

She flinched. "That's not humorous, Your Grace."

"I am never Your Grace when I am in your bed, Marlena. And I might be smiling, but I'm not trying to amuse you. I'm serious. I want to marry you. I came to your bed with you for one reason only. I don't want you going through the rest of the Season searching for a husband when I know you are the lady I want to marry."

Marlena couldn't move, couldn't take her gaze off his face, but that didn't keep a stab of pain from piercing her heart. Had he actually said the words she most wanted to hear but could never respond to?

"I didn't expect silence from you," he said.

"I didn't expect a proposal. I can't marry you," she said, looking away from him.

He took hold of her chin and gently forced her face toward him again. "All right. I suppose I should have first told you that I love you, Marlena." He pressed another soft kiss to her lips. "I do. And I'm damned jealous, too. I didn't want any other gentleman dancing with you, bringing you a glass of champagne, but I had to stand by and watch them do it. I knew the first day I saw you I felt differently about you, but I didn't want to believe it could be true. I still can't believe you captured my heart so quickly."

His affectionate words made her want to bury her face in the warmth of his chest, confess everything and hope, or even beg him to forgive her. But she couldn't face him knowing what she'd done. She'd never wanted him to know what she'd done.

"Don't say any more, please," she said, feeling as if her chest were about to cave in on her heart. She tried to move, to get off the bed, but he put his arm around her waist and held her so she turned away from him again.

"Look at me, Marlena."

It was difficult, but she acquiesced. Rath loving her, wanting to marry her, should be the most wonderful feeling in the world. Instead it was heartbreaking.

"I wouldn't be asking you to be my wife if I didn't love you and want you with me and not with anyone else. I hesitated downstairs because I didn't want to take your innocence. Not because I was unsure."

Marlena felt tears rushing to her eyes. She hoped they

wouldn't collect and spill onto her cheeks. With everything else she was feeling right now, she didn't want Rath to see her cry. Her cousins had always said, "She could cry, but she couldn't let anyone see her do it."

"Stop," she whispered. "I don't want to hear any more. I can't marry you."

"I know you love me, Marlena."

"Yes," she whispered, feeling as though her heart was crumbling in her chest. "I do love you, but there are things about me you don't know."

He gave her a crooked smile. "There are things about me you don't know, too," he answered. "Things I wouldn't want you to know."

"But I couldn't live day after day with you not knowing the secret I carry between us, and I can't tell you because it involves other people."

"You don't have to," he said, staring into eyes now pooling with tears. "I already know who Miss Honora Truth is."

Chapter 22

Silence stretched between them as she stared into his eyes. She was calmer than he expected her to be when he told her he knew who Miss Truth was.

He understood her not immediately agreeing to marry him. It was what he'd expected. As she'd said, she wasn't the kind of lady who could marry him with a secret between them. Just as he couldn't. He had to tell her he knew.

"How did you find out?" she softly asked.

"I admit it took me a while, but I finally figured it out the day Mrs. Abernathy saw the mice."

Her brows formed a frown. "You waited a long time to tell me."

"I didn't want you to know that I knew Miss Honora Truth is really Miss Eugenia Everard."

"Eugenia? No," she said unequivocally and rose from the bed.

This time he didn't try to stop her. He watched her. Her long, golden-red hair was a mass of tangled curls swinging over her shoulders and covering her breasts. She was gorgeous and she was his. He wanted her back on the bed beneath him again. Yet he knew she wouldn't allow that to happen until this issue was settled between them.

Marlena grabbed her chemise from the floor and quickly slipped it over her head. Rath rose and stepped into his trousers.

"You must have known I would find out," he said. "Or at least thought there was a possibility."

"Why would you think that?" She found her stays and slipped them on over her shift and turned her back to him. "The column is almost three years old."

"Griffin, Hawk, and I have been trying to find out who she is since she revived the secret admirer letters. And if I ever find out who the blackguard is that started the rumor at White's, I'll see to it he never starts another rumor or anything else."

Marlena remained quiet with her back to him, struggling to pull the laces on her stays tight enough to tie at her back. It reminded him of the first day at her house when she'd turned away from him and tried in vain to untie the ribbon at her throat. He would never forget how sensual it was to watch her do that.

Rath walked over and took hold of the laces of her stays. She tried to move away from him, but he said, "I took the damned things off you, Marlena, I can put them back on. Hold still."

Thankfully, she dropped her hands and let him lace her while he continued to talk. "I don't want you angry with me because I figured out Eugenia is Miss Truth."

"She's not," she said softly.

"You don't have to worry that I'll take some revenge against her. I won't. Though it's certainly deserving. She's delicate enough as it is. But you can't deny it. I saw some of her writings in your drawer that day when you were trying to find a place for the smelling salts. I now know you must have been reading it for Miss Everard before she turned it in, as it wasn't finished."

"It's not Eugenia," she said again.

"I didn't realize what it was at first, but then I read it again after Miss Everard fainted outside that day. She had the scandal sheet with her. I thought it sounded familiar, but at the time, I thought it was because Miss Truth keeps writing the same old gossip. But then there were other things as well."

Rath finished her stays, and picked up her dress. He walked around to face her, and held it out.

Marlena took the dress without meeting his gaze and said, "Thank you, but you're wrong."

"Miss Everard had Miss Truth's books and her scandal sheet."

"A lot of ladies have them and read them," she said, slipping her dress over her head and then straightening it over her body. "Even Lady Vera has them."

Rath buttoned the flap of his trousers. It bothered him that Marlena kept denying what he knew to be true. "Miss Everard is frightened every time she sees me."

"No."

"She faints when she sees me," he said, leaning against the bed and shoving his foot into his boot.

"Not anymore," Marlena insisted. "She's fine now. You've seen her at her house. She didn't faint."

"She and her sister looked as if they were about to bolt out of the house and I'm surprised they didn't," he said with irritation at her stubbornness growing. "There is no use in you defending her anymore, Marlena. I know that her sister was one of the young ladies who received a secret admirer letter from the rakes, and she is doing this to get revenge for her sister."

"It's not Eugenia."

Tears pooled in her eyes again. That surprised him. "Then Miss Truth is her sister, Mrs. Portington, or perhaps they are even doing it together."

"It's not Eugenia, or Veronica. It's me. I'm Miss Honora Truth."

Standing on one foot, he stuffed his other foot into his boot quickly and rose to his full height. What she was doing—trying to protect the sisters—was admirable, and he loved her all the more for trying. "That is not going to work, Marlena. I won't let you take the blame for either of them."

"I'm not." Her voice was calm. "I won't lie to you. It's me. It was my idea from the start."

He picked up his shirt. "You didn't receive a secret admirer letter. Mrs. Portington did. You would have no reason to dredge it up and write about it. You are covering up for them because you have always tried to help them and you are doing it now."

"Not this time." Marlena stepped into her shoes, lifted her shoulders, and said, "I had just turned seventeen when I moved in with Justine. Eugenia needed a friend, and so did I. It didn't take long to realize how unhappy she and Veronica were. Eugenia told me the story of the secret admirer letters the Rakes of St. James had sent to the young ladies making their debuts. As you said, Veronica was one of them. All were embarrassed and reprimanded by their parents for going to meet a secret admirer. Some had their virtue questioned and at least one, Veronica, made an unhappy match, but nothing ever happened to the rakes. That seemed unfair to me."

Rath's hand tightened around his shirt as what she was saying started to make sense. That scared him. "You want me to believe you heard this story and decided to start a scandal sheet."

"Yes," she declared. "It's true and it's just that simple. Not everything has to be complicated. I wanted to do something to help. I knew very little about scandal sheets but I knew how to write and compose and knew I could learn fast what I didn't know. The sheet didn't sell very well until I wrote about the rumor that was started at White's, and then the number of sales each week soared. I hadn't intended to continue with it for as long as I have, but . . . There's the truth of it."

Rath had remained quiet and let her talk, not wanting to believe her, but he did. Marlena had been taught not to be afraid of anything by her cousins. "Damnation," he whispered aloud. Miss Truth wasn't the timid Miss Everard or her sister. She was Marlena. The strong, beautiful lady standing before him. The one who had captured his heart with her wit, loyalty, and kindness toward her friends. The one he loved and wanted to marry had set out to punish him and his friends.

Maybe she wasn't through with him.

A burning heat started in Rath's chest. He stepped closer to Marlena. "Did you want me to take your innocence today to punish me yet again?"

"What? No."

Rath threw his shirt to the bed. "Damnation, Marlena, this is too important for us. Don't lie to me about it. You knew I had vowed never to touch an innocent, yet you knew how desperately I wanted you. I kept saying no, but you held out your hand to me."

"I did that because I wanted to be with you, too."

"Did you? I'm wishing I could believe that right now, instead of thinking this was a part of your revenge, too.

Were you thinking it would be a good way to force me to marry you, not knowing that I loved you and already wanted to marry you?"

"I don't know how you could even think that," she said, her voice rising.

"I have good reason to. Perhaps you even suggested to Mr. Olingworth that he contact me to be your guardian. Is that how far back your deceit goes?"

"How could it?" she asked. "I didn't even know who you were then."

"It sounds reasonable to me, Marlena," he said angrily. "You just admitted you started the scandal sheet as soon as you arrived in London. Why am I not to believe this day was planned, too?"

"Because my feelings for you are pure," she insisted. "I have not betrayed you concerning my feelings. I would have never written about you if I'd known I'd meet you one day and fall in love with you."

"It's not just about me, Marlena. You wrote about my friends. About Lady Sara and Lady Vera, who has been so kind to you."

"I had no idea what lovely people Lady Vera and the Duchess of Griffin were when I started the column. Just as you had no idea young ladies would be harmed when you wrote your letters."

Rath's anger and frustration continued to build, not just toward Marlena but for all that had happened since he'd met her. "But I didn't do it intentionally. You did. You admitted that when you wrote about the rumor that started at White's, your sales soared. Didn't you know that would put Griffin's sisters in danger from mischief-makers? Lady Vera might still be at risk from someone wanting to in some way harm her to get back at us."

"No. No," she answered just as passionately as he'd spoken. "I mean yes, it crossed my mind, but I didn't think anyone would harm a duke's sister. Who would be so bold as to try?"

"You, Marlena."

She flinched as if he'd struck her. He saw that his words wounded her deeply. They were harsh but he was powerless to take them back.

"I never wanted them in danger," she argued. "I didn't think they would be. I was seventeen. I didn't think a gentleman would ever set mischief upon a lady. That's what rakes do."

Even though he was angry with her, she could still amaze him with her boldness. In a softer voice he answered, "Yes, I guess we do it, too."

"I can't put my bad behavior off to having had too much brandy to drink or wagering with my friends."

"I have never tried to excuse what I did, Marlena. Lady Vera and Lady Sara were as innocent as the ladies we sent letters to."

"I understand that now and I am deeply sorry. Lady Vera told me she was actually accosted by Lord Henry."

"And you were going to dance with him," Rath ground out. "I probably should have let you."

"Justine arranged that dance. And whether or not you believe me I've felt remorse since first meeting Lady Vera. No, since first meeting you." She took in a deep breath that seemed to swallow down a sob. "I had hoped to end the scandal sheet after the first Season, but I kept doing it. For that, I'm sorry."

Rath sensed she wasn't telling him everything. What else could she know? What had she left unsaid?

Rath tensed again. "Marlena. You know who started the rumor at White's, don't you?"

She swallowed hard.

"Someone at the publishing company. Who? Tell me who they are."

"So you can throttle them?"

"Hell, yes!" he answered quickly. "You may have been seventeen and naïve, but the men in White's weren't. They knew exactly what they were saying and what might happen because of it." He took hold of her upper arms and looked fiercely into her eyes. "Marlena?"

"I can't tell you."

His hands tightened. "You mean you won't tell me."

"All right. I won't."

"Why? You gave yourself to me this afternoon. You said you love me. That should have meant something to you. Even now you could be in the family way because of what happened between us."

"I'm not so innocent that I don't know that, but I also know that it is unlikely after one time together." Her gaze swept up and down his face. "No matter what else we've said to each other, I want you to know I gave myself to you because I'm in love with you."

"Yes. If what you say is true and you love me, as I believe you do, you'll tell me who started the rumor so we can put all of this behind us."

"No," she said, pulling away from his grasp. "If you can't put this in the past as it stands now and forgive who started the rumor, you can't forgive me."

He let go of her. "That's not true." The words were almost a whisper and right now he wasn't sure they were truthful.

"I'm sorry, Rath. I don't really know where redemption comes from. Ourselves, others, or a higher place, but this I do know, I won't betray anyone else. Through *Miss Honora Truth's Weekly Scandal Sheet,* I've done all the betraying I'm going to do."

Marlena turned and walked out of the bedroom.

Chapter 23

He could be a rake if he accepts your heart and
then breaks it in front of you.

⊸∘⊰

*MISS HONORA TRUTH'S WORDS OF WISDOM AND
WARNING ABOUT RAKES, SCOUNDRELS, ROGUES, AND
LIBERTINES*

Whatever is it that you keep working on, Marlena? I've hardly seen you put it down since we returned from the duke's house."

Marlena didn't look up from her embroidery work. When she'd sketched the garden scene she didn't realize how much detail she'd put into it. How much time it would take to finish it. She didn't realize how important it would be to her, and how every stitch had to be perfect. Every color had to be vibrant because the flowers were her friends.

Unlike those that were already springing up in the garden, these flowers would not die. They would always be with her. Always reminding her of the duke and what he meant to her. And maybe one day her heart wouldn't constrict every time she thought about him.

She'd tried hard not be sad around Justine. The last

thing she needed was her cousin questioning her about her moods. But it was difficult when Justine mentioned his name. The hope she'd had that he could forgive her for not telling him everything was waning. She hadn't seen him at any of the parties or dinners she'd been to since she'd left him at her home that afternoon. She'd even asked Lady Vera about him, but she hadn't seen him, either.

"Are you not going to answer me?" Justine asked.

She looked up at her cousin. "I'm sorry. I suppose I have been concentrating too severely on this." She laid it down. "See, I've put it aside now. Are you happy?"

Justine smiled. "Yes. Now, will you look at me?"

"I am looking at you," Marlena said. "Your dress is lovely."

"Dear girl, I have my cape, gloves, and bonnet in my hands, do I not?"

Marlena studied her cousin. "Yes. Where are you going?"

"We, my dear. *We.* I told you I'd like to take a ride in the park today. The sun is shining, and I doubt it will last long. I want to take advantage of it. I told you to get ready. It's the Season. Everyone should see us riding about in the park. How do you ever expect to catch the eye of a gentleman if you don't go where people, and gentlemen like Lord Henry can see you?"

Marlena smiled. "I've told you I have no interest in Lord Henry or anyone else right now. Could you please go by yourself today? I've been out of the house every day for what seems like months. Sunshine or no, I don't want to go."

"Did you intend to make that rhyme? Never mind. All right. I'll take Tut. Unlike you, he enjoys looking out the window at all the people."

"You know I'd rather walk if I were going to the park."

"Pity. It looks so much better from the coach. And so do I."

Marlena went back to her stitching, and Justine and Tut soon left for their ride. All too soon Marlena realized her mind was no longer on the embroidery and she laid it down. She put on her cape, gloves, and straw hat and went into the garden where the air was cool and crisp. It was more peaceful for her than the drawing room. And certainly more so than her bedchamber now that she'd been there, in her bed, with the duke. The memories were far more vivid than she'd thought they would be. She still couldn't walk in the door without seeing him standing in front of her with just his trousers and boots on. He was a magnificent man.

And he had been hers for such a short time. His anger was to be expected, which was why she'd never wanted him to know what she'd done. Why she would never tell him about Mr. Bramwell. Rath admitted he would like to throttle him.

Marlena sat on the bench where she and Rath had first kissed. She supposed everything would remind her of him. The herbs were green, the trees were budding, and green sprouts had popped up everywhere signaling spring's arrival. In truth Marlena supposed she'd always been alone since her parents died. She'd had those who'd nursed her and cared for her before she'd gone to live with her aunt Imogene, uncle Fergus, and the boys who'd taught her so much. She'd had Mr. Olingworth who'd educated her and taught her to be a lady. Veronica and Eugenia had taught her how to be a loyal friend.

The duke had taught her how to love. What being in love meant.

Leaving him that day in her room, with hurtful words between them, had been excruciating. It seemed to have left a hole in her chest where her heart should have been.

It devastated her to think he believed she'd lured him into her bed for revenge. That he blamed her for the scandal sheet, the harm to Lady Vera, and not telling him who started the rumor, she could understand. She deserved his anger for those things. But his thinking she let him make love to her so she could exact more revenge was the most hurtful of all.

She wasn't unhappy, nor was she distraught about their coming together for their afternoon of sweet loving and passion. How could she be dismayed by something she'd wanted so desperately from the man she loved with all her heart? She treasured every moment they were together. She would always remember the extraordinary feelings he'd brought to life inside her. How he'd shown her how he could make her feel, and how she made him feel. She would not forget one single touch or kiss of their time together.

There had been nothing about her identity as Miss Honora Truth in any of the newsprints or other scandal sheets so she had to believe he hadn't told anyone. Yet. Maybe Rath hadn't decided what he wanted to do about it. Maybe he was looking for someone else to take over his guardianship of her.

Marlena's head hurt from all the thoughts she'd crammed into it. There was, at least, one thing she could remove from the crowded spaces in her mind, though: The morning had brought her the signal there would be no babe from her time with the duke. That had calmed one of her fears.

Marlena lifted her face to the sky. The sunshine was as warm and comforting as the duke's embrace; the fresh air reminded her of him, his kisses, his caresses, his—

"Marlena! Marlena."

The side gate burst open and Eugenia rushed through waving a piece of paper. She stopped abruptly when she saw Marlena sitting on the bench. Her eyes widened and she looked around the garden. "Is the duke here?" she asked softly.

"No." Marlena smiled. "I'm alone. Come sit with me and tell me what you are so excited about. And look at you. Out here without a cape or gloves. What's happened?"

"I have my shawl but didn't want to take time to get anything else."

"You must have been in a really big hurry."

Eugenia's eyes were glistening with happiness. "If I get cold, we can go inside. I couldn't wait to show you this." She handed Marlena the sheet of vellum. "You must read it right now. Out loud, please. I want to hear it again."

"All right." She unfolded the sheet and read.

"My dear . . ."

Marlena looked up. It was from Mr. Trout. She and the man never addressed or signed their letters to each other. That way their names were safe should one of their letters ever fall into the wrong hands.

"Yes, it's from Mr. Trout," Eugenia said "My maid forgot she had it in her sewing basket this morning. He finally answered us. Read on."

"It is with much gladness I tell you the publication of your book has gone extremely well. It has sold out and we are in the process of printing more. I will be adding fifty pounds into your account on the date this note is addressed."

"Fifty pounds!" Marlena exclaimed and looked up at her friend. "That's a fortune! I can't believe it."

"I know!" Eugenia squealed with glee. "Keep reading!"

"You can expect generous additions in the future. Yours truly."

Marlena leaned back in the bench, stunned. The

breeze fluttered the edges of the paper. "I can't believe it earned us that much."

"It must be true." Eugenia reached over and hugged Marlena. "Your book has done so well they are printing more. I'm thrilled for you!"

Marlena patted Eugenia's hand affectionately. "You now have enough money for the extra things you and Veronica need. And it looks as if there will be even more coming in to see you through the summer, autumn, and some of the winter too."

"It's so wonderful the book has done so well. I feel bad taking all the money. You've never taken a pence."

"You know how it's helped you. So don't mention that again."

"I don't need extra things for the Season now. You gave me quite enough." Eugenia sighed. "I don't even want to attend anymore."

"Why do you say that? I've seen you dancing with several young gentlemen and you seemed to be having a wonderful time."

"I do like to dance, but you know my heart already belongs to Mr. Bramwell. I don't feel right encouraging anyone else."

"Yes," Marlena said sympathizing with her. "I know what you mean."

Her friend's pale eyes blinked against the breeze. "I don't know why Veronica won't let him call on me."

"You do know, Eugenia. He's not a gentleman. He's below your station in life. If you married him you would never be accepted in the *ton* again, and you know that would break Veronica's heart."

"And what about my heart?" Eugenia said, sounding angry for the first time. "Is it all right for mine to be broken as long as Veronica's isn't? Besides, her heart is already broken because of her husband. Must mine be shattered, too?"

Eugenia's passion surprised Marlena, yet heartened her. She liked seeing her friend sounding stronger about what she wanted. "That's not what I meant, but you do make a very good point."

"And Mr. Bramwell makes more money than Mr. Portington's allowance."

"Maybe you can revisit this with your sister at the end of the Season. If you find no one you think you can marry, you can tell her you've tried. Maybe she will be more accepting then."

"I would like for her to care about what I want. She knows Mr. Bramwell would be a much better provider for me than Mr. Portington has been for her."

Marlena decided to stay quiet about that.

Eugenia went on, "You aren't happy about attending the Season, either, are you?"

"Not really," Marlena said honestly. "Like you, I want a man I can't have."

"The duke."

Eugenia was never one to be very perceptive, so Marlena asked, "How did you know?"

Her friend laughed. "You were kissing him."

"Oh, yes, I'd forgotten that."

Eugenia's eyes widened in disbelief and she said, "You forgot the Duke of Rathburne kissed you?"

"Heavens, no," Marlena said. "Never that. I had forgotten you witnessed part of it."

"Only part of it," Eugenia teased. "There was more."

Marlena looked down at her gloved hands. "You were kind not to question me too much about it afterward."

"The truth is, I didn't really want to know. I was envious."

"You? You fainted every time you saw the duke."

"No, jealous that you had the nerve to let him kiss you, and I hadn't let Mr. Bramwell kiss me."

"Everyone is different, Eugenia. And I am two years older than you. Besides, it would be a very boring world if we all thought alike and did everything alike, don't you think?"

"I know. But tell me, is it as amazing as I think it will be?"

"Kissing?" Marlena asked, though she was quite sure that was what her friend was talking about.

Eugenia nodded.

"Yes. It's more so. You can't dream about how wonderful it will feel. You must experience it to really know."

"I thought so."

Marlena folded the letter from Mr. Trout and handed it back to Eugenia. "Since we have such good news from the publisher today, I can now tell you what I've been dreading to share with you."

"I know what it is. It's been coming for a long time. You're going to stop writing the column, aren't you?"

"I have to."

"I know you've wanted to for a long time. I can't be anything but grateful you've written it so long."

"There were times I enjoyed it. And writing the book about rakes was enjoyable, too. I'm truly glad it did so well. I know the money has assisted you with household matters, but it really hasn't helped Veronica control her bouts of despair or her problems with Mr. Portington."

"We had such hope when we started, didn't we."

Marlena nodded and brushed a strand of hair behind her ear. "And there's one other thing I need to tell you today. The duke knows I'm Miss Truth."

"Oh!" Eugenia rose as if to flee.

"Don't worry," Marlena said, pulling on Eugenia's hand and forcing her back onto the bench. "Sit back down. He doesn't know anything about your part in it other than you know about it. He thought you might have been the one writing the sheet, but I assured him it was my idea and I started it, which is the truth."

"But I helped get it to the publisher each week."

"A minor part, and I'm not sure little details like that were important to him. I didn't betray your sister's trust in all the things she told that had happened to her concerning Mr. Portington. None of that matters since he has only gotten worse. Not better."

"That was kind of you not to tell."

"As you know, he does know Mr. Portington spends way too much money on his collection of oddities. At one time I thought there might be hope for him about that, but now I don't think anything will change."

Eugenia nodded.

Marlena sat back in the bench and sighed. "What he very much wanted to know— which I refused to tell him, of course—is who started the rumor at White's." Marlena put her gloved hands over Eugenia's and looked steadily into her eyes. "He must never know that we asked Mr. Portington to take Mr. Bramwell to White's, and that he is the one who started the rumor. Should he ever ask you about that, you must remain strong and not tell him."

"I would probably just faint if he asked me."

Marlena laughed. "Yes, I'd say that would be the perfect thing for you to do. I think he's come to expect it. He'd undoubtedly be disappointed if you didn't."

Eugenia's face turned serious. "Do you think he would hurt Mr. Bramwell?"

Marlena had to be truthful. "I really don't know. Though he's lived most of his adult life denying it, I do think he's a gentleman. But even gentlemen have been known to call each other out for a duel over a perceived wrong."

A tremor shook Eugenia. "A duel. He might challenge Mr. Bramwell?"

"I'm telling you I don't know, which is why you must remain quiet about this. Gentlemen are much more likely to let a lady's bad behavior pass than a man's. Mr. Bramwell started the rumor because we asked him, and he should never be punished for it."

"Thank you for telling me that. But none of this seems fair to you, Marlena. You have taken all the guilt upon your shoulders."

Adding on to anyone else's guilt would not absolve hers. She supposed the only thing she could do was go to Lady Vera and Lady Sara, admit her wrongdoing, and apologize. To Eugenia she said, "The fewer people who are upset about this, the better."

"It hurts terribly, doesn't it?" Eugenia said.

Marlena looked at her curiously. "What?"

"Loving someone you can't have."

"Yes," Marlena said softly, and turned her face up to the bright-blue sky once again. "It does."

Chapter 24

He could be a rake if he's so set on being right, he
can't see what is right in front of his eyes.

A longing that went bone-deep had settled over Rath.
He placed his razor on the chest and washed
the remaining soap off his face and neck. He then took
the towel and threw it to the bed as hard as he could.
Damnation, he missed Marlena. He'd told her he loved
her. He'd asked her to marry him, and what had she
done? Confessed she was Miss Truth. The gossip columnist who had plagued him for almost three years.

That, he could live with. He'd never really been affected by the gossip anyway. She admitted she was only
seventeen when she started it. If Marlena hadn't been
afraid of cemeteries and swamps before she went to live
with Olingworth, or frogs, snakes, bees, and other things
that lived in a garden when she was a ten-year-old girl,
there was no way she was going to be afraid of starting
a scandal sheet when she was seventeen.

He could see her loving the idea of doing something so outrageous. Especially to three gentlemen she thought had ruined a lady's life and had never been held accountable for it. All that, he could understand. Hell, he'd already forgiven her. That was easy to do. He loved her. But whoever had started that rumor had put Lady Vera and Lady Sara in danger. She wouldn't tell him who that was. That was what he couldn't accept, but it didn't keep him from wanting to go to her. To see her and be with her.

After the scandal sheet, he could understand her not wanting to betray anyone else. But the two of them wouldn't be able to live with the matter unsettled between them. They both knew that. So he had stayed away from her and away from the parties where she'd be. Dancing with other gentlemen.

He pulled on his shirt and stuffed the tail of it into his trousers, then reached for his neckcloth. Of course the publisher and everyone who worked there had denied any knowledge of who had started the rumor. He'd realized that this would be the case when he went there, but he'd had to give it a try.

"I'm sorry to disturb you, Your Grace."

"You're not, Sneeds," he mumbled, trying to tie the neckcloth.

"Would you like some help with that, Your Grace?"

"No."

"Very well. There's a young lady here—"

Rath swung around. "Miss Fast?"

"No, sir. Her name is Miss Everard and there's a young man with her named Mr. Stephen Bramwell."

Bramwell had been the young man Mrs. Abernathy had sent to the club to find him. "What the devil are they doing here?" he asked, more to himself than to his butler as he turned back to the mirror.

"They wouldn't say, Your Grace. I tried to send them away, telling them it was too early for a social call and they would have to send your secretary a letter and arrange an appointment if you deemed it necessary. But the young lady seemed quite adamant that you would agree to see them, and, and—".

"And what?"

"I felt quite sure the young lady might faint right there on your front steps if I didn't at least agree to come up and make you aware of their presence."

Rath snorted a laugh. "That's Miss Everard. And she's right. I will see them. Show them into the drawing room and tell them I'll be down shortly."

"Right away."

Rath finished his neckcloth and donned his coat. Why were they here? Had Marlena sent them to plead her case? No, he dismissed that idea the moment he thought of it. She wouldn't do that. If she wanted to talk to him she would have come herself. Maybe something had happened to her? No, more than likely it was Mrs. Abernathy who'd sent them.

"Best I get down and find out," he said to himself as he walked out of his bedchamber.

Miss Everard and Mr. Bramwell rose and greeted Rath properly when he entered the drawing room. Miss Everard looked paler than he'd ever seen her, and he was sure she was shaking like a leaf in a summer storm. After all the smelling salts and sachets he'd purchased for Marlena's house, he actually had no idea if he had any in his own house should Miss Everard need it. Mr. Bramwell didn't look much better but he managed to hold himself up straight, hands behind his back, and give the appearance of being strong. Still, Rath was sure he saw the man's knees knocking.

"Sit down before you faint," he said.

They both took their seats on the settee rather quickly. Obviously their legs were as weak as he suspected. "Thank you, Your Grace," Mr. Bramwell said. "We know it's early but we needed to catch you before you left for the day."

His voice was almost as shaky as his legs, Rath thought.

"The first thing I'm going to do is pour you both a drink. I know it's early, but I don't know why you're here. I fear I may never know if you don't settle your nerves. You both look like you're about to collapse."

Rath walked over to a table and poured a little splash of brandy in two glasses. He then opened a cabinet, took out a bottle, and poured a little splash of it into another glass. He walked over to them and handed one to the young lady.

"I've never had a drink, Your Grace."

"It won't hurt you. It's sherry. Not as strong as brandy but it will help steady your nerves. Small sips."

She looked down at the glass and then over to Mr. Bramwell. He nodded and she took a sip. Her eyes widened and she sucked in a deep breath.

"Keep drinking," he said. "It'll start tasting better and get easier to swallow."

She looked at Bramwell again. He nodded to her as he accepted the glass from Rath. He promptly took a sip and said, "We've talked about this—me and Miss Everard. We decided there's something we thought you should know."

So maybe Mrs. Abernathy didn't send them. "All right," Rath said, making himself comfortable on the settee opposite them. "What can I do for you?

"I don't want you blaming Marlena for being Miss Truth," Miss Everard said in a soft, timid voice.

"I don't," Rath said, and knew it was true. "She was young, rash, and bold enough to try anything."

"But there are other things about why she did it that you don't know," Miss Everard continued. "She wouldn't tell you because she would be breaking a promise she made to Veronica. She didn't want to do that."

That had his attention. "What things?"

"Veronica hasn't always been the way she is now." She glanced at Bramwell again, and he nodded again. "She didn't used to be nervous and full of despair and sometimes spending days in bed. During her first Season she was beautiful, happy, and enjoying her life. Many beaus sought her hand."

Rath noticed that Miss Everard's countenance changed when she was talking about her sister. She smiled and seemed to get a little color in her cheeks.

"She was the belle of almost every ball she attended," Miss Everard continued. "Our father was told to expect several offers from very suitable gentlemen to come for her hand. But then the scandal of the secret admirer letters came out—" Miss Everard's smile faded and her voice turned soft again. "A prank, some called it. But it was more than that to Veronica."

Miss Everard stopped, took a sip from the glass, and sucked in another deep breath as she settled her gaze back on Rath. "After that no offers ever came for her hand. Our father went to one of the gentlemen to ask why. The man said Veronica was so lovely, he'd thought she'd be above wanting a secret admirer. That had been one of the things that drew him. But then he'd discovered that she was like all the rest, so he wouldn't be offering for her after all. No other gentlemen did, either. Fearing she might be left like a dried weed on a shelf, she accepted Mr. Portington's offer. He was older. Studious and had a good allowance. She thought she would have children to fill her life and make her happy. And she was accepting of her life the first year or two of her marriage."

Rath swallowed hard. It wasn't easy sitting quietly and letting this young lady tell him to his face how one of the ladies had suffered because of those damned letters.

"But Mr. Portington started buying more and more things. Papa passed and I moved in with them. The house became crowded. There wasn't enough money to pay for coal and food. Mr. Portington kept saying everything would be fine. But it wasn't. Veronica became very unhappy. She had hoped to one day have a babe to love, but Mr. Portington—"

Miss Everard looked to Bramwell once more. "Mr. Portington gave up the marriage bed. He became more interested in adding to his fossil collection than his wife, his home, or his financial status. Now Veronica has no love, no children, and she never will because he forces her to sleep in the room with me."

Damnation.

Her words came faster. "Marlena thought, if she could show Veronica that someone had sought revenge against you and the others, it would help her not be so depressed and sink into despair, but by the time we realized the scandal sheet wasn't going to help Veronica with that, she and I had become dependent on the money it brought in to keep us in our house. Marlena never took a pence from the scandal sheet or the book. She gave it all to us. All she's ever done is help us. Please don't be mad with her. She wanted to end it after the first Season. She only kept doing it to help us so we wouldn't have to give up our home."

"Thank you for telling me this, Miss Everard. I admit that Miss Fast gave me few details. I have a different and better understanding of this after listening to you."

Rath watched her swallow hard before saying, "Veronica doesn't know I'm here. She wouldn't like that I've told you about her marriage. She doesn't want anyone to know there's any trouble or that she shares my room instead of her husband's. It would shame her. I wanted you to know how her life has been affected. Marlena doesn't know I'm here, either. Just Mr. Bramwell."

"I won't say a word about your visit."

"Thank you."

"That's not all, Your Grace," Mr. Bramwell said, shifting uncomfortably in his seat.

"Go on," Rath said to the shaky young man.

Bramwell rose, downed the brandy, and winced. He placed the empty glass on the table in front of him and said, "Miss Fast wouldn't tell you, and I appreciate her honor but for her sake you need to know I am the man who started the rumor in White's that night about the Duke of Griffin's sisters, and I'd do it again. I don't regret it."

Rath rose, too. His hand tightened on his glass. "Those are troubling words, Mr. Bramwell."

"I stand by them. I wanted to confront you earlier and tell you, but I couldn't. I promised Eugenia, Miss Everard, that I wouldn't. I couldn't betray my promise to her." He looked at her and gave her a hint of a smile. "She's too important to me." His attention returned to Rath. "Because she is confessing, I asked her if I could as well."

Rath looked at the thin slip of a man who was so frightened, it seemed even his eyeballs were shaking. "You are a tradesman, are you not? How did you get into White's?"

"I am not a member of Society but Mr. Portington made arrangements for me to enter White's with him. He wasn't aware of what I wanted to do. When Eugenia told me what she and Miss Fast were doing I wanted to help.

I asked Mr. Portington if he could get me into White's as I'd never been and always wanted to go. It wasn't a place he'd frequent often but he agreed. When we were leaving I spoke loudly so others could hear me. I said, 'The Rakes of St. James always get away with everything. They've never had to pay a price for their scandalous behavior years ago, and it's time they did.' Mr. Portington mumbled something about I should speak lower and be careful what I said. But I spoke even louder and added, 'Wouldn't it be fitting if something happened to ruin the Duke of Griffin's sisters' first Season.'"

Bramwell reached over and took the glass from Miss Everard, finished off her sherry, and placed the glass by his. She rose to stand beside him. "Now that you know, you can do your worst to me. I'm ready. Take my business, challenge me to a duel, or take my life if you want for what I've done to the Duke of Griffin's sisters. I won't be apologizing for what I did to help Eugenia and Miss Fast."

Rath leaned forward and grabbed Bramwell by the neckcloth and pulled him up to his face. Miss Everard gasped and whispered for Rath to please let go of him.

"You put Griffin's sisters in danger," Rath said in a voice that was low and meant to strike fear. "Physical danger."

"I'm sorry for that," Bramwell struggled to say.

Rath's hand tightened on the cloth. "Lady Vera may still have someone want to harm her because of what you said."

"You needed to know that your misbehavior had consequences, too. Some young ladies were hurt by your letters. None physically that I've ever heard. Still, there were serious aftereffects. And you were to blame."

"And that's the only reason I'm not going to challenge you right now."

"Your Grace?"

Rath looked over to Miss Everard and knew she was an innocent victim, too. He let go of the man and stepped back.

"Veronica said the only thing people in the *ton* said was rakes will be rakes." Miss Everard's voice was stronger than Rath had ever heard before. "Because you were dukes, the three of you went on with your lives and you were never held to account. Veronica is in a loveless marriage that she thought would at least give her children. Her husband has his fossils, his bones, his studies of them. She will have nothing after I marry."

Rath remained silent. Thinking on all he'd heard.

"You need to take a hard look at what you're giving up—Your Grace," Miss Everard said. "Marlena. You don't deserve her but she wants you."

Rath stared at the two sets of eyes looking at him and saw all the damage he'd done. "Miss Everard, I'm sorry I sent the secret admirer letter to your sister and all the other ladies. It was thoughtless, and I thought harmless."

She nodded once. "I've said all I came to say," she said. "What you do about Marlena is your own business. I just don't want her to be as unhappy as my sister and I have been."

"And I stand by my words, Your Grace," Bramwell added.

"I stand by mine as well."

Rath turned toward the door and called "Sneeds?"

"Yes, Your Grace," he said, walking in.

"Show Miss Everard and Mr. Bramwell out."

Rath walked over to the decanter and poured himself another splash. It was a little early in the day to be hitting the bottle for the second time, but he had a lot of thinking and planning to do.

A lot to make up for.

Maybe going back and remembering some of the things his father had told him about being a gentleman might help. All the emotions of anger and revenge that had been swirling around inside the past few days were impossible to fathom right now, so he didn't try. He would let them go. All of them. The only emotion he kept was his love for Marlena. It welled up inside him and wouldn't be denied.

One thing he was sure of. He wouldn't stop until he got her back. No matter how long it took.

Chapter 25

He could be a rake if he has a difficult time admitting he was wrong.

Miss Honora Truth's Words of Wisdom and Warning About Rakes, Scoundrels, Rogues, and Libertines

"I find it very unusual that the Duchess of Griffin didn't invite you to tea, too, Marlena," Justine said, walking into the drawing room dressed in one of her new visiting day dresses.

It certainly didn't bother Marlena. She was happy for Justine to be out of the house for a couple of hours. She'd been trying to work on her last Dear Reader column and Justine was always around and always talking. A little peace and quiet would be appreciated.

"You must have said or done something to upset her. It's just puzzling that you didn't get an invitation."

A pain gripped Marlena's stomach. That was highly likely. Had the duke decided to tell the other two rakes and their wives what she'd done? Had he told Lady Sara and Lady Vera, too, that she was Miss Truth? If so, she could understand them shunning her. Everyone else would, too.

Marlena inhaled three deep breaths. Let it be so. She was tired of fretting about it. She had thought about going and apologizing to Lady Vera and Lady Sara—all of the people she'd written about over the years—but there were simply too many. And the thought too overwhelming.

"Perhaps she will tell me today what it is you have done. Can you think of a time you might have offended her?"

Many times.

"I probably said something, Justine. You know I'm not always as discreet as I should be. And the Season has me weary."

"Ha!" Justine said. "Who could be weary of balls and dinner in beautiful homes? Going to parties and dancing with gentlemen will be a part of your life from now on. You'll get used to it."

Marlena smiled at Justine's enthusiasm. She couldn't think of any man but Rath. Just the thought of continuing to go to parties and dancing with gentleman she had no desire to dance with was almost more than she could bear. And, every morning she woke wondering if it would be the day she received notice that Rath had turned her guardianship over to someone else.

"I do wonder why the duke hasn't been over," Justine said absently. "You haven't heard from him, have you?"

"No," she said, and she didn't believe she would. "I see your carriage has driven up. You don't want to be late for the duchess' house."

"No, no. If you get lonely while I'm away, you can always play the piano or work on that garden scene you've been stitching for weeks now."

"It's finished," she said sadly. "I hated for it to end. Perhaps I'll start another."

"Parties, my dear girl. Tea parties, card parties, and even those walks in the park you enjoy so much when it's freezing. Now that the weather is better and warmer, you must get out and do more."

"I will," she said softly. "I will have to."

After Justine left, Marlena sat down at her secretary and pulled out paper, quill, and ink. She might as well get started.

As winter ends, spring begins. Gone are the barren trees, snowy landscapes, and frost-covered ponds. And when spring ends, summer will begin. So it is with life and so it is with scandal sheets.

The loud clank of the door knocker made Marlena jump. Tut started barking like a fiend. Then she heard Mrs. Doddle's footsteps. "Mrs. Doddle," she said quietly as the woman passed by the doorway.

"Yes, miss?"

"Whoever it is, send them away. I am not accepting callers this afternoon."

"Yes, miss."

Marlena went back to her work. *It begins and it ends. I must say good-bye.*

She didn't like that. So she started again. *The Season always brings us new gossip, and the first column of* Miss Honora Truth's Weekly Scandal Sheet *has what will be the biggest gossip of the Season. This will be the last one.*

Marlena looked at that and laughed.

"Well, it appears you haven't missed me."

Marlena's heart jumped to her throat and she almost stumbled over her chair rising at the sound of Rath's voice.

"I didn't mean startle you."

He looked so handsome standing in the doorway in his dark-blue coat, camel-colored trousers, and those boots that made him look ten feet tall. Holding Tut again. The little dog was trying to lick his chin. It wasn't fair that Tut loved him, too. She wanted to run to him and throw herself into his arms, but that couldn't happen. No matter the cost, she couldn't give him what he wanted. She wouldn't give up Mr. Bramwell.

She looked down at her scandal sheet. Her chest tightened for a second or two, and then she realized she didn't have to hide it from him anymore. He knew. She put the quill in the stand and said, "Perhaps you've decided to make a habit out of startling me."

"I wouldn't want to do that." He put Tut down.

Marlena squared her shoulders. She was doing her best not to let her mind run wild with thoughts of why he was there. She waited for him to tell her, but all he did was stare at her. Had he given her guardianship to someone else? Had he told Lady Vera about her? Had he told everyone?

"What can I do for you?" she finally asked.

He walked into the room and stood before her. She felt she should move away from him, but being so near was too tempting. "It's good to see you, Marlena."

She turned away from him to stare out the window. She'd just thought the same about him but she wasn't going to admit it.

"I thought you might like to know a few things that I've been doing," he said.

She looked back at him. "That depends on what it is. I'm sure there are some things you could tell me that I wouldn't care to hear."

"That's true, but I don't believe I have anything like that to say to you today."

Her heartbeat increased even though she didn't want it to. "Very well. Would you like to sit down?"

"No. I'd like to walk in the garden with you, if you

don't mind. Do you have a shawl nearby? It's not very cold out today."

"Yes, right over here."

Marlena picked up her gray woolen shawl and was going to put it on her shoulders but the duke grabbed hold of it and insisted on helping her with it. She smelled his shaving soap, and her stomach jumped. She prayed he wouldn't touch her. She didn't need or want any more of his touches to think about and dream about. She had too many memories right now.

Tut followed them down the steps and into the back garden. The grass and shrubs were showing their spring green colors and the sky had patches of blue among the stormy looking gray clouds.

"I see some buds but no flowers are open yet," Rath said.

"Soon," she said, walking beside him, holding on to the ends of her shawl as if they were some kind of lifeline for her. "But surely you didn't come here to see my small garden."

"No." He stopped as they neared the bench along the yew hedge, and so did she.

"I wanted to tell you that everything is now in motion for Mr. Portington to open a museum. Members of The Royal Society have inspected some of his extraordinary relics and are eager to get started helping him prepare a building."

Her heartbeat increased again. "And you and the other two rakes are still going to finance it?"

"Yes, and we have others who want to join us as well."

"I'm pleased." She looked away again, finding it difficult to continue to look into his dark eyes. She didn't want him to see how much she loved him, wanted him, and wished things could be different between them.

"There is one other thing I wanted to tell you about Mr. Portington."

"All right," she said, wishing she could stop the jittery feeling in her stomach.

"I mentioned to him that this museum would be a great legacy to leave to his son."

"He doesn't have one," she said.

"I know. He told me. He considers his wife very delicate, and he hasn't pursued children fearing for her frail health and taking to her bed at times."

"Yes," Marlena said confidently, "but she takes to her bed because he spends his monthly allowance on odd things and she's afraid he will never come to her bed and give her children," Marlena declared and then immediately clamped her mouth shut. "I shouldn't have said that."

He smiled and her heart and her hands warmed. What was he doing smiling at her when she was so distraught at losing him she was telling him about Veronica's private life?

"It's all right, Marlena. You are not telling me anything I don't already know."

"You know?"

He nodded. "And I wanted you to know that Mr. Portington is now very much interested in having a son or daughter to leave his museum to."

Tears welled in her eyes. "Really? You know this."

"Straight from his mouth."

Marlena was so happy for Veronica she wanted to hug Rath and kiss him, and tell him how much she loved him. But she remained as stiff and stoic as she could under the circumstances.

"That is welcome news." Her throat felt tight. It wasn't easy to hold in the emotions she was feeling. "I thank you for letting me know."

"Now I have some news that I don't think you or Mrs. Portington will approve of, but it's not the first time I've done something that others disapprove of."

Her heart started pounding in her ears. This was it. What was he going to do to her for writing the scandal sheet, the book, and for not telling him about Mr. Bramwell? She could handle it. Whatever it was.

"That can be said of most people, Your Grace. Just tell me what it is." *And put me out of my misery.*

"I offered Mr. Bramwell and Miss Everard my carriage-and-four to elope to Gretna Green. They left about five hours ago. At this point, it would be impossible for anyone to catch them and stop their marriage."

The breath left Marlena's lungs but she managed to whisper, "What!"

"I know it was rather presumptuous of me. And I didn't do it for Mr. Bramwell, but for Miss Everard. I felt it the right thing to do under the circumstances."

"What circumstances? There are no circumstances that would warrant that. He is a tradesman. He's—"

"In love with Miss Everard. I have no reason to like the fellow, but she does. I did it for her."

She grabbed hold of her the ends of her shawl. "I'm not one given to the vapors but I think I have to sit down," she whispered.

Rath took hold of her arm and walked with her over to the bench.

"Are you all right? You're not going to faint, are you? Do I need to get the smelling salts?"

"Oh, heavens no," she whispered as she looked into his eyes. "My cousins would disown me if I ever fainted. It's just that you don't know Veronica. She will take to her sickbed over this and she may never get out."

"Mr. Portington knows. He helped me plan it."

"What?" She gasped. "He did that to his wife?"

"He thought it was the right thing to do, too. He will tell her wife tonight and will take care of her while she adjusts to this news."

Rath was smiling gently at her. She felt limp, like a ball of yarn that had been rolled out. Wait—something wasn't right.

The day brightened as the sun came from behind a cloud. Marlena looked deeper into Rath's dark eyes. "How did you know about the two of them? Eugenia faints every time she sees you."

"No more secrets, no more distrust or worries between us, Marlena. They paid me a visit and told me everything."

Marlena rose from the bench. "Everything? You—that he—"

"Everything," he said, taking hold of her shoulders. "Bramwell admitted he started the rumor at White's."

Marlena gasped but Rath kept talking. "Eugenia helped me see that, even when a young man thinks he's just having fun with a young lady, there can be consequences for bad behavior that can last a lifetime and sometimes affect others. Men should always be careful what they say and how they treat a lady."

She looked down at his hands on her arms, and he slowly removed them. "So you didn't try to strangle him when he told you he was the one who started the rumor?"

He smiled. "I did. But only for a few seconds and my hand was only around his neckcloth and not his throat. He wasn't harmed."

"I'm glad."

"But there something else I have to tell you."

Every time he said that her heart jumped and her stomach squeezed.

"I really don't know if I can take any more news from you. And Justine will probably return shortly."

"No. I asked Esmeralda to ask her over and keep her all afternoon."

Her breath leaped. "You planned that?"

He nodded. "I wanted to make sure I had plenty of time alone with you." He reached into his pocket and pulled out a copy of her book.

"I wanted to return this."

She just looked at it and that feeling of pride made her stand a little taller. She had written a book and had it published. And it had sold very well. Maybe she'd done one thing right.

Marlena managed a little smile. "I told you it wasn't necessary to return it, but since you never read it it's just as well. I can give it to someone else."

"But I *did* read it."

She met his gaze. She wasn't quite sure she believed him. "You did?"

"I told you I would."

"I guess you finally found the time," she answered, feeling miffed that if he had read it, it had taken him this long.

"I admit that, when I first saw the book, I thought it drivel."

Well, that was about as blunt as a person could get.

"And then I decided I wanted to read it and think on the things you alleged in your book before I got back to you about it. I wanted to talk with others about it. I wanted to know if a man was, indeed, a rake if he touched a lady inappropriately as you suggested in your book. I wanted to know if a man was, indeed, a rake if he had a card game with his friends rather than a ride in the park with the lady he was interested in, and many of the other things that you state."

Had he really done that? Talked with others about what she'd written?

"Whom did you ask? Your friends? The rakes?"

"Various people, including friends who are now happily married and no longer rakes, Lady Sara and Lady Vera, Esmeralda, Loretta, and Eugenia."

Eugenia, too?

Marlena was suspicious of him. What was he getting at? She didn't even know why he was telling her this. That he'd read it was enough.

But pride made her ask, "What was your conclusion?"

He smiled. "You were very brave to write the book, Marlena. I hope every lady reads it and knows how a gentleman should treat her and that she will stay away from rakes like me."

The sun was warming her back and sparkling in the duke's eyes. He was chasing away the gray clouds in the skies and in her heart. "You have never been a rake to me. You have always been a gentleman."

"Even the last time we were together in your bedroom, here in your house? You know I planned it for us to be alone together."

"I was never unwilling at any time. I knew exactly what I wanted, and I wasn't disappointed."

"May we go back to a conversation we were having that day?"

No, she didn't want to. She was liking the way she was feeling now. Not how she was felt when he was angry and she had to say good-bye to him.

"That depends on which conversation it was."

He smiled and laid her book on the bench behind him. He gently moved his hands around her waist and pulled her up close. Marlena felt herself leaning into him, and he moved still closer to her.

"I believe I had said I love you and I want to marry you, but you never gave me an answer."

"I believe we had some very strong unresolved issues between us that seemed unsurmountable."

"We did." He moved his face closer to hers. "But your friends, the ones you would not betray, came to your rescue. I'm glad they did. They took all the blame."

"That doesn't absolve me. When I said my love for you was pure, I meant it, but my life is not guilt-free. I have written gossip, true or not, about people I've never met. I am not blameless, Rath."

The corners of his lips lifted. "Neither am I. I am a rake. I liked what I read from Miss Honora Truth between the pages of your book. You have done a good service for ladies, but I've decided I want Marlena between the sheets, not Miss Truth between the pages." He pulled her tighter to his chest and looked deeply, seriously into her eyes. "I want you to marry me, Marlena. Help me be the gentleman my father always wanted me to be."

Marlena's heart swelled. She had thought she'd no chance at happiness if Rath was out of her life. Now she had him, the man she loved asking her to marry him. The man she would honor above all else.

She could hardly breathe, let alone speak, but somehow she managed to whisper a yes. And then a stronger, louder, and happier, "Yes!"

Rath pulled her tighter. "You know I would have had to force you if you hadn't said yes."

"Because you are a rake."

He shook his head. "Because I know I can't live without you. And—" He hesitated.

"And what?" she asked, suddenly fearing his answer.

"I need someone to make sure my gardener takes care of the grounds of the Rathburne Estate."

She laughed. "Are they large grounds?"

"You can make them bigger if you want," he answered.

"Then I think I should like to go there someday."

"After we're married, or before," he asked with a teasing grin.

Marlena laughed. "After, of course."

Rath caught her up in his arms and sealed their promise with a kiss so passionate Marlena felt she was melting in his arms.

He was warm and strong.

Whack! Whack!

"Hellfire!" Rath let go of Marlena and turned just in time to see Mrs. Abernathy's parasol ready to strike him again.

"Justine, no!" Marlena exclaimed, trying to move between her cousin and Rath. "What are you doing? Put that down before you hurt someone."

"I will not let him ruin you, Marlena." She held her weapon up as if ready to go after Rath again. "You may be his ward but you are my charge and in my care. I will not let him lead you astray and leave you shamed and disgraced."

"But he's not."

"Let me explain, Mrs. Abernathy," Rath said.

"What is there to explain?" she said, her eyes bulging. "I know what you were doing. It's shameful what you've done. Pursuing me like you did, feigning interest in me. And only because you wanted to get your hands on my innocent Marlena. I won't have it!"

"No, no, he didn't," Marlena argued. "I won't let you accuse him of something that's not true."

"Because you don't know, dear girl. You couldn't see past his handsome face and charming ways."

"You are not being fair, Justine."

"Please, Marlena," Rath said, "let her have her say. She needs to say this."

"Yes I do, and I will. I saw you two walking in the garden together at your house. And later how you tried your best to get her alone. Oh, yes, I was aware of that. I saw the way you held her when you danced at the ball. Her first dance that should have been with the gentleman Lord Henry. Oh, yes, I was aware of it all. And today, I was very suspect when the duchess invited me to tea and not Marlena. I knew you'd had a hand in it and I was right. You are her good friend and that you would involve her in your schemes is deplorable."

"I am guilty of all you say, and more."

Justine didn't look surprised. "I knew it. I knew you were trying to fool me with sweet confections and coming to see Marlena when my back was turned. I knew you wanted to be alone with her today. I don't know how many times you came when I went for a ride in my carriage. The carriage you gave me so I would use it and leave you free to come and see Marlena whenever you wished. Well, Your Grace, I'm telling you right now, your days of trying to seduce and ruin my cousin are over!"

"I agree, Mrs. Abernathy," Rath said, and then turned and smiled at Marlena. "I just told Marlena that I love her and want to marry her. She just agreed to be my wife."

"What?" Justine's word was almost a croak as her hand flew to her chest.

"It's true," Marlena said, smiling and feeling happier than she'd ever felt. "We are going to be married."

"I hope I can count on you to live with us and continue to be her trusted companion," Rath said. "Or if you prefer, I can set you up in a house of your choosing in Mayfair."

Justine dropped her parasol. "Mayfair? With my carriage?"

"Of course," Rath agreed.

"Why, yes," Justine said as she touched her hair. "Yes, of course I'll continue to be her companion."

"Perhaps there is someone you'd want to tell. I mean, since your carriage is waiting."

Marlena took hold of Rath's arm and looked lovingly up at him. "He's my guardian, Justine. He won't do anything to harm me."

Justine smiled. "Of course, he won't. I do believe there are a few ladies I'd like to tell about your coming nuptials since I have your permission, Your Grace."

Rath bent down, picked up her parasol, and handed it to her.

"I shall return in an hour or two."

As soon as Justine was out of sight Rath caught Marlena up to his chest. "You do know I never had designs on Mrs. Abernathy, don't you?"

Marlena frowned and then smiled. "Of course, but I'm not sure she will ever believe that."

"I think you might be right, but I believe she will accept the house in Mayfair rather than live with us."

"Oh, I know she will. It's her dream come true and you are my dream come true. I love you, Rath."

"And I love you." He bent his head and captured her lips with his.

My Dear Readers,

Endings are never easy and seldom welcomed. But endings come, be it the end of spring, a satisfying read, a bottle of port, or a life. So it is with this salutation that I end *Miss Honora Truth's Weekly Scandal Sheet*.

We have it on good authority that the last of the Rakes of St. James is to be married by the end of the week to Miss Marlena Fast, his ward of only a few weeks. I have decided to retire from my weekly column and possibly think about my next book. Thank you to all who have followed me these three years. I do hope we meet again in the scandal pages or in a book.

MISS HONOR TRUTH'S WEEKLY SCANDAL SHEET

Epilogue

He could be a rake if he gives a young lady the
surprise of her life.

❧

*Miss Honora Truth's Words of Wisdom and
Warning About Rakes, Scoundrels, Rogues, and
Libertines*

Rath watched Marlena talking to Esmeralda and Loretta, sipped his champagne, and smiled. He wasn't
surprised the three duchesses had settled into a good
friendship during the past year and a half. He only wished
the Rathburne, Hawksthorn, and Griffin Estates weren't
so far apart. It was easy for them to get together during the
spring in London for the Season, but in the winter months
when they resided at their country estates it was harder.

Marlena hadn't minded the isolation of the Rathburne
Estate and small nearby village. She had all the gardens
and grounds she wanted, and she enjoyed walking in them
with her and Tut.

He looked around the room. One of six that had been
partitioned in the building and the biggest, since it was
also the entrance into The Portington Museum of History.

What a nightmare it had been to get it finished. Rath had workers busy night and day for weeks to make the opening date they'd set. He might have to partake of another glass of champagne in celebration though the damned stuff gave him an awful headache the morning after.

All the displays had been roped off. A necessary barrier in the museum that Portington and the Royal Society had insisted on. Rath understood. It was for the best. There was always the possibility someone would want to pick up one of the smaller fossils or clay pots, or touch the very sharp sword or some other valuable artifact from the past. The pieces needed to be preserved for history and not broken by those who couldn't contain themselves.

And then there was the huge warehouse-style room on the first floor that was filled with crates and under lock and key—the Megalosaurus eggs and more, all awaiting certification, which Rath believed would happen one day. Maybe in the distant future when more was known about the unknown history of the earth and its inhabitants—human, reptile, mammal, insect, or any other species.

Portington was an odd fellow to be sure. But he was wise not to want anyone touching his possessions. Rath smiled when he looked over at the man standing beside his wife, who was hoping her dress hid that she was with child. Mrs. Portington hadn't wanted to miss the opening of her husband's museum.

Standing close beside her was her sister. After much wailing and time, Mrs. Portington had finally forgiven her for marrying beneath her. Miss Everard—no, Mrs. Bramwell—now looked as if she didn't have a timid bone in her body. Rath's gaze stayed on Mr. Bramwell for a few seconds. Rath wasn't sorry he'd offered his coach for them to elope. It was the least he could do for Miss Everard after making her faint so many times. And he liked seeing her happy. Rath would never like Bramwell, but then he had no reason to see the man often.

Everyone in the room thought the welcoming committee was there and waiting for the invitees to start arriving. The Duke and Duchess of Griffin, and the Duke and Duchess of Hawksthorn. The Portingtons, the Bramwells, and Mrs. Abernathy were standing near the entrance eager to see and speak to everyone who entered.

Rath kept watching the door, too. They were late. They were supposed to arrive before the museum opened to the guests. He was beginning to worry so he took another sip of his champagne.

"Are you listening to me, Rath?" Griffin asked.

"No, I can't say I am."

"I thought as much. You can't keep your attention off Marlena."

"Can you blame me? She's beautiful."

"She is, so go stand by her."

"Yes, please," Hawk said. "So we can be by our wives, too. They are much better company than you are."

Rath grimaced and then grinned. "I can't believe you were the two I offered to share my port with when I first entered Oxford. I should have kept the whole bottle for myself and left you dry."

The three of them laughed as they walked over to their wives.

Rath slid his arm around Marlena and gently pulled her close to his side. "Should we stand closer to the entrance?" he asked.

"I don't think so," she answered, looking up at him with a smile. "This is Mr. Portington's night. I think we should stay in the shadows."

"The shadows? Hmm. That is an interesting turn of phrase."

"I'm glad you like it."

"And I'm glad you now write poetry and short stories and not scandal sheets."

"I'm glad, too. Though I sometimes wonder if—"

"No," Rath said.

"Not even another book of words, wisdom, and warning?"

"Miss Truth no longer exists. However." He stopped.

"Yes?" she asked with a hopeful look in her eyes. "However what?"

"I don't think I would object to you thinking about the possibility of a book of words, wisdom, and warning about gardening."

Marlena laughed. "Yes," she said, touching his arm and giving it a squeeze of appreciation. "I could do that. Why hadn't I thought of that?"

He smiled. "Perhaps you can now that you no longer have to worry about Mrs. Portington or Mrs. Bramwell."

"That is comforting and I owe Veronica's happiness to you, Griffin, and Hawk for giving them this wonderful and educational museum."

"Sometimes I do miss it when you don't call us the Rakes of St. James."

"In that case—" She smiled, rose on her toes and lifted her face to his. "—perhaps you should do something scandalous and remind me you are a rake."

"I think I will." He lowered his head toward hers to kiss her when out of the corner of his eye he saw the door open. He turned. "At last," Rath said softly. He leaned away from her and turned toward the entrance. "Marlena," he said. "Look who has arrived."

She followed his gaze. Her lips parted. Her eyes widened. "It can't be," she whispered. She took a step and faltered.

Rath took hold of her arm and steadied her. "You didn't," she whispered breathlessly.

"I did," he smiled. "It took a while, but I found your aunt Imogene and uncle Fergus, and they have brought two of their sons with them. The other three are well but have families of their own and couldn't make the journey. I know you've missed them and wanted to see them again."

Marlena threw her arms around Rath and buried her face in his neck as tears of happiness threatened. "I can't believe you thought to do this for me. I—I don't know what to say."

Rath took hold of her upper arms and forced her to look at him. "I love you, dearest wife. I want to do things for you that make you happy. I think the only thing you have time to say is *I love you*. They are looking at you with smiles and waiting for you to go to them."

Marlena dried her eyes and sniffed, too. "I love you, Rath." She reached up and kissed him quickly on the lips and then ran toward her family.

Rath smiled.

Dear Readers,

I hope you enjoyed the third book in my *Rakes of St. James* trilogy. It has been a delightful series to work on. I based the whole premise of this trilogy on the very real foundation that most, if not all, young ladies like the thought of having a secret admirer. I have especially enjoyed writing *It's All About the Duke*.

The fossilized dinosaur eggs mentioned in this book are a figment of my imagination. In fact, the word *dinosaur* wasn't used until 1841, so I never used that word in this story. However, Mr. William Buckland was a real person, and he discovered Megalosaurus bones in 1819. They weren't given the scientific name until 1924.

When I first heard that, in the twenty-first century, we have fossilized dinosaur eggs from centuries past, I found it fascinating and knew I wanted to use them in a book one day. This storyline gave me the perfect outlet. I did most of my research on dinosaur eggs online, but my husband and I were fortunate enough to see and hold in our hands some that were, at the time, in a private collection. These specific dinosaur eggs have since been donated to a museum.

During the Regency, it wasn't uncommon for women and men to live together as strangers in a loveless marriage, as was the case for Mr. and

Mrs. Portington. However, it's always difficult to write a happily-ever-after ending for my hero and heroine and not let other characters have a happy ending in the book as well.

If you missed either of the first two books in the Rakes of St. James Series, you can still go to your favorite local bookstore or any online e-retailer and get a copy of the first one, *Last Night with the Duke*, and the second, *To the Duke, with Love*.

I love to hear from readers. You can email me at ameliagrey@comcast.net, follow me on Facebook at FaceBook.com/AmeliaGreyBooks, or visit my website ameliagrey.com.

Happy reading,
Amelia Grey